IRVING STONE

whose magnificent storytelling genius
recreated the life and times of Michel-
angelo in THE AGONY AND THE
ECSTASY and Vincent Van Gogh in
LUST FOR LIFE, now brilliantly
evokes the blazing, turbulent age of
Eugene V. Debs—the fabulous pio-
neer labor leader whose private life
was as violent and impassioned as
the dedication that raised him to the
heights of greatness . . . and drove
him to the depths of public scorn. . . .

"IRVING STONE'S BEST"
                    —*Kirkus Service*

Irving Stone

Adversary in the House

A SIGNET BOOK from
NEW AMERICAN LIBRARY
TIMES MIRROR

SIGNET TRADEMARK REG. U.S. PAT. OFF. AND FOREIGN COUNTRIES
REGISTERED TRADEMARK—MARCA REGISTRADA
HECHO EN CHICAGO, U.S.A.

SIGNET, SIGNET CLASSICS, SIGNETTE, MENTOR AND PLUME BOOKS
are published by The New American Library, Inc.,
1301 Avenue of the Americas, New York, New York 10019

FIRST PRINTING, JULY, 1969

PRINTED IN THE UNITED STATES OF AMERICA

For Jean, who endures

THE BOOKS

BOOK ONE

HOME IS WHERE YOUR DREAMS LIVE

HE STOOD AT THE WINDOW IN A LONG FLANNEL NIGHTGOWN, brushing his suit carefully so that the dust would fly into the open air of Wabash Street. The October sun was just over the horizon. His young brother, still asleep in the black walnut bed, rolled over, groaned, opened one eye.

"What time is it, Gene?"

"A little after five."

"Come back to bed and let a fellow sleep."

"There's something more exciting to do than sleep, Theo."

"You say that every Sunday morning, but all you ever do is brush your clothes."

Gene took his pan of water back to the wardrobe, running a damp cloth inside the drawers to get out the last particle of dust.

"Don't you want to come with me, Theo? We painted the town red last night."

Theodore bolted upright in the bed. Gene returned his shirts, collars and neckties to the black walnut wardrobe which his mother had brought over from Alsace, then quickly slipped into an old pair of trousers and a sweater. Though he was not quite twenty he was already an inch over six feet and growing so fast that his mother swore she could watch his clothes creeping up his ankles and wrists.

"Every member of the club was out till two o'clock this morning, putting up notices of the Ingersoll lecture, and they're all in red paint."

9

Theodore sprang out of bed. He was only eleven but already he was sprouting upward, lean and hard like his big brother.

"Why didn't you say so, Gene? You know how I hate to miss anything."

He fell on his hands and knees, fishing out the pigskin trunk in which he kept his clothes. Their father had brought all his worldly possessions to America in this trunk, both arriving waterlogged after sixty-three days in a storm-tossed sailing ship.

It took Theodore only an instant to get himself into his clothes. The brothers went quietly down the front flight of stairs. The ground-floor grocery-store window said D. DEBS; the neighborhood called it Debity Debs both for the pleasure of euphony and because Daniel so often commented, "I will debit your account," when an unfortunate customer had neither an account nor existing cash.

The air was brisk and fragrant with the autumnal scents of the surrounding woods. They struck out for the heart of town, the older boy slowing his stride a little for his brother, the younger speeding up a bit more than was comfortable. Soon they passed the first sign that Gene Debs and the members of the Occidental Club had printed by hand during the week.

LECTURE! TONIGHT!!
October 17, 1875
TERRE HAUTE OPERA HOUSE
COLONEL ROBERT G. INGERSOLL
will deliver an address on
AGNOSTICISM and TRUTH!!
The World's Most Challenging Topic!
Can You Afford to Miss It?
Time: 7 P.M.　　　Admission: 75¢–25¢
Auspices: OCCIDENTAL LITERARY CLUB
Bring the Whole Family

As they continued their walk Theodore saw that every available surface of Terre Haute's stores, office buildings, factories and warehouses had been plastered with the posters, though a sense of delicacy had prevented the members from pasting the announcement of the arrival of Agnosticism on the expansive and highly inviting walls of the town's churches.

The Debs boys themselves had grown up as religious tourists. Their parents being of different faiths, they had forestalled any possibility of dispute by saying to their sons: "Here's a nickel, go to Sunday school," without indicating which one they were to attend. Gene, and later Theodore, would wander out on the street, join the first boy he encountered, and go to Sunday school with him. Their parents asked no questions when they returned, and it was just as well, for no matter what road they took to the varying churches, they somehow managed to pass Scudder's confectionery.

"Do you think people will come to hear Ingersoll, Gene?"

Gene flushed, spots of color appearing in high relief against his fair skin. His usually gentle, hypersensitive eyes, which changed color according to the emotion spinning through them, turned from their calm blue to a determined and purple-radiated gray.

"I don't know, Theo, it's a gamble. The other members wanted Christine Nilsson, the Swedish singer, but I had to do something exciting. What's the good of starting a forum just to listen to people sing?"

"Gosh, I hope it goes over, or it'll take you an awful long time to pay the club back that three hundred and fifty dollars."

Their tour of inspection brought them to the bank of the Wabash River. Just beyond the covered bridge were some overhanging willows. The two boys stripped and plunged into the stream for a splashing swim, enjoying the cold October water against the warmth of their bodies.

As they opened the grocery door they were welcomed by the scent of their mother's fresh-baked coffee cake. Their father was at the table in the dining room behind the store, as were their two younger sisters, Jenny and Emma. Daniel Debs was a handsome man with a finely modeled head and an austere chin beard. His deep-set eyes, spaced widely behind the long Roman nose, were compassionate and gentle. His face lighted up as his two sons entered the room.

"Gene," said Daniel, "I think you're in the wrong business; you should get a job with Patrick and Lapish as a sign painter."

Theodore rushed to his brother's defense.

"But Gene had to get those signs up, Father. It was the only way to make sure Terre Haute knew about Colonel Ingersoll."

Marguerite Debs came in from the kitchen with a platter of ham steaks and fried eggs which she set down in the center of the table, then kissed each of her sons good morning. She had on a large gingham apron tied around the middle to protect her Sunday black merino; her white hair was brushed sharply back from the temples and there was a happy smile on her face at having her brood together.

Gene loved her deeply. For years he had called her by the affectionate nickname of Daisy. She had a wide, expressive mouth, exact replicas of which her two sons had inherited; when she pulled it slightly to one side, the better to declare herself, everyone in the Debs family knew that the law was about to be laid down.

"You've been swimming again," she observed as she ran her fingers through Theodore's damp hair. "Isn't it getting late in the season? And why don't you take towels with you?"

These were purely rhetorical questions; the boys knew that no answers were necessary. Gene patted her hand, then turned to his father.

"You were out early this morning. Did you shoot anything?"

Daniel looked around the room with an expressive gesture, as though to say, I take with me one of the greatest guns ever made in Europe; I am a crack shot; the woods are full of animals; and they ask me if I shot anything. Aloud he said quietly, "Oh, I think you might find some things in the bag: quail, pheasant, prairie chickens . . ."

Their sister Louise came in with hot rolls, jams and coffee, and the seven members of the Debs family seated themselves around the one board for the first time since last Sunday's dinner. Only the oldest sister, Mary, was missing. She had married a nurseryman several years before, and lived amidst greenhouses on the outskirts of town. The mother sat at the foot of the table, Daniel at the head. Opposite Gene and Theodore were the three girls: Jenny, the plain and the studious, who had already announced that she was going to be a schoolteacher; Louise, the plump, quiet and domestic; Emma, the pretty, the saucy, the smart, in whom all of Marguerite's maternal efforts had come to a magnificent conclusion. They were not a beautiful crew but they had open, friendly faces, wide, honest eyes and softness of speech. Hovering over the table and the room and the house of their lives was a tactile sense of solidarity: their mother's gift. To Marguerite Debs her family was all of the world. She rarely stirred out of her house, she had chores from dawn until the last member of the family was asleep, slipping through her day quietly, effortlessly. She had never forbidden quarreling among her six children; it was her love of family which permeated them.

Daniel was the first to excuse himself, going upstairs to the little parlor where, in a glass case in a corner, he kept his leather-bound volumes of poetry. He took the books out one by one, dusted them carefully, opened each to its table of contents, his eyes glowing as he noted the authors and poems included. The cleaning done, he rearranged the volumes for new combinations of design and color and put them back. This poets' corner was his life insurance, his dream of the future, for when he was old, and his children grown, and there was no longer need to load barrels of flour and beans weighing one hundred and seventy pounds into his wagon and then carry them on his back across muddy sidewalks and up rear porch steps, he would retire, sit here and read all these beautiful lines.

Gene, too, had his sanctum, a corner of his bedroom where he had rigged up an old kitchen table as a study desk. Here he kept the few books he bought out of his earnings as a clerk. He asked Theodore to tell him when it was eleven o'clock, then closed the door behind him, sat down at the desk and opened one of the five-cent tablets in which, in a neat and fastidious hand, he wrote out his thoughts and reactions to each book as he went through its pages. He had little education: he had gone to work in the railroad yards immediately after grammar school; his reading was haphazard. He read books as he stumbled across them, as they accidentally became available, as their subject or title excited his imagination; rarely did they bear any relationship to each other or fill out an entire field of knowledge.

He opened the copy of Voltaire's *Philosophical Dictionary* which his father had given him for his birthday. In the adjoining parlor he could hear Daniel and his Alsatian cronies playing band music. Daniel, who had played the cornet in Alsace, believed that music was the most important part of his children's education; he had bought a cycloid piano from Kussner's Palace of Music, but none of the children had taken to it, and the only thing that persisted after all these years was the monthly bill from Kussner's.

In the midst of his reading Gene heard the knock on his door. Theodore came in.

"It's five minutes after eleven."

"Past eleven! But it couldn't be. I just started . . ."

"You're going to miss Colonel Ingersoll if you don't get down to the train."

— 2 —

Walking over the path he had worn to the Union Depot during the four years he had fired for the Vandalia Railroad, which ran between Terre Haute and St. Louis, Gene saddened again at the tragedy which he had heard had just befallen Robert Ingersoll's only son: young Ingersoll had become so addicted to the reading of paperback romances that he had gone insane, been taken to an asylum and died in a cell. Nor was this Ingersoll's only misfortune: only the Sunday before a Terre Haute minister was quoted in a local newspaper as telling how Ingersoll's two daughters had become maudlin drunkards, and had been saved only by publicly repudiating their father's heresy and going back into the bosom of the Presbyterian Church.

Gene decided that Ingersoll must be torn and embittered, with deep-set tragic eyes and a stooped, wasted figure. True, the photograph sent by the lecture manager had shown him as a big, jovial man with a healthy and happy face; but Gene had been warned of the tricks of lecture managers who sent out photographs which had been taken years before, or idealized for sales purposes.

His swift strides faltered for a moment as he wondered how he would approach this rebel, about whom he had been reading. How unlike Daniel had been Ingersoll's father. To Minister Ingersoll all mankind had been evil, damned in conception and born into everlasting sin. The Devil was ever-present, inside one's head and body as well as outside; burning hell-fire was as close and inescapable as one's reflections in a mirror; life was a hideous and revolting journey along an unswerving road of lust and concupiscence, ending in the pits of eternal damnation. Robert's mother had died when he was only two, and so there had been no one to intervene. At home the Sabbath had begun on Saturday afternoon, and no voice or head could be raised out of the blackness until Monday morning. Having no assembled congregation on which to work during the week, John Ingersoll rehearsed on his two sons: they were flogged half to death for taking a few apples hanging on the road side of an orchard, and the skin was worn off their knees while their father endlessly prayed for their repentance. The two boys might well have hated their father, but instead they had pitied him, and hated orthodoxy instead.

Rounding a corner, Gene faced the familiar mustard-colored wooden depot. When he was fourteen he had gone to work for fifty cents a day scraping paint off the Vandalia cars that stood in these very yards; after a year he had substituted for a missing fireman, and kept the boilers up so well that he had been given a permanent job handling the stormy end of a scoop. Frequently his run would end at midnight at some isolated spot along the tracks, a hundred miles from St. Louis. Then the crew would pile wearily into a little shack and throw themselves fully clothed upon soiled bunks for a few hours of unconsciousness. But even at fifteen he had little patience with sleep; when the last of the men began to breathe regularly he would get up, light a candle and read the book he had been carrying in the rear pocket of his overalls. Once a brakeman awakened just before dawn, leaned up on an elbow and watched him.

"What are you doing, son?"

"Studying."

"You mean you'd rather read that book than sleep?"

"Yes, it's more exciting."

"One of us is a danged fool," the older man had said as he settled back, "and I'll betcha it ain't me."

These had been exhilarating but danger-laden years for the boy. Every day there had been another accident: engines colliding head on, trains being hurtled from their tracks in the icy darkness, the crash of freight cars, the slipping of couplings. Yet railroaders rarely left their work, any more than the coal miners around Terre Haute refused to go into the pits because there were frequent explosions.

The Terre Haute and Indianapolis train puffed across the last mile of prairie and came to a stop with considerable more noise than Gene knew was necessary for the arresting of the engine. Some twenty passengers swung down from high platforms, were greeted by friends or relatives, and disappeared. There was only one man left standing on the platform. A kind of panic overcame Gene. Ingersoll had missed the train! It was not so much that he had lost the club's money and would have to replace it from months of tedious labor, but the Occidental Literary Club would have been made to appear ridiculous.

While these fugitive thoughts were chasing through his mind, the lone occupant of the station, an enormous fellow with a red-cheeked face and hearty smile, came up to him.

"Are you by any chance Eugene Debs?"

"Why, yes. . . ."

"For a moment there I thought I'd be left waiting at the church."

Gene seemed stunned. The man asked quietly, "Is something wrong? Has the lecture been canceled?"

"No, no . . . it's just that . . . you didn't look . . . I didn't recognize . . ."

"Didn't you receive the circular with my picture on it?"

Gene winced as he replied, "I might as well tell you the truth, Colonel Ingersoll. I was looking for an unhappy little man who could hardly carry his suitcase because of the weight of his burdens."

Ingersoll's eyes twinkled.

"Was there one misfortune in particular that you were thinking about? My son, for instance?"

Gene stared at Ingersoll unbelieving, for he could see that the colonel was laughing quietly to himself. He whispered an almost inaudible yes.

"I wouldn't worry about that story too much, Mr. Debs. My only son did not read a great many novels. He did not go insane. He did not die. *I never had a son!*"

Gene gazed steadily into the other's eyes for a moment, then joined Ingersoll's hearty laughter.

"You mean that people hate you so ferociously that they will fabricate these stories out of thin air?"

"Thin air, and gaseous."

Gene picked up Ingersoll's valise with one hand, and with the other he took the older man's arm. They began walking up to the Terre Haute House. Gene had never been with anyone who radiated such a sharp sense of good will and well-being; it was not only his magnificently rich voice which heartened with its sound before one had gathered its import; nor was it solely his flashing eyes, at once so penetrating and confiding; it was something inside the spirit: a comprehension of the human world, perhaps, and the indestructible joy of the lucky one who had found his work in life.

"I really get off easy, Mr. Debs. You must remember that only a few years ago men, women and even children were imprisoned and tortured for expressing doubts about organized religion."

By now they had reached the front of the Terre Haute House. The early morning sun vanished behind grayish clouds, and there was a sharp scent of rain in the air. Gene looked upward, anxiously.

"If it starts to pour, we're going to be in trouble. Terre Haute doesn't like to get its feet wet."

"Either in water or new ideas, eh?"

"Quite so. Your manager made me sign a contract that I would pay you the full amount in cash before you went on the lecture platform. . . ."

Once again Ingersoll laughed heartily.

"My manager is my brother-in-law. He lives in perennial fear that his sister won't get enough to eat. If you don't make any money you can forget about my fee. I really oughtn't be paid for spreading my own beliefs, I ought to pay people to come listen to me."

— 3 —

On the way home Gene stopped at Gloria Weston's to deliver the three lecture tickets Mr. Weston had asked him to reserve. Gloria lived in the corner house on Tenth Street, just down from the Debs grocery. For years she had waited on the stoop each morning for Gene to come by and walk her to school. Gene had always liked Gloria, liked the fresh, pert dresses her mother sewed and starched, the cascade of live-wire copper hair tumbling down the back of her head, the infectious laughter.

She was raking in the patch of earth in front of the Weston house, a smudge on her cheek, when Gene came up.

"Gene, how delightful!" she exclaimed. "You're just in time for lunch."

"Now, Gloria," he protested. "I didn't come for lunch. I came to bring the tickets."

"But you always said you loved Mother's corn fritters."

Her voice was soft, low-timbred.

"I didn't know your mother was making corn fritters for lunch," he chided, "and you know I didn't know she was making corn fritters. . . ."

"Well, you do now." She linked her arm through his and led him up the short flight of wooden steps.

Gloria was seventeen. She had sparkling green eyes, a tilted nose. When he was with her Gene seemed to be laughing all the time. It would have been hard for him to say at what he was laughing: perhaps the turn of a phrase, a man chasing his hat across Canal Street, the confiding way in which she slipped her hand into his as they walked through the fields of a Sunday morning. Gloria was small, hardly reaching his shoulder, but she had an attractive figure, with delicate ankles and a full bosom which, unlike most Terre Hautians, her mother refused to strap down as though it were a confession of original sin.

Gloria liked people and houses and food, and liked the warm, autumnal sun of Terre Haute touching the yellow leaves with rays of light and knocking them off their brittle stems; but best of all Gloria liked Gene Debs. To his great embarrassment she persisted in telling him he was the handsomest boy in Terre Haute. Everyone knew that she intended marrying him on his twenty-first birthday.

The furniture in the Weston house was covered in bright colors, the windows framed by hangings of gay chintz. Mrs. Weston made no attempt to keep her home fanatically scrubbed, as Marguerite Debs did; it would have been futile in any event, since hundreds of people passed through it in the course of a week, friends bringing their friends.

"Mother," cried Gloria, "Gene says he smelled your corn fritters as he went by the house, and couldn't resist coming in."

Gene laughed, "Well, if you insist," and ran his fingers fondly through Gloria's hair.

Mrs. Weston waved a plump forearm liberally sprinkled with flour.

"She probably plucked you right out of the street on the grounds that you loved fritters."

Gloria dropped down on the sofa and motioned for Gene to sit beside her.

"All you people ever think about is food," she twitted. "I want to hear about Colonel Ingersoll. What was he like?"

A voice called out from the stairway, "Wait a minute, Gene. I want to hear about this too."

Gloria's father came running down the stairs and into the parlor, an open pamphlet in his hand. Paul Weston seemed middle-aged to Gene, perhaps because he was as bald as the rear of a Greek statue, though he was only thirty-eight. He was a lawyer, but an unambitious one who took no cases which involved quarrels, disputes or trouble. Terre Haute's social stratification was as unbendable as the Vandalia's rails, with no way for the members of one group to come into contact with the other; Paul Weston and his wife were known as traitors to their class, the original and now wealthy settlers who looked with contempt upon the new settlers, such as the Debses. The Westons had become so déclassé that they had even moved into the wrong part of town; except for this, Gene and Gloria could never have met.

It was raining when Gene left the Westons, and it was in a steady downpour that he called for Colonel Ingersoll several hours later. Backstage the Opera House was shadowy and musty-smelling, with only one wall lamp illuminating some torn scenery. He had had a difficult time finding anyone willing to introduce the speaker; he had been turned down by the mayor, two councilmen, the principal of the Rose Polytechnic Institute. Only the Rev. Peter Hanford, a slight, sandy-haired widower, had been willing to risk the task.

Gene introduced Colonel Ingersoll to the minister, wished them both good luck and hastened out the side alley. When he entered the theater and took the seat he had reserved for himself in the midst of his family, he was astounded to see that the Opera House was a sellout. Even the side boxes, which perched like floating red velours angels on the gilded walls, were filled with the town's leading citizens. While gleefully congratulating himself on having made enough money to buy a library table and chairs for the clubroom, Gene perceived that this audience was behaving in a very different fashion from those that came to hear Lotta, or to watch Tom

Thumb, or Joe Jefferson play *Rip van Winkle*. There was no bright conversation, no laughter, no waving to friends, but only a kind of constricted whispering and a tense, attenuated overtone of foreboding.

The Rev. Mr. Hanford opened the center curtains; he was exactly half the size of Ingersoll, and appeared like a bantam leading a tiger on a string. There was scattered applause from members of the Occidental Club, and from the town's few iconoclasts; but the hostile silence from the majority of the audience was much louder and more eloquent. Gene felt in the pit of his stomach the waves of hostility which must be pulsating upward against Robert Ingersoll.

But if the speaker felt any antagonism he gave no sign; after the introduction he walked around the podium and leaned across the candlelights, his big, handsome face radiant with good will. It appeared as though this were the happiest moment of Ingersoll's life, when he stood before a tightly woven and tightly shut mass of a thousand minds that hated in advance every skeptical word and unorthodox sentiment he would utter. Gene wondered how this could be. But as Robert Ingersoll's voice rolled out over the audience, as he challenged the sacrosanct precepts of the age: the Divine Revelation of the Bible, the existence of a blazing hell, the relentless warfare being waged between the Deity and the Devil over every last human act; as he denied that the brain must remain a sealed and quaking chamber throughout the terror-stricken centuries, as he spoke of the transcendent glories of the free and open mind, Gene came to grasp the miracle: the father had been the bow, pulling mankind backward; the son was the quivering arrow.

And Gene Debs knew what it was that made Robert Ingersoll different: he was without fear, mankind's closest companion. Fear that he might not find a place for himself, make good, be accepted, be successful. Fear that he might not fit in, conform, keep up. At every step of the road another new fear, as though the world were a vast jungle closed in by matted terrors. Fear, the synonym of life, the poison in the well, the face in the mirror, the mask in the coffin.

— 4 —

When Gene reached his desk at Hulman & Cox, Wholesale Groceries, Monday morning, he found a letter propped against his inkstand. It was signed Joshua Leach, Executive Secretary, Brotherhood of Locomotive Firemen. The message was short: Mr. Leach would like to speak to Mr. Debs at Hulman's after work that evening.

No railroader ever gets the rhythm of wheels over rails out of his blood, even though he may leave the trains many miles and years behind. Each man's beat has a different cadence, determined by his own inner cycle rather than the varying structure of the lines; never exactly the same in any two heads, unchanging throughout a lifetime. For Gene it was a clackety-clack, clackety-clack, click-clack, click-clack; clackety-clack, clackety-clack, click-clack, click-clack. All day he felt the moving wheels beneath him.

He had plenty of time to wonder what Joshua Leach could want of him, for the work at Hulman's was of the simplest nature. He could tell what time it was by the odors being hauled into storage: at eight o'clock when he sat down to his desk there was the strong scent of coffee bags being piled lumpily on the floor above, and by eight-thirty the coffee invoices were on his desk, ready to be entered in his ledger; at nine o'clock came the sweet stuff: maple syrup, molasses, sugar, candy, all meticulously tabulated in his book by ten o'clock; then came the barrels of durables: the beans, barleys, flours, rice; at eleven came the pungent sacks of peanuts and the cases of pepper, paprika, cloves. Directly after lunch came the bottled goods: the soda waters, vinegar, coal oil, cleansing fluids; at three o'clock came the fragrance that sent the clerks to the water tap: the barrels of lager beer with their bungs slightly awry.

His thoughts raced faster than any engine he had ever stoked. He had always been a little shamefaced about stepping down from the excitement of a fireman's cab to the brackish backwater of a clerk's desk. His mother had spent sleepless nights because so many firemen were being killed and maimed; she had gone to Hulman, from whom Daniel bought most of his groceries, and secured the promise of a job for her oldest boy. When he gave the word that he was quitting the footboard, the firemen had condoled with him for being obliged to give up the roundhouse with its smell of hissing steam.

Gene alone knew that he had utilized his mother's anxiety to be disloyal to his brother tallow pots, that when he slipped out of his overalls for the last time, scrubbed the coal dust from his hands and face, it had been with an emotion compounded of triumph and escape. For the fourteen hours of labor a day had begun to brutalize him; his fast-growing young body had cried out for rest and sleep when he so desperately wanted the few remaining hours for reading, for study, for a quenching of his thirst for knowledge.

He still spent some of his spare time down at the yards

where the Vandalia and Terre Haute and Indianapolis lines merged, for somehow he felt closer in spirit to his friends there than to his fellow clerks at Hulman's. He enjoyed the colorful patois of the railroaders, which sometimes flashed around bends like a swift locomotive, sometimes puffed up grades like a slow freight. There was always a welcome for the gentle, lanky kid who had been a full-fledged fireman at the raw age of fifteen. One evening while crossing the tracks he had encountered Denis O'Hern, a huge, lumbering fellow who had been shoveling coal for years without losing an ounce of his superfluous fat. Denis's one ambition was to become a locomotive engineer, and to this end he had studied and worked conscientiously. That night Denis looked very gloomy.

"What's the matter, Denis?" asked Gene.

"Ah, life is hard, me boy, full of the unexpected."

"You mean you failed that engineering test again?"

"No, me boy, I passed it, glorious-like."

"That's wonderful, Denis!"

"It would be, me boy, but I have no watch, and the company won't give me the engineer's job without I have a good watch."

Gene had put his hand over his breast pocket where he felt the fine, reassuring bulge of his own engineer's timepiece. It had taken him a year of fanatical saving to gather together the money for the watch; but there it was, out of his pocket without a second's thought, and into Denis O'Hern's hand.

"No, no, me boy. I can't take your watch."

"But I have no real need for it, Denis. There's an alarm clock goes all the time in my head. Wake me up any time during the night and I'll tell you what hour it is."

Denis rubbed his hand caressingly over the heavy silver mechanism.

"I'll return it, me boy. Just as soon as I start drawing me new pay."

Denis had not returned the watch, nor had he made good as an engineer, for his eyes went blind from watering at the first scent of danger. But everyone on the Vandalia Railroad knew the story of Gene Debs's watch; and everyone knew, too, of the overcoat he had taken off his own back that bitter night in January when he had seen young Ray Eppinghauser come out of the trainmen's shack, where the men kept warm over a brazier, and plunge through the snow toward his train, the collar of his thin suit coat turned up around his neck.

"Ray, where's your big coat?" Gene had asked. "It'll get down to thirty below on your run tonight."

"Serves me right if I freeze to death," groaned Ray. "I got drunk last night, and somebody swiped my coat."

"Here, I have another one at home," said Gene. "You'll never make it that way."

When he had reached home, his teeth chattering and his face blue with cold, his mother had wept. She had bought him the coat for Christmas, only two weeks before.

"If you felt sorry for him," she protested, "why couldn't you have given him your old coat? Why did it have to be that brand-new one, so warm and beautiful?"

"But it happened to be the one I had on, Mother. Ray would have come down with pneumonia if I hadn't given it to him. Besides, that old coat is still warm."

"Ray Eppinghauser is no good," retorted his mother. "He gets drunk, loses his coat, and then you think you are responsible . . ."

Gene had put his arm about his mother and kissed her cheek.

"Now, Daisy, I couldn't let him freeze just because he had one too many. Ray is as God made him."

"Yes, he is as God made him." She kissed him. He saw that there were tears in her eyes. "And so are you, my son."

By now he had been at Hulman's for a year; he had tangled with a good many books, yet he knew that at twenty he was still unawakened, that nothing had come into focus for him. Only that summer the Occidental Literary Club had been the Wabash Ball Team; Gene had played right field, where he had caught the few fly balls hit to him, but had been so gawky chasing ground balls, with his long arms and legs flying like a swarm of cranes, that his fielding and batting averages were sometimes interchangeable.

But if he had been a spotty fielder, he was far and away the best organizer on the team. When there were schedules to draw up, trips to be made, benefit games to be played, everything was turned over to Gene Debs. When the members decided to convert from the britches of baseball into the long pants of literature, Gene had gone to the president of the Vandalia Railroad, Riley McKeen, who had provided the boys with baseball equipment, and McKeen had given them rent-free a big room which ran the length of one of his buildings.

"I could give you your chairs and table and some books, too, Gene, but I think it's about time you boys began earning things for yourselves."

For his first meeting Gene had carried a load of wooden boxes from Hulman's to the third-floor meeting place to serve as chairs; since they had no books or magazines they had not sorely missed a library table. Gene had arranged a debate for that night: *Fatalism versus Free Will,* and the fifteen members of the club, all of them poor boys whose education had ended with Gene's at the academy, had slugged it out for three hours. If they came out with more bumps and bruises than they did at the end of their ball games, they also emerged with the first rudiments of how to defend themselves in the rough-and-tumble of open debate.

As he closed his ledger and tidied his desk a few minutes before six o'clock, he saw a man coming down the aisle with the unmistakable lurch of the trainman who spends the larger part of his life squaring off against the pitching movement of an engine; for like the sailor, the railroading man never gets used to the fact that land can stand still under his feet. The short, thickset man with the shock of gray hair pitched to a halt and asked:

"Are you Gene Debs? I'm Joshua Leach."

Gene stuck out his hand, and when it was clasped in Leach's he felt the stubs where two fingers should have been: railroaders needed no secret grip to identify members of their order, the way the Knights of Labor did. Leach was a full head shorter than Gene, but twice as thick across the shoulders and hips; he linked an arm through the younger man's and began talking even before they had left the brick warehouse. Leach shoveled words into a conversation like coal into a furnace.

"Couple years ago up at Port Jervis we had a bad time: a locomotive exploded, killed one of our boys and blew off another one's arm. Their wives had no money to bury 'em, so us firemen got together and kicked in enough cash to bury Bill Cooper and take care of Andrew's family till he could get work. Before that meetin' broke up I got an idea. I said, 'Look, men, we're all in the same fix: tomorrow night a wheel might break on the tender, or a rail split and it'll be your widow or mine who won't have enough money for a decent burial. Why don't we make this an organization? Every man chips in a few cents a week out of his pay, then when one of us gets hurt or killed, there's money in the kitty to take care of our families.'

"That's how the Brotherhood of Locomotive Firemen started. We won't be satisfied till every tallow pot in the country joins us. We're forming a local here in Terre Haute. The boys said you were our man."

Gene was so astounded he half stopped, but Leach's pow-

erful arm propelled him onward without a break in their
pace.

"But . . . but I'm not on the footboard. I quit a couple of
years ago. . . ."

"We need a man who can read and write and talk the
words when talking's called for. I'm asking you to take
charge."

It had sometimes seemed to Gene that his pursuit of wisdom was as unfruitful as that of ground balls. He hadn't the
faintest idea of what he was, what he wanted from life, or
what was going to happen to him. So far all of his energies
had been undirected. He had no articulate desires or personal
ambitions, yet some driving force from deep within his nature had caused him to wonder if he were going to be a clerk
at Hulman's all his life. Or perhaps a head bookkeeper, or
manager of purchasing?

But this offer of Joshua Leach's, this was an opportunity to
be of service, to begin with a new project and help it grow.
He turned to Leach, his mouth slightly raised on one side.

"Count me in!"

— 5 —

Supper was catch-as-catch-can in the Debs household.
Theodore and his young sisters ate at five so that they would
have several hours for their homework. At six Marguerite set
out her husband's food, then relieved him in the store. At
six-thirty she served Gene and Louise, home after work, and
at seven she sat down in the kitchen to finish what was left of
the food, while Louise washed the dishes and the two women
exchanged news of the day.

After supper Gene boiled a tub of water, scrubbed himself
with a hard brush, then shaved. There was plenty of face to
shave: the clean lip above the wide, warm, expressive mouth;
the long, slightly hollowed cheeks running rhythmically into
the powerful chin. He was fussy about his shaving: the sideburns had to have as sharp an edge as his finely honed razor,
all shadow beneath his underlip had to be removed as relentlessly as on the high cheekbones.

He carefully wiped the long steel blade, then parted his
tow-colored hair in a deep cleft on the left side, brushing it
back over his left ear, but combing it forward a little on the
right side, over the high brow. His eyebrows were slashes of
black, always a surprise in his otherwise gentle face, but they
provided an illuminative frame for his deep-set, widely
spaced blue eyes.

He put on his good black suit and under it his starched

white shirt and collar, with the black satin bow tie stuffed under the two cutaway wings.

"You're going courting," said Theodore, who had been watching the elaborate dressing process.

"What makes you think so, Theo?"

"Why else would you get so clean and put on your Sunday clothes?"

Gene went to the front window and brushed his coat into the night air.

"I'm going to a locomotive firemen's meeting."

"In those duds! Don't make me laugh."

"No fooling, Theo. I'm going to be secretary and I thought I ought to dress up the meeting."

Theodore's eyes opened wide with admiration. "Gosh, that's wonderful."

Gene reached the meeting a few minutes before eight. He was in such a high state of excitement that when he passed Austin's hardware store he could not resist going in and buying the beautiful bone-handled penknife he had been admiring for many months.

Joshua Leach was standing outside the building; Gene greeted him with a barrage of questions.

"Tell me about us: how long have we been in existence? How many locals are there? What's our program?"

Leach grinned to himself; Gene Debs had already taken hold.

As they started into the meeting room Leach murmured, "You know, of course, there's no pay . . ."

"Pay?" repeated Gene blankly.

They were greeted jovially by the firemen, but Gene's heart sank as he entered the room, for he had forgotten in the two years since he had last seen it what a filthy and gloomy hole it was. The ceiling had originally been a chocolate-brown plaster, and the walls had been covered by yellow paper, but the roof had leaked and the chocolate-brown ceiling had turned black and the yellow wallpaper was streaked with every ugly color available to a rain-soaked pattern. There were a dozen dirty and broken canvas chairs standing around, an unswept floor littered with cigar butts, ashes and matches. The windows, all locked tight, were blackened with years of dirt, the presiding officer's desk was splintered and discolored. The air was stale and foul.

Within the next quarter hour about twenty firemen entered the room, sitting down in the chairs and on the soot-covered window ledges. Some of them had just come off their runs, the coal dust packed with perspiration into the furrows of their faces. They hadn't wanted to come, but every last man of them had worked with Joshua Leach and somewhere along the line benefited from his friendship.

Leach hit the desk two or three times roughly with the bones of his palm, then began speaking:

"Brotherhood is the biggest word in the language, boys; means everyone pitchin' in and workin' together to make us a real benevolent society. I herewith declare the Terre Haute Lodge of the Brotherhood of Locomotive Firemen organized. You told me this morning that Gene Debs was your man, and so he becomes official secretary. He calls the meetings, keeps the records, collects the dues, which are fifteen cents a month, and sees that your lodge hooks up with the national office. In just a minute now we'll handle all the questions you want to ask." He turned to Gene. "But first, Mr. Secretary, will you make a record of the names of everybody attendin' this meetin' and open a set of books."

It was ten o'clock by the time Gene reached home. Everyone was asleep except Theodore, who had been lying awake waiting for his brother's return.

"Tell me about it, Gene. Did you have a big crowd? Are you really secretary? What was it like, the meeting?"

Gene was warmed by his brother's enthusiasm, but then it had always been this way. Theodore seemed to live more vividly in his big brother's life than in his own.

"Well, it was . . . all right, I guess. We've got our local, but the three questions you popped at me when I came in the door were three questions more than the whole twenty men wanted to ask Josh Leach. This union is for their own benefit, but darned if they showed the slightest interest."

"You mean they didn't want to join?"

"I wouldn't blame them if they didn't. Why do they always have to meet in a pigsty and be surrounded by dirt and ugliness and broken-down walls and furniture, just because they're workingmen?"

Theodore gazed at his brother in silence, watched him carefully take off his good suit, hang it neatly in the wardrobe, then fold the starched shirt back into its laundered position and tuck it away in a drawer. Then Gene straightened up and whirled on Theodore.

"The answer is they don't have to!"

The superintendent at Hulman's loaned him buckets and brushes. He and Theodore spent all day Sunday pulling down the meeting hall's torn and blistered wallpaper, then scrubbed the dirt off the windows. During the following two evenings they gave the room a coat of light-colored paint. Daniel agreed to donate two reproductions from his *Paris Illustrated* collection. The room began to take on a cheerful atmosphere.

At a secondhand store Gene found some lengths of green carpet that were clean and not too worn. On Thursday night he gave the floor a coat of shellac and on Friday night laid the carpet. At the secondhand dealer's he also found two Morris chairs which he could not resist buying. Theodore asked:

"Are you keeping track of the money you're spending, Gene?"

"No, I'm not."

"How will you know how much the treasury owes you?"

Gene laughed. "There is no treasury, so I guess it can't owe me anything. You see, Theo, I have no right to spend any of the lodge's money until the membership authorizes it; but if I don't spend the money I'm afraid I won't hold the membership. That's what's known as a dilemma."

"That's what's known as practically all the money out of your savings account," replied Theodore.

Gene rented folding chairs from an undertaker and covered the rickety chairman's table with green felt. In the basement under the Debs grocery he found a refectory table which had collapsed and been discarded. He and Theodore built new legs onto it and carried it over to headquarters late one night after their father had gone to sleep. Mr. Hulman gave him the wholesale price on a barrel of beer. Gene downed his supper hastily because he wanted to stop downtown and buy the latest newspapers and magazines to place on the table.

Theodore hovered over him while he once again dressed in his Sunday finery.

"Do you think they'll like it, Gene?"

"Of course they'll like it; it's the first time they've had a clean, comfortable place to meet. After the dues begin coming in I'll buy writing tables and good chairs and plenty of books and we'll use it not only as a meeting place but a club —just like the Occidental Club." He stopped and looked at his brother for a moment. "Gosh, Theo, I wish I could take you with me; you worked so hard, you're entitled to come."

"It's all right," replied Theodore wistfully. "I'll wait up for you."

It was a little after seven when Gene reached the meeting hall. He grouped the magazines and newspapers on the refectory table, set out the glasses and opened the carton of pretzels which, to his astonishment, Hulman had contributed to the affair. Then he sat down in very dignified fashion at the table, spread open his minute book on the green felt and waited with happy expectancy for the arrival of the firemen.

The firemen were late. Eight o'clock came and no one had arrived. At eight-five Gene looked at his watch again, and then at eight-ten. By eight-fifteen he was beginning to grow puzzled; by eight-thirty he had become anxious; and by eight forty-five it had dawned upon him that no one was coming; that *he* was the Brotherhood of Locomotive Firemen, that all by himself he would have to lounge in the comfortable chairs, read the current magazines, eat the pretzels and drink the barrel of beer.

He did none of these things. He sat very still and very stiff behind the green felt table, his blue eyes half sad, half angry. At nine o'clock sharp he opened his notebook, pounded on the table with his mallet and announced:

"The meeting will come to order. The secretary will read the minutes of the last meeting."

He then read the minutes of the previous meeting. When he was finished, he asked aloud, "Are there any corrections? If not, the minutes stand as read. The meeting is now open for old business. If there is no old business, the meeting will go on to new business. Is there anything further on the agenda? If not, the meeting stands adjourned. Next meeting same place, same time, two weeks from tonight."

He stood up and pounded the green felt with his mallet.

He was determined to find out where the Terre Haute firemen were that night. He found them exactly where they had always been: having a drink in the saloons, playing cards in the back rooms, fast asleep at home. He did not let the firemen see him, and he spoke to no one in his rounds of the town.

This time Theodore had not even bothered going to bed. He ran quickly into the hall when he heard his brother coming up the long, side stairway. Before Theodore could say a word Gene announced:

"It was a bust!"

Theodore stood still, confused, searching his brother's anguished face for an explanation.

"Nobody came, nobody! Not even one fireman to carry the word that the windows had been washed and the walls painted, that there were chairs to sit in and books and magazines . . ."

He sat down heavily on the edge of the stairs.

"You can't force men into a union; they've got to come in of their own free will. Since I'm no longer a fireman, what right have I to tell them what's for their good? Frankly, Theo, I'm stumped."

— 6 —

When the members of the Occidental Club gathered in their clubroom to count their assets, they found they had earned four hundred dollars from the Ingersoll lecture, after expenses, and that Major O. J. Smith, Civil War hero, Horace Greeley liberal and owner of the *Gazette*, had given the club a ringing salute for its courageous contribution to Terre Haute's intellectual life.

The lecture's one unfortunate aftermath was that the Rev. Peter Hanford's Board of Vestrymen asked for his resignation. Gene made straight for the parish house. He stumblingly offered his apologies.

"No, no, Gene," interrupted the minister, "I'm a grown man and I can take responsibility for my acts. It's just that . . . Clarissa and I . . . we wouldn't know where to go. . . ."

Clarissa was the minister's beautiful small daughter. She had soft blond hair and big powder-blue eyes.

"We've lived here since Mama died," she cried.

Gene shifted about, miserable at what had happened. "Let me talk to Major Smith at the *Gazette*. Since he approved the lecture, surely he must disapprove your being dismissed for it."

Major Smith gazed up at the plaster bust which adorned the top of his roll-top desk and murmured, "That's one of the things Horace Greeley fought so hard in the *Tribune:* intolerance."

The next morning the *Gazette* streamer read, BIGOTRY IN TERRE HAUTE. The Rev. Peter Hanford's vestrymen were called upon to prove that they were not medieval fanatics. The board knew the editor as a fighter, and so they backed down.

"But only temporarily," the Rev. Mr. Hanford told Gene.

Riding the success of the Ingersoll lecture, Gene recommended that the Occidental Club next invite Susan B. Anthony, who had recently landed in an upstate New York court for casting a ballot in an election. The prosecuting attorney had said:

"The defendant, Miss Susan B. Anthony, voted for a representative of the Congress. At that time she was a woman; there is no question but that she is guilty of violating a law of the United States."

The judge had given Miss Anthony the choice of paying a hundred-dollar fine or going to prison. Susan B. Anthony rose to her feet and delivered herself of a brief oration which

Gene had clipped from the Terre Haute *Gazette* and read to the Occidental members.

" 'All I possess is a ten-thousand-dollar debt incurred by publishing my paper, *The Revolution,* the sole object of which was to educate all women to do as I have done: rebel against your man-made, unjust laws that tax, fine, imprison, and hang women, while they deny them the right of representation in the government. I shall work on with might and main to pay every dollar of that honest debt, but not a penny shall go to this unjust claim.' "

Daughter of a Massachusetts Quaker who was read out of meeting for unorthodoxy, young Susan had been raised in the heresy that a woman's brain could be as sharp and useful an instrument as that of a man. However, when she went into the world as a teacher she learned that women were fourth-rate citizens; they were kept out of the professions, the colleges, the advanced crafts and businesses, deemed good enough only for the lowest-paid manual labor; except for those who could wheedle their way through feminine wiles, the women of America were as enslaved in spirit as the Negroes.

Attractive, intelligent, an excellent cook and housekeeper, Miss Anthony had denied herself love, marriage, children, security, had spent her years beating about the country on wretched trains and carriages, enduring incredible privation, the thousand ignominies bestowed upon her for challenging a man's world. She had faltered only once. This came after years of working for the freedom of the Negro and his right to vote, only to be betrayed by the Abolitionists, who consented to the word "male" being written into the Fourteenth Amendment, which gave the franchise to the illiterate male Negro while withholding it from the educated white woman.

As Gene quickened his steps toward the railroad station to welcome her to Terre Haute he knew that her quarter century of rejection and defeat had not embittered her, for had not Colonel Ingersoll told him with his warm smile that opposition warmed one's blood, made living an exciting and romantic adventure?

This time he had no difficulty in recognizing his lecturer as she stepped down from the train, for she was a tall, spare woman of fifty-five, with rapidly graying hair pulled back severely over her ears, and spectacles sitting on top of a straight-ridged nose. Her strong face was lined, her eyes had the quality of being withdrawn from the possibility of hurt yet leaping forward to the possibility of combat. Her expression as she stepped onto the platform seemed to Gene to be masked: sharp, pale, cold. Nor did she unbend when he rushed up to her, explaining:

"Miss Anthony, I'm Eugene Debs of the Occidental Club. We're happy to have you with us."

She nodded, courteously but coolly, and it was not until a moment later, when he recovered from his first shock of seeing that Susan B. Anthony was no Robert Ingersoll, that he realized why this woman, standing so rigidly erect before him, was refusing to remove the mask: off to one side, on the station platform, stood a group of Terre Haute women pointing at her and giggling derisively while their male companions looked on with contempt.

"Come, Miss Anthony," he said. "We'll find a carriage just outside the station."

The woman turned and gazed at him for the first time.

"You're the young man who arranged my coming here, are you not?"

"Yes, Miss Anthony."

"For twenty years I have been fighting for an opportunity to speak in Terre Haute, and it was always refused me."

"We'll pack the Opera House for you tonight."

For the briefest instant Gene saw her eyes flash.

"Is it far to the hotel?"

"No, just a few blocks."

"Good. We shall walk."

As they made their way uptown, the Sunday morning loiterers called out insolent and offensive remarks. Gene's face grew red, and he wondered with a reverential awe how this woman could have stood twenty-five years of unabated abuse, and still walk beside him unfalteringly, her head high, her eyes flashing. What kind of impregnable inner armor did she possess?

When they got to the corner of State Street, a group of beer drinkers was waiting for them. Gene murmured, I think it would be better . . . if I got on the other side . . ."

"Stay where you are," the woman replied. "I have traveled over the face of this country a thousand times without protection, and I'm too old to begin now."

As they came abreast of the leering men, one of them snickered, "Why ain't you wearin' your bloomers today if you want so bad to be a man?"

Another threw back his head and laughed raucously. As he brought his head downward he spat a mouthful of tobacco juice full into Susan Anthony's face.

Rage seized Gene. Though he knew nothing about fighting,

he pulled back a clenched fist. His arm was caught in a firm grip.

"Don't strike him," said Miss Anthony. "Once you resort to force you put yourself on the level of these ignoramuses."

The group of men drew back. Gene and Susan Anthony continued down the street in silence, Gene's insides quivering while she took a white handkerchief from her coat pocket and wiped her cheek.

After what had happened to the Rev. Mr. Hanford for his introduction of Colonel Ingersoll, Gene decided that he himself would introduce Susan B. Anthony at the Opera House. That evening he called for her shortly before eight. He led her backstage, then went to the peephole in the curtain to see how well the theater was filling up. He gasped aloud when he saw that the house was empty; row after row of dark, blank spaces, extending back through the high gallery. Numbly he counted the faces in the audience: not even the Occidental Club members had come. Aside from the solid phalanx of the Debs and Weston families, the audience consisted of exactly fourteen Terre Hautians, most of them women schoolteachers.

When he turned he saw that he had no need to explain: the gaunt woman with the militant eyes already knew what had happened.

"Miss Anthony, you don't have to . . ." he stumbled. "There's only a handful of people . . . if you feel it's not worth your while . . ."

Her eyes blazing, she said tightly:

"Do you think I am not used to this? Do you think I haven't traveled hundreds of miles through snowstorms, without food or even a chance to change my clothes, only to find that ridicule has kept every last person away from the lecture? Don't you think I know that women's suffrage has lost its news value? I will work just as hard on ten people as I will on a thousand; if there is no one out in front, then you go out there, and I'll give my lecture to you alone. Ah yes, it's easy to be the opposition when one has big audiences; the difficult thing is to stick to the job when all you get is silence. But listen to me, Mr. Eugene Debs, that's the best way to fight, when you stand alone, when you have nowhere to turn, and so you go upward because that's the only direction available. Now get on out in front if you want to hear me, because I'm going to begin my lecture."

Gene closed his eyes and stood for a considerable moment

seeing before him the picture of the empty Opera House, and of his own empty union hall. He, too, knew what it meant to be rejected.

— 7 —

Susan B. Anthony's visit had impressed upon him that the easiest and most possible fight was not always the best possible fight. He winced when he remembered that only a few weeks before he had imagined he could build a union with a barrel of beer and a bucket of paint. Now he realized that he would have to build it with bread and butter.

Gene tried to explain this to the family as they sat around the Sunday dinner table. When he said that being secretary of the firemen's local would have to be a full-time job, his mother looked at him with a touch of concern in her grave brown eyes. He added quickly:

"No, no, Mother, I don't mean I'm leaving Hulman's; what I mean is that I am going to have to organize this new job very carefully so that I will have every evening and all day Sunday to work at it."

He turned to his father, waiting for him to speak.

"This business of unions, Gene," he said slowly, "I don't think I approve of them."

There was a silence in the room. Daniel's favorite picture, which hung on a wall in his bedroom, was of a war veteran standing in a ditch by the roadside asking alms. Gene knew that to his father this picture was the symbol of suffering humanity, which gave everything: its youth, its idealism, its fighting strength, only to become exhausted, unwanted, pushed aside: mankind a mendicant, begging by the side of the road.

"You should be the first to approve of a union, Father," replied Gene, at a loss to understand his father's objection. "The purpose of the firemen is to work together to benefit each other. All of your favorite writers in the poets' corner would have approved."

Daniel shook his head slowly. "Don't misunderstand me, son. I don't disapprove of your work, it's the basic idea behind it. . . ."

"You disapprove of men banding together, to help themselves and their families?"

"Men should be free of alliances and entanglements; once these firemen do what you call 'band together' they will use force to attain their ends."

"No, no, we have no intention . . ."

Daniel broke in.

"If the locomotive firemen did not want things, they would not trouble with a union. At first they will try to get them by appeal, by logic, by petition. But are they going to give up their ambitions when they find persuasion ineffective? Gene, nothing good ever came through the use of violence; what we take by force can be wrested from us by force; the only way a man can enrich his life is through his inner spirit. Once he resorts to external means he is no longer free. True freedom means to stand alone."

"To follow your philosophy," replied Gene, "you'd have to live in a cave, like Rousseau's man of nature. You couldn't have a wife or children or a home or a grocery store, or even be a citizen of a country."

Daniel looked around the table and saw that the six members of his family were waiting for his reply.

"These are the imperatives," he answered quietly. "But beyond the family and the minimum state, without which we would be savages, man must not join, for every time he joins something he gives away something, and another loop in the rope is fastened about him."

This discussion was a little abstract for Marguerite, who had been juggling the practicalities in her mind.

"If you're going to have so much to do, Gene, you'll need space to work in." She turned to her husband. "Daniel, you never use that little storeroom out behind the shed. We could clean it out and make it into a workroom for Gene. Yes?"

Daniel now found himself in the uncomfortable position of abetting an idea which he disapproved; but for Daniel, disapproval and opposition were not bedfellows. By nightfall Gene and Theodore had emptied the room of its piled-up flour and sugar sacks, boxes and crates. By the end of the week the room had been whitewashed; Gene moved in his desk and chair, and set up his books and stack of notebooks. He then walked down the block to get Gloria and proudly showed her his new office.

The next Sunday morning when he went out to begin work, he found her there, tacking up red-and-white checked gingham curtains. He burst into hearty laughter. Gloria, standing on tiptoes on a chair gathering the gingham curtain to one side with a white tieback, turned around and demanded:

"Are you laughing at me or at the curtains?"

"But, Gloria, it's just too silly. Gingham curtains don't go in union headquarters."

"You mean the members won't like it?" she teased.

"Yes."

"What members won't like it?"

"Just you wait and see," he grunted. "We'll have plenty of members. Every last fireman in Terre Haute."

She reached over the chair. Gene put his hands under her arms and brought her down slowly in front of him. Her body was warm and supple under his fingers. Neither of them moved. Her green eyes laughed up at him mockingly.

"Let's make a bargain, Gene. As soon as you have a quorum you take a vote, and if a majority of the firemen disapprove of my curtains, I'll take them down. No extra charge."

"You're an imp," he replied, "but a lovely one. I guess that's why I always end up by doing what you want."

They had kissed only a few times during their years of friendship: once or twice at Gloria's birthday parties, on Christmas morning when exchanging gifts. But there had been one kiss a year before, when they had been walking home on a warm spring night after a ball in town, that had been sudden and violent, when their lips and their bodies had clung to each other, and the night and the city had been blotted out. That kiss had stirred Gene deeply, too deeply he told himself, for he had been only nineteen, earning ten dollars a week as a clerk at Hulman's grocery concern. Love was something he read about in Balzac and Dumas and Victor Hugo; it was an emotion he would one day feel and a world he would one day enter, but of necessity he was very far away. Who was he, and what was he, what did he know of life and where would he fit into the seething pattern about him? He wanted to find his proper place in the world, to be of some use. All these things were in the future, five years, ten years, fifteen years, how could he tell?

His thoughts came back to Gloria. He kissed her gently. She stood quite still, then slipped out of his embrace.

"I have to be getting back now," she murmured. "We're all going down the river for a picnic in Father's boat. You couldn't come with us, could you?"

"I'd like to, Gloria, but I really must work."

She went to the door, then turned and looked at him for a moment, her figure silhouetted sharply against the morning sun.

"I'm happy for you, Gene. I know you will make something really good out of all this."

Impulsively he went to her, put his arms about her waist and kissed her full on the lips. She clung to him, her arms about his neck.

"I do appreciate the curtains, Gloria," he murmured. "You're always doing nice things."

Gloria enjoyed a serious moment, but she liked to end it on an upbeat of pleasantry.

"You can sew curtains for me sometime, Gene," she said, and was gone.

He closed the door behind her, stood for a moment feeling good inside himself, and happy. But there was work to be done, much work.

He had undertaken the task of assembling the names of every locomotive fireman operating out of Terre Haute. He already had sixty-five names. Most of the men he had worked with, and could call his friends, yet he knew that it would be futile to ask each one separately, as a personal favor, to come to a meeting to discuss the Brotherhood. The idea was too new, too vague, too untried. First he would have to educate himself in the values of unionism, and once his faith had been buttressed by knowledge, he would be able to pass on that conviction to the men.

He must bring into being an organization which at the moment existed only in his own mind. Since the men had rejected the union, they probably thought that the local had died a-borning. Gene picked up his pencil and began writing a letter to disabuse them.

DEAR FRIEND:

I had looked forward to seeing you at the last meeting of the Terre Haute Lodge of the Brotherhood of Locomotive Firemen. Of course, I know that there was a good reason for your absence; you were probably out on a long run, but quite frankly the meeting labored under a disadvantage because you were not there to participate in the discussion.

He laughed aloud at this last line, then murmured, "And that's no lie!"

"What's no lie?" asked Theodore, from the door. "And who put up those fancy curtains? Bet Gloria's been here."

"You're too smart for your britches," grunted Gene. "Here, sit down and write the rest of this letter for me while I speak it out."

Theodore slid quietly onto the wooden chair. "I don't see how you ever got through school. Nowadays they wouldn't let you out of the fourth grade with this handwriting."

Gene's thoughts were turning over too fast for him to hear Theodore. Instead he replied to something he himself had been thinking.

"You're right, boy; that letter is no good. As soon as the firemen learn that they all got identical letters they'll throw them away. I have to write to each one separately, mention his wife and children, recall something that happened while we were on a run together. Then when I start to talk to him about the Brotherhood, he'll know I'm talking to him personally. Catch on, Theo?"

Theodore, who had been counting the names on the list before him, exclaimed, "You mean you're going to write sixty-five different letters? Your beard will be longer than Father's by the time you get through."

"Tell you what we're going to do, boy. From now on we're going to throw away all the clocks and all the calendars. We're going to treat time as though it were a stick of Gloria's molasses taffy: the harder you pull on it, the farther it stretches."

— 8 —

It took Gene and Theodore a full week to write the sixty-five letters, not only because of the sheer volume, but because Gene was feeling his way carefully, using only those arguments which might appeal to each individual. He remembered the winter night that Ed Garrity had lost three fingers of his left hand while helping a trainman with a defective coupling. Ed had wept openly while Gene bandaged the stumps with strips of his torn undershirt, wept in anticipation of the day when a real terror would materialize: when he would lose either or both legs and be nailed to a porch rocking chair for the rest of his life. It was easy to know how to appeal to Ed Garrity: tell him about the accident insurance, how, if he had an accident, he would be provided with a doctor and artificial limbs, so that he could get around again.

But you couldn't talk to Charlie Masterson that way: huge, blond, devil-may-care Charlie who laughed at defective couplings, split rails, boasting that no railroad built could cut him up in little pieces, that when they buried him, all of Charlie Masterson would still be stuck together. However, it was the talk of the footboard of how crazy Charlie was about his young wife, how he would slave any number of extra hours to keep her from washing the family clothes. Talk to Charlie then about the life insurance that would be paid to Mrs. Masterson if Charlie should be killed, saving her the physical drudgery inherited by every laboring man's wife.

Karl Hoffer, the bachelor, loved beer busts: talk to him about the union's holiday outings. Dino Franchetti had eleven children and was hard pressed to keep their stomachs filled:

talk to him about more pounds of beef, loaves of bread, bags of garlic and boxes of spaghetti. Henri Letescue was dominated by hatred against the bosses who had refused to care for him when he had been scalded by live steam, refused to restore his old wage on the grounds that he was no longer as fit: talk to Henri about the strength of cooperative action.

But rub the eraser end of his pencil as he might across his forehead, Gene could think of no outstanding characteristic of Sam Balker or Mack Hurger to which he might effectively appeal. As for Bob Christopher and Dad Jenkins, they were tired, apathetic creatures who long ago had shoveled their last vestige of interest into the furnace along with the coal.

"We'll get more scientific as we go along," he told Theodore. "Before we send these letters out we'll set up an index file, listing the kind of argument used on each fireman. When a man comes into the union, we'll know our letter was a good one, and we'll try that same argument on someone who turned a deaf ear to us."

Theodore was having the time of his life. He had always adored Gene, and Gene had had the kindness never to shut out the youngster from activities for which he was too small or immature. When Gene had played for the Wabash ball team, Theodore had been the official scorekeeper. Now he was sergeant at arms of the Occidental Literary Club, and already he had become amanuesis for the firemen's local.

"That's a pretty high-flown title for a kid your size," commented Gene with a warm grin.

"I can't even pronounce it," replied Theodore.

Their mother pushed open the door of the little office.

"I see you boys are busy at it," she called, and when Gene and Theodore turned their long, lean faces up to her from the desk, so alike with their clear eyes, their long, straight-ridged noses, their wide, expressive mouths, she was filled with pride, pride at their clean-cut, open-faced, honest manner; pride in their lean, straight, strong limbs; but most of all pride in their love and pleasure in each other.

Whatever else may happen to them in the world, she thought, they will always have each other. Sometimes that's all a person needs, no matter how severe his trials: one human being who loves him and is utterly loyal.

"Theo, it's nine o'clock, time for bed."

"Aw, Ma; we're right in the middle of a letter."

"Then finish it, and off with you. You must have eight hours of sleep if you want to grow as tall and strong as your brother."

That was the clincher; Gene and his mother smiled at each other as Theodore sprang up.

Marguerite Debs went to the little rough desk, gazed at the litter of pages and put an arm about her oldest boy. Gene gently pulled her down in his lap. She sat for a moment with her cheek on her son's. Born of a prosperous Alsatian family, she had crossed the Atlantic by herself as a young girl when her boyhood sweetheart, Daniel Debs, had written her from the New World that he was lonely and needed her desperately. She and Daniel had moved to Terre Haute, Indiana, because they were told it had a large Alsatian colony, and was going to become the Porkopolis and railroad center of the Midwest. But even as they arrived in the bitterly cold, wind-lashed winter of 1851 there were signs that Chicago, to the north, would become the focal slaughterhouse and railroad yard of the nation.

She had borne ten children in almost as many years. Four of them died of malaria, of Wabash shakers, of disease so swift and mysterious in nature that the child had been buried before the illness had been named. Her first children had been born in a little clapboard dwelling on North Fourth Street, the front room of which also had been turned into a grocery store. The flimsy structure was called a shotgun house because the rooms ran straight back in a row. Wooden strips had been nailed across the window of the second-story bedroom to keep baby Gene from falling out.

Terre Haute had grown slowly, painfully; even though Marguerite helped her husband in the store, giving it every hour she could spare from her children, there was rarely any profit that could be figured in silver or gold; the wages for their work took the form of food which the store supplied them, and the shoes and clothing for which they bartered sacks of flour and sugar.

But she had not counted profits in terms of columns in a ledger. Her profits had been her daily happiness with the gentle Daniel, whose only vices were his impracticability in business and his cornet playing with his Alsatian cronies of a Sunday afternoon. Her profits were in her six children, who loved her deeply; her gain was in this handsome boy, with the gentleness of his father, his father's taste for learning; hypersensitive to suffering, a nature abundant with love for people and excitement in the world about him.

". . . a kind of . . . well, purpose," she heard Gene saying. "There's double pleasure in useful work. I don't mean that the job at Hulman's isn't . . ."

"Is there a future in it, Gene?" she asked solicitously.

"Well, it's given me direction, and a great deal of work that needs doing. That's a future in itself, don't you think?"

As she was about to leave the room, she turned. "Weren't you invited to that party at Gloria's tonight?"

He jumped up, exasperated at himself.

"Confound it. I remembered that party all week, and just tonight I had to go and forget it."

Gloria opened the door for him. She was wearing a blue satin party dress with a tight-fitting bodice and flaring skirt, her hair wound on top of her head.

"We've all been waiting for you, Gene," she exclaimed.

She led him into the parlor where about twenty of her young friends had been playing Going to Jerusalem, then called out, "Mother, come and play a waltz for us. I want to dance with Gene."

Paul Weston was sitting by the window in carpet slippers and a worn black velvet smoking jacket which had been given to him as a birthday gift by his wife some fifteen years before. Paul didn't smoke, but he always slipped into a jacket before picking up a book, as though it were an armor protecting him from intrusion by a more practical world. Now he laid down the book and went into the hallway to get his viola, which had been leaning precariously against the mirrored hatrack. Gloria slipped gracefully into Gene's arms. Everyone at the party knew she was Gene's girl, that she had never looked at another boy since she was twelve. Everyone in the room knew that they loved each other and that they belonged together. Gene was glad he had come.

When the waltz was over Mrs. Weston jumped up and exclaimed, "Gloria, if you want fudge you're going to have to put it on right away."

"All right, Mother. Come on, everybody. The one who helps the most gets to scrape the pans."

"Leave Gene with me," her father protested. "I haven't talked to him about this Susan B. Anthony lecture yet."

Gene saw Gloria's eyes become serious for an instant. He sat down on the piano bench alongside Mr. Weston, who was quietly plucking his viola. Then Paul Weston laid his bow on the piano top.

"Gene," he said, "you've got the makings of a lawyer. Why don't you come into my office and read law for a year? You could pass the examination easy at the end of that time."

Gene was too surprised to answer. He had never thought of himself as a lawyer. Paul Weston mistook the astonishment for reluctance; he quickly added: "I'll pay you the same wage you get at Hulman's."

"Why, Mr. Weston," exclaimed Gene, "no one ever pays a clerk any wage while he's reading law."

Paul Weston blushed a trifle.

"Your mind is logical and disciplined, Gene. Besides, your personality would be good with juries." He rose quickly, leaned his viola against the mantelpiece, then came back to the piano bench. "You're twenty now, aren't you? By the time you're twenty-two you could be a practicing attorney. I'll make you my partner, we'll divide up, even-fifty."

To Gene this seemed a generous offer.

"That's extremely nice of you, but I don't know, I never thought about the law."

Paul Weston ran his fingers amusedly over the velvet smoking jacket from which almost all the nap had been worn.

"I don't blame you, Gene. I know I'm not a howling success, and I haven't made a million."

"Oh, Mr. Weston, please, I think you're about the finest and happiest . . ."

". . . but I'll reform, Gene. I'll take all the cases that come to me, even if I don't like them, criminal cases, too. The first thing you know we'll have a roaring practice."

Gene sat quietly, thinking. There was money in being a lawyer, if one wanted money; there was professional status, open roadways to politics, industry. He wondered why it was that it had taken only a few moments to tell Joshua Leach "Count me in!" while Paul Weston's offer, which provided a thousandfold more promise, left him unmoved.

— 9 —

It was unbelievable that not one among the sixty-five firemen bothered to answer his letter or to fill out the membership card and insert it in the stamped and addressed envelope he had enclosed. As far as any result was concerned the mailbox in which he posted his letters might have burned down or taken wings and flown away.

Under the light of his round lamp with the green glass shade, he and Theodore had just finished marking the sixty-five cards in the file with "No Result."

"I can't understand it," groused Gene. "If I had asked them for money . . . but I didn't."

"Maybe they couldn't read my chicken tracks," suggested Theodore anxiously.

Gene poked him playfully in the ribs.

"Don't you believe it, boy. What was wrong with those letters was my thinking, not your writing. I guess I've forgotten how too talk to them."

"Why don't you ask Joshua Leach?"

Gene was perturbed. "No, no, Theo. I'd be ashamed to tell Josh. He might lose confidence in me, or just let the Terre Haute local go until a better time."

"Then you'll have to ask Ed Garrity and Johnny Nichols and Mack Hurger themselves."

"That would only put them on the defensive. What time is it, Theo?"

Theodore yawned. There was no heat in the little office, and he had on only a light shirt. His lips were blue.

"Bedtime, I know that much."

"I've got an idea. I'm going out."

They walked up to their bedroom together. Theodore was undressed and asleep before Gene had slipped into his old leather jacket. He turned the wick down low, covered Theodore's shoulder with the quilt and walked down the long flight of stairs.

His first stop was the Old John Garb saloon, hangout of railroaders. As he pushed open the swinging doors and looked into the mirror backing the bar, he saw the faces of a dozen men for whom he had waited so anxiously at the first meeting. Karl Hoffer was proclaiming that Governor Samuel Tilden had done such a great job busting up the Tweed gang that he'd be elected president the following year. Chris Demurray ridiculed the idea:

"That whisky makes you talk foolish, Karl. The Democrats're never going to elect a president again, it's always going to be Republican."

Percy Kubsch, who had been firing with Gene on the night that they had barely missed death from an oncoming engine, cried out:

"Look who's here, boys, old Gene Debs, back to join us! Casper, draw a large beer for Mr. Debs."

Gene walked through the heavy sawdust covering the floor. After he had been treated to two beers, he bought a round himself. The beer was strong, it made his head swim, but he faithfully held to his determination not to mention the union unless someone else brought it up. He soon perceived that nothing could be further from the men's minds than the Terre Haute local.

The following evening he went down to the row of bungalows across the tracks where many of the trainmen's families lived. He called first at the house of Bennett Minshall, a young chap with whom he had chummed during his years on the footboard. Minshall had been married only four years, but already he had three children and his wife was big with the fourth. Their house consisted of a front porch, parlor with two rockers, a kitchen and a single bedroom in which the three children were already huddled in sleep in one big brass bed. The walls and floor were unpainted board, but Florence Minshall kept them scrubbed down to the grain. Prior to the depression of 1873 Ben had earned one dollar and forty cents a day, but his wages had now been cut fifteen cents a day. Like all firemen he had to be away from home almost half of the time, during which he was obliged to pay for his food and lodging; Florence was left with eighty cents a day on which to maintain her family.

Bennett was reading the evening paper when Gene knocked and walked in.

"Gene, you old coot!" he exclaimed. "Haven't seen you for ages. What have you been doing with yourself?"

Gene asked himself, Is he joking? Aloud he replied, "Oh, I've been holding down that chair at Hulman's. But I don't have to ask what you've been doing, Ben!"

Ben and his wife laughed heartily.

"Florence, let's have a cup of coffee with old Gene. I'll make it."

He went back into the kitchen. Following an impulse, Gene blurted out, "Florence, I've got to ask you a question, but you must promise not to tell Ben."

Florence wondered what kind of a secret Gene Debs could have.

"I won't tell."

"Then did he say he got a letter from me?"

"A letter? What about?"

"The firemen's union."

"Ben never said he got a letter from you about any union."

Gene drank six cups of coffee that evening in six different homes; never once did anyone bring up the subject of the union. To his chagrin he saw that this was nothing deliberate on their part. Neither the firemen nor their wives were sufficiently interested to talk about the organization.

He trudged home. His whole body felt cold; he wanted to snuggle against his brother for warmth and comfort, but he lay rigidly on the edge of the mattress, staring up at the stippled ceiling above him. Lying there, unable to sleep, he became convinced that he lacked the necessary skills: it took training and experience to become a master craftsman in any field. Why should this not be true in working for unionism?

His four years as a railroader had served as high school; now the tiny room behind Daniel's grocery store became his college. The minutes and the hours slipped away under the light of his mother's lamp, for at last the knowledge he was seeking was to serve a specific purpose. As he gathered about him the few books on labor unions he learned that before the beginning of the nineteenth century there were no factories, no large-scale employment and no unions. A man owned his own tools; in the rare cases where there was an employer, he worked at the bench alongside his three or four employees. The Industrial Revolution, which replaced hands with machines, was supposed to advance civilization through the cheap production of creature comforts; actually it had plunged mankind back into the jungle.

The first trade union in America was established in April of 1803 by the New York Society of Journeymen Shipwrights; it was not until three years later that the New York City House Carpenters formed the second union in the country, and not until eleven years later, 1817, that the New York Typographical Society followed suit. Means of communication were slow at the beginning of the century, but not so slow, Gene thought, that another five years must pass before this idea spread to Boston with the first union of the shipwrights and caulkers in 1822, and still another five years before the printers organized in 1827 in Cincinnati.

One other fact he saw at once: the most intelligent and highly skilled of the workers were the first to form their unions; the unskilled, the laborers, had achieved not a single union in the full seventy-five years of the century. A furrow creased his brow; for to him it appeared that these had needed unionism the most!

He set up a sheet of brown wrapping paper on one wall of his room and drew it off into squares. On the left-hand side he put the job the worker was doing; in the first column he set up the hours, in the next the wages, in the next the ratio of employment to unemployment, in the next the proportion of accidents, and what responsibility the employers took for them; and in the last column the conditions under which the men worked.

He wrote hundreds of letters to existing unions, to employers, to libraries, newspapers and magazines. Because of the difficulty in acquiring information he found it a fascinating contest: each piece of submerged or untabulated material that he routed out, fitted another fragment into the puzzle he was attempting to turn into a portrait of the workingman in America.

He knew that there was one fundamental question that had to be asked and answered before he could go any further in his work: *How were improvements secured?* If the government of the United States considered it one of its functions to improve the working conditions and living standards of the eighty per cent of its people who earned their way by wages, then the need for unions was lessened. If the employer was interested in the permanent welfare of his worker, then again labor unions had no great usefulness.

Until he answered this question for himself he would be like a carpenter without a hammer or a tallow pot without a shovel. Once again he set up a chart on the wall but he soon found that he had wasted his energies; for there were few compartments to be filled under the heading of "improvements granted by ownership" or "improvements provided by government legislation." Occasionally an owner or a manager gave his employees a six-day week because he wanted them to go to church on the Sabbath, raised their wages in times of prosperity, didn't dock them when they were sick for a day or a week. President Van Buren, needing ships, had signed an order making it illegal to work shipwrights in any government yard for more than ten hours a day. But ninety-nine per cent of the alleviation won by workers had been accomplished through their own sacrifice and hunger.

When Gene read about eight-year-old children chained to machines, women working eighty hours a week, fainting from weakness in the dark holes in which they were employed, it mattered little to him that these people were long dead. He possessed no calloused skin into which he could retreat when he heard of human suffering; it was not possible for him to say, as the youngsters of Terre Haute did when they passed a dead cat or dog in the gutter: "Not in my family!" Somehow all the dead cats and dogs in the gutters were in his family; and somehow all of the human race was in his family; the past never died for him, and this was doubly true when he checked the material on his charts and saw that the past was just a shorter word for the present.

— 10 —

One Sunday afternoon he heard a knocking on the door, but it was too faint to penetrate the intensity of his concentration. There was a second tapping and after a moment the ¹oor opened slowly. Gloria came into the room. She had been out in the sun that morning and her hair was still vibrant with light. Even in the abruptness of Gene's transition from work to welcome he saw that she was growing more beautiful each day, her face and figure thinning down to maturity, her green eyes deepening.

"Gene, you shouldn't be indoors on such a lovely spring day. You should be taking me for a long walk out to the Indian Burial Ground."

She raised her arms slightly for him to lift her onto the desk.

"I can't put you up there, Gloria, you'll be sitting all over the labor movement."

"Didn't you tell me that one of the major objectives of trade-unionism is a six-day week?" she twitted. "You had better take your best girl walking on Sunday."

Gene put his hands under her arms and lifted her onto the desk. She was light, almost ethereal, yet when he felt her warm, strong flesh under his fingers, and felt the fullness of her figure against him, there was nothing ethereal about her.

"You keep a lot of charts, don't you?"

"Yes."

"You know everything that happened, and when?"

"Everything!"

"Then would you consult one of your charts and find out when you kissed me last?"

"My charts only go back to the beginning of the century."

"Those are the nicest words you've said to me for a long while," she sighed.

He turned his face slightly and before he knew it his lips were on hers; her mouth was so alive, so sweet, he felt that this was the most important, the most beautiful thing that could happen to anyone. Gloria murmured against his cheek:

"You'll come out for a walk? It's so lovely along the river now."

With the deepest reluctance he made the painful movement of stepping back so that his lean chest no longer harbored the softness of her bosom. Miserable, he murmured:

"No, I can't, Gloria."

"Oh, darling, why not? You work so hard all the week at Hulman's. And then every night here. You must have a few hours of pleasure. You'll become ill. You can't work all the time."

Gene dropped heavily into a chair, ran the back of his hand over his eyes.

"I am tired."

"Then it's settled."

She jumped off the desk, took his two hands in hers and tried to raise him from the chair.

"Gloria, I started so late, I'm like a child amongst these

books. The most elemental things I don't know . . . there are
great blank spaces . . ."

"But, Gene, you're young, you're not even twenty-one yet,
you have all your life to do this work. You don't have to
finish it all today, this week."

Gene held her hand against his cheek.

"I'll never get it finished, Gloria. Not if I live to be a thousand. So many have tried and they end up with nothing. . . ."

"Then if you're going to end up with nothing in your
work, I'm not going to let you end with nothing in your life.
At least you'll have memories: you'll remember that on a
warm spring day in 1876 you walked hand in hand with your
girl along the Wabash, with the poplars green and lovely and
the whippoorwills calling across the river."

Gene dropped her hand; he had a sharp pain at the back
of his head. Gloria waited for a moment, then said quietly:

"Gene, you mustn't become a fanatic. They do no good,
either to themselves or to anyone else."

He rose, went to the table, straightened out some papers.
When he spoke it was gently and the pain was gone.

"It's not fanaticism, Gloria. Every new fact I find, every
new conclusion brings me joy. Can't you understand? It
means that I've got a job. It means that I'm being useful.
That's why I'm happier than I've ever been in my life."

She stood gazing at him, her eyes troubled. She was deeply
interested in this union he was trying to build and the work
he was doing because she saw that it made him happy. She
had wanted him to be happy because happiness is a fertile
field for love. She wanted him settled, so that he would begin
to think in terms of permanence. She was not ambitious for
him to make a great deal of money; that had never been an
objective of the Weston family; nor did she feel that he had
gone backwards by working for the firemen's union, as her
wealthy cousins had warned her. She knew that Gene liked
her, that he cared for no one else. It had been natural for her
to assume that, like every other young man in Terre Haute,
he too would marry his best girl when he was twenty-one.

What was now slowly filtering through her consciousness
was the realization that Gene Debs had no need for marriage
at this early age; that he had need for a good many other
things first: work, understanding of the world about him, a
sense of being useful, of growing into a job where he could
serve.

She turned away, went to the door, opened it slightly and
stood there with her head down, crying noiselessly.

He had never seen her cry. He went to the door, wrested

her hand from the knob, took her in his arms. A tremor went through him when he saw how beautiful she was with the tears in her eyes.

"Please don't cry, Gloria," he said, "we'll go for our walk. There's nothing in the world I'd rather . . ."

It was a moment before she answered.

"No, Gene. You want to work. You have so much to do. You must never let a girl's tears divert you."

"Gloria, honestly, I'd love to go out along the river."

"I'm jealous, that's all," she cried.

Before he could answer she had gone out the door, leaving him alone. He stood there irresolute, then half stumbled to his chair and sat with his long arms and legs drooping, his senses in turmoil.

— 11 —

Gene had insisted upon paying Susan B. Anthony's railroad fare and hotel bill out of his own pocket. The club was now in debt for the rent of the Opera House and for the circulars. He boldly wrote to Jenny Lind, who was the rage of the East, asking her to come to Terre Haute. In reply he received a perfunctory refusal from Miss Lind's manager, but the following day there came a telegram which read:

> COLONEL ROBERT INGERSOLL JUST TOLD
> ME ABOUT HIS MEETING TERRE HAUTE
> UNDER YOUR AUSPICES. WILL BE HAPPY
> SING FOR YOU DIRECTLY AFTER CHICAGO
> CONCERT.

He had scored a great scoop: the highest-priced tickets were bought up even before they were printed and hundreds stood at the back of the hall and in the aisles to hear the Swedish nightingale. Gene was able to pay the Opera House two rentals, settle his poster bill, and put back into his own savings account the expense money he had paid out to Miss Anthony. Not even to Theodore did he dare mention that, magnificent as was the voice of Jenny Lind and grateful as he was for the funds, he had enjoyed infinitely more the voices of Robert G. Ingersoll and Susan B. Anthony.

But if the affairs of the Occidental Club prospered, with more young men coming up to the third-floor meeting hall each week to put down their twenty-five cents annual membership dues, Gene's union was doing very poorly indeed. At the end of three months he had accumulated exactly two members: Denis O'Hern, who joined in lieu of returning the watch Gene had loaned him years before, and Ray Epping-hauser, who signed his membership card as a token payment on Gene's overcoat.

He gathered together his accumulation of facts and fired with a marksman's rifle. The letter he sent to Terre Haute firemen was couched in simple and direct terms; it showed how much each union in America had gained for its members over a period of years; how the wages, hours and working conditions in non-organized fields had remained static. He ended with a bold declaration:

Do you want higher wages? Do you want a shorter work week? Do you want safer working conditions? No union in America has ever failed to achieve these ends. What others have accomplished by working together we can accomplish here in Terre Haute.

Dino Franchetti walked over the evening he received his letter, signed his application blank in Gene's office and dropped a silver dollar ringingly on the table. Ed Garrity scrawled on the back of his membership card, "Gene, maybe if we had a union years ago I wouldn't-a lost my fingers." Johnny Nichols passed him on the street early one morning and handed him a signed card, saying, "It sounds like a good idea, this joining together."

Fourteen firemen joined in a rush. Exultant, Gene imagined that it would be a matter of a few days or a few weeks before the balance of the sixty-five men would be members. Then the flow stopped, as abruptly as it had started; the letter and the fresh enthusiasm were a week old and had apparently lost their power of persuasion. Shameless now, Gene waited for the men to drop off their tenders at the end of a run, pursued them to obscure saloons, interrupted tense poker games. He reviewed the case for the union, challenged objections, pleaded. But those men who had wanted to come in were already in; the rest wanted no part of the Brotherhood of Locomotive Firemen.

He was working in the little storeroom at eleven o'clock one night when he heard footsteps come running up Wabash Street and swerve in his yard. The door was thrown open without a knock. Henri Letescue burst into the room.

"Gene, there's been a bad smashup . . . the single track in that new cut. Two engines collided head on."

Gene sat motionless, his body half twisted in the position he had taken when the door was thrown open.

"They're getting up a relief train. I thought you might

want to go along . . . might be a couple of the union boys."

Gene jumped out of his chair and ran to the yards. He swung onto the coal car just as it started moving. Engles, the superintendent of the Terre Haute and Indianapolis, was on board; he looked upset and worried. No one spoke.

It took forty minutes, going at the top speed of twenty-five miles an hour, to reach the wreck. The two engines were standing half-way up on their haunches, interlocked like battling stallions caught in a death grip. By the side of the roadbed a tarpaulin was stretched over several bodies. Gene went quickly to it and moved the canvas aside. There were three men lying on the ground: the two engineers, both of them horribly mangled, and big Charlie Masterson; Charlie who had boasted that railroading would never cut him up in little pieces.

Gene heard a deep groaning behind him. He ran back to a little copse of woods where a group of men were working over a prostrate figure. The breath almost went out of him when he saw Bennett Minshall, his face green and twisted in agony. One of Ben's legs had struck against the steel edge of a car and been amputated as neatly as though by a surgeon's knife. Someone had applied a tourniquet. Ben opened his eyes, recognized Gene.

"Gene," he cried, "get me home, quick, before I bleed to death."

"You're all right, Ben," he said, "we're taking you back to the hospital now."

He had no right to give orders. He didn't even know that he was giving them, but he said in a voice that no one would have dared to ignore:

"Pick him up! Easy . . . down the track now . . . get that engineer. We're taking this train to Terre Haute as fast as we can."

The superintendent was still inspecting the mechanical wreckage. Henri Letescue located the engineer and within a matter of seconds they were backing as swiftly as they had come.

It was several hours later when he left the hospital. The doctor assured him that Ben's chances were good.

It was past three in the morning as Gene walked the dark streets, his heart aching for Ben and Ben's pregnant wife, his children, aching for Charlie Masterson's wife, who would be left destitute. Neither Charlie nor Ben had come into the union; there could be no life insurance for Mrs. Masterson, no money to tide over Ben's family until he could go back to work. He tormented himself with the thought that the fault had been his own; he must have chosen the wrong argu-

ments, made invalid points, aroused their suspicion or antagonism. Even if he had done nothing to keep them out, he had
done nothing to bring them in. His was the responsibility and
his the failure.

He found himself in front of the Minshall house. Everything was dark inside. He walked quietly up the steps and sat
on a rocker on the porch; when this got too cold he opened
the unlocked door and went into the dark parlor, finding his
way silently to a chair. He heard no sound behind him but
suddenly there was a voice very close to his ear. It was Mrs.
Minshall.

"There's been an accident, hasn't there? I heard an engine
several hours ago. There's nothing scheduled this time of
night . . . and Ben's out somewhere on his run."

Gene rose, reached out his long arms to hold the woman
firmly by the shoulders. If he didn't convey the news, a messenger would arrive from the company within an hour or
two.

"Yes, there was an accident."

He felt her shoulders sag under his arms.

"Ben's not dead, Gene?"

"No, no, Florence. He's all right, I brought him in myself.
He just . . . hurt his leg."

Trainmen's wives know that there are very few hurt legs in
the industry. Either your leg is untouched, or you lose it.

"He's lost his leg," she said. Then suddenly, sharply: "Not
both legs, Gene."

"No, only one. Believe me, it's only one."

He moved quickly as she fainted. He caught her and carried her to her bed. Then he ran next door. Mrs. Tuell took a
quick look, cried to Gene:

"Put some hot water up to boil, quick!"

Some minutes later, while Gene sat in the cold parlor
watching the dawn gray out the blackness of the night, Mrs.
Minshall was delivered by her neighbors of a premature
child. The baby died within a few moments. Gene swayed
with the movement of the cars beneath him: clackety-clack,
clackety-clack, click-clack, click-clack, clackety-clack, clackety-clack, click-clack, click-clack. He rose and walked home,
stiff, cold, miserable.

By seven-thirty he was back in the yards. The superintendent was an expert Chicago dispatcher who had come up on
the office side of railroading. He wore the same heavy black
suit month in and month out regardless of the weather.

"What do you want, Debs?" he asked brusquely.

"I want to talk to you about Charlie Masterson and Ben Minshall."

"Come back later. I'm busy now cleaning up the mess they dumped in my lap."

Gene controlled his flush of anger.

"Mr. Engles, I'm due at work in a half hour."

"What gives you the right to talk for Masterson and Minshall?"

"I'm secretary of the fireman's local."

Engles dug into a drawer on the right side of his desk and tossed a sheet of names at Gene.

"Show me their names on this list."

It was only a second before Gene replied quietly:

"Every fireman operating out of Terre Haute is a member of the Terre Haute local."

Engles made derisive sounds, half rose from his chair and glared across the desk. It was said around the yard that he had rails in his body instead of blood.

"We ought to make the engineers and trainmen pay for those two locomotives."

"Men don't kill themselves for the pleasure of it, Mr. Engles," replied Gene. "Not when they have wives and children at home. When two locomotives crash head on, that means your signal system has broken down. And that's the fault of this office, not of the men running the trains."

His voice was firm, his manner sure.

"I claim your company should give Masterson a decent burial and pay his wife a thousand dollars insurance. I claim your company should pay Minshall's hospital bills and give him five hundred dollars to tide him over."

Engles studied Gene with a furious pity.

"Do you know how much it will cost to replace those two engines?"

"I'm interested in human cost, not machine cost."

"You're not interested in machine cost! Of course you're not, because you're not responsible! You don't have to satisfy directors and stockholders. You'd be mighty interested if we had to shut down, if we had to throw all those men out of work because we couldn't make the railroads pay and there were no more trains running across America."

Gene fished in his pocket, pulling out a crumpled newspaper clipping.

"Here's a story Joshua Leach sent me from the San Francisco *Bulletin*. It describes the homes that are being built for Leland Stanford, Mark Hopkins and Charles Crocker on the top of California Street hill. Stanford's home is finished, at a two-million-dollar cost. Crocker's is going up to two million three hundred thousand. Mark Hopkins's is going to cost three million. That's over seven million dollars to put roofs over three families, all of it taken out of railroads. You can't tell me that giving Charlie Masterson a decent burial or paying Minshall's hospital bill is going to stop the trains from running."

Engles sat staring at the clipping. When he spoke his manner was conciliatory.

"If it were only Charlie and Ben we could do it, Debs. But there are men getting hurt and killed every day of the week . . ."

". . . and their families are all entitled to protection."

Engles shook his head.

"You seem to have some misguided idea that trains are run for the men who work them. Get wise; they're run for passengers and freight. We didn't bring your firemen into the world and we didn't bring them into the yards asking for jobs. If they'd stop hitting the booze and handle their jobs better . . ."

Gene knew that the firemen were hard drinkers but the insinuation that the men had been drunk on the job and had killed each other was more than he could stomach.

"I want a funeral for Charlie Masterson, a thousand dollars for his wife, doctor bills for Ben Minshall and five hundred dollars to tide him over."

"I can give you absolutely nothing."

"Then we'll sue for negligence."

Engles relaxed. "Now be your age, Debs, you know the law of the land: the Fellow Servant Rule says that the company is not responsible for accidents caused by fellow workmen."

Gene was stuck. He swallowed hard.

"You've got to give me the promise of a job for Ben," he cried.

"Did I say I wouldn't?" replied Engles, who knew a good compromise when he had flushed one. "We'll stake him out as a crossing guard. My clock says it's five minutes after eight, Debs; if you don't get over to Hulman's right fast you'll lose your nice soft job behind that desk."

Gene winced under the implication that he sat behind a comfortable desk while firemen risked their lives. He turned and walked out of Engles's office, defeated . . . defeated by a man's heartless indifference to the fate of other human beings. But even as the door closed behind him his nature rejected the cynicism: Superintendent Engles's coldness and cruelty were a false front masking . . . fear: fear that he would be blamed for the accident, fear that he would be made responsible for the heavy loss, fear that he might have to go to his employers and ask for money for Charlie and Ben, be fired, disgraced. . . . Fear. Man's birthright. His death shroud. Fear.

Although he was already late for work he went to the roundhouse and passed the word that the firemen would gather that night.

— 12 —

He arrived at the meeting room a half hour early. Twelve of the members were already there; the other two were out on runs. Most of them were in their overalls, their faces as black as coal miners'. For these men who rode the tenders, death was literally just around the turn; no one had to remind them that it was the merest accident that Charlie Masterson lay dead in his little front room and Ben Minshall lay on a hospital bed while they sat in these chairs, for the moment whole.

Gene had no minute books with him, nor did he open the meeting formally. Somewhere between the door and the opposite window ledge against which he leaned he began to talk, for all he knew in the middle of a sentence; for he had been talking furiously to himself inside his head all day. He told the twelve silent, unmoving men of his interview with Engles; then, not knowing how he slipped into the sentence, or even that he had made the decision in his mind, he said:

"There's no one can help them but us. We've got to bury Charlie and pay his family the thousand dollars insurance. We must take care of Ben's bills and pay him five hundred for the loss of his leg."

There was a twisted, almost breathless pause while the twelve faces looked up at him, baffled by his words. Dino Franchetti was the first to speak:

"But Charlie and Ben wasn't members. They never paid into no insurance fund."

"They were members," replied Gene stubbornly, "only they didn't know it, they didn't get around to signing their application blanks."

The firemen searched in their minds for Gene's meaning. Johnny Nichols murmured, "You'll never get National Headquarters to shell that money out of their treasury, Gene."

"We're not going to ask National Headquarters," he persisted. "We must take care of our own boys."

Henri Letescue lifted his weight heavily to his feet and said, "See here, Gene, this thing's for the men who believe in it, for the men who put out dues that their wives could be buying steaks with. We feel mighty sorry for Charlie and

Ben, but they wouldn't come in. You did everything in your power . . ."

Gene shook his head, sadly.

"I must have used the wrong arguments, Henri."

He went to his desk, put his elbows on the green felt and held his face in his hands. After a moment someone said from the rear of the room:

"Gene, you're talking about almost two thousand dollars. Where would we get that kind of money? Two thousand dollars! At a dollar and a quarter a day, that's fifteen hundred work days, Gene. We got kids at home, too."

Gene took his hands away from his face but instead of seeing the men in front of him he saw Ben's wife lying on her bed. When he spoke his voice came from neither his larynx nor his abdomen, but from his heart.

"They tell us that all men are brothers; this is not so. But some men are brothers; Charlie Masterson and Ben Minshall are your brothers. When there was work to be done, they were at your side to do it; when there was no work, they suffered and starved beside you. They knew which muscles in your back ached so bad you couldn't throw another scoop of coal; and when you ate bad food and had the runs, they know how you leaned against the cab to keep from fainting in the weakness and the heat. When your pay was cut, theirs was cut, and their children had as many bites less of beef and bread as your children. If you were too ill to do your job one night, if you were late, if you took a drink too many, they covered for you. There is nothing you could do or feel that these men haven't done or felt, nothing they could not understand and sympathize with. You have sweated together before blazing ovens, and frozen together in roadside shacks; you have been crushed and maimed, yes, and killed together. This is brotherhood. So long as we have this, we are not alone on the earth. But once this brotherhood is gone, we are no better than those animals, human as well as beast, who devour each other. Our jobs can vanish, our money can be used up, our health and strength can disappear, there can be nothing left to our security . . . but while we have brothers, brothers we do not abandon, and who do not abandon us, we are secure on this earth, we cannot be destroyed."

The next day at noon Gene went to see Riley McKeen. McKeen was a maverick: born into money and culture, he wore them both informally, like his specially made silk shirts and loose-fitting suits. McKeen enjoyed people for their flavor and cared nothing about the town's social stratification. He was sitting with his feet up on the desk, and Gene noticed amusedly that there was a hole in the sole of one of his shoes. In Terre Haute he was known as the finest rich man that ever lived. He was always the first name on any collection list and no one ever went to him for a favor that he didn't get. He was a chunky man, florid of complexion, with walrus mustaches.

McKeen was fond of Gene, liked the way the boy had organized the Occidental Literary Club, put over the Ingersoll lecture and come back strong from the Anthony discouragement.

"What can I do for you, Gene?"

"I'd like to tell you a story, Mr. McKeen. I know you'll be interested because it has to do with people."

McKeen's male secretary came in with a tray of crackers and a bottle of milk. McKeen took the tray, then said, "Archie, bring another glass for Mr. Debs. He's lunching with me today."

Archie laughed, said, "Mr. Debs, you picked the worst restaurant in town."

McKeen sat back in his chair, slowly sipping his milk as Gene told him about Masterson and Minshall, told him about their wives and children, about the long period of layoff just the year before and the desperate straits the families were in.

McKeen put his half-empty glass down on the desk.

"Yes, Gene, that's an interesting human story. How much do you want?"

"We figure we need eighteen hundred dollars."

The sympathy vanished from McKeen's face. He came down abruptly in his swivel chair.

"Gene, that's too big a bite to put on one man. I'll contribute two hundred and fifty dollars to the fund."

Gene's face reddened.

"I guess I didn't make myself clear, Mr. McKeen. It's generous of you to offer a contribution but we want to pay everything ourselves. I've got a paper here with twelve signatures on it, all reliable firemen. Mine will make thirteen. We want to borrow eighteen hundred dollars from your bank at the regular interest rate and pay it back, so much a month."

McKeen turned away in his swivel chair and gazed out the window. After a moment he called out, "Archie!" When Archie came in McKeen wrote something on a slip of paper and murmured:

"In cash."

The two men sat in silence, not looking at each other. In a few moments Archie was back with some bank notes. McKeen handed the packet to Gene.

"Thank you, Mr. McKeen. I want you to know you'll never lose a penny on this loan."

"No, Gene, I don't expect I will."

"Now if you'll give me the paper to sign."

"Paper? Oh yes. Suppose you just write on this sheet, 'I owe you eighteen hundred dollars,' sign your name to it and then clip that sheet of twelve names to the back."

Gene did as he was instructed. He was too excited to realize that McKeen was making him a personal loan, that there wasn't a bank in the world which would have considered those thirteen signatures as collateral.

Late that afternoon the Rev. Peter Hanford read the burial service over Charlie Masterson. Gene delivered the thousand dollars in cash to Mrs. Masterson and the five hundred to Mrs. Minshall in envelopes marked *Brotherhood of Locomotive Firemen, Terre Haute Local.*

The regular union meeting was not scheduled for ten days. Gene spent the intervening evenings studying reports on railroad accidents, drawing up crude charts to indicate the kinds of accidents which happened most frequently, and under what conditions. At the next meeting he intended to ask for a committee to determine the causes.

On the night of the meeting he was detained at home, helping his father arrange a showcase of good French wines for which Daniel had just secured the agency. He reached the headquarters at ten minutes after eight. Sitting grim-faced on the chairs and window sills and leaning around the walls were all of Terre Haute's firemen.

No one said hello when he came in, no one looked up. The air was tense.

Silently he strode to his desk. It was covered with papers, green-backs, silver and gold pieces. Dazed, uncomprehending, he ran his fingers through the papers, saw they were filled-in application blanks, some of them going all the way back to the first batch he and Theodore had mailed.

Slowly he grasped what had happened. Every man in the room had become a member. Without even trying to make an estimate of the amount of money on the table, he knew that it was many times the required dues: folded greenbacks that had been hidden from light for years, stored in sugar jars against an emergency; gold pieces that had been withdrawn from circulation and had been lying in some secret bureau drawer.

Standing there, gazing at the solid phalanx of men looking toward him, Gene Debs knew that his local had at last been born. Born like everything else worthy of life: in pain and blood.

BOOK TWO

PASSIONATE PILGRIM

To GENE IT WAS EXCITING NEWS THAT THE FIREMEN WERE
to have a press of their own. He had confidence in the power of
the written word; here was an opportunity for education, for
building unity among the members; and here, he felt, was the
chance to wage the fight against two evils which he believed
had done labor the most harm: drink and strikes. He knew
that the firemen drank to escape the drudgery of their world,
but he knew also what a heavy price they paid for this momentary illusion that they had dissolved their iron chains in
the magic liquid of alcohol. He thought the magazine ought
to print short stories in which firemen were the heroes, articles about life on the railroads, also good technical material:
"How to Run a Locomotive," "The Art of Firing."

William Sayre, a Chicago newspaper reporter, was going to
edit the magazine of the Brotherhood of Locomotive Firemen. Sayre wrote Gene asking him to contribute an editorial,
but a jingle had been running through his head all day while
he entered figures in his ledgers at Hulman's. Except for his
jottings in the notebooks he had never done any writing, yet
good and serious writing had always been one of the household gods. Had not Daniel Debs given his first son the middle
name of Victor, in honor of the immortal Victor Hugo?

Gene sat at his desk in a high state of expectancy. He took
a fresh sheet of paper and wrote down:

I Have Drunk My Last Glass

No, my comrades, I thank you—not any for me;
My last chain is riven—henceforth I'm free,
I will go to my house and my children tonight
With no fumes of liquor, their spirits to blight;
And with tears in my eyes I will beg my poor wife
To forgive me the wreck I have made of her life.
I have never refused you before? Let that pass,
For I've drank my last glass, boys,
I have drank my last glass.

The editorial did not get itself written; he tried a dozen versions during October before he was even partially satisfied.

The weeks of November seemed to crawl by, for he was wild with desire to see the first copy of the *Locomotive Firemen's Magazine*. At last he came home to find a packet awaiting him; with shaking fingers he gazed at the bright cover, a group of firemen standing before a giant locomotive, and over their heads a banner which proclaimed the philosophy of the order: *Benevolence, Sobriety and Industry*. He turned quickly to the editorial page, his lips moving while he read his own sentences. "Many persons have asked 'What is the Brotherhood of Locomotive Firemen?' We answer them in this wise: An Order for the protection and elevation mentally, morally and socially, of all classes and denominations of mankind who step on the footboard. Our aim and belief is to place such men upon the locomotive engine as have received their education through our Order, to give to the public a class of men whom trust can be reposed in." They had also printed his poem.

He pressed a copy into the hands of Theodore, then gave one each to his mother and father. There was one copy left over; he slipped into an old sweater and walked quickly down the block to Gloria's house.

He sprinted up the Weston stairs, grasped the knob and pushed on the door to open it; but the door stuck. It was the first time he had ever known the Weston house to be locked. He stood gazing at the knob bewildered, then realized that if he wanted to get in he had better knock on the clapper.

Paul Weston opened the door. Instead of being in his jacket and slippers he was neatly shaven, wearing a necktie and his tight-fitting Sunday suit. There was a note of constraint in his voice as he said:

"Hello, Gene, this is a surprise."

Through the archway Gene saw that Mrs. Weston was at

the dinner table; he also saw a strange back blocking the view of Gloria, who sat opposite. As he walked into the dining room he noted that Gloria was wearing a silk dress, her hair braided like intertwined copper wire. She rose, walked around the table and put out her hand for his.

"Gene, how nice you came. We'll set a place for you."

He felt somehow unhappy. "No, I've had . . . we just finished . . ."

"You can't have been home more than five minutes," she protested.

The conversation had taken place a few steps from the well-dressed stranger. Paul Weston said, "Mr. Harkness, may I present our old friend, Mr. Eugene Debs?"

Paul's sentence ended with a rising inflection, as though he were asking permission for the introduction. Mr. Harkness rose, turned to Gene and extended his hand. As Gene grasped it he was filled with admiration for the Weston guest: for Harkness was a man magnificently put together; thick black hair combed back to the neckline, large dark eyes in a handsome face. Gene could see the outlines of his powerful shoulders and chest under the expensive cloth. For the first time in his life he stood in awe, embarrassed by the fact that he had slipped into a sweater with holes at the elbows, that he had taken off his necktie and left it on his desk, that in his enthusiasm he had not even troubled to comb his hair.

"Mr. Harkness is a railroad attorney from Chicago," Paul Weston was saying. "He came down to settle a little matter."

Gene saw that Paul was impressed by Mr. Harkness, and he was surprised, since Weston's life had been a flight from the wealthy and socially prominent of Terre Haute. Perhaps it was the impression Harkness gave, of a man who had battled his way upward with his fists and brains, that had captivated the family.

"Gene, do sit down and join us," urged Mrs. Weston.

"Thank you, but I'm not dressed; Mother is expecting me back right away. I just came over to . . ."

He limped to a halt, feeling suddenly that his enthusiasm had been juvenile; that he could not show the *Locomotive Firemen's Magazine* to the Westons under Mr. Harkness's worldly eyes. For just a flashing, bitter instant he had a sense of how crude and childish the magazine was, with its blatant cover and amateurish content.

He murmured his apologies, told Mr. Harkness that it was a pleasure to meet him, and went through the arch. Gloria got to the door before him.

"Gene, why are you running away? You haven't even told me why you came; it must be something important."

She glanced down and saw the brightly colored volume in his hand. Her face lighted with pleasure. She looked quickly toward the arch, leaned up and pecked his cheek. "The magazine has come at last. Did they print your editorial?"

Miserable, Gene could only murmur, "Gloria, please let me go. You have a guest. I'll come back again tomorrow night."

Too disappointed to return home, he decided to show the first issue to the Rev. Peter Hanford. Clarissa answered the door, and Peter Hanford led Gene into his study. It was a quiet, pleasant room filled with books on philosophy and religion. He motioned Gene to a chair.

"The board has engaged a young man to serve as my assistant, and he is very subtly taking over my functions."

"Are they still fighting the Ingersoll battle?"

"The funeral services I conducted for Charlie Masterson gave them fresh impetus."

Gene rose. "But why hasn't a clergyman the right to comfort the family of a man who has just been killed?"

"My congregation felt that I had injured their social status. Parenthetically, my church board includes several directors of the Terre Haute and Indianapolis. They thought I was taking the side of the workingman against the railroad."

Gene could only shake his head sadly.

"I'm out now, Gene," the minister continued; "no one has said anything, Clarissa and I haven't been given a dispossess notice yet, but within a matter of a few months my young assistant will have taken over all the duties and there will be nothing for me to do but move."

— 2 —

He had been at Hulman's for more than two years now, and although he had received the regulation one-dollar-a-week raise every six months, he was still doing the identical clerical work that had been given to him on his first day in the office. He did his job well, but it was obvious that he had no desire to undertake more difficult tasks or greater responsibility. Young men who had come in after him had been promoted and were receiving larger salaries. Gene was afraid of promotion and larger salaries; he needed every spare ounce of energy for the union.

Hulman's five-year-old son had taken a liking to the tall, blond fellow with the infectious laugh. Every time he came into the building he ran to Gene's desk. Gene was telling him

the story of the engine that got mad and ran into the woods
to hide from its engineer, when Hulman came to claim him.

"Gene, why don't you ride home with us?" he asked.

It was now past six, and the long narrow office was empty.
Gene swooped the boy up, sat him astride his shoulders and
walked out to the Hulman carriage. Hulman leaned toward
him and said quietly:

"Gene, you're a bit of a puzzle to me."

"Sometimes I'm a bit of a puzzle to myself, Mr. Hulman."

"You have a great deal of natural ability, but apparently
you don't want to get ahead."

Gene's eyes met Mr. Hulman's.

"It isn't that I don't want to get ahead . . ."

"Does the union pay you enough wages to make up for
what you could be getting from us?"

"Oh, I don't get any money from the union, they can't
afford it yet."

Mr. Hulman pulled his head down sharply.

"Mind you, I approve of your work for the Occidental
Club and the fireman's local. In fact I think they're good
training for you. But do they have a future?"

Gene launched into an enthusiastic account of the possibilities of unionism. Hulman let him go on for several moments
before breaking in.

"That's all fine for the firemen, Gene, but what does it
mean for you, personally?"

Stumblingly, with a soft, eager, embarrassed smile, he murmured, "Well, there's so much to be done. You know yourself, Mr. Hulman, how desperately the railroad men need organization."

"I don't think it wise to try to change people's character,
Gene, but one day you're going to be obliged to be practical.
You may not want to, but the world and circumstances will
force you to, and then you must not be caught off base."

When Gene did not answer, Hulman went on. "Somewhere, sometime you're going to have to start thinking about
yourself, that's only common sense. Idealism is a luxury you
can't afford in this competitive world."

They had driven up the long circular driveway of the Hulman home, the carriage wheels crunching along the wide
gravel pathway. The driver lifted the little boy out of the
seat. Gene and Hulman sat quietly in the rear of the carriage.

"I admit the truth of what you are saying, Mr. Hulman,
but I don't know what to do about it. I'm completely happy.
I'm enjoying my work. I have everything I want; and my father is doing better since he put in that line of French wines."

"And you're not frightened about the future? You're not afraid that you're throwing away your best years?"

Gene thought a few moments before answering quietly, "No, I'm not afraid, because I think there will always be plenty of the kind of work I like to do."

"And the things that money can buy?" Hulman made an expansive gesture which embraced his carriage, his beautifully matched horses, his spacious grounds and the white-columned home.

"I don't seem to find much time for them, Mr. Hulman." Gene laughed because he knew this answer was the most ridiculous of them all. "When I was a boy I used to go along with my father on the community hunts. The other men seemed to hunt for the pleasure of the kill: they shot hundreds of prairie chickens and then left them to spoil. When Daniel had enough game to feed his family, he stopped shooting. I guess that's the way I feel about money."

On his way home from Mr. Hulman's he stopped at a bookstore and bought a copy of *The Preparation and Delivery of Speeches*. As secretary of his local he would be expected to speak at the Indianapolis convention of the Locomotive Firemen.

Oratory was a great art, almost as well loved as concertizing.

"Theo, you've got to help me," pleaded Gene. "I don't want the delegates to know it's the first time I've spoken from a platform."

Theodore opened the little book and read, " 'No other element in the delivery is more deserving of attention than the voice, the qualities of which are Purity, Strength and Flexibility.' " He looked up grinning and murmured, "Now let me hear you be pure, strong and flexible."

"The pure and strong parts I understand, but how do you be flexible?"

Theodore exclaimed, "First you must get set! 'The normal position is usually about three feet from the front of the platform. If too far forward, the speaker suggests undue familiarity. On the other hand, if he stands more than three feet back from the edge of the platform, he will suggest timidity.' "

Theodore jumped up, paced off three feet from the desk, which brought him almost to the door, then said, "Stand here. 'The head should be up, the body erect, the shoulders square and at right angles to the audience.' "

"All right, I'm set," said Gene. "Now you sit behind the

desk and pretend you're a wildly cheering audience of tallow pots."

It had taken Gene only an hour to memorize his speech, for he had written it out of a full heart. If, as his father had warned him at the outset, every union must ultimately devolve into a striking force, then unions could not survive. Strikes were the industrial equivalent of force and violence; in any war, both sides had to lose; better to achieve even the smallest fragment of their program than to bring down upon their heads the censure of industry, the press and the public, end with chaos, bitterness and disgrace.

Before he realized it he had reached the end of his plea.

"Why don't you take it over and try it out on Gloria?" suggested Theodore. "You could ask her about things like purity and undue familiarity."

Gene was feeling exhilarated. The idea sounded good.

"Thanks. I'll bring you a report."

But when he arrived at the Weston house he found valises standing in the hallway, and Mrs. Weston throwing covers over the parlor furniture. Gene had opened the door and walked in without announcing himself; he now stood perplexed, listening to Gloria call from upstairs:

"Mother, if we're going to dine at the Bismarck Hotel, won't I need an evening gown?"

Getting no answer to her question, she came running down the stairs, her eyes ablaze. She pulled up short when she saw Gene standing there, a sheaf of papers in his hand and a puzzled expression on his face.

"Oh, hello," she said.

"Are you going somewhere?"

She hung the gown over the banister and came slowly down the last half-dozen steps.

"We're going to Chicago. Father has some business . . ."

Mrs. Weston came out of the parlor. "Isn't it wonderful, Gene? Mr. Harkness invited us for a whole week."

Gene was more startled than Gloria when his voice came out of him dry and hoarse.

"It's nice . . . you're going to have a vacation."

Gloria had regained her poise.

"Mr. Harkness said he had no right to ask Mother and me to stay home alone. I've never been to Chicago, Gene, and I've heard so much about it."

Paul Weston called down from the head of the stairs.

"Why, Gene, how nice of you to come and wish us bon voyage."

Gene could think of no answer.

"He couldn't have come to say good-by, Father," said Gloria, "because he didn't know we were going." She turned back to Gene and spoke in a low voice so that her parents would not hear. "It was all so sudden; the telegram came only a couple of hours ago; and I haven't seen you for more than a week."

This time Gene could not reply as he had so many hundreds of times before, "I have been busy." In fact, he couldn't say a thing.

— 3 —

The first reports to reach him about the strike of trainmen in Pittsburgh told of peaceable demonstrations in the streets, with considerable portions of the population joining against the highly unpopular Pennsylvania Central Railroad. However no trains moved out of the city and before long a division of Philadelphia militia was ordered in to clear the tracks and enable the trains to roll. The militia, marching toward a railroad crossing, suddenly came face to face with a large crowd of strikers and their sympathizers. Some of the demonstrators had stones in their hands, and let them fly. Soldiers were struck, an officer gave a command, militiamen fired. Some thirty men fell. For the first time in twelve years, since the end of the Civil War, Americans were killing Americans.

By nightfall thousands of people were in the streets, many carrying guns and torches. They set fire to the railroad yards surrounding the roundhouse, burned the machine shops, a hundred locomotives, sixteen hundred cars. The strikers claimed that the damage had been done by the hungry and unemployed who had thronged into Pittsburgh; the railroads charged that this was a vast conspiracy organized by the unions to terrorize the companies and take over the roads.

Gene was heartsick. He would have liked to be on the scene; but he could not leave his job, nor would he have had any function there; for the firemen and brakemen who had struck against another slash in wages had resisted all efforts to be unionized. To him it seemed a wanton piece of irony to be attacked in the national press for violence which the Brotherhood had officially repudiated, and for the conduct of men who had refused to join their union.

Beaten, cowed, abandoned, the men returned to work, at the lowered wage.

It was against this background of tension and bitterness that Gene donned his one good suit and set out for the Locomotive Firemen's convention. He had no money to spare for a railroad ticket, nor would he have spent it on a coach seat if he had. He climbed up into the cab and rode to Indianapolis with the engineer and fireman.

His bright excitement over attending his first convention dimmed as he entered the auditorium. A pall hung over the meeting. The first reports were given by glum, almost furtive men who seemed to be looking over the shoulder of their thoughts for fear there were spies behind them. It was not until one courageous delegate cried, "The program we set up here will be successful 'When the frost is on the punkin and the fodder's in the shock,' " that the men unbent, laughed and applauded, for they had all read the poem by some local poet the night before in the Indianapolis *Journal*.

Gene silently blessed the versifier, for it was his turn to go out on the platform and make his maiden flight. In his memory he heard Theodore reading from the book on oratory, " '. . . three feet from the front of the platform . . . voice pure, flexible.' "

Joshua Leach was introducing him to the two hundred assembled delegates with his usual "heave it in and get away" manner.

"This is Gene Debs, the towheaded kid I put in charge in Terre Haute. I told you he'd make good."

There was a sharp interest in the youngster on the platform. Leach sat down and Gene was on his own. At twenty-two he was just half the age of the youngest delegates, and the only one present who wore no mustache. The hall was small, the high windows letting in a diffused light. To Gene it seemed that the men facing him were not two hundred disparate individuals, but one man, one mind, one hope. To his astonishment he found he had already begun speaking, and that he was breaking the rules: he was too close to the edge of the platform, his tall frame was bent over toward the delegates: the voice that came from deep inside him had little need to think about pureness or flexibility.

He told the delegates that the Brotherhood of Locomotive Firemen was of vital interest and benefit to the commercial world. He portrayed a railroad as an architect of progress, its roadbed as a pathway of enlightenment. He elaborated the responsibility placed upon railroad workers, then deplored the low wages of these same skilled men, so low that they could scarcely provide their families with the necessities of life; he drew his fullest round of approval when he charged the cut in wages with responsibility for the recent strikes which had terrified the nation. Then he enunciated his belief that the Brotherhood was a benevolent society, committed to the philosophy of "resist not evil."

"A strike signifies anarchy and revolution, and the one of but a few days ago will never be blotted from the records of memory. The question has often been asked: Does the Brotherhood encourage strikers? To this question we most emphatically answer: No! To disregard the laws which govern our land? To stain our hands with the crimson blood of our fellow beings? We again say no, a thousand times, no!"

He had expected confirmation. Instead his words plunged into a deep silence. As the men shifted in their seats, moved to one side the better to see him or to blot him out, he realized that the air about him had grown perceptibly cool. He stumbled through his closing sentences, feeling the delegates withdraw from his words, withdraw from his presence, saw them gaze up at the little windows or hunch forward in their seats and stare down at the floor. Joshua Leach's eyes were turned away as he left the stage. Somewhere, somehow, he had failed, he had let his brothers down.

He went out through a side door and walked for several hours in the cold night air. He had intended to remain in Indianapolis the next day, but now he felt he could not face the delegates again. The thought of personal failure did not sadden him, only the realization that he had not measured up.

He heard several church bells commingling the news of midnight. Only then did he realize that the streets were deserted.

No, not deserted, for there ahead of him was the sound of footsteps, and the form of a man loomed big in the darkness. They came toward each other like two ships on an otherwise empty sea; the skipper of each could observe that the other was rudderless and bound for no port. Neither moved to let the other by, but stood grinning as though this were a long-planned rendezvous.

The other was in his mid-twenties, Gene guessed, with a face as round as an Indian pumpkin, his corn-colored hair shocked to right and left of what probably been a part several days before. He wasn't fat, he wasn't even round, but he gave the impression of a roly-poly, and certainly he must have had his spectacles on inside out, for they had the effect of magnifying his own jolly blue eyes instead of the things those eyes were supposed to see.

"Ah," exclaimed the stranger, "there's another soul in Indianapolis who roams the streets after midnight. Are you a burglar or a poet?"

"A burglar."

"Good, then that leaves the category of poet for me. My name is Jimmy Riley. The first time an Eastern magazine prints one of my poems, I shall include my middle name in the signature."

"My name is Debs, Eugene Debs. Nobody's ever going to pay me for a poem, but my father gave me the middle name of Victor, after Victor Hugo."

"Ah," exclaimed the stranger. "Your father must be a poet too, his name is Walt Whitman."

"Whitman is a bachelor; my father has a grocery store."

"Do you know Indianapolis by night? Cities are like people when they're asleep: you can look behind these false fronts of wood and brick and plaster. You can read their innermost secrets, you can tell their age, you can see whether they are pure of heart or evil in their desires."

"I haven't thought of it that way. In fact I wasn't thinking about Indianapolis, or the walls or houses."

"You have been disappointed in love," murmured Riley. "We shall go to your sweetheart, we shall read her my beautiful verses, we shall soften her stony heart until she forgives you and holds you to her breast."

Gene found himself chuckling.

"True, I have been jilted, but not by one person; by two hundred."

"Magnificent," exclaimed Riley. "All my life I have longed to meet a man who could love two hundred women. I could love two hundred poems, if I had written them all myself . . ."

"They are not women," replied Gene. "They are delegates, union delegates."

Riley stopped short, linked one arm through Gene's and gazed up at him. "You are a union delegate! You are an executive, a man of affairs. You are in control of your every emotion. You know exactly what you will be doing a week from Thursday at three-seventeen in the afternoon."

"I will be making entries in Hulman and Cox's ledgers. What do you do for a living?"

"I live for a living. I breathe, I sleep, I walk in the woods, I write verses. What more must a man do to live?"

"Eat."

"You are a materialist, my friend. I am a troubadour. I sing my little ballads and people cover me with flowers, give me the choicest of wines and the second joints of the fowl."

"Have you by any chance a poem in your vest pocket?"

"My sweet, innocent friend, I might be found in the streets without a hair on my head or a stitch of clothing on my carcass, but never in all my life would I be found so naked that I would not have one poem in my pocket."

They had come to a little park with a string of billiard-green benches edging a graveled path. The chill and sickening sense of failure left Gene's heart.

"Let's sit down," he said; "read me the one you like the best."

"They are all the best," replied Riley, and pulled out from his pocket papers of all colors, sizes and functions. "Would you like to hear *The Frost Is on the Punkin* or would you prefer *Old-Fashioned Roses?*"

Gene laughed again, for with the moon shining on the thatches of Riley's corn-bond hair, he looked as though he were the frost on the punkin, incarnate. Then he remembered the delegate who had quoted the poem.

"Say, did you write that one about the fodder in the shock?"

"Who else could have written it but a troubadour who has roamed the steppes of Indiana?"

"One of the delegates at the Firemen's Convention quoted it tonight. Got a big hand, too."

"My poem . . . quoted at a convention," said Riley ecstatically; "and when I think of all the unkind things the papers have been saying about labor unions!"

"Why haven't the Eastern magazines printed your work?"

"You have to have a great name to get your poems printed."

"What about a great poem, wouldn't that help?"

"Not in the slightest. I once wrote a poem called *Leonainie,* signed it with the name of Edgar Allan Poe and sent it in to the Kokomo *Dispatch.* They published it under his name. Doesn't that prove my point?"

"Was it a bad poem?"

"Certainly not. I can't write a bad poem."

"Then you see, it was your great poem they wanted, not the name of Edgar Allan Poe."

"My young friend," mourned Riley, "you have me momentarily confused."

"How would you like to come over to Terre Haute and read your poems for the Occidental Literary Club? We'll pay your expenses and give you half the profits, if any."

Riley sprang off the bench, threw his sheaf of papers into the air. "This is a turning point in my life. I shall not wait for an Eastern editor to accept one of my poems. This is an occasion far more auspicious, propitious and . . . do you know any other words that end in 'ishous?'"

"Delicious! How about two weeks from tonight? I'll announce it as readings from original poems by Jimmy Riley."

The man looked up at Gene quietly, gratefully.

"If it doesn't require too much extra printing," he pleaded, "would you mind putting in my middle name, Whitcomb?"

The tonic of Riley's personality had cleared Gene's head, lightened his burden of inadequacy. There could be no doubt that the delegates would think of him in Joshua Leach's words as a "tow-headed kid," charge him with being as naked of experience as of mustache.

"I'll tell you one saving grace about youth, Mr. James Whitcomb Riley," he murmured aloud: "It's not incurable."

— 4 —

By the time he returned to Terre Haute, pictures and stories of the Pittsburgh fires and the clashes between workingmen and troops had been headlined on the front pages of the newspapers, together with pleas for federal and state legislation to outlaw the "willful bands of labor." He walked to the union meeting with a heavy heart and sense of foreboding. As he entered the room he saw that vandals had wrecked part of the furniture, that the desk was lying on its side, and there were jagged holes in the carpet and in the plaster on the walls. He righted the table, picked up a folding chair and sat tapping his gavel on the torn felt surface. The room was airless; he went to the window, but the lock had been smashed. He searched in his pocket for the knife he had purchased so exultantly the night Joshua Leach had summoned him to the meeting, thrust the big blade under the wood frame and pushed upward. He exerted too much pressure, and the blade snapped in half.

There was no need for him to look at his watch to know that the minutes were speeding by, that it was nine o'clock, and that not one member had turned up for the meeting. He was back where he had started; only then he had been fired with the enthusiasm of a new venture, he had been a scientist experimenting in a laboratory. It seemed to him that he was twenty years older instead of just two: the fun and excitement were gone: the game had assumed the features of war.

He picked up his minutes book and notes from the convention, closed the door behind him and went to the yards. Dad Jenkins and Sam Baker were polishing their engines prior to going out on their runs. They pretended not to see him, but Gene had been a fireman long enough to know that everyone working in a roundhouse knows who goes in and out of the big front doors. He made for the station house. As he crossed the tracks, Dino Franchetti came toward him. Gene stopped in front of the wiry little Italian.

"Hello, Dino," he said.

But Dino passed without looking up. Gene stood for a long time, his head down, his eyes unseeing, his long arms and long legs seeming to hang in mid-air, unbased. He heard a voice speaking behind him, a strange voice. He did not turn, but listened to the words.

"Excuse me, Mr. Debs, the superintendent of the Terre Haute wants to see you in his office."

The voice stopped and the voice went away. After a while Gene blinked his eyes a few times, gulped, and made his way slowly back to the superintendent's office. Engles was sitting behind his dispatcher's desk, a green eyeshade strapped tight over his eyes.

"Terre Haute's getting to be quite a big town, isn't it?" he asked.

"Growing every day."

"And the state of Indiana is one of the biggest in the nation?"

"So they tell me."

"With all these thousands of square miles around you, and all the interesting places you could be, why do you pick out the Terre Haute and Indianapolis railway yards?"

Gene caught more from Engles's tone than words.

"You believe in private property, Mr. Debs?"

"Indeed I do."

"Then suppose you get off our private property and stay off! We don't want you around here any more. Neither do the firemen."

"Have they told you that?"

"We know what's in their minds better than they do; they're just a bunch of bohunks with barely brains enough to shovel coal." Engles rose in rage. "I'm issuing an order to you, Debs: stay off this property or I'll have you arrested."

Gene shook himself vigorously. A look of incredulity and amazement came into his eyes. He stared straight at Engles.

Engles lowered himself into his seat. "You'll also find yourself fired from Hulman's."

"And how will that happen?"

"If we don't haul Hulman's freight, he goes out of business."

Gene glided around the desk, stood towering over the man in the chair.

"My apologies," he murmured. "I have underestimated you. I didn't realize how resourceful you were. I can see now why you have become a superintendent: you have ideas, originality, daring. I predict a great future for you."

"That's more than I can predict for you."

Gene walked home slowly, his hat in his hand, letting the autumnal breeze cool his feverish head. He slipped through the side entrance into his little office, walked to his desk, turned up the wick of the kerosene lamp. The light came up slowly. He had a feeling that he was not alone in the room. He whirled about. Huddled in the corner next to the door, his face drawn and his eyes wide, stood Dino Franchetti. The two men stared at each other wordlessly. Then Dino came to Gene.

"Gene, we are swine, but you must forgive us. They have threatened to fire us if we do not quit the union. Worse, they will use the black list. We will not be able to get a job on any railroad in the country. They told us if anyone is seen talking to you . . ."

Gene's first reaction was overwhelming relief: the men had not abandoned him and unionism of their own accord; they had been terrorized. Against their own decision he would not have known where to turn; against the company's intimidation he would know how to work.

"Dino, my friend, sit down. Now listen to me, Dino. They cannot make their threats good. If they discharge every fireman in Terre Haute they cannot move their trains."

"They will bring them in from Chicago, from Minneapolis. They will fire the trains themselves."

"Dino, don't you see, this is the opportunity they have been waiting for—to break our organization. They would make up that Pittsburgh damage joyously if those riots could be used to break every trainmen's union. You have done them no harm. What do we ask of them except a few extra dollars in pay? A few safeguards to keep you from being killed? But they don't want you to have the right to ask for anything, Dino; not even a penny's worth."

Dino looked up at him, his eyes frightened.

"Gene, I have eleven bambinos. Do you know how much spaghetti eleven mouths can cry for?"

Gene had no eleven mouths to feed; his own stomach would be fed by his mother and father if an emergency arose. He put his bony arm around Dino's shoulder, pressing his fingers strongly into the little Italian's flesh.

"You are right, Dino. Do not know me if you pass me in the streets, and I shall understand. But just as sure as you're sitting in this room with me, that union will not be destroyed. You will come back into it. You and the other sixty-three men, the firemen all over the country, will come back, and one day those eleven mouths of yours, Dino, will have more to eat, and a bigger, warmer home to live in, and money for education and doctors and for some of the decencies of life because you came back into your union."

He felt stifled. He went down to the river, walked along the bank of the Wabash. For the moment he was defeated. He had an open, honest, uncomplicated nature, trusting, rich in faith. He had no ulterior motives or hidden schemes; there was little that came into the recesses of his mind that could not be spoken out in meeting. From his earliest days he knew that if you believed in something you stood up for it, you fought for it, you were open and unrelenting in your drive, you took the consequences if you were wrong, but if your cause was a good one eventually you would accomplish some part of your objective. For him the tragedy was that once again the unions would be driven underground, obliged to resort to secrecy, to cabalistic ritual, to meet in dark and hidden places, afraid of their employers, afraid of the police, afraid of traitors in their midst, afraid of their own laws and government.

Terror was abroad in the land again. His thoughts went back to the night he had heard Robert Ingersoll and realized that fear was the dominant emotion of mankind, was born with him, died with him, was his ever-present comrade, shadowing his every step, hurting, maiming, amputating, freezing, from the cradle to the grave, converting the race of man to a breed of cowards, sick in body and sick in brain from the unconquerable fear. And that was how it would be with these men: fear rode again, cracking the whip, numbing their courage, their resolution, their intelligence. This above all must be conquered, for here was the great enemy, the eventual destroyer of man: fear.

When Gene reached home the next evening he heard voices in the dining room behind the store: his father's voice, and a hearty booming laughter. He swept into the room, saw the table covered with one of Daisy's most beautiful cloths, the heavy family silverware, and the Limoges dishes her family had given her to bring to America.

"Welcome home, Gene Debs," boomed the big voice, and Gene found himself exchanging broad grins with Robert Ingersoll.

"Colonel Ingersoll! Only today I was thinking of . . . Why didn't you let me know you were coming?"

"I didn't know myself until a few hours ago."

Although it was only two years since Gene had seen him, he felt that Ingersoll was looking considerably older. Afterwards the two men went to Gene's workshop. Theodore was already working at the desk.

"I hear you're having some trouble," said Ingersoll. "Tell me about it."

Gene talked about his efforts to build a fireman's local in Terre Haute; and how it had now vanished into thin, poisoned air. "I'm stumped," he concluded.

Ingersoll sat on a corner of the desk. "I can give you one clue from my own experience. You plant and cultivate, irrigate and fertilize, and nothing happens; then history begins moving, impelled forward by its own imperatives, and soon it comes to your field. One morning you wake up, and lo! you have a full, fine crop where the night before there seemed to be only barren rows!"

"I . . . I suppose you're right."

"Are you suffering a little from disillusion, Gene?"

"Yes, to be frank with you."

"But that's perfectly natural, my boy. The idealist is always torn between disillusion and inner resolve. One of the bitterest lessons I had to learn, Gene, was that the job always has to be done over again, every day."

Gene was aghast. "You mean that no matter how completely a work is accomplished . . ."

"It doesn't stay accomplished," broke in Ingersoll. "If it did, we would all be living in a Utopia by now."

"But if a man knows that to be true, how can he continue?"

"Because if he doesn't carry on, if he doesn't renew his efforts every day of his life, then only the grasping and evil people remain active." His left arm had been lying across the corner of the table. He leaned over it and spoke in a low tone. "Oh yes, they let me speak now, but, Gene, whom am I convincing? In every city and hamlet in America clergymen are still preaching black hell, teaching hatreds of other religions, paralyzing the minds of little children by threats and intimidation—yes, Gene, the same kind of threats and intimidation that the superintendent of the Terre Haute and Indianapolis used against you."

"But you haven't quit!" exclaimed Gene. "You go on fighting."

Ingersoll shook his head in a vigorous denial.

"Ah, Gene, I've quit a hundred times. Once a group of people I had been teaching turned against me as an infidel, as a dangerous disciple of the Devil. I broke down. I said that I was through forever."

"Then what happened?"

A smile came over Robert Ingersoll's open, forthright face. "Wendell Phillips came to see me. I didn't even know he felt friendly toward my work. But some way he had heard that I was in trouble. He spent an evening with me and told me some of the things he had undergone in his fight to free the slaves: mobs, beatings, hangings in effigy. When he left, I knew that I could never give up no matter what happened. For you see, Gene Debs, the fighting spirit is handed down from generation to generation, not through relationship of blood, but through relationship of idea, of spirit. It was a living torch Wendell Phillips brought me that night; it keeps a light burning in the vast and encroaching darkness. You understand what I'm telling you, Gene?"

"Not exactly, Colonel Ingersoll, but I know that I do feel better. I'm ready to start all over again."

"I have a rabbi friend back home who quotes a line from the Talmud which I find helpful in times of discouragement: 'It is not upon thee to finish the work; neither art thou free to desist from it.' "

With that he arose and made his adieus, refusing Gene's offer to accompany him to the station.

Gene and Theodore sat in the quiet for a long time, then they heard the whistle of the late night train on its way to Chicago.

"Gene, what did Colonel Ingersoll come to Terre Haute for?"

"I don't know, Theo. Some kind of business, I suppose."

"He arrived on the four o'clock train, and he was in our house just a few minutes later. Now he's on that late train for Chicago."

Gene turned his head to one side, gazing at his kid brother for a moment.

"Theo, I believe you're right. Tired as he is, and sick of trains, he made that hard, dirty trip . . . because he heard I was in trouble. Theo, I have a great idea. Get out your pen and ink. We're going to invite Wendell Phillips to Terre Haute."

— 5 —

Despite the loss of his members he resumed his life as a practical trade unionist. He subscribed to the *Iron Moulders' Journal, Cigar Makers' Official Journal,* the *Labor Standard* of New England and the *National Labor Tribune* of Pittsburgh. He bought the New York *Times,* Chicago *Tribune* and San Francisco *Bulletin* in order to know what was happening in the great railroad centers; he wrote sharp editorials in the *Locomotive Firemen's Magazine*. Two injustices provided immediate targets: the dollar and twenty-five cents a day wage to which the firemen had been reduced during the 1873 depression was still in effect, even though business had recovered; secondly, the men were required to go to the roundhouse two hours every day, without pay, and polish their locomotive before they went out on their run.

Since he had been barred from the Terre Haute and Indianapolis yards, he wrote Superintendent Engles a letter in which he asked that the line restore the old wage scales and pay the fireman extra for the two hours of polishing in the roundhouse. Engles replied quickly but curtly that polishing engines had been part of a fireman's job as long as there had been a railroad; that he couldn't pay extra for that particular work any more than he could raise wages, for the railroad was losing money. To this Gene replied with a telegram that if the Terre Haute and Indianapolis were losing money, it was being badly managed: he had the haulage records and he knew that the line carried more freight and passengers than ever. He offered Engles a proposition: if in six months he could bring in a report proving that the union firemen gave better service and were involved in fewer accidents, Engles would then be obliged to raise the wages of everyone belonging to the local.

Engles ignored the rebuttal.

Gene walked rapidly across Terre Haute to Riley McKeen's estate. A servant led him into the library where McKeen was stretched out in a big leather chair, his feet up on a hassock, sipping a whisky-soda and reading Gibbon's *Decline and Fall of the Roman Empire*. The library was lined with a cherry-red mahogany. Gene guessed that there must be five thousand volumes.

Laying his book down on the table, McKeen asked Gene what he could do for him. The local had repaid the eighteen-hundred-dollar loan, giving McKeen a renewed confidence in the younger man. Gene told of being ordered away from the Terre Haute offices, his letter to Engles and the reply he had received. McKeen listened closely, then commented, "It's not the man's fault. Gene; he's the buffer between the employees and the owners. The more work he can get for the less money, the stronger he stands with his bosses."

"Tell me, Mr. McKeen, am I being unreasonable? Shouldn't these men be paid for that two hours of labor in the roundhouse?"

Slowly McKeen answered, "Yes, I think they should."

Gene slid into a chair, his knees week. "You mean you'll pay them extra for those two hours?"

His gratitude was so pathetic that McKeen sprang up and began pacing the room.

"Look, Gene! Don't fall into the fallacy of thinking that everyone who owns or manages industry is a son of a bee. Management has its troubles too: for the past few years we haven't been able to pay dividends, and the stockholders are screaming that they could be investing their savings elsewhere and getting a good return. Every day we need more capital, more tens of thousands, because engines and cars are getting more expensive; we have to re-lay hundreds of miles of track, but the money is hard to get. Try to remember that we're not all ogres, or misers gloating over our millions."

"I'll remember that, Mr. McKeen."

"What good would it do me to make an extra thousand dollars a year and feel that it came out of the hides of the Vandalia crews?"

Gene could not comment.

"You see all these books, Gene? They tell the history of the world. A hundred years from now when people pick up a book of history and read the name of Riley McKeen, I don't want them to turn around and spit. When the time comes for me to check my locomotive into the roundhouse, I want to be able to say I never took advantage of any man because he had less power or money than I had."

McKeen sank back in his chair, took a long draft of his whisky. "Tell you what I'll do, Gene, I'll take the offer you made to Engles. Come back in six months and prove to me by the record that the union firemen are doing a better job, and the Vandalia will give your men preferential hiring. I'll do better than that. I'll sign an order raising the union firemen to one dollar and forty cents a day basic pay. That'll bring the irregulars into your local so fast you won't be able to keep track of them."

He had looked forward to his work for the evening, but when he finished supper he found it difficult to get up from his chair, and he had to overcome the greatest reluctance to go out to his office. When he sat down to his desk and began mulling through the disorganized papers, a distaste rose in his chest that had reached the proportion of nausea by the time it got to his throat. He went to the door, opened it and stood gazing out into the starlit Terre Haute night; and he knew what he wanted, actually for what his whole system was aching: to hold Gloria's confiding hand in his, to see her lovely face before him, her eyes eager, excited, laughing at him, laughing at the goodness of life.

He found himself walking down Wabash Street, mounting the Weston steps, reaching out his hand for Gloria's, hearing her exclaim:

"Gene, I was just thinking about you. It must be thought transference or something."

His eyes feasted hungrily on her shining red hair and on her mouth. He linked his arm through hers, held her against his side for a moment, then said:

"Could we take your father's boat? I'd like to go miles and miles away from Terre Haute, away from everybody, just the two of us."

A flash of surprise and pleasure lighted her face.

"Of course. I'll ask Father for the key. I'll get some marshmallows and the coffeepot."

It was cool on the Wabash, but they sat side by side, each pulling on an oar, and soon they were at a secluded beach, and Gene had gathered wood for the small hot fire which he confined within a border of stones. They sat across from each other, their legs folded under them Indian style, while Gloria brewed the coffee and he toasted marshmallows on willowy branches.

"I'm so tired of myself and my jobs and everything I've been doing," he said. "You don't know what a joy it is to sit across from you and think about how lovely you are in the firelight, instead of what the Cigar Makers' Union proposed at their last convention."

Gloria laughed gaily.

"I'm glad I can compete with the cigar makers."

"Tell me everything you've been doing since I saw you last; I'm hungry for the slightest detail about you."

"Eddie Deutsch proposed to me last Sunday."

"Eddie . . . proposed . . . what?" he asked dully.

"Proposed marriage, of course."

A rage drenched his mind as swiftly and unexpectedly as an Indiana rainstorm.

"Eddie Deutsch! But that's ridiculous. He has no right . . . what encouragement could he have had?"

"None, but he said I had a twentieth birthday coming, and when a woman is twenty she's a spinster."

"You, a spinster!"

"Your sister Mary was married at seventeen. By the time she was my age she had two children."

"Gloria, you're the last woman in the world to be a spinster."

She threw her head back sharply, her eyes blazing.

"I wish you would reassure Mother and Father on that point," she said. "Every time you're invited to supper you beg off at the last moment because you have to write an editorial for your magazine, or go to a meeting, and I had to miss Susie's birthday party because the streetcar men went out on strike and asked you to negotiate for them."

"But I settled that strike fast, Gloria, and they had been deadlocked for ten days."

"No, no, Gene," she broke in. "You don't understand. I'm proud of you and your work. I agree that it is more important to settle a strike than to take me to a dance. And it's wonderful that you got a contract for the drivers, they now have security. But what security have I?"

She turned away so that he could not see her face. When she spoke again her voice was low and quiet, and she had managed to bring back to it a note of banter.

"Don't mind me, Gene," she laughed. "I know you have to go your own way and do things by your own methods. It's getting late, we'd better start back for home."

He stood unmoving; he knew that he had loved Gloria from the beginning of their childhood friendship; and in some dim, forbidden chamber at the base of his consciousness he sensed that he would never find another Gloria Weston, never find anyone so lovely, so desirable, so superbly suited to his nature and his needs. Many of the Terre Haute boys he had grown up with were already married, had children; many of them earned no more than he did at Hulman's; for the most part they were happy and contented with their lot. Then why did he not take Gloria in his arms, kiss her full on the mouth in declaration and avowal?

He couldn't: his life was so uncharted, his need for work and freedom so overwhelming. If only he were going to remain at Hulman's, he could ask for a promotion, start a little home: everything would be happy, normal. But he knew that he could not stay much longer behind his clerk's desk, that he wanted his full time for his real job. Deep in his consciousness he sensed also that he wanted to devote his entire life to unionism and to the civilizing cause that it embodied. He knew now the history of labor, and he had just lived through a virulent anti-union drive; his future would be troubled, filled with conflict and terror. What would he have to offer Gloria? His love? The mere fact that he stood here, not taking her in his arms, not comforting her or reassuring her, but rather telling himself that the future was too chaotic to risk marriage, didn't this indicate that he did not love Gloria with

the wholehearted, passionate rapture he had read about in literature? And somehow he understood that this wholeheart-
edness, this passion, this rapture was reserved for his work.

Could he offer Gloria a fragment, a residue, a life of uncertainty because he would forever be wedded to something
he loved more than he did his own wife?

— 6 —

A message summoned him to Major Smith at the *Gazette*.
Smith was leaning back perilously in his swivel chair, turning
the bronze head of Horace Greeley over and over in his
hands, his face dark. He did not speak when Gene entered;
instead he thrust a printer's galley at him. Gene read that the
Rev. Peter Hanford's congregation announced with regret the
resignation of their pastor, and paid high tribute to his years
of service.

"But what happens to the man, Gene? Do we have to
stand by and watch him driven out of town?"

"No, Major, I think we can keep him here," Gene replied
earnestly. "He doesn't require a large salary or elaborate surroundings; perhaps we could open a simple non-sectarian
church for him? I believe I could persuade the firemen to
help."

Major Smith dug into one of the cubbyholes in his roll-top
desk, extracted a checkbook and filled in a number of blank
spaces above the lines, then handed it, heavily wet from his
stub pen, to Gene. It was for five hundred dollars. "That
seems like a small price for religious freedom in this town.
Let me know when you are ready to open your church and
we'll give it a double-page spread."

In his search for a church for the Rev. Mr. Hanford, Gene
found a former vegetable store behind the Union Depot. It
was in bad shape, ". . . but that's a blessing to us," the minister said, "otherwise we never could have afforded the rent."

"All it needs is hot water, soap and paint," replied Gene.

He and Theodore helped on Sundays, but the Rev. Mr.
Hanford worked without interruption for weeks, until the
room glistened under its coat of white paint and shellacked
floor. Major Smith kept his promise; everyone in Terre Haute
knew that the All Faith Church was opening, and the entire
Debs family went to church together for the first time in
twenty years.

The All Faith Church did passing well, with perhaps thirty
or forty adults attending Sunday morning service. Peter Hanford was content, for he had almost a hundred youngsters in
his two Sunday afternoon classes. The firemen's local contin-

ued to contribute a few dollars a month, to which Gene
added from his own pocket, saying to Theodore:

"Unless I am misinterpreting the story of Christ, this is the
kind of church He meant to organize."

Only Clarissa seemed unhappy in the two cheap rooms she
and her father rented in the house of an old couple. Clarissa
was pretty, and Clarissa was headstrong; her father had neither the knowledge nor the will to be stern with her. There
were disquieting rumors about Clarissa.

Gene sent out his union notices regularly, went to the
meeting hall, sat the full hour and then returned home to his
desk. The few dollars left in his local treasury he sent to
Sayre for subscriptions to the magazine, not only for those
members whose subscriptions had run out, but for those who
had never been willing to part with the price of the magazine.
The men must be kept in touch with the union's doings; in
their minds they must never come to believe that their national was any the less strong because this particular local
was sick abed.

The firemen had been ordered to keep out of the union
hall, but no one could order Gene to keep out of the firemen's homes. Many of his evenings he spent with the men
and their families, not embarrassing them by ramming the
union down their throats, but talking of simple and friendly
things. He knew to an eighth of a pound and half of a penny
how much of the poorest grade of hock meat and bones they
could buy, to the last pint of milk and thin slice of bread
how much nourishment could go into each of the children;
how much longer the threadbare clothing on their backs
could endure their wiry bodies.

The men went out to work, they escaped the leanness of
the larder, the cries of the children; but the wives had to remain at home, anguished over spindly children who were de-
veloping rickets. To Gene economics was not a series of
ledger books and figure columns: it was human pain, human
suffering, human endurance: for over everything, the mud-
filled, rutted streets, the shacks, the plain unpainted board
rooms, the faces of the people, was fear: fear that they could
not go on, that death would strike, that little as there was
today, tomorrow there would be even less.

His battle to keep his local alive was rooted in his passionate conviction of what unionism could do for these families
through cooperation. He studied the social landscape with
clear eyes: religion was interested in reconciling the laboring
man to his fate on this earth, promising him spiritual reward

in heaven. Government was big game, worth millions to the hunters in control of the railroads, the industrial corporations, the banks.

Then who was left to look out for the people? The workers who were at the mercy of every wind of chance, the very first to suffer when depression came, the last to gain when prosperity flushed the nation; what management called the mudsill, the necessary brute labor whom it would be gratuitous and impossible to elevate? Only themselves! If their union went, they were abandoned; either the men pulled themselves up by their own concerted effort, became self-reliant, intelligent, strong, or they remained in slavery. His own union was all unions in microcosm; what happened to his local and to the Brotherhood of Locomotive Firemen would reflect on workingmen all over America who were trying to organize to better themselves. He vowed an unrelenting determination never to let his organization die.

But despite his efforts the Brotherhood of Locomotive Firemen was crumbling fast. Locals vanished by the dozens; hundred of members drifted away; subscriptions to the magazine fell so low it was operating at a loss. The union was in debt, the magazine was in debt, the entire national venture faced bankruptcy, dissolution, the ignominy of failure.

To see this beautiful effort in a death struggle was as painful to him as the death of someone he loved. He became depressed. Only laughter refreshed him; laughter and a sense of the infinite variety in human nature.

When James Whitcomb Riley tied the reins loosely at the dashboard, Gene asked, "Don't you want to know where we're going?"

"The horse can find lovelier spots than we can; besides it isn't where you're going that's important, it's how much fun you have while getting there."

Gene chuckled as he stole a glance at young Riley sitting beside him in the buggy. Riley heard music and saw poetry in everything about him, spinning verses about the honeybee and the butterfly, the tree toad and the cricket, the hollyhocks and the clover blossom.

"How did you get into this verse-writing business anyway?" Gene asked.

Riley thought for a moment before he replied.

"It was like this, Gene. I had been abroad, and was on my way to Indianapolis. I looked up at the sky and decided that it was just as blue as it was in Italy. The trees were just as green on the Wabash as they were in France. It came to me that it wasn't necessary to get out of sight of Indiana or the

Hoosier farmers to find the poetry of life."

"You're so sympathetic to those who earn their living by their sweat, Jim; then why is it that you never protest against poverty? Burns and Shelley did."

"That's the difference between us: you think people can improve their lot. I like to search for the beauty in things as they are."

Gene thought back to the reading that Riley had given the evening before at Dowling Hall. There had been only a handful of club members, for no one had heard of James *Whitcomb* Riley.

"Is it as easy to write those poems as you make it sound?"

"Easy! It's like grinding sausage meat with bones in it."

"You mean you were tired when you finished writing:

"I only pray for simple grace
To look my neighbor in the face
Full honestly from day to day—
Yield me his horny palm to hold,
And I'll not pray for gold. . . ."

Riley sat back and wagged his head with relish as he listened to his own words.

"I sent the poem to a couple of fancy magazines in the East but they just snorted it back to me."

"Then would you let me publish it in our *Locomotive Firemen's Magazine?*"

"Delighted! You are now the owner of a poem."

Because he and Riley had become close friends, Gene asked, "Jim, have you ever been in love?"

"Yes, I'm in love."

"Tell me about her."

"Well, she's great-bosomed, fertile, swiftly changing in mood, sometimes light and gay and shining as the sun, sometimes cruel and black and rain-lashed."

"In short," laughed Gene, "Mother Earth."

"I've never met a woman that I've enjoyed more than the sight of that sunlight dusting through the green foliage. By the way, you wouldn't have any idea what time it is, would you?"

"Are you being interested in the time?"

"I'm not, but I promised to give a reading in Indianapolis tonight."

"Indianapolis! But there's only one train left."

Gene picked up the reins of the horse and peered about him, trying to recognize the terrain.

"You wanted the mare to lead us," he laughed, "and now we're lost. Suppose you tell her to take us back to the station."

When next he stopped by the Westons' to drop off some magazines he found Ned Harkness in the parlor, sitting on the sofa with Gloria. Gloria was in an apron, and it was obvious that Harkness's visit had been unexpected. As Gene entered, Harkness broke off in the middle of an earnest sentence, the unfinished half dangling in mid-air like a broken wire.

"The ubiquitous Mr. Debs," murmured Mr. Harkness.

Gene wasn't sure what "ubiquitous" meant but he had a feeling that it could be no compliment at this particular moment. With equal asperity he replied:

"Are you practicing law in Terre Haute now, Mr. Harkness?"

Harkness showed his white teeth in a smile that seemed to Gene devoid of pleasantness.

"No, but it would have its advantages." He turned to Gloria and added meaningfully, "Very great advantages."

"Gene, do sit down here next to me," said Gloria quickly, patting the sofa beside her. "It's such a long stretch up to where your face is."

"I just came to tell you . . . that is, I want to leave these magazines . . . for your father. . . ."

He stayed another moment or two, promised Gloria to look in the following evening, and departed. He went back to his workroom, but there was pain at the rear of his skull. The print in front of him blurred when he tried to read it.

There was a faint touch of fingers on the door and Gloria was inside, the door closed behind her, leaning against it with a frightened expression in her eyes. Gene sat still, half turned in his chair.

"Gloria, what is it? What's happened?"

He rose, took her by the hand and led her to his chair at the desk. She got up, walked about the room, touching things, the red-and-white curtains she had hung at the windows, the books she had given him for birthdays and Christmas, his batch of five-cent notebooks, the pictures of Paine, Voltaire and John Brown, the nailed-up grocery boxes with their files of correspondence. Gene watched her, watched every move of her lithe figure, every changing expression on her face. She was trying to tell him something, yet when the words came out they were about irrelevancies. He wanted to help her, for he perceived that she was undergoing a mortal struggle, wanted with all his might to banish the redness from her eyes, the dryness from her lips; yet he was restrained by a force stronger than the knowledge that he was failing her. Then she had left, refusing his offer to accompany her, slipping out quickly.

He could not bear to be in the room after she had gone. He went upstairs, undressed quickly, slipped into his side of the bed with a minimum of disturbance so that he would not awaken Theodore. He lay on his back staring at the dark ceiling.

A few days later he read in the *Gazette*:

GLORIA WESTON MARRIES
PROMINENT CHICAGO ATTORNEY

Gloria and her parents had gone to Chicago the Sunday before; the wedding had taken place at St. James Church; the bride would make her home in Chicago where Mr. Harkness was a rising and highly regarded railroad attorney.

This was what Gloria had tried to tell him. Harkness had proposed. After all, she was twenty now, Terre Haute was beginning to call her a spinster. And he was no help to her. He had wanted to hold her but not be responsible for her. She had wanted one word, but he had given her nothing, nothing!

He was conscious of a deep silence about him. He looked up. All eyes were on him, mother's, father's, Theodore's, Jenny's and Emma's. They had known this was going to happen; they had seen the story in the paper; and now they were anxious for him. He jumped up, went into his bedroom, closed the door behind him and stood staring out of the window over the fields, seeing Gloria's beautiful, sensitive face before him, seeing Harkness's bulky form, the powerful features, the dominant eyes, the line of square, squat teeth. Every fiber of him ached. He swayed as the heavy freight beat over the rails: clackety-clack, clackety-clack, click-clack, click-clack.

His mother was standing by his side. She slipped her arm about her oldest son's waist. He turned to her, lowered his head onto her shoulder and wept unashamedly.

— 7 —

It was Sunday afternoon, and the Debs family was having coffee in the parlor. Jenny put down the newspaper she had been reading as she exclaimed:

"Say, that's a lot of money for the job of city clerk. It pays fifteen hundred dollars a year."

Theodore asked, "What does a city clerk do, Gene?"

"Oh, he prepares tax duplicates, issues vouchers for bills, probably keeps a record of the council meetings."

"Is that hard to do?"

"No, I shouldn't think so."

"Then why don't you go after the job?" asked Theodore in the same tone as he would ask, Why don't you go after your raincoat?

"Thanks for the compliment, Theo, but you have to get yourself elected."

"Other people seem to get themselves elected," retorted Jenny.

"But who would vote for me?"

"The railroad unions would," replied Theodore. "And all those streetcar men that you helped get their strike settled."

"Everybody at Hulman and Cox would vote for you," added Jenny.

"And what about the Occidental Club boys and their fathers?" asked his mother. "The club has a hundred members now."

Gene got up and began pacing the room.

"Mind you, not that I wouldn't like the job: anybody would, but I'm no politician, I don't know how to make street-corner speeches."

"All the Alsatians here would be loyal, Gene," said his father. "I'll put up a big sign in the store: MY SON IS RUNNING FOR CITY CLERK."

Gene came to the head of the table, spread his fingers out on it and leaned toward his family.

"Ladies and gentlemen of the nominating committee! I am deeply touched by your vote of confidence. What's more, if Susan B. Anthony's Woman Suffrage Amendment were only passed, I'm sure you ladies would vote for me. But as it is, I have a powerful lot of correspondence waiting for me out on my desk. Now any time you would like to nominate me for governor, or president . . ."

He went out to his workroom. About an hour later Theodore came in and announced belligerently:

"Gene, I'm sure you could be elected. I been asking around the neighborhood about the fellow who's got the job now. Nobody seems to think he's done so wonderful, he never had any clerking experience before."

"Theo, you're not serious."

"Why not?"

Gene pushed back in his chair, hung his long legs over one edge of the small desk and gazed up at the blank ceiling for a considerable time. When he brought his head and his legs down again, his decision had been made.

"You seem to have it all figured out, Theo, so I'll try, if you will be my election manager."

It wasn't as difficult as he had imagined: he went to the City Hall, learned that he needed signatories, secured them in the space of two days and filed his application to run for city clerk. The family then sat in a huddle over the dining table, figuring out a campaign poster. Mary and Louise Debs each sent a check to defray expenses. When the posters came back from Patrick and Lapish, Gene's name had been spelled with two *b*'s: Debbs. The family was crestfallen. Jenny looked at Theodore.

"Don't blame me," cried Theodore. "I didn't do it. There was only one *b* on the paper I handed to the printer."

"Now, now," said Daisy, "people are going to recognize Gene even if he does have an extra *b* in his name."

Everyone in the family worked night and day. Theodore bought several hundred government post cards, secured a copy of Bailey's *Terre Haute Directory,* and wrote notes to everyone listed as a mechanic or laborer; Mary and her husband, Ernst Zobel, made a tour of their business associates; Jenny and Emma unabashedly went from house to house with little printed cards showing Gene's picture and record; Daniel gave a campaign speech to every housewife who came into his store, and staged a beer party for all of the French people in the town.

Two nights before election the Occidental Club turned out full blast with torches and placards reading: ELECT GENE DEBS CITY CLERK! PUT OUR GENE IN THE CITY HALL! They picked him up at his house, marched him through the main streets of Terre Haute, ending at the square. Everyone cried for a speech. Eager hands pushed him up onto a small platform.

"My constituents," he cried, "If you elect me city clerk . . ."

There was a spontaneous burst of applause.

"I promise that I . . ."

The Occidental Club broke out with three cheers.

"And that the duties of city clerk will be . . ."

The band burst into "Auld Lang Syne." The meeting was over.

On the day of the election Major O. J. Smith published a warm-hearted approval of Gene in the *Gazette*. "Mr. Debs is a finely built young man of twenty-four, is active, hard-working, painstaking and inspired by a most laudable ambition to succeed in all he undertakes. He has a good voice to read the record of the Council and writes a neat, plain hand, with which to keep it. His habits are excellent, his manners are pleasant, and his qualifications first-class."

Eugene Victor Debs received three thousand votes, while his opponent polled only half as many. Now there would be money to help Jenny finish her course at the Indiana State Normal; there would be extra funds with which to help rebuild his union; he would have Saturday afternoons off to devote to his other activities.

Daniel's French band played happy music while Gene's many friends thronged in to shake his hand and wish him well. Mr. Hulman and his fellow clerks formed a circle around him while Mr. Hulman said:

"Gene, we want you to know that you're starting on your new job with the best wishes of everyone here. As a little token of our esteem we bought you this farewell present. Every man standing around you chipped in to buy it."

Grave, unsmiling, Hulman handed him a jewelry box. Gene opened it to find a gold watch and chain. He was deeply touched.

"You're all very kind, and I want you to know that next year, if I'm not re-elected this watch will help me to get to my desk at Hulman's on time!"

Everyone laughed.

There was much handshaking and wishing of good luck and soon the house was empty. Gene sat at his desk in his little office fingering the gold watch and thinking ironically that now he was in a position to marry Gloria: a year ago, at twenty-three, it would have been too soon; now, at twenty-four, it was already too late. In the quiet of the room he thought back over the years. He had done so much, and so much had happened to him; he regretted nothing . . . except . . . Gloria. Should he have been bolder, less questioning of what the future held, married her when the time was ripe for Gloria to be married?

Even now the answers were elusive: he had a good job for a year, but his union was gone, his work had been fruitless, his efforts to revive the local might prove of no avail.

— 8 —

Gene was shocked at Will Sayre's appearance: his cheeks were hollow, he had developed a jumping nerve at the corner of his jawbone. Nor did it take much prompting to find out what had wounded Sayre so mortally: the city newspapers were calling him a socialist, a radical, a revolutionist. He could not have been more hurt if he had been charged with being an embezzler or murderer. His reaction was automatic: the moment he saw himself accused of incendiary influence his stomach turned over, he suffered sharp cramps, and within an hour he had been prostrated.

"Gene, how much abuse can one man absorb? Every time they call me another name, it's like sticking a sharp knife into me."

Gene formulated his thoughts carefully, editing them in his mind in the same manner that he rewrote at his desk when he was doing an article for their magazine.

"Will, when a man calls me a scoundrel, I ask myself: Is he right? What is his motive? If he had no basis in fact, then my skin is whole, and every knife he throws at me falls to the ground."

"But I have no way of answering them. I send letters and articles to all the papers, but they refuse to print them. Gene, you know I'm not a socialist! I believe in private property. I've never written or published one word in the magazine that was incendiary."

Gene hardly knew how to quiet his editor, for it was apparent that he had no armor of attitude with which to shield himself from falling blows: he was simply not constituted for controversy. Gene said to himself, Some men are and some men ain't; some men can take it only when they know they're right, some withstand it even better when they know they're wrong. Aloud he said:

"Your trouble, Will, is that it's so long since you worked for a city newspaper that you've forgotten what they're published for: not the dissemination of news, but the accumulation of profit. You have got to keep a screen before your mind, a screen that will let through the fine grains of truth while keeping out the rocks of slander."

"But what's it all for, Gene? A magazine that's a failure? That nobody wants, not even the firemen themselves?"

"You mustn't say the firemen don't want it; they do, only they're confused and frightened. Without it, they have no voice, they hardly exist."

"I'm willing to fight, Gene, but I want that fight to be in my work, my efforts to create a good magazine, to get first-rate copy, to make it informative and entertaining, and serve a valuable purpose. My God, isn't that struggle enough?"

Gene put an arm about his comrade's shoulder; it did seem that anyone who worked for human equity undertook a double task: the duties of his particular job and the fighting off of the wolves who devour freedom. To himself he vowed, I'll not let my enemies cut my strength by falling for that game. The only time I'll be hurt is when I fail in my own work.

Before Sayre left Terre Haute, Gene had become associate editor of the *Locomotive Firemen's Magazine*. It meant more work piled up on the desk in the little office, but it was the only way to keep the magazine running. The fact that he had been elected to the position of city clerk reflected an aura of prestige and respectability over the magazine and his non-existent local.

He checked his calendar and saw that it was more than six months since he had spoken to Riley McKeen. At that time he had spread word among the former members of his local that McKeen would raise wages on the Vandalia if he could be shown an improved record. He had impressed upon the men that this was a chance not only for a higher wage, but for recognition of their union. The Pittsburgh riots were fading in memory, the newspapers had shifted their barrage from unions to some other topical evil, and responsibility for the destruction of the Pennsylvania Railroad property had been distributed almost equally among the strikers, sympathizers, unemployed, state militia, private police and the Pennsylvania Railroad itself. During the course of the past year a revolution had also been taking place inside the railroad dynasty: the fifteen hundred separate short lines connecting the towns of America were consolidating rapidly, and as each company's haul became longer its need for reliable engineers, trainmen, firemen and brakemen became urgent.

Now his tally sheets showed that during the period of trial the number of absentee firemen had been cut by almost eighty per cent, there had been no bursting boilers, only two charges of drunkenness had been brought against the men.

"You don't have to show me the record," said McKeen at the bank. "Our bookkeepers know when we've stepped up service and cut down costs."

"Then you're satisfied that we've fulfilled our part of the bargain, Mr. McKeen?"

"I promised you a basic daily wage of one dollar and forty cents. I'll also pay five cents an hour for the polishing work in the roundhouse."

That night he and Theodore sent out penny post cards to all the union firemen working for the Vandalia, informing them that they were now receiving a dollar and fifty cents a day.

The following morning a messenger came to Gene's desk at the City Hall.

"Mr. Debs, Mr. Engles wants to see you."

Gene sat studying the city tax sheets in front of him. Engles had never consulted him; Engles had forbidden him to come around; if he were sending for him now, it could only be because the Terre Haute and Indianapolis wanted something.

"Tell Mr. Engles that he can see me here on his lunch hour if he wishes."

At twelve o'clock Gene went home for his big meal of the day; he returned to the City Hall at ten minutes to one. Engles was sitting in a chair waiting. Gene dropped into the chair behind his desk, then asked:

"Can I do something for you, Mr. Engles?"

"I suppose you know we lost five of our best firemen to the Vandalia this morning."

Gene's mouth assumed his mother's crooked smile.

Engles was talking very fast. "You know about our consolidation plans. We're extending the run of our trains several hundred miles. We want our firemen to stoke the whole run, lay over a day and come back again on one of our trains. The men don't want to be out for four days at a stretch. You've got to get those firemen on the Terre Haute trains for me."

Gene's first triumph turned bitter on his lips: for this was no longer a hard man sitting in front of him, laying down the law; this was a frightened creature whose job was in jeopardy. And Gene Debs had no defenses against human suffering.

"All right, Mr. Engles. I'll ask the boys to make the long run, but the Terre Haute and Indianapolis is going to have to make concessions, in writing."

"We are prepared to meet the raise in the Vandalia's wages," said Engles quickly.

"The men must be given room and board allowance for the time they are away from home; and they must be given an adequate rest period when they return to Terre Haute."

Engles nodded.

"You guarantee to recognize the Brotherhood of Locomotive Firemen."

Engles's face froze. "I can deliver it all, except the recognition of the union."

Gene's anger flared. "You're asking me as head of the union to keep the men on your trains, yet you're unwilling to recognize the organization that you want to do the job. What kind of logic is that? What kind of justice?"

On Saturday night Gene sat in the meeting hall at his old desk with the tear in the green felt and faced a roomful of men. In the four years since he and Theodore had painted these walls, Terre Haute had grown as a railroad center; more locomotive firemen were living in the city than ever before. Notices had been posted about the Vandalia's wage increase and preferential hiring for the members of the Terre Haute local. There were some forty new application blanks on his desk, and a hundred dollars in dues.

He had plowed his field, bided his time; circumstances had combined to bring his plants to fruition. He now had the only full-bodied local in the national organization.

And in his hand was a telegram from Joshua Leach asking him to come at once to Chicago.

He no sooner dropped off the caboose in the railroad yards than one of the firemen called out, "Gene, Josh is waitin' at the roundhouse."

Joshua Leach was walking around in circles, not a difficult thing to do in a roundhouse, but it was the pattern of his thought rather than the design of the building that was to blame.

"What's the trouble, Josh?" he asked. "You look as though you lost your last lodge."

"Worse than that, boy." He looked around quickly, then continued on in an undertone. "Will Sayre has disappeared."

"Disappeared? You mean just plain vanished?"

"Hell no. He's run away . . . and taken every last dollar we had in the treasury."

"How much did he take, Josh?"

"About three thousand dollars."

Gene thought back to his last conversation with Sayre. He alone knew that Will Sayre's heart had been broken; that he had taken the money, much of which belonged to him in back wages, in order to flee into respectability.

"That's not all," continued Leach. "We're in the hole twelve thousand dollars, including eight thousand to the printer. Some of our death beneficiaries haven't been paid. I doubt if there are fifty active lodges or a thousand dues paying members."

Gene's breathing halted: they once had had sixty thousand members!

"What are you going to do?"

"The executive committee has a plan. Come on, let's go to the hotel."

Gene found his hotel room crowded with the executive committee of the Brotherhood of Locomotive Firemen. Several of the men threw anxious glances at Josh.

"What is this, a wake?" asked Gene.

"It is if you don't come through," replied Grand Master Arnold.

"Come through with what? The last time I looked at my bank balance, I had sixty dollars to leave to my heirs."

"We don't want your money, Gene," said Leach; "all we want is your life."

The executive committee was sitting on the two available chairs, the bed, the table and the bureau. Gene stood in the center of the room.

"Come on, boys, out with it."

"First of all," said Arnold, "you are now editor of the *Locomotive Firemen's Magazine.*"

"Secondly," said Leach, "you're the secretary-treasurer of the organization."

"Now wait a minute," cried Gene. "I'm holding a full-time job as city clerk of Terre Haute, I'm running your magazine and I'm trying to hold my local together. . . ."

"That's exactly why we're putting the job up to you," said Leach. "There's no one else can do it. We're in debt, the magazine we just made you editor of don't exist no more, and the Locomotive Firemen won't exist no more unless you can do for us what you did for the Terre Haute local."

"Get off the bed," said somebody, "and let Gene lay his carcass down. Maybe it'll help him think."

Gene stretched out full length on the bed, his ankles and feet sticking through the brass railing at the end. He locked his hands under his head and stared up at the ceiling, through the roof of the hotel and all the way back to that first convention in Indianapolis when some of these same men had turned away from him because of his youth and inexperience.

How could he add still another job to his already crammed life? To run the magazine and to be secretary-treasurer meant that he would have to be on the road constantly, reviving locals, holding their affairs in the palm of his hand, forming new lodges, inducting thousands of new men, fighting the battles of the locals and the national all over the railroad empire. How could he possibly do it? If he doubled his efforts at the City Hall, and doubled them for the magazine and then multiplied them a thousandfold to reconstruct the national organization into a vigorous and creative union, when would he have time to live? To love? To eat or sleep? To get one tenth of his work done in any twenty-four hours?

He bolted upright in the bed. The men who had been smoking their cigars in silence turned to him.

"I can't do it, boys. I'd like to, you know my whole heart and soul are in this movement. If I were triplets I'd take the job. If I were even twins I'd try it; but short of being four guys in one, the whole thing is impossible, and you know it."

"Yes, Gene, we know it," replied Arnold quietly. "No one man can do this task alone, even on full time and full pay."

"Now wait a minute, I didn't say anything about pay, it isn't the money that . . ."

"Oh, stop it, Gene," admonished Leach. "You've been working for the union for five years and spent every penny you've earned on us. How in the hell could we ever think it's wages that's stopped you?"

"Gene is right," continued Arnold, as though no one had interrupted him. "We're dead, and we might as well arrange for funeral services." He looked around the room from face to face and said solemnly, "We tried hard, boys, but events were against us. It was just too soon. Maybe we'll be able to try again in another ten years, maybe our kids will be able to put it over."

No one spoke. Gene lay out on the bed with his eyes closed. He felt that there was nothing more brutally meaningless than death, death of something or someone you loved, you had given birth to, you had nurtured, you had planned and built and invested with your own blood and muscle and bone. Clackety-clack, clackety-clack, click-clack, click-clack. Without knowing that he had somehow passed over a line, he heard himself say:

"The national offices will have to be moved to Terre Haute."

"Yes, Gene."

"Every dollar of our debts will have to be paid."

"Yes, Gene."

"Every cent you've got in your pockets goes into the pot."

"Yes, Gene."

He picked up Joshua Leach's hat, took a wallet out of his coat pocket and dumped forty dollars into it, then passed it from member to member, waiting until they had put in not only their greenbacks but their silver and nickels and coppers as well.

"Just one thing more," he said. "If I remember our constitution, the secretary-treasurer must be elected by the order, meeting in convention. Do you think you can get me elected?"

"We'll try," replied Joshua Leach with a quiet smile. "We have summoned delegates from every local still functioning. They're waiting for us in the meeting hall."

Gene's eyes shot open in surprise.

There were about fifty delegates seated glumly on hard,

narrow chairs. Arnold and Joshua Leach pushed Gene in through the open door ahead of them. Every man in the hall rose and cried:

"Gene Debs! Gene Debs!"

Gene turned to Arnold. "What does this mean?"

"It's very simple, Gene . . . we elected you before you got here."

Gene could only whisper, "Oh, you did!"

— 9 —

On his way home he stopped at Indianapolis to inspect the office he had inherited. The one dingy room held an obsolete black walnut writing desk, an address ledger with the names of former members, and an old iron safe, barren except for three blackened pennies. It wasn't much to go on, yet he turned the three pennies over and over in his hand, deriving a symbolical pleasure from them. How could one say that the organization was dead or destitute? Had not great ventures and great fortunes been founded on less than this? He dropped the three pennies into a vest pocket and patted them securely. Then he put the address book into his coat pocket and continued on to Terre Haute.

He told his family nothing of what had happened in Chicago: there was just too much work to be done before he would even know whether there was a Brotherhood of which he was an official. That night he wrote to the printer in Dayton telling him that the *Locomotive Firemen's Magazine* had been moved to Terre Haute. The printer informed him by return mail that the Brotherhood owed him eight thousand dollars.

"If I don't threaten to sue, it's only because there's nothing and no one to sue."

Two crucial things had first to be accomplished; he had to pay off a considerable part of the printer's debt, and he had to assure the firemen and their families that they would undergo no second bankruptcy of the order's funds. Once he could guarantee the safety of their money, people would no longer be either afraid or unwilling to pay it in. The only way to accomplish this was to post a bond. But with what? He didn't have a dollar to his name except the salary he was earning. He took his problem to the only banker he knew.

"I need about ten thousand dollars, Mr. McKeen. If I send the printer four thousand dollars in cash and a note for the other four, I'm confident he'll release the magazine to us. And if I can put up a bond with you for six thousand dollars against my insurance funds, I'm sure that will give the firemen and their families confidence in me. What I wanted to ask you was, how does a man get ten thousand dollars in this world?"

McKeen laughed as he replied, "Different men get it in different ways. If you were a manufacturer, I would suggest that you float a stock issue; if you were a real estate manipulator, I would suggest that you take out a mortgage on your land."

"But seeing as how I am secretary-treasurer of a half-defunct union?"

"Then you'd better get ten signatures around town guaranteeing the loan."

"Do you think there are ten men in Terre Haute rash enough to back me?"

Riley took a form out of his desk, wrote something on it and replied, "Now you only need nine."

Gene had less trouble than he had anticipated: his father signed, Mary's husband signed, Mr. Hulman and Mr. Cox each signed, and so did the mayor of Terre Haute.

So astonished was the printer in Dayton to receive a cashier's check for four thousand dollars that he sent Gene the old plates, illustrations and title prints. Now that the magazine once again belonged to the union, Gene found nothing but small foot presses in Terre Haute. For the moment he was baffled.

"It's a good thing I didn't know about this before I borrowed that ten thousand dollars," he told Theodore. "How can I bring the magazine to Terre Haute when we have no way of printing it here?"

"That's easy," said Theodore. "Borrow another ten thousand dollars and buy yourself some big presses."

"Maybe I can talk somebody else into it."

He put on his hat and walked down to Moore and Langen, the only professional printers in town. He had given them the Occidental Club business on tickets, circulars and programs.

"Mr. Langen," he said, "you're throwing away a lot of important jobs by not having a big press. You know yourself how much of the local business goes to Indianapolis and Chicago . . ."

"That's true," replied Langen. "However, those presses are mighty expensive."

"Suppose you had a guaranteed job that would meet the cost of those presses month by month, and everything else you got was profit? I'm bringing the *Locomotive Firemen's Magazine* here to Terre Haute. I can give you an initial print

order of five thousand; by the end of the year we should be
running twenty thousand."

Langen looked at Gene for a moment, then said apologetically, "You always paid your bills for the Occidental Club,
Gene, but I heard tell that the Locomotive Firemen's Union
isn't so flush."

"No, Mr. Langen, we're not rich, but we're not destitute
either. We just sent a four-thousand-dollar check to the former printer in Dayton."

"Tell you what I'll do, Gene. I'll canvass the town, see how
much big work there is to be had."

"Fine!" exclaimed Gene. "Now there's just one thing
more."

"What's that?"

"A union magazine can only be printed by a union shop."

Langen gazed at Gene in cool silence. Then he said with a
strange smile:

"Gene, no one can accuse you of lack of nerve. That time
five years ago, when you hired Colonel Ingersoll to come
here, I thought you'd go into debt for the rest of your life,
and be ridden out of town on a rail. All right, boy, if you
ever walk into this shop and see a big printing press, you'll
know that the men handling it belong to the printers' union."

In the earlier years he had outsprouted his clothes so fast
that Theodore inherited them before his older brother had
made a permanent impression at the knees or elbows. Theodore's face and figure were such authentic replicas of his own
that when Gene saw him coming down the street in a suit,
shirt and tie which he himself had been wearing only the year
before, he had the impression that he was gazing into a tall
mirror.

Theodore didn't mind taking Gene's hand-me-downs in
clothes because in his spirit he was intensely independent: his
opinions were his own. Participating in each other's secrets,
sharing one room, one bed as they did, it was as though they
were two parts of a whole rather than separate individuals ca-
reening their separate ways through life. For the past few
years Theodore had done little playing with the boys of the
neighborhood; his excitement came from his brother and his
brother's work. Even his schooling had become stale, because
his work with Gene had taken him into the mature world of
conflict, of challenging ideas; he had to stretch himself to
keep up, and the youngster found this more stimulating than
playing baseball.

One evening he announced, "Gene, you can't do all this work by yourself. I'm going to help you."

Gene was thinking his own thoughts.

". . . of course . . . just like you always did . . . in your spare time."

"Full time."

Startled, Gene turned his head.

"Sooner or later you'd be hiring somebody to help with the books and the mail and the printer's copy."

"You're going to keep on with school, boy."

"But what can I learn in school that's half as interesting as I learn from you?"

Gene smiled grimly. "The family's in better circumstances now, and we can afford to give you some education. We want you to rise in the world, make something of yourself."

"You mean become a railroad lawyer?" asked Theodore.

The question was fresh, but germane; when Gene remained silent Theodore said more gently, "Seems to me you've had several chances to rise in the world, and instead you hung onto the coattails of the firemen's union, even when there was no union."

"Mother and Father won't approve."

"Suppose we leave it up to Mother?" asked Theodore. "If Daisy says I have to go back to school, I'll go."

Gene was certain their mother would send Theodore back to school, but when they found her on the back porch, rinsing out the family's long winter underwear, and made her dry her hands and come sit for a moment in the parlor and drink a cup of coffee with them, she fooled her oldest son completely.

"I don't know what you're going to do, Gene, but I have confidence in you. I know you'll be able to handle whatever the future has in store for you. I want Theo to become that way too. The best thing you boys can get out of life is working together, being loyal to each other."

Gene's voice was gruff with love and embarrassment as he turned to Theodore.

"All right, then, you are now an employee of the Brotherhood of Locomotive Firemen. We'll pay you three dollars a week and you can have it every week that there's three dollars in the treasury. You're in charge of the office during the day while I'm at the City Hall; you open the mail, prepare copy for the printer, wrap and post the magazines . . ."

— 10 —

Time had had a rigidly compartmentalized nature: there were seven days in the week and he had always known what day it was; there were twenty-four hours in the day and he could have given you the precise moment in the hour. But now time became fluid as the flowing Wabash: in the ever-present heat haze of unfulfilled labors, days and nights merged into each other, weeks and months became indiscernible.

Once he had the magazine under his wing, the next task was to straighten out the insurance tangle. He found that there were five unpaid beneficiary claims; that the locals in these five towns should have vanished into coal smoke was natural and inevitable. He therefore risked most of his remaining cash to pay up the claims. With each check he enclosed a personal letter of sympathy and an explanation that the union and its funds were now under his particular care.

The results were immediate: firemen's wives from three of the locals sent in their husbands' back dues and insurance money.

"Well, well," murmured Gene, fingering the greenbacks. "The first take on our new investment. Not that the money isn't welcome, boy, but do you know what's happened? Three dead locals are now alive again. We've got to pursue these women, see that they spread the good word around."

Except for occasional news notes or articles that he whittled out of Grand Master Arnold and Joshua Leach, he had either to write or select the material for the entire sixty-four-page volume of the magazine. He no longer had time to think of style, no longer an opportunity to wonder if he were expressing what was closest to the hearts of the firemen and their families.

He had lived through five troubled years; he could no longer publish stories about firemen saving little girls on the tracks, or verses about men having taken their last glass. He gave them interesting stories by Victor Hugo and Mark Twain. He ran literary articles on Longfellow and William Cullen Bryant; he published political speeches by Patrick Henry and Daniel Webster, by Gladstone and Garibaldi; he briefed the teachings of Thomas Carlyle and Charles Darwin; and he interspersed these stories with humorous anecdotes about Spoopendyke's Bathing Suit, and Jerry, the Obstinate Mule.

No issue went forth without its plea for each lodge to buy

technical books and magazines, to keep its meeting hall open day and night so that the firemen might utilize every spare moment for study. In his editorials he knew that he was being more preacher than teacher; when he had worked on the railroad, the firemen were despised by management as "drunken rowdies," "unprincipled, worthless creatures." Slowly the habitual drunks were being replaced by younger men who kept their eye not only on the 140 point of the steam-gauge mark, but also on the three dollars and fifty cents daily wage being paid to engineers. The brunt of his fight was still to gain respectability for his enginemen; unashamedly he preached moralisms: "Self-respect is the cheapest and best commodity in the world." "If we are true to the spirit of manhood, failure can never be our lot." "The man of work some may hate, but all respect."

A good part of his efforts were directed at the hiring superintendents who obliged firemen to sign an agreement saying they would not join the union. He had to convince these superintendents that the union was good for the railroad as well as the firemen; that "Our organization means to assist in the solution of the labor problem by honest adjustment of differences: arbitration, not war."

He wanted his magazine to become both a textbook and a campus; he wanted it to become the voice of labor.

He was running a one-man show, and if the magazine reflected all of the inadequacies and contradictions of a one-man show, it also displayed all the strength of unified and passionate authority. His control enabled him to throw out the black lists, get rid of vituperation and name calling, start a woman's department which printed recipes, the latest styles in dresses from New York and advice on how to repair furniture. Where Will Sayre had been on the defensive, writing long editorials in which he denied that the Locomotive Firemen were anarchists or socialists, Gene went on the offensive, glorifying the firemen's job, publishing complete engineering courses for home study. Above all the pages were saturated with his confidence, with his undying determination that the Locomotive Firemen would not perish, but would grow day by day into a powerful and useful union.

During his first year of its life the magazine cost him nine hundred of his fifteen-hundred-dollar city clerk's wage. He considered the money well spent.

Once again the grocery boxes nailed to the walls were filled with letters, each one different in approach and tone, but all of them dominated by the same compulsion: Your local must come back to life! As the months passed each file got thicker, but he was not discouraged, for once in a while a letter would come from an old member, or a new fireman, asking for insurance, wanting to know when the local in his town would meet. Anyone unguarded enough to write such a letter was immediately named secretary-treasurer of his local and instructed to go among his fellows and bring them into the meeting hall.

Of personal life he had none. He started work at six in the morning and finished at three the next morning, never fully knowing when he got into bed or out of it, whether he had taken off his clothes and crawled under the blankets or merely thrown himself face downward on the pillow; never knowing what it was he was eating, or which meal of the day. His grip was always packed, ready to depart on a moment's or an hour's notice for Elmira or Nashville if word were flashed that he was needed: to tramp through a railroad yard in the rain or sleet half the night, to be ordered out of the roundhouse as an agitator, to be put off a train while attempting to deadhead over a division, sometimes into a midwinter snowbank.

Never did he come home empty-handed, without a new convert, a new member, a new local: track hands, shopmen, telegraphers, switchmen, brakemen, all turned to him because they had no organizer, and they were all the same to him, all his children, because they worked on the railroad. When he was introduced as a labor leader at a meeting of trackmen in a shed in Sheboygan he was on his feet in an instant, crying out:

"I am not a labor leader. If you are looking for a Moses to lead you out of this wilderness, you will stay right where you are. I would not lead you into the promised land if I could, because if I could lead you in, someone else could lead you out."

So he rode the engines over mountain and plain, was fed from the dinner pails of swarthy stokers, slept in the cabooses, the rhythm of wheels over rails singing in his blood. clackety-clack, clackety-clack, click-clack, click-clack. With Gloria gone there was not even an occasional moment of hand holding or a bit of awkward dancing about the parlor. This was no life for a woman, certainly not for a wife; that it might not be any kind of a life for a man either never entered his thoughts.

On one of his rare Sunday mornings in town he met Major Smith at the All Faith Church. Smith was very debonair in a new pearl-gray spring outfit. After the services they walked back to the Debs home together.

"You know, Gene," the editor said, after viewing the files of the Brotherhood of Locomotive Firemen, "you're a strong combination of executive, shopkeeper and missionary."

"I wish the combination were as successful as it is strong," mourned Gene. "I've already distributed three issues of the new magazine and sent out two thousand pieces of personal mail. Every now and then I catch a stray member."

"You're not discouraged, my boy?"

"Discouraged, tired, broke . . ."

Major Smith settled himself in a chair, rested his fedora with its soft brim on a pile of unanswered mail. He made an incongruous picture as he leaned his fashionably tailored figure across the desk that had formerly served as a kitchen table. His eyes were friendly as they rested on the boy.

"I'm moving my plant to Chicago, Gene. That's going to be one of the greatest printing centers of America because it's a focal shipping point. I want you to see the new wooden lugs I've invented for the type face. They're so much lighter and less expensive to ship that I'm sure we're going to develop a tremendous business."

"You do well with everything you undertake, Major."

"Thank you, Gene. My idea is that after a while we'll graduate from printers into a press association; we'll write our own news stories and features, set them up into a kind of boiler plate and ship them all over America."

"It sounds like a wonderful idea."

Smith laughed. "You're the only young man I know who wouldn't already have been figuring how he could get into this and what part of the millions he could corner for himself."

Gene sat on the edge of his desk, his long legs crossed and dangling.

"Gene, I want you to come in with me. You're a progressive, and so am I. The thing for us to do is to make a lot of money, then you can go back to the labor movement well protected."

"Major, how can a progressive think in terms of making a lot of money?"

"There's nothing anomalous about that, Gene; the progressives are the ones who should be the most successful because their minds are open to new ideas, radical experiments."

"I can't afford the time to make money."

"But don't you see how much more effective you can be?"

Gene walked the floor. "Unions aren't built on money;

they're built on faith. If they have to be supported with outside funds they will collapse the minute the last outside dollar vanishes."

"Gene, your editorials are always about the need for mass education."

"As long as the workingman is ignorant and management is educated, it will have the advantage."

"Then don't you see? This development of inexpensive plate is going to help mass education enormously. As it is now, only rich people can buy a lot of books; magazines and newspapers are far too expensive. We can bring the cost of printing down to a half, a quarter, yes, Gene, and if we keep moving forward vigorously, we could produce printed matter at such a low cost that every man, woman and child in America could afford an education. Isn't that as valuable as unionism?"

Gene knew that Smith was not fabricating the dream. What he promised, he delivered; and what a magnificent opportunity to put the right kind of thinking into Major Smith's new boiler plate. Seeing Gene thoughtful and interested for the first time, Smith quickly interjected:

"You see, Gene, there are many ways of doing the job you want done. Don't give me your answer now. I want you to come to Chicago with me this week end."

The following Sunday they walked through the streets of Chicago in the brisk morning air to the building the newspaperman had purchased. It took only a brief inspection for Gene to realize that he had invested a sizable fortune here; that the setup was so good there was little possibility of failure.

"I can see that you like the plant, Gene, and the idea behind the business. I'm not offering you a job, boy, I'm offering you a partnership. I want you to be general manager of production. You'll have a drawing account and stock in the company, twenty-five per cent of the stock. That shows how much I think of you. Within a few years you'll be rich, you'll have influence and power, you'll be able to walk into the meetings of railroad managers, yes, and boards of directors. You'll be able to work from the top instead of the bottom, and though it sounds cynical, my boy, that's where things are accomplished."

Gene stood silently, his eyes surveying the presses.

"Think it over," said Major Smith, "take a walk around the lake. Meet me here in a couple of hours."

The off-lake wind was strong in his nostrils. In rhythm with his long strides was the pleasant thought of being successful, of owning two suits of clothes and having a hundred dollars in the bank. Major Smith's printing plant and press association would grow at a steady pace; it was pleasant to think about working at something in which he would not forever be fighting so desperately to achieve so little.

Then he was no longer thinking of the proposed partnership: he was thinking of Gloria. Just being in the same city with her filled him with her presence as completely as it had when she had been in the same room with him in Terre Haute, moving about quickly and gracefully. As he walked along the streets of the North Shore, with its proud and handsome homes, he could hear her low, gentle voice inside the silent houses. And he was sick with longing for her.

When next his thoughts became conscious he found that he was in a poorer part of the town, with the houses narrow and soot-covered, the noise of the freight hogs clanging up and down. Automatically his feet had led him to the railroad yards. He made his way to the roundhouse, where he met old friends, and soon he was talking railroading and unionism. Here in Chicago the hatred of the men for their lines and their bosses was more bitter than in Terre Haute. He was saddened at the thought that skilled workmen, who should have taken pride in their work and been motivated by feelings of guardianship over their machines, loathed the greater part of their waking hours because they felt they had been judged unworthy of their hire. To be worthy of his hire a workman must be given sufficient pay to keep his family in the decencies; any other definition was meaningless. They were being deprived, thought Gene, of that one skeletal without which a man becomes a sagging contour of flesh: his joy in his craft, his job, his contribution.

This he told the men; this they understood. He forgot to be sick with longing for Gloria. Major Smith and the dream of wealth vanished.

— 11 —

He found Frank Karnorski, vice-president of the Brotherhood, sitting on his doorstep. Even before the man spoke he saw that something was askew.

"What hit you, Frank?" he asked.

"The vice-president of the Pennsylvania Railroad."

"What in blazes were you doing within ten miles of a vice-president of the Penn?"

"I was asking him to issue me an annual pass."

"Annual pass!" exclaimed Gene. "Are you crazy? Since

those Pittsburgh strikes, the Pennsylvania won't even employ union engineers!"

"Well, I didn't see what I had to lose. But that dirty so-and-so McCrea, he was on top of me before I saw him get out of his chair, and the first thing I knew I landed on my face in the outside office, with the clerks giving me the hee-haw."

Gene controlled his anger long enough to say, "Frank, don't you know you never ask favors from your opponents? If there's any favors to be done, you do them. You don't humiliate yourself and your order. . . ."

Then he sat down to think the thing through. The railroads carried not only passengers and freight, but stories as well; the yarn about the Locomotive Firemen's official who was thrown out bodily by the Pennsylvania Railroad would be clackety-clacking along the rails of the country within a matter of hours, and it would cover the full ninety thousand miles of tracks almost as fast as the telegraph. He must not allow this to happen, for within a week the Locomotive Firemen's Union would be the butt of ridicule and derision in every roundhouse in America.

"McCrea operates out of Columbus, Ohio, doesn't he?"

"Yes, why?"

"Because you're going back there."

"Not me!"

"You'll follow me into that office. Before you leave you'll have your annual pass."

There was a freight pulling out for Columbus within the hour. When Gene climbed aboard the cab he was greeted by trainmen, who then turned to Frank and said, "What's this about McCrea throwing you out?"

"Don't believe a word of it," Gene cut in. "McCrea just asked Frank to bring me back so we could discuss the matter."

He caught a few hours' sleep on a bunk, washed in the cold water of a cracked bowl, and the moment the offices of the Pennsylvania Railroad opened he swung through with Frank at his heels. An office boy tried to stop him, but he pushed open a little gate in a low railing, picked up a chair, put it down at the corner of McCrea's beautiful mahogany desk and began waving his index finger under the vice-president's oblong beard. As soon as McCrea could recover from his astonishment he cried:

"Who the devil are you, and get that dirty finger out of my face!"

It was not difficult to perceive that behind McCrea's long beard and black coat there was a bull-like torso.

"If that finger is dirty, Mr. McCrea, it's with honest coal dust. I notice I don't see any signs of work on your lily-white hands."

McCrea's hands weren't lily-white, they were tough and calloused and sunburned, for he had come up the hard way, from the ranks; but Gene knew this kind of man, knew that he had to slug it out with him, insult for insult, blow for blow.

"I don't know who you are but I threw that partner of yours out of here yesterday and I'll give you exactly sixty seconds to get out before I dump you on the sidewalk."

He put his hands on the desk in front of him and began to push forward on them. Gene followed suit. The two men leaned across the corner of the desk, their faces not an inch apart, looking for all the world like two bull moose ready to tangle horns. Frank shrank back to the railing, while outside the clerks gathered in a semicircle to watch the contest. But if animals can smell fear in human beings, other humans can smell its absence twice as fast. McCrea settled back slowly into his chair.

"Who are you and what do you want?"

"I'm Eugene V. Debs, executive secretary of the Locomotive Firemen. I want the Pennsylvania Railroad to stop black-listing our men, to stop thinking they're a favorite instrument of God, to stop terrorizing everybody that works for them, and to issue annual passes to our officials."

"Your name may be Debs," replied McCrea, "but it's the only part of that harangue that has any truth in it. We don't black-list firemen, we just refuse to employ the drunks and irresponsibles; we don't terrorize anybody, that's not our business, our business is to push trains down railroad lines. As for passes for your officials, you don't even have a union any more."

"McCrea, I'll wager you that the Locomotive Firemen's Union is still in existence when the Pennsylvania Railroad is just a bad memory in people's nightmares."

"Get out of here, Debs, before I heave you out."

Gene's wide mouth pulled to one side.

"Mr. McCrea, you're apparently a man of violence. Picking on my unsuspecting partner here yesterday must have given you a lot of pleasure, made you look like a real man to your office staff. Since throwing people out gives you such great pleasure, I wouldn't mind letting you do it to me . . . only I can't let you throw out unionism, Mr. McCrea."

"Unionism! I spit at the word. It's just another word for anarchism, socialism, criminalism."

"We're guilty of many things, Mr. McCrea, but we're the merest amateurs compared to the Pennsylvania. When it comes to underhanded methods, evasion of the law, and double-dealing with your own customers, you people are geniuses. If you would use any considerable part of your resourcefulness in running your railroad efficiently, there would be plenty of profits and high wages for everybody."

"I suppose that's why you want us to hire union firemen, so that you can tell us how to run our business."

"Mr. McCrea, where you employ men to run your industry, those men become your partners. Surely you don't think you could operate railroads without man power? Then why is it so absurd for those men to want a say about the conditions under which they work?"

"Sounds to me like you believe in socialism."

"On the contrary, I would never have anything to do with a labor union that entered into any socialistic movement. We don't want to take your pretty trains and tracks away from you, Mr. McCrea. We just want to put healthy, happy, alert men up in the cabs."

McCrea let out a string of curse words that lasted for a full three minutes. Gene leaned back in his chair and marveled at the performance. Then he continued:

"There is no crime on the legal or economic agenda that hasn't been committed by the Pennsylvania Railroad. And now that I look at you, sitting back there in your full hatred and contempt of the men who help you make your millions . . ."

For the first time McCrea's armor was dented.

"Now just a moment, Debs. No one can accuse me of hating our workmen! It's those firebrands who burned up our property in Pittsburgh . . ."

"Those weren't union men, Mr. McCrea, and I can prove it to you."

"If you can do that, I'll take the unions back on my road."

"If those had been union men in Pittsburgh and West Virginia," said Gene, "they'd have been strong enough to keep you from reducing their wages once again. . . ."

McCrea leaned back in his chair and laughed.

"They'd never let you teach logic at Harvard."

"They wouldn't let me sweep out the dormitories at Harvard, but that's not what you and I are discussing."

McCrea leaned across the desk, but this time in a more friendly fashion.

"Now that you bring up the subject, what in the hell are we talking about?"

"Railroad passes," replied Gene. "I want the Pennsylvania Railroad to issue annual passes to the officers of the Locomotive Firemen so that they can ride in cleanliness and comfort while going about their duties."

"That's the equivalent of an executioner asking a condemned man to sharpen his ax."

"That's obsolete thinking, Mr. McCrea, and belongs to the eighteenth century. Before that luxuriant beard of yours is two inches longer, you'll be quite happy to have the Locomotive Firemen running your trains, because they'll be doing a fine job for you."

McCrea sat for a moment stroking his long beard. Then he called to one of the clerks.

"Mr. Bullock, will you kindly issue annual passes to these two gentlemen."

There was an audible gasp from the clerks outside the railing, the first really pleasant sound Gene had heard since he entered the office.

"Thank you, Mr. McCrea, you're very kind, but just make that one pass for my partner here."

McCrea leaned so close that Gene could smell the aromatic oil he rubbed into his beard.

"You mean to say you beat your way here from Terre Haute and risked getting thrown out on your broadside just to get that lick-spittle friend of yours an annual pass!"

"Oh no, Mr. McCrea. I also wanted the pleasure of meeting you."

McCrea broke into a broad grin. Gene could see what a charming man he must be in his own circle.

"You're a fighter, aren't you, Mr. Debs?"

"No, sir," replied Gene meekly. "My father brought me up to resist not evil. I'm against all force and violence. My philosophy in life is to turn the other cheek."

McCrea rose.

"I respect a fighter," he said. "That's how I managed to rise in the world, fighting my way upward."

Mr. Bullock returned with an annual pass in his hand. McCrea indicated that he was to give it to Frank. Gene said good-by. McCrea seized his hand in a bearlike clasp.

"How much money does the union pay you to make these ridiculous demands, Debs?"

"Fifty thousand dollars a year."

"You're lying!"

"Why, Mr. McCrea, do you think I would risk my life in

such lions' dens for anything less than fifty thousand a year?"

McCrea studied Gene for a moment, then asked softly, "You mean you're a volunteer? That you get nothing at all?"

"I wouldn't say nothing at all, sir: travel broadens one, and meeting cultivated gentlemen, with a magnificent vocabulary like yours, always extends your knowledge of the world."

McCrea's delighted laughter followed him all the way to the sidewalk.

This story traveled farther and faster than the one of the day before, reaching the outermost dead ends of the railroad empire. Wherever railroaders gathered they told the story of how Gene Debs matched wits with McCrea of the Penn; and they laughed, laughed as they shunted freights, drove the fast expresses down the line, as they oiled the wheels and filled the water tank and made their repairs in the roundhouse. And as they laughed, their courage rose.

By the end of the year Gene had four thousand members and a hundred active lodges. He paid his last dollar of debt and told himself that now there was smooth sailing ahead.

— 12 —

He did not know how long she had been coming to the house before he noticed her, which astonished him all the more when he finally did take a full look at her Junoesque stature. Her name was Kate Metzel; she carried herself with the air of one who knew an inner secret which made her a princess; though she could not reveal the source of her knowledge, anyone who had the good fortune to chance upon it would immediately agree that she was indeed a regal being. Some people in Terre Haute mistook this for arrogance; attractive men had been frightened away by what they thought to be Kate's coldness, her feeling of superiority.

Gene found the diversion of an engaging woman not altogether unpleasant. Since Gloria had left Terre Haute he had known no young girls. He enjoyed his sisters' high-spirited talk about the eligible men in Terre Haute, their stories of the bicycle-climbing contests west of the town, of the new fast set which was riding tandem with one horse in front of the other, of the Saturday afternoon trotting races. Sometimes when he seemed pale from being too much indoors Emma would plead with him:

"Gene, do come picknicking this Saturday afternoon. It would do you good to get some sun on your face."

No matter how late he returned from a meeting now, he always found Kate still chatting with the girls or sitting in the parlor sewing with Daisy. There was a bad block just west of the Debs house with only gas lamps on the corner to illuminate the railroad crossing. When Gene was out of town Kate expected Emma to walk her across the dangerous area, but after a time Emma grew tired of the chore. One night, returning late from a meeting, he came up the long flight of side stairs in time to hear Emma exclaim:

"Look here, Kate, if you come every evening and stay until you're afraid to go home, you'll have to go alone. I'm not a policeman."

He wondered why Emma was being so cross with Kate. True, Emma was always saucy and independent, but after all she and Kate were good friends. He made a little joke as he came into the strained atmosphere of the parlor and told Kate that he would see her home.

It was pleasant to have an attractive woman by his side, to have her shoulder touch his lightly, accidentally, as they stepped down off a curb, to have her take his arm confidently, securely, as they crossed the dark tracks. His world was so utterly masculine: at the City Hall with the councilors and the businessmen, at the union office with his firemen. On his frequent trips over the lines to address meetings, to sign up hesitant members, he looked only into the faces of men, faces hardened and lined by years, drenched with labor and anxiety. But Kate was not hard, she was soft: her arm and shoulder were soft against his, her cultivated voice was soft and melodious against his ear, her eyes were soft when she looked at him, not arguing, not resisting, not asking for any one of a thousand tasks to be done, but just saying quietly and pleasingly:

I am Kate Metzel and you are Eugene V. Debs. I am an attractive young woman, and you are an attractive young man. We both live in Terre Haute. I am a superior creature and you are a superior creature. Both of us will rise high in the world and become important. One day I shall tell a man that I love him, and one day you will tell a woman you love her. One day I shall marry, and one day you will marry. In the meanwhile it is very pleasant walking along the street with you like this, safe, guarded by your presence and your courage and your bigness; pleasant to hear you tell me of your work; work which you and I know very well will bring you great success and achieve everything you want, for you are too superior a person to fail. As one superior person to another, I like you for this. I am Kate Metzel, and you are Eugene V. Debs. I am an attractive young woman . . .

Kate had a big, open aristocratic face, a trifle heavy under the chin but otherwise handsomely molded, with clear gray

eyes harboring no nonsense, cool and logical in the objectivity of their gaze. But the most beautiful thing about Kate
Metzel, which everyone in Terre Haute admired, was her
lovely skin: arousingly smooth to the touch, with a subtle
warm coloring which started low on her cheek and spread
upward with the artistry of Rubens's brush. Gene also admired her crisp, immaculate cleanliness.

Despite the fact that Kate's stepfather had been unwilling
to spend any money on her education, she was at all times a
cultivated lady. By a religious reading of the fashion magazines from the East, and a close, albeit distant scrutiny of the
life and habits of high society, she had developed a rigorous
savoir-faire. If she did not always wear her impeccable manners with the ease and comfort of a pair of old shoes, this
was due only to the fact that they were newly acquired and
hard come by. She had a stately walk, and by the very precise movements with which she sat in a chair, or draped a
napkin delicately across her lap, one knew immediately that
here was an aristocrat.

He found that he was looking forward to getting home at
night, and to the long Sunday afternoons when he would take
an hour or two off, have coffee in the upstairs parlor while
Daniel played music and Daisy visited with the other mothers
of the neighborhood who came in for her freshly baked
coffeecake and the news exchange of the week. If Kate enjoyed his company more than she did that of Emma or Daniel or Daisy, she gave no outward sign. No one knew exactly
how it had happened, nor what it signified, but she somehow
had become an intimate of the family. Gene asked her out
not at all, yet before long he found that he too had become a
close friend of Kate's, that she knew everything he was
doing, as well as the story of its day-by-day progression.

If she had made demands upon him, Gene would quickly
have ended the relationship; since he had lost Gloria, and
taken over what seemed to be the unionization of the entire
railroad industry, he had ever less thought of romance.

By summer, sufficient dues were coming in for him to rent
his first office. He found it over Riley McKeen's bank, with a
big room in front for himself and Theodore, and a small room
in the rear with a teller's cage, behind which he put a former
engineer whose hand had been hurt in a crash. Gene quickly
trained him to handle the insurance funds, several thousand
dollars of which were being deposited each month by hand
and by mail.

If Gene was always working, always rushing, spending his

few spare hours on a freight going to Toledo or Louisville,
using three out of every five dollars he earned at the City
Hall for union stationery and stamps and printing bills, Daisy
and Daniel did not tell him that he was foolish or misguided.
If he was growing thin, losing his hair at the ever-broadening
V part where he applied the brush, if he resigned from the
Occidental Club for sheer lack of time, if he had no group
of intimates or social life, his parents did not choose to confront him with these omissions: his life was his life, he was
living it up to the hilt.

And in this life he had chosen he had a partner: Theodore,
with whom he discussed everything, to whom he could grouse
and complain under the burden of pent-up emotions, setbacks
and failures. Theodore had a lively sense of humor. Gene
rarely had the impression that his brother was nine years
younger, inexperienced in the ways of the world. Since there
was never a word of discouragement from Theodore, no
slightest thought that they were toiling for insufficient reward,
Gene was aided and abetted in his magnificent folly.

They still rose at five and went swinging off through the
woods with matching strides, for Theodore had reached six
feet, a long lean windmill of endless vitality. After all these
years they knew every plant, every tree; they knew every new
bud that thrust its way through the ground, every new bird
that built a nest. Something in the deep quiet of the woods, in
the awakening of the life about them, in the springy, life-giv-
ing texture of the earth under their feet flowed up through
their legs, into their abdomens and chests and arms and
shoulders and brains. This was their hour of release, when
they sang and laughed and told anecdotes; this was their
medicine, their catharsis, their elixir: from it came their indestructible strength.

Daisy had the daughters of her friends in for Sunday
coffee and sat them next to Gene in the parlor. Later he
would take his mother in his arms and say:

"Now, Daisy, stop being a matchmaker. I didn't try to
marry you off."

"You know I never interfere in your life, Gene, but you're
approaching thirty."

"You'll never get rid of me, Daisy, until you put me out
bag and baggage. I'm married to the Brotherhood of Locomotive Firemen, and I'm having little children all over the
place: we have five new lodges down in the Southwest."

His parents laughed because he thought he was being
funny, but Daisy protested, "It's coming time for you to have

a family of your own, Gene. There's trouble and heartache in marriage, but there's even more happiness."

"If I'm not convinced already by living with you and Daniel all these years, I'll never believe it. But you must let me do things in my own good time."

Daisy kissed his cheek, murmuring, "Of course, my son. You know what is best."

What he particularly liked about Kate was that she was not the gushy, talky kind. Her voice was full-bodied, and she used the most punctilious pronunciation. He found this particularly pleasant after the idiom of the locomotive firemen and the patois of merchants wanting things done quickly at the City Hall. The nature of what she was saying could neither quicken nor retard Kate's speech, nor could emotion cause her to slur a single consonant. By the time she had finished a third of her sentence, Gene knew what the rest of it would be, but Kate was in no hurry: he heard every vowel and diphthong right up to the ultimate period, for Kate went on the immutable assumption that everything she said was of equal importance; there were no hills or valleys in her pronouncements; all of them were eminences.

Vivacious Emma could not stand the long, slow enunciation. "Oh, Kate, do hurry up. We're all way ahead of you."

But Kate would not be dissuaded. She was known to be strong-willed; no one had ever been able to influence or change her.

"She wears stiff-laced corsets on her spirit," Emma complained to Gene. "That's why she walks and talks so stiffly."

"That's neither fair nor generous on your part, Emma," Gene protested. "She's had a difficult time, her stepfather never cared for her, he wouldn't let her go to school or . . ."

"I see she's been telling you the story of her life."

"Why do you dislike her so, Emma?"

"I just can't stand that Teutonic immovability. The boys around town call her 'the mountain that Mohammed went to.' "

"I don't know; I kind of feel sorry for her. She's been pretty much alone since her mother's death. Her half brothers and sisters are clannish; they've driven her brother Dan to drink . . ."

"Somebody certainly drove him to drink; I saw him rolling around the gutters only the other night."

Gene persisted. "She's got a strong spirit in her, one which overcomes all hardships, and I admire her for it."

Emma looked at him shrewdly, then turned away.

"Very well, Gene," she murmured, "I'll say no more. If you like Kate, we all like her."

— 13 —

She came into his life at a happy time. By the end of his second year as executive secretary of the Brotherhood of Locomotive Firemen, Gene Debs was able to announce that they had one hundred and fifteen lodges, five thousand members and a surplus of ten thousand dollars in the treasury. Upon hearing this startling news, the convention promptly set his salary at two thousand dollars a year and gave him an expense account so that he would not have to pay for postage and stationery out of his city clerk's salary. The magazine had eight thousand subscribers; the railroad owners' publication declared it to be the best edited in the labor field.

He never relaxed his vigil. On a trip to Chicago he passed the office of O. S. Lyford, superintendent of the Chicago and Eastern Illinois Railway. Lyford had the reputation of pushing his men hard, but giving them a square deal. Following an impulse, he walked into the superintendent's office and introduced himself. Without looking up Lyford replied:

"I'm busy. Can't talk to anyone now."

"You should never be too busy to speak to a representative of the Locomotive Firemen."

Lyford bounced up from his chair, stuck out his hand and exclaimed: "Do you represent the Brotherhood of Firemen? Glad to see you." He pushed Gene down into a chair. "Our master mechanic informs me that in the last two years he has not been compelled to discharge one of your members for drunkenness or neglect. Why, before, we used to have to fire two or three firemen every day of the week."

"Good! Now maybe you can do something for me in turn."

"Glad to."

"Then cancel the lease on your depot saloon. For the sake of a few dollars every month, you put liquor in front of every trainman just before he has to start out on his run. How does it make sense to fire a man for yielding to the temptation you stick under his very nose? It now costs you three million dollars to build a hundred miles of track, and another six hundred thousand dollars to run trains on them. For the sake of a small rental you endanger not only three and a half million dollars of property, but the lives of thousands of passengers. What kind of economics is that, Mr. Lyford?"

"Bad." Lyford shook hands with Gene. "Drop in every

time you're in Chicago. If I don't get rid of that saloon next month, stay on my neck until I do."

But if there were superintendents who welcomed the Brotherhood, there were managers throughout the country who refused to employ any fireman belonging to the union. To these men he addressed editorials which drew sympathetic newspaper response in half a dozen railroad cities.

"Railroad managers who will not employ members of the Brotherhood of Locomotive Firemen are not men of common sense. They are the enemies of the roads they control and the foes of society. They would have their employees destitute of intelligence and independence, cringing, fawning slaves, devoid of manhood and ready to do their bidding, as if they were chattels."

His magazine built the self-respect of men who had been despised. The membership soared, six thousand, eight thousand, ten thousand. With the money that came into the treasury he hired Samuel Stevens to work as an educator, and Stevens traveled to every part of the United States explaining the purposes of the Brotherhood, founding new lodges every time he dropped off a caboose. By the time the 1882 convention was called in Boston, the Brotherhood had grown so respectable that it was welcomed by rousing speeches of approbation from the mayor and from the governor of Massachusetts. Gene's salary was raised to three thousand dollars a year, and as an added tribute Terre Haute was named as the next convention town. After serving for three years as city clerk, he would no longer need the salary to support his outside activity.

The fruits of hard labor were sweeter still because he now had money to build a good library, and an occasional hour when he could swing along the shore of the Wabash, hand in hand with Kate, or take her to a concert at the Opera House. Nothing had been said between them about love or marriage, but people began to take it for granted that they were engaged.

One day Kate asked, "Eugene, do you think you'll stay in politics?"

"But I've never been in politics."

"Why, of course you have. You got yourself elected city clerk three years in a row."

"Oh, that! That was just a technical job, and I had had a lot of experience at clerking."

"But you won by bigger majorities every year, Eugene. You could be elected to any office you wanted."

Gene laughed.

"I'm serious, you'd have no trouble being elected to the state legislature. From there it's an easy step up to Congress . . . and the Senate . . ."

"Whoa! Whoa!" cried Gene. "You're disposing of the rest of my life. I don't want to be in politics. That's a bad place for a union official."

"But think of all the good you could do."

"Good is never handed down from above, Kate. As the unions grow stronger, they will accomplish their own good. There is no other way."

"But you don't mind if I think you would make a wonderful United States senator?"

He put his arm about her broad shoulder, which came almost to a level with his.

"Who am I to deny you the right to your own opinions, Kate?"

She turned full-faced to him, smiling warmly. There was a radiance in her face.

"And who are you to change them?" she asked softly.

On September eleventh the Locomotive Firemen delegates began to pour into Terre Haute. Gene went down to the depot to welcome the governor of Indiana. That afternoon a procession formed at the corner of Third and Walnut streets, with the police corps marching first, then the Ringgold band, followed by the Riley McKeen High School Cadets; next came the Veterans of the Civil War marching in full regalia, after that the Occidental Literary Club, the delegates, the City Council, with its distinguished guests, then the entire Terre Haute Lodge, ending with the municipal fire department. Gene walked between the mayor and the governor.

The Opera House was filled. Grand Master Arnold rose to his feet and cried, "I cannot refrain from accrediting to your fellow townsman and our grand secretary and treasurer, Brother Eugene V. Debs, praise for the great victories we have gained."

There was a storm of applause, after which the speeches began in earnest, Governor Porter telling the assemblage, "Your honored secretary lives here and is held in not less esteem by his fellow townsmen than by your Brotherhood, which regards him so highly."

As Gene and his friends left the hall at midnight he was stopped at the sidewalk by two men. They had planted themselves directly in his path.

"Mr. Debs," said the shorter and stockier of the men, "how would you like to run for the state legislature?"

"I wouldn't."

The stocky man took up the argument. "We could get you the Democratic nomination in a jiffy."

"Gentlemen, I appreciate your kindness, but I've already got a job."

He started to brush past. The taller of the two politicians, who had a soft voice and an engaging manner, murmured, "There must be a good many laws your union would like to see passed, Mr. Debs. Once we elect you, you can introduce the bills into the legislature."

"Say, Gene," cried one of his friends, "we've been trying for years to get that Co-Responsibility bill introduced. Maybe this is our chance."

"A good man can go a long way in politics," continued the smooth speaker; "two sessions in the state legislature, three at the most, and we'll have no trouble in electing you to Congress. Two or three sessions there, and we'll move you up to the United States Senate . . ."

There was a cheer from the crowd. Gene replied, "Gentlemen, you're drunk!" He pushed the two men away with a movement of his hand and forgot the incident.

Not so the Democratic party. The men were back in his office the day after the convention had disbanded and the Terre Haute papers had lavished praise upon its own hospitality. Word had spread throughout his local that the Democrats wanted to nominate him; he found himself caught between the urging of the politicians, the firemen, his family and Kate . . . and no logical reason he could offer to refuse the nomination.

He was completely unprepared for the national storm that greeted his acceptance. Samuel Gompers, powerful head of the Cigar Makers' Union, issued a blast denouncing the entrance of labor officials into national politics, on the grounds that the unions in turn would be crushed by the politicians. Terence V. Powderly, organizer and head of the powerful Knights of Labor, the only national organization of working people of all kinds, wrote an impassioned approval of Gene's nomination, claiming that when all workers were sufficiently educated to elect their own government officials they could then pass laws which would bring the workers' society into effect. Newspapers in New York, Chicago and San Francisco asked:

IS EUGENE V. DEBS A TREND?

Gene found himself in the anomalous position of agreeing

with Gompers, who had blasted him, and disagreeing with
Powderly, who had approved him. The only pleasure he got
out of his candidacy was that the campaign posters now
spelled his name with one *b*.

He did even less to get himself elected to the legislature
than he had for the office of city clerk. Riley McKeen told
him:

"It's no use spending your time and money; nobody knows
that better than I. When I ran for the United States Senate I
invested a fortune in my election, only to be defeated by a
man who was richer than I was."

Kate Metzel didn't feel that way. Her numerous half
brothers were successful businessmen in Terre Haute; the entire family was regarded with awe bordering on consternation
at their alchemist methods of turning a hundred dollars and
an empty lot into fortune-making properties. They could not
withstand her urgings to invest a thousand dollars in Gene's
campaign and to plead his cause among the conservative circles of the city.

She took charge of the campaign headquarters on Main
Street, mailed out thousands of pieces of literature, worked
night and day. Gene was touched by her loyalty; he only
wished that he could be as interested in the outcome as she
was. When the results came in, and he found that he had
been victorious by a considerable majority, he could not be
so ungenerous as to say that he wished he had been defeated.

Flushed and happy, Kate faced him across the board tables
of the campaign room, after everyone else had wrung his
hand and left.

"Congratulations, Mr. Representative! I know this is only
the beginning of a long and wonderful career. In a few years
you'll be in Washington, and then you'll really be in your element."

Could he do less than take her in his arms, tell her what a
wonderful job she had done, how grateful he was? And that
he loved her . . . ?

On the Sunday morning of his wedding he shook Theodore
by the shoulder while it was still dark. Theodore groaned,
rolled over, and asked what time it was.

"After four. Time to get up."

"I'm not the one being married."

"Come on, boy, I want to take a long walk in the woods."

They slipped into their old clothes, walked through the
streets in the darkness, and were soon winding their way
along the familiar trails, listening to the birds sing at the first

light of an early dawn. They were both feeling the sense of
impending separation.

"It sure will be wonderful to have you gone," said Theodore. "Now you won't wake me up any more at two in the
morning with your icy feet."

"Yes, and every time I look for a new necktie, it won't be
wrapped around your long turkey neck."

They were silent for a moment, and then Gene said, "This
marriage isn't going to make any difference between us.
You're still my pard. Nothing will be changed."

"Yes, it will, Gene, but we'll survive the changes. Come, if
you're getting married this morning, we'd better hurry back."

St. Stephen's Episcopal Church was lovely in the early
morning, with the sun streaming through the stained-glass
window and falling upon the flowers on the altar. Kate, too,
was beautiful in a costume of fawn-colored cashmere, the
collar and cuffs of crimson velvet, her hat and gloves repeat-
ing the crimson tone. They were catching the seven-fifteen
for Indianapolis, after which they were going on a honeymoon tour of New York, Pittsburgh, Philadelphia, Boston,
Baltimore and Washington.

Kate's trousseau had been made by Madame Gorunder in
Louisville, and comprised dresses and bonnets for every occasion. Gene wondered if she knew that most of the social
functions she would attend would be receptions by the locals
of the Brotherhood of Locomotive Firemen.

BOOK THREE

A MAN'S CASTLE

THE BROTHERHOOD DID HANDSOMELY BY THEM: A COMMITTEE from the seven Chicago lodges brought a magnificent suite of mahogany parlor furniture, upholstered in blue, olive and gold plush. The furniture was so handsome that it made Mrs. Koopman's on South Sixth Street, where they had rented rooms, look a trifle shabby. On Friday another living room suite arrived from the boys in St. Louis. Already they were the owners of three bedroom sets, one each from Buffalo, Pottsville and Indianapolis. Boston sent a mammoth silver pitcher, Kansas City an elegant silver water service. Every day gifts streamed in from the locals: Brussels carpets, Persian rugs, a French clock, dining silver, china, glassware, a chamber set, lamps, pictures, bric-a-brac of every description.

"Why, it's enough to furnish a huge house," Gene exclaimed. "What are we going to do with it all?"

Kate smiled meaningfully.

"Leave that to me, dear."

In January he left for the state capital. The first day he took his seat in the hall of the legislature he was puzzled by the continuously soft sibilance coming from all sides; by watching closely he perceived that the muted sound was the expectoration of tobacco juice into each man's handsomely engraved spittoon. He had taken to the Capitol with him a portfolio of papers containing notes and memoranda on the bills he intended to introduce, also a batch of union mail and manuscripts on which to work if there should be a lull in the legislative proceedings. To his astonishment the other men's desks were as bare of papers as a fireman's hat of feathers. He soon learned that the important work was done in committee: in somebody's hotel room over a poker game and a case of bourbon.

During the early days he buttonholed each legislator, patiently presented the case for Co-Responsibility, documenting his thesis with charts and diagrams. He found a few men who were sympathetic to his aims; others were amused by his naïveté in the ways of state legislatures. They said to him in fatherly tones:

"Now, take it easy. Rome wasn't built in a day. Just relax, son, and everything will come out all right."

He did not take it easy; he didn't know how. He secured a check list of every man in the legislature, went to his hotel room early in the morning or late at night, made it plain that he would not be tossed into the wastebasket like the unraveled butt of a dead cigar. And then it was he found that each man had certain bills he wanted passed; he rarely got a direct answer to his plea, but always the oblique:

"Debs, how do you stand on that bill permitting private sale of the mineral deposits in state reservations?" or, "There's a very fine group in our state who think it would be advisable to legalize betting at the race tracks. . . ."

The need to secure a majority vote on the Co-Responsibility bill loomed large in his mind. If he wanted the legislators to take his bill seriously, then surely he must lend an attentive ear to the next man's cause.

The legislature met for only an hour a day. He had no other office in Indianapolis, and so he remained behind, running his union from the desk in the Capitol, answering the letters forwarded to him by Theodore, writing his pieces for the magazine. Darkness fell, the janitors came in to wax the desks and polish the spittoons, and still he sat there, his index finger splattered with ink.

At the end of three weeks of hard work he had lined up enough votes to get his measure passed in the lower house. Jubilant, he returned home for the week end to report the good news.

The three-room apartment upstairs at Mrs. Koopman's was small, but Kate walked with her head high, ignoring the fact that it almost touched the low ceiling. Even in this tiny flat, thought Gene admiringly, she carries herself like a princess, moving as slowly and majestically as though these rooms were a royal suite at Buckingham Palace.

He watched his wife set the table for dinner. This was no swift, let-'em-lie-as-they-fall process, as it was in the Debs household. The beautiful tablecloth had to be shifted half a dozen times until it sat exactly right, the silverware was given a final polish in the kitchen before it was laid out with infinite ceremony, making sure that each goblet was at the right distance from the napkin. The low vase of flowers was artistically arranged; the sparkling butter dish, the cut-glass bowls of jam, all were appetizingly distributed.

He grew worried over the food on the stove, and asked, "Wouldn't you like me to watch the pots?"

"Dear no, you must never go into the kitchen."

"But something might burn."

"Nothing ever burns for me."

The religious ritual over the table had been going on for an hour. Gene was ravenous, but he knew better than to try to hasten his wife. At length she emerged from their bedroom, her apron off, her hair freshly brushed, wearing a crisp percale.

"How serene and lovely you look, Kate."

"I'm glad you think me lovely, but why shouldn't I be serene?"

"Well, you know, fussing about a kitchen, over a stove."

"My dear, there's no need for a woman ever to be flustered or untidy just because she's keeping house. If we're systematic, there's a place for everything, and everything in its place. . . . Now sit down, Eugene, I'll bring dinner in a moment."

Gene sat, but it was not for a moment. He heard a variety of sounds from the kitchen, plates being set out, a carving knife being sharpened, pots being moved. By any rough estimate he knew it must have been a half hour before Kate emerged, beaming over the picture of a carved roast set in the middle of a big platter, surrounded by a ring of small, browned potatoes, with carrots leading from the roast to the potatoes like spokes of a wheel. She set the platter down in the center of the table and then sat with her hands in her lap, gazing at the tableau in happiness and triumph. He could not resist going to her side and kissing her.

"It all looks so beautiful, Kate."

"It is a pretty picture, isn't it?"

He returned to his seat, helped himself generously to the roast, potatoes, and carrots, stabbed a three-decker forkful and put it in his mouth. The food was stone-cold. Now he understood why Kate had not been worried about anything burning: the heat had been turned off an hour before. In the

brief instant he sat there with the cold piece of meat and potato in his mouth, a kaleidoscope flashed through his mind:
his mother and sisters dashing in, holding sizzling pans by
cloth holders, crying out, "Get it while it's hot!" Pictures of
Gloria and her mother emerging excitedly from the kitchen,
their cheeks flushed from the heat.

"Is something wrong, dear?"

"Oh no, no, I was just thinking how nice it was to be home
again."

He began chewing mechanically, for the food was not only
cold but flavorless. He noticed that Kate was eating almost
nothing at all.

"Aren't you hungry, Kate?"

"I'm very rarely hungry."

"But you went to so much work."

"Oh, I enjoyed every minute of it, Eugene."

He had been intending to consume all the food on his plate
so that she would not see that he did not like it, but now he
understood that this was not necessary. He stopped eating
with half of his dinner untouched; Kate said nothing, she did
not even seem to know that he had eaten very little. At that
moment he came to understand something important about
his wife: it was the ritual of the act that engrossed her, the
ceremonial preparation. What happened from that point forward was of little interest to her; she had done her job, and
now it was up to other people to enjoy it or not, according to
their desire.

After supper Theodore arrived. When Kate disappeared
into the kitchen, closing the door behind her, Gene asked
Theodore for a full report of the activities flowing over his
desk. By the time Theodore had reached the middle of his
recounting, the wheels that had been gyrating in Gene's
head since he had reached the legislature began to slow
down. He jumped up, went to the kitchen door.

"Kate, I'm going for a walk. Be back in an hour."

He was too preoccupied to observe that his wife did not
want him to go. "Come along, Theo."

Theodore noted that Gene walked hesitantly, that he had
no conception of where he was going, circling whole blocks,
turning off into side streets that led nowhere. They passed the
block-square county courthouse with its tremendous four-way
clock cupola, then followed the giant sycamores along the
Wabash until they came to the covered wooden bridge with its
inverted V-shaped roof, pitch-dark at this hour of night, pleas-
antly redolent of the animals that had crossed during the day.

At the end of the bridge, just before they were to emerge

into the night, Gene seized his brother under the arm, exclaiming, "Let's go back!" Now his pace was swift as they passed along College Avenue, heavily tree-lined. When they passed the Rose Polytechnic Institute with its myriad of turrets and spires, Gene came to a sudden stop.

"The higher it goes, the grander it gets. Who do you suppose the architect was trying to impress?"

"God, probably."

"Look, Theo, I've been a fool. Yes, and a scoundrel too."

"For instance?"

"For instance, I've made a flock of corrupt bargains."

Theodore knew better than try to get his brother's steam gauge up to 140 before the boiler was ready.

"I don't even know how it happened, boy. I didn't realize what I had done until I got back here to Terre Haute, took a look at your homely mug, heard your voice telling me about the new members from Kansas, and the local that died aborning in Minnesota. It must be something they mixed into the building materials of that Capitol: no thoughts can reach your head except the kind that go through political plaster."

"You mean you became a politician?"

"Oh, Theo, if you could only know some of the bills I agreed to vote for!"

"Isn't that the rule of politics: you give away something you don't care about for something you do care about?"

"I don't know, boy: once I get outside that capital, I'm no politician."

Once again he seized his brother by the arm. They struck across town, toward home.

"I'm taking the morning train back to Indianapolis. I'll repudiate every one of those swaps . . ."

"Just a minute, Gene: what happens to our Co-Responsibility bill when you get through laying about with a broadax?"

"I don't know, boy. I'll just have to find another way."

The other way was not easy to find: the men with whom he now broke his vote pledges said, "Well, if that's the way you feel about it!" or simply turned away in silence.

There was a saying in the railroad yards that the first plank of lumber was the hardest to pull out of a flatcar. Gene won his first new convert by taking the man, a lawyer from Greenfield, into the home of Mrs. Ula Hartigan, whose husband had been killed two years before when the Terre Haute and Indianapolis rails had split under the intense summer sun. Mrs. Hartigan now did the neighborhood wash. Her oldest daughters, twelve and ten, helped boil the water in the big kettles, rinse and iron the clothes.

"The company would accept no responsibility for the accident," Gene told the lawyer, "and so the Hartigan family is shackled to these tubs. You and I wouldn't want that to happen to our wives and children."

"No, Mr. Debs," replied the lawyer soberly, "I wouldn't want this to happen to my family."

The antagonism he had incurred by renouncing his bargains slowly evaporated. He spent the long hours of the afternoons and evenings with the men whom he felt he could somehow reach, and at the end of what seemed an interminable month he had garnered a dozen promises to support his bill if he could bring it to a vote. One morning he rose before the bong of the gavel had finished echoing.

"Mr. Chairman, I ask for the right to speak on a matter of personal privilege."

"Refer him to his committee," snapped someone from the other end of the hall.

The Greenfield attorney stood up, saying, "Mr. Speaker, I ask that Eugene V. Debs be heard. No man on this floor can raise a legitimate reason why he should be hushed down."

Gene delivered an impassioned appeal for the railroaders. The men who had promised to fight for the bill rose and spoke their convictions. Gene asked for a voice vote. In his emotional excitement he could not understand why so many of his sternest opponents smiled tolerantly while voting for his measure. He soon learned why: the Senate quickly added a dozen amendments which emasculated the law. The following day Gene rose on the floor of the House, his lean frame bent over at the waist, for the first time speaking in a voice which penetrated the political plaster.

"Mr. Speaker, I wish to withdraw my Co-Responsibility bill from this legislature. I have wasted a good deal of your time and mine—wasted it because I forgot the ever-present railroad attorneys who do the thinking for the Senate. I am resigning from this House in protest over what has happened."

He picked up his papers, stuffed them into his portfolio and strode out of the chamber. In the deep silence behind him he heard only the hissing sound of tobacco juice snaking its way to the cuspidors.

— 2 —

Kate knew something was wrong by the heavy steps on the stairs. She put her crocheting into the basket on the dining-room table and hurried to greet him. Even as she kissed him, she saw that his face looked drawn and tired.

"Eugene, are you ill?"

"No. I'm all right. Or I will be after a few hours in Terre Haute."

"What happened? Is the session over?"

"Oh no, it's still going full blast, doing nothing."

"But if it's still . . . then why are you home?"

"Because I quit."

"You . . . what?"

"Resigned. Retired. Withdrew."

"But, Eugene, you can't resign from a legislature. You were elected."

"No more politics for me. Ever."

She stared at him in utter disbelief, then burst into tears, ran into the bedroom, closed the door behind her and threw herself face downward on the bed. Gene stood for a moment by the dark circular table; he had not realized that his action would have such a crushing effect on Kate. He went into the bedroom and sat on the edge of the bed.

"Kate, don't you want to hear my reasons? Don't you want to know what happened?"

She only wept the harder. He felt contrite. Out of the past he heard Gloria's tearful voice saying, You must never let a woman's tears divert you. He wanted to take his wife in his arms, comfort her, nestle her head on his chest and say soothing words of love, but she seemed so formidable, there was so much of her to suffer. He put his arm around her shoulder and tried to lift her. She would not be budged. After another few moments her weeping subsided and she sat up.

"Eugene, I'm sorry I broke down this way, but it was such a shock . . . it meant so much to me."

"What did, the legislature?"

"No, no, I mean your whole political career. Everyone said you had the makings of another Senator Daniel Voorhees, and in a few years they'd be calling you the 'tall sycamore of the Wabash.' "

"I chopped myself down."

Kate stared at her husband, dumfounded.

"You have just thrown over a brilliant political future, and yet you can sit there and make bad jokes!"

"Theo always said that a bad joke was better than none at all."

"Please don't quote Theo to me, Eugene; I don't look to children for my wisdom."

She straightened her shoulders, drew herself to her full stature.

"Eugene, you realize that this is a failure on your part, don't you? The legislature can't change its methods overnight just to suit you. It was up to you to conform, to adapt yourself. Then after five or ten years . . ."

"Oh, Kate, you wouldn't sentence me to that legislature for ten years!"

". . . you could slowly but surely have changed their methods."

He thought carefully before answering.

"You're right, Kate, I went there to do a specific job, and I failed. There is never any excuse for failure, but sometimes there is an explanation; if I intended to devote my life to politics, then I would have to work the slow and hard way, become a politician. But, Kate, I don't like politics, I'm no good at it."

"Nonsense! You could be good at anything you wanted to."

"Thanks for the vote of confidence, my dear. What I meant was, politics is not the right road for where we want to go. I think we must grow strong within ourselves first, and when we do, the legislators will put through our program because we will elect them."

"Eugene, all my dreams and plans for you are shattered. Now I suppose you'll have to go back to that union!"

"Go back? I never left it."

"You could have, if you had seized your opportunities."

"Kate, I went to the legislature only for the union, it was part of my job."

"But, Eugene, you want to rise in the world . . ."

"I rise in the world . . . every morning at five."

"Will you please stop those wretched puns! Every successful man uses his early jobs as rungs on a ladder."

"If you could have been there with me, Kate, you would have seen that the Indiana legislature wasn't a step up from the Locomotive Firemen."

She persisted, her voice deliberate.

"After a couple of sessions, if you had made a good record, you could have been elected to Congress."

"The weather's too hot in Washington."

"Eugene, I can't understand why you laugh at our most serious moment."

Gene slowly twisted the ends of the bedspread between his fingers. His voice was quiet.

"It's for a good reason, Kate: I'm trying to show you that

you mustn't treat every turn of the wheel as though it were a matter of life and death. I'm completely happy with the Locomotive Firemen."

Aghast, Kate cried, "You mean you're willing to spend the rest of your life as an . . . an employee . . . of a *union!*"

Her scorn was not on the word "employee," where he would have guessed it would be, but on the word "union." If she despised the people and the cause he worked for, then this was more serious than he had imagined.

"Kate, surely you don't disapprove . . . ?"

"It's just that I don't think you're in your element among working people, Eugene. That class is for those unfortunates who can't rise out of it. But with your capabilities you could go into business, make a lot of money. Everybody would respect you and look up to you. Nobody cares about unions except the people who sweat for a living. It's just that I hate to see you throwing yourself away, when you could become an important person. Why, Eugene, if you worked half as hard for yourself as you do for those firemen, you'd be a wealthy man in a few years. You could build a big home on the outskirts of town. You could move in the best society."

His heart heavy in his chest, Gene could think only that this argument must stop. In the same gentle voice he would use to a child he replied:

"I'm already the richest man in the world, Kate."

"You, rich?"

"Yes. I have you. Love is worth more than all the tea in China."

Thwarted by the oblique thrust, and tired now, she put her arm about her husband's neck.

"Oh, Eugene, I do love you, but sometimes you're so hard to understand." She kissed his cheek, then went to the door of the bedroom. "I'll get you some supper, right away."

Sitting alone in the darkened bedroom, Gene thought, I had everything I wanted in life. I was happy with Daisy and Daniel and Theo, with my work. I had no need of love or marriage or a house of my own. How did I get into this thing, anyway? Life is funny: with Gloria I failed to act and lost; this time I acted, and I am losing . . . what? Freedom? But that's nonsense. Marriage is good for a man: a home of his own, and children.

At the thought of children, his gloom vanished.

— 3 —

It was good to get back to his own job, to the office with

the charts on the walls, to the daily problems of the railroad men, to the files of correspondence which showed him that slowly but surely he was making progress. He was writing steadily now, reading every book on economics that he could find. Because of the phenomenal growth of his organization, the solidity of his finances, and the good reputation it enjoyed among the managers, the Brotherhood of Locomotive Firemen became a model for new groups trying to unionize. Again he was out on the road, and every new stop brought a request for a meeting.

One day a brakeman by the name of Osterhout made the long trip from Oneonta, New York, to see him. "Debs, the brakemen at Oneonta commissioned me to get full information on organizing."

Gene spent the day preparing the draft of a constitution, then showed him how to set up the books, the check-system files on membership. Late that night he walked Osterhout to the station. As the train pulled in he asked the conductor, a friend and member of the Brotherhood of Railroad Conductors, to carry Osterhout over the road.

"Glad to, Gene! Any friend of yours. Come aboard, Osterhout."

"Incidentally, Osterhout is interested in organizing a Brotherhood of Railroad Brakemen, and he ought to be encouraged in that work."

The conductor broke into sarcastic laughter.

"Brotherhood of Railroad Brakemen? Judas Priest! What next?"

The sarcasm rang in Gene's ears long after the train disappeared from view, echoing a flaw in the unionism that stratified men by their trades. The engineers, thinking themselves kings, looked down on everybody else; the conductors, considering themselves white-collar workers, despised the firemen; the firemen thought they were more important than the yard crews. Everybody who worked at railroading ought to belong to the same union.

"All for one and one for all." He knew it was a distant dream, that everyone would have to suffer much, from the lordly engineers down to the humblest trackwalkers, before this idea of brotherhood could be broached.

Despite the undercover efforts of the Brotherhoods of Engineers and Conductors to keep what they called "those laborers" from creating a union, the first lodge of the Brotherhood of Railroad Brakemen was founded in Oneonta and named the Eugene V. Debs Lodge. Osterhout made another trip to Terre Haute. "You are the founder of our Brotherhood," he said with a flourish, "and I have come to bring you this ring as a small token of our appreciation."

He slipped the ring onto Gene's finger. Gene gazed at the ruby in its heavy gold setting.

"This ring must have cost the boys a fistful of greenbacks."

He slipped the ring off his finger, dropping it into Osterhout's pocket. "Tell the boys I'm grateful but that I said they should give it back to the jeweler and use the money to organize new lodges."

Two months later he was working with a new local in Scranton, Pennsylvania, when one of the firemen said, "Gene, the mayor heard you were in town, wants to see you."

Preoccupied, he asked blankly, "Mayor . . . wants me?"

"Terence Powderly, head of the Knights of Labor. We've elected him three times on a Greenback-Labor ticket."

Walking up to the City Hall, Gene recalled the fantastic rise of Powderly from switch tender and car repairman to the General Master Workman of the Knights, the most powerful labor organization in the country. The Knights had been formed seventeen years before by some garment cutters in Philadelphia. Only thirty-seven years old, self-educated Terence Powderly had accomplished the double miracle of bringing the formerly underground organization into the open and being the first head of a labor group to be elected mayor of a big city.

Mayor Powderly sprang up from his desk and came halfway across the mahogany-paneled room to clasp Gene's hand.

"We've known each other for years," he cried in a rich and laughing Irish voice. "Here, sit on this leather couch beside me."

Gene found himself engulfed in the dynamic energy of Powderly; his deep blue eyes were sparkling, his cheeks were a hearty red, and he wore dashing handlebar mustaches, rakishly curled at the ends.

"I expected one day I would walk into your office as mayor of Terre Haute, just as you walked into mine."

Gene told him of his own futile attempt to be a legislator. "Mind you, I'm not trying to justify my failure; it's just that I agree with Samuel Gompers that trade-unionists don't belong in politics."

At the mention of Gompers' name Powderly's eyes snapped with anger.

"Gompers! That grubby little worm, eating out the insides

of a black cigar! He thinks that if he can win his men a few
cents more an hour he's getting them into heaven."

Gene leaped to Gompers's defense.

"He may not be getting them into heaven, but he's taking
them out of the hell of those tenement sweatshops."

"No, no, Gene, he goes begging with his hat in his hand:
'Please, Mr. Employer, be so kind as to raise our wages, and
cut our hours, and improve our working conditions. . . .'"

"But these are legitimate trade-union objectives!" cried
Gene. "Through them the working people are slowly being
brought out of slavery!"

Powderly jumped up, began pacing the room, generating
electric voltage.

"You've used exactly the right word, Gene: slowly: at a
snail's pace, so that maybe in five hundred years, or a
thousand . . ."

"Looka here, Mayor Powderly, the history of our country
shows that the trade-unionist has always gained more for the
men than the reformer."

Powderly threw back his head and laughed, rubbing his
index finger up and down the deep cleft in his chin.

"Now, now, Gene, you're not going to frighten me by the
use of the word 'reformer.' My ideal is to reform America,
not by begging for five cents more an hour, but by abolishing
wages altogether. Why should we waste our genius on such
trivialities as fresh air in factories when we are in process of
educating the working people of America to take over their
own industries."

Gene was aghast. This is revolution, he thought.

Not long after he quit the legislature he returned from an
early morning walk with Theodore to find Kate upset.

"Gene, where have you been?"

"In the woods with Theo."

"You were gone when I awoke. I couldn't imagine that
you should want to leave me . . ."

"Theo and I never miss an early morning walk."

"But you're married now."

"Would you like to come with us, Kate?"

"Eugene, you know it's not proper for a woman to go
walking foolishly in the woods at five in the morning."

"Then why should you object if Theo and I . . . ?"

"Because people will talk."

"What could they possibly find wrong to say about it?"

"That you prefer your brother's company to your wife's."

"Oh no, Kate! Who could conceivably criticize a man for loving his kid brother?"

"Gene, you're now an important person in your community; you can't keep on with your childhood habits."

"Not even with the good ones?"

"That's irrelevant, and you know it. Marriage changes a man's life. You've got to settle down. If you continue to walk at five in the morning, folks will call you eccentric."

"My friends won't call me anything of the sort, and my enemies wouldn't bother with so mild an epithet. So stop worrying, Kate, and put breakfast on. You'd be surprised what an appetite I have."

Kate went into the kitchen, but he could see by the expression on her face that the discussion had been only temporarily recessed. It was resumed a few Sundays later when she returned from services at the Episcopal church, took off her hat, coat and gloves and put her purse in its niche in the bedroom bureau. He suggested that they start out for the Debs home early so they could buy Daisy a bouquet of flowers.

"Eugene," she said, "you weren't intending that we go to your parents' home every Sunday, were you?"

"Well, it's nice to be with the whole family once a week. Sunday dinner has always been a great pleasure to Daisy. And I notice you are thoughtful enough to help with the dishes, so you see it's no burden."

"But had you thought it might be a . . . burden . . . to me?"

Gene put his hat down and searched his wife's sentence for some possible meaning.

"You always enjoyed the family's company. You came nearly every night and every Sunday for months on end."

"But we have our own home now, Eugene. It's time you broke away from Daisy's apron strings."

"Broke away—from Daisy? And Daniel? Why, I love them better than anything. . . ."

"You are supposed to love your wife better than anything. . . ."

"From the time I was old enough to see and hear they've given me every tenderness."

He was thoroughly aroused now.

"Eugene, you know I'm not a snob. But having Sunday dinner in a dining room behind a grocery store."

"You mean Daisy's cooking is tasteless because it's served behind a grocery store?"

"Now don't start quarreling with me about things I never said. If you happen to like French cooking, Daisy is a wonderful cook. Personally I enjoy the German flavors more. It's just that we're doing our best to rise in the world now. And there's something distasteful to me about eating Sunday dinner as though we were grubby shopkeepers."

"A thousand times you've asked me to open a shop so that I could become a successful businessman. But now a shop that has raised six children and gotten us all off to healthy, happy starts in life becomes grubby. When did you suddenly discover this, Kate? Certainly eating behind a grocery shop never impaired your appetite before we were married."

"That's a cruel thing to say, Eugene, and it isn't like you."

"How can a man know what he is like when he hears everything he's grown up with being attacked?"

She saw that her argument had jumped the tracks before it left the yards. She slipped her arms about his waist.

"Eugene, all I'm saying is that Daisy and Daniel have earned something better than life behind and above a grocery store. I think they ought to buy a lovely home for themselves. I think you ought to help them. Daisy and Daniel have probably been wondering, now that you earn three thousand dollars a year, why you haven't offered to help take them out of that . . ."

He was all contrition; he had done Kate an injustice.

"Kate, forgive me. Sometimes I'm a little slow in understanding you. Maybe you're right about the folks; maybe they have been waiting for me to suggest something. Get your purse and hat, we'll go over to the house and talk to them after dinner."

"Eugene, would you mind terribly going alone? I have a splitting headache. I don't want you to be worried, but I'm just going to have a cup of tea and lie down. The family's expecting you, and I know you don't like to disappoint them."

After dinner he and Theodore stood with Mother Hubbards over their Sunday clothes, drying the dishes as Daisy took them out of the soapy pan and passed them through the tub of boiled water. On the last trip in from the dining room Gene murmured, "Stand by me, Theo, I've got a little business to transact with Daisy."

"If you know in advance that you need help," replied Theodore, "It looks to me like you're going to lose."

"No, no, Daisy's been waiting for this for a long time."

He went to his mother, rested his lanky frame against the drainboard.

"Doesn't this house seem awfully big to you now, Daisy?"

"I hadn't noticed it," she replied.

"I think there's too much work around here for you. You ought to take it a little easier."

"Why Gene, I'd love to. You get here early next Sunday morning and cook dinner for us."

Theodore burst out laughing.

"What I'm trying to say, Daisy, is that you must run up and down those outside stairs at least forty times a day."

"Fifty." She finished the last of the silverware, piled it on the drainboard, rinsed her hands in cold water and dried them. "You have something on your mind, Gene, what is it?"

He took a deep breath; he really had no heart for this task, but it was obvious that it had to be performed.

"I think it's time you and Daniel bought yourselves a home, like one of those new cottages they have been building in the Cedar Woods tract. Where you can walk from the dining room into the parlor without going into the street and up a flight of stairs."

Daisy cocked her head at her son, then lifted one corner of her mouth ever so slightly.

"Who's been talking to you?"

"Nobody's been talking to me. I earn three thousand dollars a year now. I could help you buy . . ."

Daisy leaned against the sink and gazed around the big kitchen. Her eyes took in the details of the cupboards that she had built and rebuilt over the years, of the new linoleum with the checkered stripe that she had gazed at so lovingly while it was in the window of the hardware store; she counted the cups one by one as they hung from their hooks, and checked the piles of dinner plates on the shelves to make sure that none was missing. Then she turned back to her oldest boy.

"This is home. This is where I watched my children grow up tall and straight and beautiful."

"She means me." Theodore grinned.

"This is where Jenny and Theo and Emma were born. If I move out of the house of my memories, Gene, what do I think about when I look at your cute bungalow with its fresh paint and fresh woodwork? That is good for you, son, because you are beginning your life. I am ending mine."

She reached her hands up to her son's long, lean cheeks and kissed one corner of his mouth. "You're a good boy, Gene, but Daniel and I don't need any help. We're happy here."

On his walk home he saw an attractive girl smiling at him from a distance; he did not recognize her until she stepped in front of him and said:

"Hello, Mr. Debs, don't you remember me? I'm Clarissa Hanford."

"Not little Clarissa Hanford," exclaimed Gene.

"No, not little any more. I'm grown now."

She had indeed grown: for though she could have been little more than sixteen, she was a full-blown woman: long-legged, ample-bosomed, her eyes worldly. When he asked if she were still attending high school, Clarissa laughed, her mouth open, her teeth flashing.

"High school! That's for children. I am out working now, making money for my clothes. Don't you think this is a lovely red dress, Mr. Debs? You don't think that All Faith Church could have bought it for me, do you?"

She threw back her head, laughed gaily for another instant, said a quick good-by and was gone down the street. He stood gazing after her for a moment, troubled.

— 4 —

Kate was singularly uninterested in his report about Daisy and the house on Wabash Street, yet he sensed that she had made some kind of decision as a result of their discussion. Her step was lighter, she moved with her shoulders back and her head held high.

The work on his desk seemed limitless. Running his hand through a box of neglected firemen's papers, he turned to his brother. "Theo, you're going to have to attend the Denver convention and present the secretary's annual report. That will give me a chance to get out from under this coal pile. Besides, it will be a good experience for you."

However Theodore returned from the convention with less enthusiasm about the firemen than about a girl named Gertrude with whom he had apparently fallen in love.

"She's warm-natured, she likes people. And what do you know, Gene, she thought the convention was exciting. She asked me to get her tickets for the visitors' gallery, and I had to tell her all about our work and what I do for the union." Theodore's cheeks flamed and his eyes danced. "She's only a little thing, Gene, like Gloria was, but she has a stout heart."

At the mention of Gloria, Gene saw her face before him. He pushed aside his nostalgia as though it were a heavy crate on a railroad siding.

Theodore was still chattering irrepressibly.

"We're in no hurry, she's only eighteen. We're going to correspond, and next summer, when the Brotherhood meets at Atlanta, maybe you could get a pass for her?"

"My dear old pard," chuckled Gene, "she shall ride on my

pass, and I'll heave coal up on the cab. That's the least I can do for my future sister-in-law."

When he reached Mrs. Koopman's that evening he found his flat in an uproar, with Kate packing barrels of dishes, a towel wrapped around her hair, and her face beaming. She embraced him with unusual ardor, exclaiming:

"Eugene, I've found the nicest little cottage! We'll have it all to ourselves. It's at 1000 North Eighth Street, you know that little yellow house set so far back from the street. And what do you think, Gene, I got it for only sixteen dollars a month: isn't that a bargain? The owner said we could move in tomorrow, it's all freshly painted."

Gene could not remember having seen his wife so happy since the night he had been elected to the legislature. He was delighted for her sake, and for his own too: these rooms were so small it had been difficult to think of entertaining. But with a whole cottage to themselves . . .

"You must help me pack."

For a week she was like a woman possessed: she had no patience to eat or sleep because of her excitement about sewing the new cretonne curtains and bedspreads, rearranging the furniture a hundred times to get it exactly right, hanging or rehanging pictures, building additional shelves in the kitchen to house her dishes and gleaming pans.

At last the house was ready, and just in time, for the Occidental Club had invited Henry George, the single-tax advocate, to lecture.

"He's coming in tomorrow on the late afternoon train, Kate, and I'd like to bring him home for a light supper before the lecture."

"But, Eugene, he's a radical, isn't he?"

"Henry George? Yes, the real estate owners think him radical in wanting to take over all the land."

"Then why do you want to invite him into your home?"

"Kate, I don't understand. Why shouldn't we have Henry George in our home?"

"I just don't think we should become intimate with people who want to tear down our form of government."

"Then you object to his lecturing here for the Occidental Club?"

"Eugene, that's unfair; I'm not a bigot. I believe in free speech and free listening. Any man that wants to express his point of view, and can get people to listen to him, has a right to speak."

"For a moment there, Kate, you had me frightened."

"But, Eugene, just because I believe in free speech, does

that mean that I'm obliged to let a revolutionary break bread at my table? When I serve a man food, Eugene, and he eats it off my plates in my brand-new home, that means we are friends, that we think alike and have the same values."

"Oh, Kate, no! I've brought all sorts of people into Daisy and Daniel's home, and I've eaten in the homes of men with whom I've disagreed nine times out of ten. If we never associate with anyone except those who share our beliefs . . ."

"You're avoiding the issue, Eugene. If my family and friends learned that I had Henry George in for dinner, they'd think I've become tainted with radical . . ."

"See here, Kate," he broke in angrily, "there are people in Terre Haute who say I'm radical just because I work for a labor union. If you're going to label as radical every idea that you don't like, then the term simply becomes a synonym for disagreement."

"Eugene, every time you lose a point in an argument, you go off into vague theorizing. I know you're not a radical, and I know that Henry George is; therefore, I say that you should remain in your element and he should remain in his. Let him eat his supper at the Union Depot. I understand the food is delicious there, and he won't have to wear himself out being sociable before his lecture."

"But you should think of this as a social coup: you're capturing the lion of the hour. Henry George has just returned from a triumphal lecture tour in England."

"Triumphal with whom? People who agreed with him? I wouldn't want them in my home either."

He was too hurt to answer: he had gone on the assumption that one of the purposes of this new home was to afford pleasant surroundings for their friends. The thought that he would have to strain the ideas of future visitors through Kate's concept of political respectability was an almost unbearable humiliation.

"Kate, please do this for me as a special favor. I promise we won't discuss a word of economics at the table. It will merely be a social visit to show Mr. George that he's welcome in Terre Haute."

There was a quality in his voice that made her stop her work and gaze at her husband in troubled surprise.

"Very well," she said, "it shall be as you wish. Tell me what time you want supper and what I should serve."

He threw his arms about her. "Thank you, Kate, it's good of you to do this for me."

He tried to kiss her, but she turned away.

The following afternoon he sounded a rhythmic beat on

the clapper, then opened the door and ushered Henry George into the parlor. He had taken only a couple of steps before he realized that something was wrong: the atmosphere was too still, there were none of the pleasant odors of the roasting chicken he had suggested for supper. He asked Mr. George if he wouldn't sit down for a moment, then went quickly to the bedroom.

The room was dark, the blinds drawn below the sills. Kate was stretched out in bed, flat on her back, her face pale and her eyes closed. She seemed so utterly still that for one arrested breath he thought she might be dead. He leaned over, ran his fingers across her brow. She spoke without moving or opening her eyes.

"Eugene, I'm dreadfully sorry . . . to disappoint you . . . but I became so ill . . . almost fainted . . . There was no one to send with a message. Please apologize to Mr. George for me, won't you? Tell him I'm dreadfully sorry . . . to be such a poor hostess. Perhaps next time."

He sat on the edge of the bed, finding it difficult to breathe. So she had won the argument after all! He rose, went to the door and stood before it, his head bowed. On the other side of the closed door sat Henry George, a man whom he admired and respected. George was no fool, he had endured public slander and abuse for too many years not to know that this cold reception was just one more affront. But wait, he hadn't told Henry George that he was taking him home to his wife for dinner! He had simply said that he was taking him home.

He opened the door, a broad grin on his face, said, "Come along, Mr. George, or we'll be late for supper," and led him straight to Daniel's dining room behind the grocery store. If Daisy and Daniel were surprised they did not show it: they were too accustomed to having him arrive with his hand under the arm of an unexpected dinner guest. Daniel, who had read *Progress and Poverty*, paid George the compliment of disagreeing with his conclusions in such a fashion as to prove that he had pondered the book's premises.

Theodore came in through the store in time to hear the end of the discussion. Gene had mentioned that he was going to take Henry George home for supper. By home, Theodore had known he meant to Kate's. He went to his brother's side, slipped an arm about his waist.

He started for home at eleven o'clock, after putting his visitor on the Pullman for St. Louis. The hall had been crowded and Henry George had made a forceful speech, though he had not convinced Gene that government ownership of the nation's land was the panacea needed to solve mankind's ills.

He walked slowly; the excitement of the meeting had been superseded by his dread of an encounter with his wife. He did not know how he was going to get into that bed and go to sleep alongside her without a discussion.

But even as he entered the black and airless bedroom, saw that Kate had not moved from her supine position in the six hours since he had left, he realized that she was genuinely ill. She had not been trying to defeat him: the thought of having someone in her home whom she hated and feared had struck her down.

If he were to tell her now that the impending hospitality to a social iconoclast had made her ill, she would only deny the charge, say that it was the too strong coffee she had had at lunch, or perhaps the strain on her eyes from sewing in a bad light. He knew that it was neither strong coffee nor bad light: it had been her husband who was the cause of her trouble, her husband who loved her but who had obliged her to do something repugnant to her nature.

Contritely he brewed a cup of tea in the kitchen, then brought a pan of lukewarm water and a towel to her bedside, where he patted her face and her hands. He raised the blinds and opened the windows, letting in the cool night air; and when he asked if she were feeling better she knew from his voice that there would be no quarrel.

She felt better at once; he was pleased when she drank the tea he brought her and asked for news about the lecture.

— 5 —

From the day of her marriage Kate saw nothing of her family, except on those rare occasions when her brother Danny rolled into town, generally at the end of a three-week spree. She had talked so glowingly about her half brothers, their financial acumen, their brilliance in business; but now that she was married she never mentioned them. They were not invited to the homes of her sisters, nor did Gene ever come upon them in his own house. He asked her if she didn't want to give a dinner for her family.

"I will when I'm ready, Eugene," she replied.

"Well, just so long as you're happy."

"Oh, I am happy here, darling. This little bungalow will do fine, until we move into our own home."

He turned sharply. "Home? What home?"

"Why, the one we're going to build for ourselves, when we're ready."

"You mean you have it all planned?"

"Of course. How can you accomplish anything if you don't have plans? Would you like to see a picture of it?"

He sank into a chair and shook his head.

"Kate, you amaze me."

"I have known for years precisely what my house will look like: the architectural style, the interior decoration, and just where every piece of furniture is going to sit."

"You mean you had someone draw blueprints?"

"I have been cutting pictures out of the society magazines; I have them all mounted in an album. I look forward to the day when I open the door of my own big, beautiful house, and you walk across the threshold."

"Suppose I don't want a big house? I don't mean that in a number of years, when we have a family and need the space, and we have more money saved . . ."

"No, Eugene, the house comes first. A house is tangible proof that you're a successful man, it will attract other successful men to you, it will bring you opportunities for advancement."

Gene grinned. "The only successful men who come to see me are union officials, and they bring me problems, not offers of advancement."

"But don't you see, Eugene, when you have a house, successful people from every walk of life will come to you, and they will be impressed! Let me bring you the pictures; when you see how imposing it is, you'll want it as much as I do."

She had already left the room. She returned in a few moments with a black leather album whose pages had originally been intended to hold photographs. She sat close to him on the sofa, and with her eyes flashing excitement, introduced him to the house.

"Here's how it looks from the outside, Eugene. Isn't it beautiful?"

Gene found himself looking at a two-and-a-half-story frame house of Queen Anne architecture with a steep roof of many gables. There was a hollow feeling at the pit of his stomach, for this was no simple workingman's home; this was a castle.

"How will you ever get enough money to build it?"

"Oh, you just leave that to me," she replied. "I already have a good sum put away in home-building bonds."

"But how could you?"

She gazed at him for a moment; her hard determination frightened him.

"I have saved it penny for penny and dollar for dollar! I've done my own sewing and washing. I've denied myself trips with you because I knew how many dollars it would take out of my savings. I've tried not to deprive you of anything, Eugene; I knew that wouldn't be fair. I've fed you well, haven't I, and kept you comfortable?"

"Oh yes, Kate. But this house, can't you see it's not for me . . . ?"

She interrupted him. "Why not? You are a natural aristocrat."

"But I'm an employee of a union. I shouldn't live in such a grand house when . . ."

"A man lives as best he can, Eugene, by honest work. If your salary can buy you a lovely home, why aren't you entitled to it? What are you supposed to do with your money, gamble or drink it away?"

Somehow she had marshaled all the logic on her side. He persisted in the face of it.

"A union official shouldn't live better than the men he represents. If he does, he's taking too much salary."

"Now really, Gene, you're forever saying that a workman is worthy of his hire. If you get only enough to live in a shack, then all you're worth is a shack. If you earn enough to build a fine house, then you're worth a fine house. There isn't a human being in the world who would dispute that, Eugene, or who would deny that your years of sacrifice and labor have earned you the right to live well. The Locomotive Firemen will be proud that you live so grandly. They'll point to your house and say, 'That house belongs to the secretary of our union. Pretty nice, eh?' It will be proof that their organization is strong and prosperous."

"Well, maybe you have a point there."

"Of course I have a point. When important people come to Terre Haute they will visit you in your big and beautiful house. It will help you get the things you want for your men."

"Those values are true in the commercial world, Kate, but I'm not in business."

"Oh, aren't you!" she laughed. "You receive about fifteen thousand dollars in dues every month; your insurance fund is handling about sixty thousand dollars a month. You take in as much as many a good-sized corporation; and you'll be taking in more every day. Before long your salary will be up to ten thousand a year. Yes, even twenty thousand a year, as your organization grows."

Aghast, Gene could only murmur weakly, "Kate, you're making a plutocrat out of me. No union could afford such sums; and what would I do with all that money if I ever got it?"

"You'd give it to me," his wife replied coolly, "and I would make excellent use of it. I would buy investment property, I would put it into the very strongest stocks and bonds, I would make you a rich man."

"But, Kate," he wailed. "I just want to earn enough for a comfortable living."

"Money is the most important thing in the world, Eugene, because it controls everything in life."

"That is crass materialism."

"You can't throw me off the track by calling names. The Brotherhood of Locomotive Firemen almost died for lack of money, didn't it?"

"Yes."

He was crushed. Kate sensed her triumph. She said more placatingly, "Eugene, it isn't as though I nag you to make more money. Now do I?"

"No, Kate, you don't."

"It's just that I want to use your salary to give you the proper surroundings. Is that selfish of me, Eugene?"

"No, Kate."

"If I had been another kind of woman, it would have been easy to spend your salary on frivolities. But when I saved five dollars or twenty dollars, I knew just what it would buy: a beautiful lamp at the foot of the winding staircase, a . . ."

Gene gasped. "You have the house completely furnished! You've been living in it since the day we married."

Kate went to her desk, drew forth her account book in the Home Builders' Association.

"Don't you see, Eugene, I'm not the kind of woman to put you in debt. Our shares in the Home Builders' Association are paying us eight per cent. If I have saved this much money, I've earned it, haven't I?"

Her argument had been honest and logical every step of the way. In a voice so low she could hardly hear it he answered:

"Yes, Kate, you have."

— 6 —

Gene was on the road much of the time, and Theodore took over the office of the Brotherhood. Because of their years of work together, the similarity of character and approach, the methods one brother evolved seemed substantially right to the other; they had also learned to compromise their differences.

They were working on a special edition of the magazine devoted to the movement for an eight-hour day when Gene bethought himself to look at the clock. It was past the dinner hour.

"Come along home with me for supper, Theo, and we can knock out the rest of this at the table."

"Does Kate expect me?"

"No, but there's always enough food."

Theodore started to say, I'd rather not. But he knew this would hurt his brother. Instead he said, "That'll be fine, but be sure to tell Kate it was your idea."

Gene threw open the front door of his house. Kate was waiting for him in the big armchair where she spent so many hours of her life watching for him to come in. This home-coming was the most important moment in her day: she spent several hours preparing for it, bathing, taking infinite pains with her hair, donning a freshly pressed white blouse or a tailored dress. Gene was not observant, he knew only that his wife was as meticulous in her personal habits as she was fanatical about keeping the house clean.

"Good evening, dear. I brought Theo home to dinner with me. We can throw another bone into the soup, can't we?"

He saw the disappointment flash across her eyes, and turned swiftly to observe whether his brother had come far enough into the room to see. Theodore had seen, but he gave no intimation. Kate regained her poise quickly.

"Of course, we're always happy to share with Theo. Won't you both sit down right away? I'm afraid the roast is already a little overdone."

If the roast was overdone, neither Gene nor Theodore knew it, for they resumed their discussion of the series of articles on *Eight Hours for Work, Eight Hours for Rest, Eight Hours for What We Will.* Neither did Gene notice Kate's absence from the table. It was not until ten o'clock, when Theodore had left for home, that he realized she had eaten nothing, had as a matter of fact set out the dessert and then disappeared into the bedroom. He found her lying sidewise across the bed in the darkened room.

"Kate dear, don't you feel well?" When she did not answer he continued, "But surely you didn't mind my bringing Theo home for supper? There's always food, and we had to get the articles laid out before tomorrow morning."

Kate picked herself up and sat on the edge of the bed. Her clothes were rumpled, her hair in disarray.

"Eugene, do you think it's fair to me?"

"Do I think what's fair?"

"Bringing your office home at night."

"But if there was something urgent?"

"You go away for days and weeks on your business, and I don't object, I don't even ask where you've been. But when you're in Terre Haute, I think I should have your few hours of leisure."

"But, darling, you do. It's just that tonight . . ."

"You leave the house at five in the morning to pick up Theodore for your walk in the woods. You're back at seven for a bath and breakfast. Before I turn around you leave for the office. If I don't put a stop to this supper and evening work, you'll be working until midnight."

"Not any more," he said, smiling. "I'm not the man I used to be for those twenty-hour chunks of straight labor."

"What have I to look forward to all day but our hours alone together? If I'm going to find Theo on the steps every time you open the front door . . ."

Gene had brought his brother home so seldom that his temper rose.

"I've brought Theo home only a few times. After all, he's my brother. We started this union together; we get a tremendous amount done, working as a team."

"You should have married him," she snapped.

His anger vanished at the unhappiness in her voice. Kate was right! What did she have of him? His excitements, his adventures, his plans and dreams, yes, even his despairs and defeats he shared with Theodore. These were things he owed his wife, for this was the stuff of which a good marriage was made. Yet he had tried: he had discussed the union problems with Kate, listed the grievances of each local against its particular line when they wrote in to him for help, tried to tell her what it was his men wanted from management. But Kate had not been interested; worse, she had seemed antagonistic. Somehow he had the feeling that she regarded the growing strength of the union as something dangerous and undesirable. His life was his work, and if his wife disagreed with the objectives of that work, if in every struggle she was hoping that the union would lose . . . !

He shook himself free of the morbid cycle of his thoughts. This was not the issue involved. Kate wanted her evenings alone with him. She was entitled to that.

"All right, Kate, I won't bring Theo home to dinner any more."

She jumped up, went to her dressing table and began brushing her hair.

"We will invite Theo often, Eugene. But let's prepare for it

in advance: give me a chance to market and set the table
properly."

He avoided meetings and night work; they sat together in
the parlor before a blazing fire. One thing he noticed very
quickly: she was highly sensitive to the kind of book he
might be reading. If it were a work of literature, *Madame
Bovary* or *The Brothers Karamazov,* or the novels of Smol-
lett or Cooper, she sat in her rocker contentedly sewing, utterly at peace. But if it were a book on political economy,
Lassalle's *Workingman's Program, The Story of Labor in All
Ages* by Simonds and McEnnis, or any one of the dozens of
pamphlets on social reform which were mailed to him from
all over the world, Kate was restless, uneasy. It sometimes
seemed to him that she was afraid the Czar's secret police
would knock down the front door, and arrest him for reading
incendiary literature.

The weeks and months slipped by. He helped the Switchmen's Benevolent Association, which had been a Chicago
local, expand to a vigorous national brotherhood. He did so
much organizational work for the Brotherhood of Locomotive Brakemen that they offered him a salary and expense account, which he turned down on the ground that the Locomotive Firemen, who had jumped his salary still another
thousand dollars a year at the last convention, were providing
him with all the money he needed.

And at last his travels brought him in April of 1886 into
the same room with the man whom he admired most in the
labor movement, Samuel Gompers, who was even now building an organization of trade unions which would be nationwide and would achieve concerted action for the welfare of
its members.

Samuel liked to boast that a Gompers was as sturdy as an
oak, which Gene found a likely figure of speech: the man
was massive about the shoulders and chest, with almost no
neck, but a broad powerful face and head, his thick black
hair chopped off at a point precisely opposite the slashing
black eyebrows. His eyes too were big, dark, strong. His mustache was black and he wore a small, square beard tuft directly below the circle of his underlip. His speech was as
strangely polyglot in its accents as the melting-pot New York
in which he had come to maturity. He looked like a crude,
bluff man who would attempt to bludgeon his way, but Samuel Gompers had seen too many union battles lost by these
methods; he had become one of the most conciliatory men in
the labor movement, winning concessions from employers be-

cause he presented his case quietly, reasonably, without intimidation.

At the moment that Joshua Leach had arrived in Terre Haute to appoint Gene secretary of the firemen's local, Samuel Gompers had been organizing the cigar makers of New York City into one local union. It had been unionism that helped the Gompers family to reach America, for Samuel's father had been a member of the Cigar Makers' Union in England, and during a depression he had drawn the passage money from the union's Emigration Fund. The Gompers family reached New York and settled in the most unsavory slums of Houston Street when Samuel was a boy. Mentally hungry, he had sought education at every possible source. He joined the Arion Baseball and Social Club where the tenement boys debated the burning issues of the day, but by far the best part of his education had been secured inside the cigar factory where he worked a twelve-hour day: by the fortuitous accident that hundreds of men rolling cigars make no noise, the workers could select one man to read aloud from the current books. Young Gompers had a strong voice, and he frequently read for longer than the usual hour stretch, in return for which the other workmen gave him a prorate of rolled cigars.

The New York Cigar Makers' Union endured bitter times. Strikes against the most oppressive of hours and conditions had been lost time and again because the union had no money, no discipline, no ties with other unions to back them up. But not even slum imprisonment in tubercular sweatshops had turned Gompers against the form of government to which his family had emigrated. In the shop with him was an older man who had taught him: "Study your union card, Sam, and if the idea does not square with that, it ain't true."

"I have followed that advice all these years, Debs: there's nothing wrong in the American way of life that can't be fixed by a union card. Half of the battles I lose with management today are results of the employers' reading that the Knights of Labor stand for socialism, hence all unions stand for socialism, and the more money they give us for wages, the more we will have for guns and barricades."

"But there's one part of Powderly's program I approve most heartily," replied Gene. "No one knows better than you how desperately working people need education, yet you resist every effort to turn the trade unions into educational centers."

Quietly Gompers replied, "Right now we are educating the public to the eight-hour movement; we are teaching America the evils of sweatshops, of tenement factories, of child labor; that kind of education brings us results. It is not our purpose to bring the workers Beethoven and Shakespeare; it is our purpose to bring good food into their kitchens and clean toilets into their factories. When we have won the economic fight, the men will be free to pursue whatever intellectual life they want. Your friend Powderly's mystical Knights are content to wait a hundred years for their Utopia; we say that every hour spent in a filthy tenement factory, and every unfed child at mealtime, is a crime against humanity, right now, right this very second."

Gene was quiet. Gompers knew agreement even when he heard it in silence. He had respect for Gene Debs; he had read the *Locomotive Firemen's Magazine* for many years.

"The world has been in slavery for eight thousand years, Debs, and trade-unionism is the one and only way to achieve freedom. The American Federation of Labor will be an object case in voluntarism: men join because they want to, employers deal with us because we can prove the economics of our case. I look to my union card, and to my union card alone."

"I should think there would be times when we could cooperate with other groups," commented Gene. "Take this struggle for the eight-hour day, we've had a lot of help."

"From whom?" demanded Gompers bluntly.

"Well, from the anarchist group in Chicago. They've broken ground."

"Gene, I'm ashamed of you, talking of union labor as though it were a beggar, walking the streets with its palms outstretched. Where you let other causes break ground for you they also break heads in the process, and you must stand responsible for their conduct. You can't control them; since when did a mendicant control an almsgiver? And sooner or later they do something to serve their own purpose. Then your united front blows up in your face."

Even as he opened his own front door on his return from New York City, some three weeks later, Gene found that Gompers's words had been prophetic.

— 7 —

Kate was hysterical with fear.

"Eugene, you didn't know any of those men, did you? Your name hasn't been linked with theirs?"

"What men? Linked with whom?"

"Those anarchists in Chicago, the ones who threw the bomb and killed all those hundreds of policemen."

"Now, Kate, suppose you sit down by me quietly and tell me what this is all about."

"They were holding a meeting in Haymarket Square for that eight-hour day of yours. The police tried to stop them, and so they threw bombs!"

"Where did you get this information?"

"It's in the evening paper. The whole country is up in arms. Oh, Eugene, if any of these men are your friends, if you ever had them here in Terre Haute, don't you see what will happen, Eugene? The Chicago police will come here after you. They'll charge you with these murders."

"Where is the paper, Kate?"

"In the bedroom."

He went into the bedroom to collect the scattered sheets. This was doubtless a new journalistic attack on the eight-hour movement. But there spread between his hands was the headline:

A Horrible Deed

At the end of a mass meeting in Haymarket Square, as a police captain had ordered the group to disperse, a bomb had exploded, wounding a large number of policemen, whose fellow officers had then fired their revolvers into the fleeing crowd.

His insides quivering, he walked back to the parlor with the paper hanging by his side. He dropped listlessly beside Kate. Her fears were deepened.

"Eugene, will they have any way of connecting you with these men?" She took the paper from him and tremblingly ran her finger down the column. "This Albert Parsons, or August Spies or Samuel Fielden?"

"No, I don't know them," he replied dully.

"Are you sure? You've never had them here to lecture, or for the union?"

"No, Kate."

Her eyes were wide with fear. "Oh, Eugene, why do you have to consort with those horrible men? Now there'll be police in our house, they might even accuse you . . ."

A sufficient portion of his mind cleared for him to turn to his wife, take her quaking shoulders in the grasp of his two long, powerful hands and say sternly, "Kate, you must get hold of yourself. I have no more connection with these men than you have."

She put her head on his shoulder, and the sobs that racked her big frame sent a tremor through him.

"Eugene, you don't know what I go through, every day and every night, frightened that something like this will happen, that there'll be killings, and they'll hold you responsible."

He lifted her head from his shoulder and held her face before him.

"Kate, you must listen to me: I have nothing to do with such things. I abhor violence. There never has been anything in my union work except a conventional trade-union program. We're a benevolent organization: our interests are in getting better wages for the men and taking care of their families when they're hurt or killed."

"Yes, yes, I believe you, Eugene, but everyone says union leaders are radicals, so what does it matter what kind of radical you are if they think all radicals are the same?"

She rose, went into the bedroom for a moment, returned with a lace handkerchief with which to wipe the tears from under her eyes. He knew that her terror was as actual as though he had been named in the afternoon paper as one of the arrested anarchists.

"For your own sake, Eugene, you've got to give up this work. Sooner or later something will happen like this horrible mass murder in Chicago, and they'll implicate you in it. If you were ever arrested, accused of these crimes, and sent to prison . . . it would kill me!"

"But, Kate, this is outlandish! How can I be sent to prison for asking a railway manager to cancel the lease on a depot saloon? I'm a businessman, the same as any of your brothers; I negotiate contracts for locomotive firemen, and I get the best bargain I can, the same as any other businessman. What possible connection can this have with bombs or killings?"

Kate was inconsolable.

Whatever hopes he may have had that the newspaper reports were exaggerated were blasted the next day when fuller accounts reached Terre Haute. He recalled his father's philosophy of anarchism. The son realized that this must have been a blow to Daniel Debs, and he hastened home to his father. The counter of Debity Debs's grocery store was littered with the Chicago newspapers. To Gene's surprise Daniel was reading avidly, but unshaken.

"Why did they have to do it, Father?" he asked. "It served no purpose, there was no provocation."

Daniel Debs looked up, his gray-blue eyes clear.

"Why did they do what, son?"

"You always taught me that the anarchists were against

violence: that's why they didn't want government, or any other kind of restraint."

"You ought to know the answer, son: they didn't do it."

Gene sank down onto a case of wine.

"They didn't do it?" he whispered. "But how can you say that? All the evidence . . ."

"What evidence?" demanded Daniel, his eyes flashing. "These men held a May Day meeting in favor of the eighthour day. Somebody threw a bomb. If you can show me one scrap of specific evidence in all these charges . . ."

"But who else could have done it?"

"People serving their own purposes, even irresponsible lunatics; but who could have gained less from it than the men who were holding the meeting?"

Daniel Debs turned away from his son.

"Watch the store for a moment. I must have a cup of coffee."

He went through the door into the dining room. Sadly Gene thought, Father is growing old. When the facts get too bitter, he can't digest them. But he hasn't lost what I've lost from that bomb, what all union men and workingmen have lost. They've blown up our eight-hour day. They've hurt our whole union movement because now everyone is going to be tarred with the same brush. Management will be suspicious, the press will turn against us the way they did after the Pittsburgh riots in '77. Every time we raise our heads they'll call us anarchists and see bombs bulging in our hip pockets.

When he returned home he found Kate gone. She came in several hours later, dressed in a dark suit and hat. She began speaking the moment she saw him.

"Eugene, I've been talking with my brothers. They'll give you a job with them, they'll even lend you some money to set you up in business for yourself. Oh, darling, they have confidence in you, and I have too: you can make a living some other way. Can't you see, Eugene, there's nothing in this unionism but trouble? Once you're in business nothing bad can ever happen to you, there will be no question of radicalism or causes, you'll be in the best element. Any man would do that much for his wife, Eugene, if he loved her."

He turned away.

— 8 —

As a direct result of the Haymarket trials and the hanging of Spies, Parsons, Fischer and Engel, Kate informed Gene that she was building her house. This was the ultimate security she must have to protect her against the insecurity of her husband's life.

"I have the money available now, Eugene. You have no objections to my going ahead?"

He offered no objection, he was almost anxious that she build: they had been married for three years now and still had no children. Looking back, he recalled that the prospect of youngsters had been one of the most important reasons he had married. Kate had been unwilling to bring children into the world until she could place them in the permanence of their own home. He did not exactly know how she managed not to have children: the people around him seemed to have them abundantly whether they were willing or no; but Kate was enormously efficient, and whatever she wanted she somehow managed.

In the meanwhile his warmth and love had gone out to every child he passed on the street: a conversation, a laugh shared, to the children on his block a bag of jelly beans on his way home from work. In the house directly opposite were two youngsters, Georgie and Aggie, a towhead of eleven and his pigtailed sister of eight. When Gene went to the station in the late afternoon to catch a train, Georgie and Aggie walked with him and waved him good-by. No matter where he went he would stop at the last town to buy toys for them and assure his welcome-home kiss.

He told himself that once Kate had moved into her own house he would not be put off any longer; for he sorely missed the warmth and exuberance of Daisy's and Daniel's home. He knew the only way he could achieve this was by having young ones of his own. He told none of this to Kate; instead he brought up a more immediate problem.

"There's one favor I must ask, Kate: build fairly close to the Union Depot; that will enable me to leave the house at the last moment and to walk home quickly when I reach Terre Haute. If you build on the outskirts of town, I'll spend hours traveling back and forth to the station."

He knew that he was asking a considerable sacrifice. There was a good residential district near the Union Depot, but the very fact of its location kept it from being one of the more desirable parts of town. He knew where Kate wanted to build: out in the exclusive section where the McKeens and the Hulmans had their rambling mansions. Yet he also knew that Kate was interested in his welfare, pursuing him down the block with a clean handkerchief or a pair of rubbers, invariably warning him when he left on a trip:

"Eugene, be careful, be careful what you say."

She sat perfectly still, her knuckles white where she gripped the edge of the chair arms. Her head was high, her face pale and her eyes troubled: for Gene was asking her to give up part of her childhood dream. The minutes passed; it was as though she did not know he was in the room. After considerable time she came out of the locked chamber where she fought her major problems. The color had returned to her cheeks, and her eyes met her husband's. She enunciated each syllable with distinct clarity.

"Yes, Eugene. You have a right to ask that much. Often you arrive in the rain and the snow, drop off a freight in the middle of the night when there is no carriage available. I can't have you trudging miles to reach home. My grandmother owns several lots on Eighth Street, off Sycamore. I know she'll give me a good price on one of them."

"That would be wonderful Kate; it's only a block and a half from the station. Thank you, darling."

She blinked back her tears and lifted her mouth to his grateful kiss.

"This is to be your home as much as mine, and it must be convenient for you. But, Eugene, let me build the house and furnish it all by myself."

"I promise I shan't bother you. I won't even go past Eighth and Sycamore while you're under construction."

He was glad that Kate had something with which to occupy herself during the ensuing months, for he was at home very little, and even during these returns to Terre Haute he was sorely troubled. His difficulties did not arise from the Brotherhood of Locomotive Firemen; on the contrary they were making magnificent progress, their membership rising rapidly, the magazine playing an ever more critical role in enunciating America's trade-union policy and progress.

He was sick at heart from a cause which he would never have believed possible: that labor could do as much damage to its fellows as ever management could dream of. Arrogance and self-interest were prevalent among the workers, the more skilled crafts despising manual labor as though it were the great unwashed.

Even in railroading, each union discouraged the formation and growth of every other union, reasoning that there was just so much pie to be cut up. Part of his success in arbitrating differences with management had been his demonstration that in every case where a union had been formed, earning larger wages and shorter hours through its organization, *the employers had made not less money, but more.* He tried to show the arrogant brotherhoods that by the same token this must be equally true of labor: a union had to produce more to earn more.

He wrote scathing editorials denouncing the engineers as the aristocrats of labor; the engineers were so flattered that they promptly adopted the slogan as their own, and began putting out literature in which they labeled themselves the *Aristocrats of Labor*. He sadly discovered that it did not take wealth or power to corrupt; advantage in any form could turn the trick.

He had done another full swing around the roundhouse: he realized that the trade union, left to itself, was too narrow and factional to achieve the kind of unity needed to accomplish the workingman's security. He now became convinced that it was no good for men to be stratified by their trades, that everybody who worked at railroading ought to belong to the same union.

He could not have foreseen the need for this a few years before, when the men had still to be taught the principles and disciplines of trade-unionism. Having learned to co-operate with their own craft, they would have the basis upon which to build vaster unions which would work for the advantage of everyone within a particular industry. The growing conflicts between the unions took him the long step from trade-unionism to what he now considered an inevitable conclusion: industrial unionism.

The new organization of management would have forced him before very long into a similar channel of thought.

Shortly after the Haymarket explosion the twenty-four railroads operating out of Chicago joined together in a General Managers' Association. Railroading had never been a competitive industry, but now, Gene saw, even the element of competition of working men would be eliminated. It could no longer be a case of the Brotherhood of Locomotive Firemen against the Great Northern; it was now the Great Northern fireman against the railroad dynasty.

In his movements over the steel rails he discussed the idea of industrial unionism with everyone from trackwalkers to the whitecollar conductors. The lower he went in the wage and skill brackets the greater was the eagerness for one big union; the higher he went the more resistance he met.

But he was in no hurry. He knew that this was a revolutionary idea which would meet opposition even more intensely from management. He had to prepare the ground first; he had to make tens of thousands of friends throughout the railroad empire; he had slowly to evolve a form and a philosophy which would be so completely right that no railroader could find the logic to remain outside its domain.

— 9 —

He arrived from Kansas one morning to find movers in front of his little cottage. Kate was directing the operation from the front porch with all the assurance of a major-domo. She tucked her arm securely under his, murmuring, "You're just in time, darling. Today is moving day."

"So I see. Are all these things being moved to the new house?"

"Oh no, no, Eugene. This old stuff has been sold. Everything in our house is brand-new."

The house had taken five months to build and another two months to furnish. During this time Kate had been a perfect tornado of energy, often arriving on the job before the carpenters or plasterers and surpervising the angle from which every nail was hammered.

They walked down Eighth Street and stood on the sidewalk in front of 451. There was a pounding in his head as he lifted his eyes to the two-and-a-half-story house which seemed huge with its bays, cupolas, dormers, chimneys. Kate took him by the hand and led him up stone steps to a wide cement porch enclosed by a yellow-and-red brick railing. She then opened the front door, which had a richly paneled top of figured glass, and said smilingly:

"Do enter your home, Mr. Debs."

Gene found himself in a large foyer. He felt weak at the knees and wished Kate would let him sit down in the big chair against the back wall. There was a handsome circular wooden staircase to his right, with a bronze Mercury on the newel, holding a gas fixture high in his hand.

"Come into the parlor, dear."

Gene walked to the Steinway piano in the bay at the left of the fireplace, touched a few notes idly, wondering who was going to play it. The fireplace was of bronze tile and next to it was a handsome maple table. The carpet beneath his feet was soft, and over it were scattered oriental rugs.

He followed her wonderingly into the library, and drew in his breath sharply at the walls paneled in cherry wood, with handsome bookcases built solid against the back of the room. The wallpaper was blue with long white flowers; there were blue chairs with a matching sofa, and in front of the grate a library table on which she had laid out his pipes and magazines and books precisely as he had left them in the cottage a month before.

Kate next led him through the open doors at his right to the dining room, explaining the details of construction as she went. He listened as would a tourist at a world's fair. She told him why the china cabinet was in the left corner from the hall, where its choice dishware and glassware would be convenient for the setting of the round mahogany table. She showed him how the reddish-tan wallpaper tied in with the table and draperies. To his astonishment he saw a brass bird cage in the far right corner, the canary in it rolled up in sleep.

"Why, Kate, I didn't know you liked birds!"

"Well, I . . . I don't exactly, but the model after which I copied this dining room had a bird cage. Let's go upstairs; I want you to see your study and our bedroom. I hope you're going to be as excited about them as I am, Eugene."

"You'd better lead me, Kate. I'll get lost in this palace."

"Now, Eugene, it isn't a palace. It's a lovely home."

At that moment his attention was caught by the hanging light dome, with its green-and-white glass lilies and cattails attached to four copper crossarms. He was so astonished at its ornateness that he kept looking back over his shoulder and tripped on the bottom step.

Kate turned to the right at the head of the stairs and proudly took him into her bedroom. It was a big room; in a bay of three windows stood an elegant dressing table adorned with Dresden vases and figurines. A heavy carved mahogany bed stood against the hall wall, with its massive bureau decorated with a silver-backed toilet set. The wallpaper was a pastoral scene, representing cottages amid groups of trees. There was a tile fireplace. Gene idly noted that although the mantelpiece held a number of Royal Worcester vases there was not a flower in one of them. Above him he saw a hanging chandelier with a cluster of colored glass grapes in each spray. Kate explained why each piece of furniture was set in the precise position it was. He had the feeling that everything was nailed down, could never be moved in any direction, for any purpose.

"Are you really going to let me sleep in this gorgeous bedroom, Kate? It's pretty swell for a simple fellow like me. I'm awfully dirty when I come home sometimes."

Kate blushed, then said laughingly, "You'll find a marble washbasin in the bathroom next door, and oddly enough, there's a tub there too."

"You think of everything, Kate."

"I try to, Eugene. But if at any time you don't want to sleep in here, there's a little room at the back you can have all for yourself. But let me show you your study. Now that you have more space at home, I hope you'll spend less time at that grubby office downtown."

The room was directly over the library, spacious and cheerful, with a gay blue-and-white checked wallpaper. Kate had had his old desk from the storeroom at Daisy's and Daniel's polished and repainted and put in a far corner. Seeing his collection of workbooks and piles of labor magazines and newspapers made him feel at home for the first time.

"This is a nice room. I think I shall be happy here."

"Thank you, darling. I tried so hard to make every room beautiful, so that you would enjoy them all. Do you think I've done well? Are you happy with the house, and with me?"

He took his wife in his arms, kissed her affectionately, told her that she had done a wonderful job. Tears of gratification came to her eyes.

"When do we move in, Kate?"

She lifted her head from his shoulder, laughing at him.

"We're in, silly. Your clothes are hanging in the closet, your shaving equipment is in the bathroom. What's more, there's food in the kitchen, and I shall serve you luncheon in your new home."

He found it pleasant to lie back in the big bathtub and study the bubbles and flowers on the pink wallpaper. It was also pleasant to sit at the table in the center of the huge kitchen, with its twelve-foot ceiling, and have Kate serve him luncheon.

"Eugene, we must give a beautiful housewarming party."

This was the best news he had heard since entering the front door; the edifice could do with a little warming.

"That will be fine, Kate. Let's invite everyone we know."

She smiled at him indulgently.

"Well, not exactly everyone, just those people who would be in their element here."

"Everybody's in his element in a nice house."

Apparently she had not heard him, for she was drawing up invitation lists in her mind.

"All of the prominent people, the old families, and of course you want to invite Riley McKeen and his family."

"Riley McKeen?" he asked in surprise. "Why would he want to come here?"

"He's your friend, isn't he?"

"Not in the social sense. We've worked together on certain problems."

"Then of course you're friends. He'll be delighted to see

that you've arrived in his set. So will Mr. Hulman and Mr. Cox."

Gently he asked, "Kate, why would all these people want to come here? We've never been in their homes."

"But now that you have a big house of your own, they'll be anxious to come."

"You mean it's the very existence of the house, the fact that it stands and we own it, that will put us in society and make all these folks want to visit us?"

"Yes, of course, Eugene," she answered with serenity. "How else do you think anyone gets into good society?"

"I don't know," he replied. "I've never been in; I have a strong suspicion that I never will be."

"That's only because you lack confidence in yourself. You can accomplish anything you want. That's why you have a wife to help you know what it is that you want in life."

Gene forbore. "All right, Kate. I'll invite anyone you say. But after you have your party, could I have mine?"

"Of course. Whom do you want to invite?"

"The boys."

"The boys?"

"The men whose dues have built this house."

She burst into a hearty laugh.

"Oh, Eugene, for a moment I thought you were serious."

"I am."

"You mean that you want a couple of hundred locomotive firemen trooping through this house, wiping their feet on the new carpet, slapping their blackened boots against the furniture, pawing over the curtains and upholstery with their dirty hands?"

"They wouldn't come direct from their runs, Kate. They'd go home to bathe and shave and put on their Sunday clothes. You'd be surprised how nice they look when they get all cleaned up. They even smell good. I hardly think you could distinguish them from that social group you're inviting."

"You always end your arguments with such absurdities that I sometime wonder how you get along on the platform in front of conventions."

"Not too bad, Kate."

"I'm sorry I laughed, Eugene. I can understand your desire to have the firemen come into your new home. It's a very generous and noble gesture on your part. But can't you see that it would simply be bad manners to flaunt your prosperity in their faces? They'll go away disgruntled, saying, 'Why is he entitled to more of the world's goods than we have?"

"Just a moment, Kate! We've reversed positions on this

matter of the firemen's feeling about my house. I didn't want to build it in the first place. But you told me that the firemen would be proud, that they'd point it out, saying, 'This is where the secretary of our Brotherhood lives. Pretty nice, eh?' If that reasoning was good enough to get this house built, it ought to be good enough to secure invitations into it for the men who paid for it."

"Really, you make it sound as though those thousands of coal shovelers are your employers."

"They are."

"Nonsense. You are over them, not they over you. If it weren't for your work, they'd still be lucky to draw a dollar a day."

From a deep well of conviction, he was able to answer her.

"If I hadn't started it somebody else would have. The unions are like the railroads in that respect; they're here to stay. No one man created them, no one man can destroy them, and nobody is indispensable to them."

He got up, paced the floor, studying its intricate pattern. Seeing that he was hurt, she veered her course, sharply.

"Wasn't I right, Eugene? Isn't this the proper environment in which to bring up children?"

Hesitantly he seated himself again at the luncheon table.

— 10 —

Grand masters and other officials were elected, served their terms, went out of the Brotherhood, frequently into newspaper work or businesses of their own. Only Gene Debs was permanent, like a lighting fixture illuminating numerous changes in furnishings. Whenever Kate learned that one of the firemen's officials had resigned to go into business, she would urge him to do the same.

"You didn't marry that organization, Eugene. You've served them now for fourteen years, isn't that enough? You keep telling me the organization is so strong and solidly entrenched that no one can ever destroy it now; then you're not so important to them any more, are you?"

He knew the answer to this, but he knew equally well that it would sound ridiculous to Kate. The locomotive firemen did not need him; he needed the locomotive firemen. Raising flowers for a living as did his sisters' husbands was very fine; selling drugs as did his wife's brothers was also fine; but it simply was not for him. When Jay Gould gave a statement to the press that in his opinion every employee of his railroad should own stock in the company, Gene quickly wrote a blistering editorial denouncing this crude joke; for Jay Gould, with his manipulated millions, paid the lowest wages to be found on any system. When P. M. Arthur, head of the Brotherhood of Locomotive Engineers, declared that he never had and never would co-operate with any other labor organization, Gene published the story of how Arthur had come to him during a strike, begging him to persuade the Knights of Labor to haul down their scabbing engineers.

This was his life, this was his romance, this was his excitement and adventure. Without it he would be nothing, and his existence would be meaningless. When anyone said to him:

"You are doing a great deal for the labor movement," he replied, "On the contrary, the labor movement is doing a great deal for me."

It was not easy to live with the adversary in his own house. No matter what the problem or issue at stake, Kate took the word of the newspaper reporter or editorial writer over his. Since she subscribed only to those newspapers which accurately reflected the sympathies of the Metzel clan, he invariably found himself and his wife at polar extremities of opinion; no amount of logic on his part, no recital of the statistics would change her mind by the slightest fraction. Anger did not quicken her speech, but slowed it even further, with every syllable precisely articulated.

The atmosphere inside Kate's beautifully furnished rooms would grow increasingly frigid, and all night he would twist nervously on his side of the bed.

Theodore feared to bring up the subject he had been wanting to introduce for many months. He was certain that his marriage to Gertrude would be a happy one. How could he say, Please don't discourage me, Gene; Gertrude isn't like Kate. Gertrude is warm-hearted and loyal, and anything I do will be exactly right with her. He and Gertrude had decided to marry that summer; half the joy would be gone out of the plans if Gene disapproved.

"What do you think, boy?" he asked his older brother anxiously. "I am twenty-six now, and Gertrude and I have been in love for five years. Don't you think it's about time?"

They had been climbing a little hill which gave them a clear view of the valley, the farmlands a rich purple where they had been freshly plowed. Gene did not look at Theodore but put his arm around his younger brother's shoulder. He quietly gazed at the sheen of the Wabash River below, then said:

"My dear old pard, you have a fine girl in Gertrude. I loved her the moment I laid eyes on her. You'll be as happy as Daisy and Daniel."

Then he returned home, packed a bag, and began his criss-cross of the nation on a hundred intersecting rails. He enjoyed the ever-changing faces of the people, the cities, the new ideologies that were springing up with amazing rapidity. The country had been convalescing from the ugly wounds of the Civil War for almost thirty years; now there was a yeast working in society, individuals trying to think their way through dead-end barriers, re-forming intellectual patterns.

When he first met Clarence Darrow in Chicago, Darrow was a struggling lawyer more interested in Ibsen and Tolstoy than in Blackstone. Darrow took him to the meetings of the Sunset Club where they were quickly involved in the crackling discussions of novels by Flaubert, Turgenev, Zola, *War and Peace, Hard Times, Crime and Punishment.* In return for these intellectual treats, Gene gave Darrow an education in trade-unionism, outlining his idea for a new railway union which would embrace everyone from section hands to engineers.

"Trade-unionism is in sad need of overhauling, Clarence. Each Brotherhood is expensive to run, and duplicates the functions of the others."

When Darrow asked what the Brotherhoods thought of the idea, he replied:

"They hate it because they're afraid it will weaken their influence; they don't want to share the fruits of unionism with the eight hundred thousand unskilled workers in the industry."

"Gene, can you unionize the unskilled workers? They must come from twenty different nationalities and speak a dozen languages!"

"As we educate them, we'll unionize them. They'll have no fear that we're trying to batten off them, for the one dollar a year dues will be voluntary: neither a worker nor a local need pay any money to be a voting member. And I have good men coming in with me as officers: George Howard and Sylvester Keliher, both former officers of the Conductors, will serve as vice-president and secretary. Lou Rogers, editor of the *Age of Labor,* will publish our paper. I haven't told my brother yet, but I think he'll come in with us when I do."

Theodore and Gertrude were sitting in Daisy's dining room talking about their wedding trip in the Rocky Mountains when Gene loomed in the doorway. For a moment no one spoke.

"Theo, you promised to send me a telegram so I could meet your train."

"I did send it."

"That's strange, I never got it."

"Kate got it."

Gene swallowed hard. His eyes went to Theodore's unpacked valises.

"Why did you bring your things here? You agreed to stay with me until you found lodgings."

"Kate didn't extend us an invitation, Gene."

Daisy broke in, "I told them to get their bags from your house and come back here."

"Then you were at my house?"

"Yes, for a little while."

Gene looked at the home-coming dinner Daisy had spread before the newlyweds.

"Didn't you have anything to eat at my house?"

"Yes, we had kidney stew."

"It was delicious," said Gertrude.

Gene thought, Not if it was the same kidney stew I had last night, it wasn't.

He brushed aside his anger, went to Gertrude, embraced her warmly, welcomed her into the Debs family. He then turned to Theodore.

"You'll come home with me now, won't you, boy? I fixed up the spare room for you. You'll be comfortable there."

"But, Gene, we couldn't go to your home if Kate didn't invite us."

Daisy returned from the kitchen.

"Gene, sit down and eat," she said. "Let the youngsters stay here. They'll be fine in your old room. Gertrude wants me to teach her how to cook."

He started to object, then saw the corner of his mother's mouth go up slightly. "We'll all be happy here, Gene. It's best this way."

He knew she was right. He sat down, tried to eat, but somehow his stomach and throat had reversed positions, and he could not swallow a bite. For he knew that the house had become The House. The collection of boards and bricks was not merely a place of shelter; it had taken on some fourth-dimensional, occult significance for Kate. In this house nothing could be changed, nothing could be moved, nothing could be suspended. Every piece of furniture, every drapery, every rug satisfied some deep-seated, long-denied hunger; that was why she could not be casual about her possessions.

When strangers knocked on the door she did not answer. If

on occasion he learned that a friend or an associate had come to Terre Haute, and he asked Kate why she had not answered the door, she would reply, "Oh, I thought it was just a solicitor." When he invited Howard, Keliher or Rogers to come in of an evening, and they sat before the fireplace mapping the constitution of the railway union, Kate bulked in the far corner, crocheting, trying to disguise the vigilant eye she kept on the guests. While he was seeing his visitors out the front door, she was already working with her broom and dustcloth, cleaning up behind them.

Yet she did not bedevil him about his habits. She suffered if he spilled pipe tobacco on the rug or threw burned matches onto the hearth, or pushed up a small chair on which to rest his feet while reading; but somewhere, sometime, she had decided that the man of the house had certain privileges. He knew that she was struggling with herself not to be upset, and rather than keep her on edge, he adapted himself to his wife's regime. In his mind there had been the idea that once he had a home the front door would be pushed open and nailed to the side wall, and then hundreds of people would move in and out, eating his food, sleeping in his beds, partaking of his ideas, laughter and hospitality.

Well, a person grows up with a lot of preconceived notions; and marriage is the graveyard of many of them.

When he could no longer abide the cold or the loneliness he would walk over to Mulberry Street, where Theodore and Gertrude had rented two rooms. Someone had given them a parrot called Colonel for a wedding present, and when they locked him in the bedroom he would call out, "The colonel wants to come into the parlor!"

"He talks about himself in the third person," laughed Gertrude, "the way famous people do."

The three of them would sit around the kitchen table, chatting and laughing over nothing more relevant than their love for each other; and then Gertrude would make hot chocolate and bake a tin of biscuits, while Colonel cried from the other room, "Gertrude, what in hell are you doing?" Gene thought, She's doing what a wife ought to do: keeping her husband happy.

By ten, his blood warmed once again, his stomach full of Gertrude's raspberry jam, he felt sufficiently revived to return home.

One night he opened the front door to find himself engulfed in a stale stench of alcohol. Poor Danny, he thought, there's no chance for him to keep his drinking a secret; he can smell up a whole depot all by himself.

Kate had put Danny to bed in the front room; her eyes were red from weeping, but she was valiantly ministering to her brother with cold towels. Danny was a red-faced, beefy man with heavy eyelids; now his eyes were almost entirely closed, and he was babbling incoherently. Gene stood behind Kate while she tried to force some medicine between his lips. He took the spoon and the bottle from her.

"That won't do him any good, Kate. It's just a hair of the dog that bit him."

She looked up at him blankly. "But it always helped him when we lived at home."

He could not suppress a tiny smile.

"These medicines are eighty per cent alcohol, Kate. You'd better rest awhile, I think I can get him to sleep."

He put his hand under her arm, lifted her forcibly and led her into the bedroom. For about an hour he sat by Danny, holding him down when he struggled to fight his way out of his hallucination, and pieced together the story of how Danny had lost his liquor store in Milwaukee by trying to drink the profits before they were rung up on the cash register; that he was now without a job or resources, and had returned to Terre Haute to get a job as a fireman from Gene.

Danny's mumblings fell away to occasional disconnected sounds, and at last he was asleep. Gene piled several extra blankets on top of his brother-in-law, then opened all the windows, and went to see how his wife was faring. He found her in the kitchen preparing dinner, dry-eyed but pale and tense. When she saw Gene she stopped in the midst of turning over lamb chops.

"Eugene, you must promise me one thing: that you'll never become a drunkard."

Gene suppressed a chuckle. "Kate, that's not me in the front bedroom. I'm down here with you, perfectly sober."

Kate was too terror-stricken to return his smile. She put down the heavy frying pan, wiped her hands on her white apron, went to Gene and slipped into his arms, her own clenched forearms hard against his bosom.

"Eugene, I know you don't drink, but you never will, will you? It's so, so horrible . . . to see a full-grown man lose control of himself."

"Now, now, Kate, stop trembling. If it will make you any happier, I will take the pledge: 'I hereby apply for admittance into the Women's Christian Temperance Union.'"

— 11 —

When his plans were well formulated, Gene walked into

Theodore's office, gazed around him musingly and said, "Mighty nice office you've got here, Theo."

"Glad you like it. Drop in sometime and I'll show you how it works."

"Kind of attached to the place, aren't you?"

"I love it better than my own mother. Why?"

"It just occurred to me this is the first place you ever worked, outside of that little storeroom at the back of the grocery. It would be kind of a wrench to move away, wouldn't it?"

"My dear old pard," drawled Theodore, "stop bushing around the beat. You're never more obvious than when you're trying to be subtle."

"I wasn't trying to be subtle, Theo. I was just wondering if I couldn't get you the job of secretary-treasurer of the Locomotive Firemen."

"What do you mean, get me the job? I've been filling that job for five years while you've been gallivanting around the country looking at all the pretty scenery."

"I'm serious, Theo. There's no one could handle the work better than you."

"Always except you."

"That's what I'm trying to tell you, boy. I'm quitting."

Theodore jumped up from his seat as though someone had ignited the wood beneath him.

"You're what?"

"I'm no more good to the firemen. I've known it for at least two years now. Look, Theo, I want to ask you a question. You have a good job here with the Brotherhood. You can stay with them the rest of your life, you'll have security, it's the kind of work you like . . ."

"You're not asking a question, you're making a speech."

"All right then. Do you want to come along with me . . ."

"Of course," interrupted Theodore.

"Now wait a minute, you idiot. I haven't told you where I'm going."

"I don't care where you're going."

Gene leaned over the desk and clapped Theodore on the shoulder.

"I have to leave for the Chicago convention now. I'll tell you about our new venture when I get back."

Theodore let him get as far as the door, then laughed. "Don't rush back on my account. I know about your plans."

"You do?"

"My boy, you couldn't hide anything inside of that head of yours if you covered it with a tarpaulin."

After a moment Gene replied quietly, "There won't be any money for wages."

"True."

"The whole idea may collapse, and we'd both be out of jobs."

"True, true."

"Theo, here I am endangering your job, your very livelihood and all you can say is . . ."

"True."

Gene laughed, picked up a magazine from the shelf near the door, flung it at his brother's head, and was gone.

It was two full weeks before he returned, exhausted from his struggle to resign from the group of men he loved best in the world.

As he turned the corner and came up Eighth Street, he saw Kate's figure behind the lace curtains of the dining room where she crocheted away her hours, keeping vigil for him. She saw him immediately, waved, and was at the front door before he could reach the bottom of the steps. She waited with her arms half outstretched and a warm smile on her face.

"This trip seemed so long, Eugene. I thought you'd never get home."

"It seemed long to me, too, Kate," he replied wearily. "I've never been gladder to be back."

"Thank you, dear. We can have a little time together now, can't we? You don't have to rush off somewhere."

"No, I can stay home awhile now. And I'll have more leisure to spend with you, that is, right at first."

"You look tired, dear. I have a pot of coffee on the stove. I'll turn the light on."

She prepared breakfast for him. He ate ravenously, remembering that for several days he had hardly touched any food. He thought how nice it would be to spend a day or a week just lounging about the house and working in the garden, passing quiet hours with Kate in a kind of holiday mood. There was an empty lot next to the dining-room porch where he intermittently planted flowers and vegetables. That afternoon he pulled weeds, but even as he yanked on the unruly stubble he knew that he had made a decision which would have inevitable consequences for his wife, and that she was entitled to know about it right away. After an hour he put down his spade, wiped his hands on his old khaki trousers, and joined his wife on the porch, leaning down by the side of her chair.

"Kate, I have something important to tell you."

She looked up quickly, half frightened, for she never knew where Gene's unpredictableness would lead next.

"I have resigned from the Brotherhood of Locomotive Firemen."

A flash of joy went across her face. She put her arms around his neck.

"Oh, darling, I'm so happy and so relieved. I knew one day you'd give up that dreadful job; I knew one day you'd see that it was a blind alley."

"Wait, Kate, you haven't heard . . ."

"I kept telling my brothers it was just a temporary thing, that you'd grow out of it. And now at last you have. Eugene, you've made me so happy; it's as though I were in a prison and you unbolted the door and let me out into the sunshine. Now I don't have to be frightened every hour you're away that you've gotten into some kind of trouble. Do you know what you're going to do next? I have a little money saved up; you will open a business here in Terre Haute: a drugstore or a florist; one of my brothers said you'd do well in the wholesale grocery business."

Kate was so rarely ebullient; the flash of joy sent a warm pink glow flooding over her lovely marblelike complexion; it transfigured her, showed him all too well how little happiness he had brought his wife, and how much anxiety and dread. Poor Kate, he thought, she got a bad bargain in me. I'm the last man in Terre Haute she should have married.

Aloud he said, "But, Kate, I'm not looking for a new job. I have one."

"You have one? It's here in Terre Haute, isn't it? We won't have to move away?"

There was real terror in her voice now at the thought of giving up her house: her haven, sanctuary, testimonial.

"No, Kate, we won't have to leave our home. I can work out of Terre Haute just as I always have."

"Oh, you're going on the road again. Why can't you settle down here like every other businessman, go to work at eight in the morning, and come home at six?"

"Don't you want to know what I'm going to do, Kate?"

Her eyes glazed with anxiety. "Eugene, tell me: what are your plans?"

"I'm starting a new union, Kate."

She dropped back into her rocker and began sobbing.

"Oh no, not another union! What good does it do to transfer from one to another?"

He took her two hands in his and held them tightly. He

had dreaded the moment when he would have to tell Kate that he was changing positions. He knew that she hated unions, and this jump from a small specialized trade union into a nationwide organization could only intensify her fear and dislike of his work. But without his knowing it an edge of excitement contoured his voice.

"This is a new kind of union, Kate. Something never tried before in the history of the world. It's going to be big and strong and important."

The sound of the adjectives lifted her from her gloom.

"Why is it going to be all these things? And what will it mean to you?"

"Take the railroad industry: there must be twenty different crafts or working groups. Every union is separate and distinct and cares not a tinker's damn for any other union. If the engineers demand higher wages, selfish firemen move up and take their places; if firemen ask for an increase, yardmen are glad to fill in for the extra money. It's dog eat dog. We're going to put an end to that, Kate. We're going to have a union in which every man works and fights for his neighbor, just as his neighbor works and fights for him."

"A union comprising all the men who work for the railroad, that could mean several hundred thousand members, couldn't it?"

"If our idea is sound, we should have no trouble getting several hundred thousand members."

"It will make you a powerful group, won't it?"

"That's what we're hoping for, enough strength inside the indus . . ."

"And rich!"

His heart sank.

"No, Kate, we'll never be rich, because there'll be no compulsory dues. A railroader, or a local for that matter, can join without putting out one penny."

"But, Eugene, that's ridiculous. Why should you let them in without dues? No business does that; if they're going to get the benefit . . ."

"Membership will be a dollar a year for those who want to pay it. There'll be no pressure brought on those who don't want to."

"How do you think you can run an organization with nobody paying dues?"

"The members will pay," he said stubbornly. "They will want to pay."

Cagily she asked, "How many of them can you count on?"

"About half."

"Then very soon you will be taking in from fifty to a hundred thousand dollars a year! And the very lack of compulsion will bring the others in."

"Yes, I think so."

"You're really very shrewd, Eugene, when it comes to understanding those men. You laughed at me when I said that you would be earning ten thousand, yes, and twenty thousand dollars a year. Now it will all come true!"

"Perhaps," he murmured tiredly, "but it's going to be a long way up to ten thousand a year from seventy-five a month."

The excitement died out of her face.

"Seventy-five dollars a month? What are you talking about?"

"About me. About Howard and Keliher. That's all the salary we're going to take for the first year, until we have a solid reserve in the treasury."

She settled weakly into her chair.

"You mean you are deliberately giving up four thousand dollars a year and going back to less than a thousand?"

"You yourself said only a few moments ago that this was a good idea."

"Because I thought it would be good for you! But if it's going to be bad for you . . . !"

He pulled a chair halfway across the porch, ignoring her automatic gesture of disapproval, and drew it up in front of her.

"Listen to me, Kate. This is the most important task I've ever tackled. It's given me new hope because I see a way of bringing security into the lives of thousands of people who have never had it before. Think what it will mean . . . Kate, you haven't been listening."

"But how can I run the house on seventy-five dollars a month? How can I continue to build up our savings?"

"You won't! You'll dip into the money we've saved to finance this new venture. That's what savings are for."

"Never!" broke in Kate. "I'll never spend a dollar of it. Savings are to earn money. Do you think I'd sell any of my stocks, when some of them are earning as much as twelve per cent?"

He laughed. "That's the first good reason I've ever heard for money earning more money without the owner working for it. Your twelve per cent interest is going to support us, Kate, while we build an organization that will oblige you to take six per cent for your savings and share the other six per

cent with the men and women who create that wealth for
you."

She could not control her tears, nor did she put her hands
to her face in an effort to conceal them. He put her head on
his shoulder, comforted her by stroking her hair and her
cheek, while to himself he said, Kate, what bad luck you
have! Every time I turn around I hurt you worse! Oh, Kate,
how much of this pain can you stand?

— 12 —

The ensuing months passed in a joyous frenzy for him.
Seven hundred railroad men attended his opening meeting in
Hirzel's Hall in Terre Haute, some two hundred joining before the evening was over. He was ever on the move, speaking a dozen times a day, starting with two switchmen over a
boardinghouse breakfast, and ending before a mass meeting
under gaslight. Everywhere he planted the idea of equality of
labor to replace aristocracy of labor; in the depression year
of 1893, where employment was falling off, and money
scarce, he took in locals with their full membership, unac-
companied by one dollar of dues.

By April he, Howard and Keliher had organized a hundred
and eighty lodges in twenty-five states. Their efforts were confined mostly to the Midwest. Two Montana men came in as
officers and began lining up the West: Martin Elliott, a squat,
redheaded proletarian out of the copper mines of Butte, and
Jim Hogan, who saw the humorous side of everything, using
laughter and satire to bring in the men who could not be
moved by serious argument. The roster of officers was completed with William E. Burns, a slender, handsome chap who
was a good fighter in an argument, and Roy Goodwin, a pro-
digious reader. Working together with Gene, Theodore and
Lou Rogers, editor of the *Railway Times*, they made an excellent organizing team.

The Brotherhoods could not openly oppose him: he had
done too much for them, over too many years. He was the
father of the brakemen's union, and they came in by the hundreds; so did his friends among the firemen. On certain lines
the switchmen's locals joined en masse, but on others, management kept them out. Among the hundreds of thousands
working for the railroads, very few had not heard the name
of Gene Debs, read his magazine, been in some way benefited by his work. He had given the railroad employees eighteen years of devotion; tales of his selflessness had been notar-
ied wherever trains were hauled over rails. They said he was

the only man in any industry in America who had earned the
confidence and friendship needed to create one big union.

And so the American Railway Union grew, two thousand
members, ten thousand, twenty, thirty, forty, the idea sweeping across railroad flats like fire across a prairie. Theodore
managed the office, Gene stayed on the road as teacher,
preacher, organizer. On his occasional stay in Terre Haute
for rest and recapitulation, he and Theodore would pore over
the charts which showed how many members they had in
each craft and in each state; then they would go over the list
of reasons why the engineers or conductors had refused to
join, and together write articles for the *Railway Times* to
answer these objections.

"We're doing fine, Theo, they're coming in faster than I
dared hope. If only we have sufficient time, before anything
happens . . ."

But there is never sufficient time: James J. Hill's Great
Northern Railway cut the wages of its trackmen from a dollar and a quarter a day to one dollar and the men walked
out. Since they belonged to no union except the American
Railway Union their leaders went to George Howard, who
was in St. Paul, demanding that he call a strike on the Great
Northern. Howard had no choice; he sent out a strike order
and a telegraphic appeal for help.

Gene and Theodore reached Minneapolis in a torrential
downpour. They changed their sopping-wet socks, then sat
around the hotel room in their stockinged feet because they
had not brought extra shoes. George Howard came in, his
black beard and face darker than the rain sheets pouring
against the window. No one bothered to shake hands.

"What state are we in?" demanded Gene.

"State of confusion," replied Howard.

"Did you try to arbitrate with Hill?"

"He laughed at me."

Gene pulled a Morris chair up to the window, his bony
knees digging into the wainscoting, the dark rain curtain providing a vivid reflector for his thoughts:

You don't make unions out of thin air; they have to be
conceived and carried and given full form before emerging
from the secure womb of darkness into a rain-swept world.
Nor did you expose them to the bitterest of the elements before they had grown strong. He had always believed that
strikes were bad medicine, that the path of labor was strewn
with the corpses of unions that were doing well until they
went out on strike. This was a premature, almost impossible

test for the American Railway Union; but wasn't every test of brotherhood difficult and premature?

He turned back to Theodore and Howard, who had been talking in undertones behind him.

"I'll try to arbitrate with Hill. If that fails, we'll have to crowd every railway man in the Twin Cities into big halls and swing them along with us."

George Howard's opinion of these two possibilities was eloquently expressed by his bleak silence.

"We'd better prepare now for the second eventuality, George. Get to the newspapermen in this town as fast as you can and tell them that we are holding up your strike order on the Great Northern until we can hold a conference of the railroad men."

"Now wait a minute, Gene; if you start canceling my orders, you'll undermine my position."

Gene put his thin arm around Howard's shoulder and held him firmly with his long, lean fingers.

"George, trust me, we're in trouble. If we fail to take the Brotherhoods out with us, neither of us will have any position left to undermine." He turned to Theodore. "How much money did we bring with us? George, what have you in your wallet?"

The three men shelled their silver and greenbacks onto the middle of the bed. Gene counted quickly and pushed it over to Theodore. "Theo, hire us the biggest hall you can find in St. Paul for tomorrow night. Then find a printer and have handbills run off right away announcing our meetings. I'm going up to see James J. Hill."

He was ushered wordlessly and soundlessly into Hill's sanctum; even his feet as they went across the soft carpet made no sound. Hill received him with a probing flash of the eyes in which Gene found his welcome, his instruction to sit down in the big leather chair and to state his business quickly. Hill had a powerful head with a massive brow and massive eyebrows, a big, bony nose and a large, warm mouth and chin partly covered by a soft beard. Gene was glad to see that he was not angry or prepared to quarrel. Sitting there in silence with nothing moving but his big eyes, he radiated so much energy that the room fairly crackled with it. Only after he had grown accustomed to the pulsation did Gene perceive that the eye which seemed sunk behind the other was of glass. When Hill spoke, Gene found his voice chesty, chained.

"Mr. Debs, I am a quick reader of character; you are not

like the usual labor agitator. Would you mind telling me briefly of your background?"

Gene sketched his childhood, his going to work at fourteen, scraping paint off railroad cars, his four years as a fireman, and then the advent of Joshua Leach and unionism into his life.

"I'm in this room as a horse trader, Mr. Hill; now I think you owe me a brief résumé of what brought you to the opposite side of this conflict."

"Fair exchange," murmured Hill. He turned in his swivel chair to the precise angle at which his bad eye disappeared from Gene's vision. "My beginnings are like yours, Mr. Debs. My father died when I was fourteen, and I worked for four years as a clerk in the village store at Rockwood. Like you, I waited almost in pain for the end of the day so I could get home to my studies. My imagination had been fired by my readings about the Orient, and I tried to get to the Pacific coast to find a ship. I landed in St. Paul just a few days too late to join a group of trappers, and so I went to work for a company running steamboats on the Mississippi. I was only a clerk, but I spent most of my time finding new commodities for the ships to carry, and new sources of fuel to keep them running. In 1875, the year you started your local, I formed my Northwestern Fuel Company. I ran steamboats, and began taking over bankrupt railroads. My friends told me I was insane, but I pushed a new line to the Canadian border, and built a system westward, until last year it reached the Pacific coast. So you see, Mr. Debs, our lives up to this moment are quite similar: I built railroads and you built unions."

For the first time a stern, almost ominous note crept into his voice.

"Now we have a little issue to decide between us: which is more important, the railroad or the men who work for it."

The fact that Mr. Hill was now a multimillionaire seemed to Gene fair compensation for his accomplishment. But in the face of the man's fortune and talent it was inconceivable that he could persist in any effort to push a workingman's wage below a subsistence level. Surely a man who had taken over two bankrupt streaks of rust in a wilderness, and converted them into an empire, would know that it was bad business to pay men less than they could live on?

"They are equally important, Mr. Hill. I've been fighting strikes and discouraging them for eighteen years now. The last thing in the world I want to do is let these men go out. I'd like to arbitrate our differences in a friendly spirit."

"But, my dear sir, we have no differences to arbitrate. It's

my task to run a railroad and get as much money as I can
for the stockholders. It's your task to run a union and get as
much money as you can for your members. Why don't we
each of us do our own job according to our lights?"

"Because at this moment your lights and mine are colliding. We have convinced our men that management will arbitrate and compromise. If you make a liar out of us, Mr.
Hill . . ."

"You will strike! What are you going to use to take men
out?"

"Words: unity, brotherhood . . ."

"Words! You can't make a fire under them, or fry them in
butter."

"True, but we can do something better: we can remake the
world."

Hill laughed heartily, as though someone had set out to entertain him with a funny joke.

"Mr. Debs, that's naïve; no one can remake the world."

"Mr. Hill, you brought railroads and people to the wilderness, converted it into prosperous communities. You're not
the right one to decry man's power to remake his world."

Hill glanced at the many papers on his desk, rose and extended his hand.

"It's been a most interesting discussion, Mr. Debs. Come
see me again next time you're in St. Paul."

— 13 —

He sat in the Morris chair all night gazing sightlessly into
the blackness. Theodore tossed and turned behind him, awakening every few moments and urging him to come to bed, to
get some rest. But Gene was undergoing the severest inner
conflict of his life: how was he to repudiate the rock upon
which his eighteen years of work was founded? How did he
tell men to strike, when he had been the country's most ardent opponent of strikes? If strikes destroyed unions, would it
not be suicide to permit the American Railway Union to destroy itself? And if the strike were successful, was he certain
he could hold it in control? Daniel had warned him long ago,
"Unions mean strikes, and strikes mean violence." He had
spilled out millions of words, in print and in person, against
all violence, even in thinking, as the workingman's worst
enemy. What did he do now, divest himself of his profound-
est convictions and his beliefs as though they were a pair of
old shoes whose soles had come loose and were flapping in
the rain?

An ash-colored dawn sifted into the street below him.

What did a man do when he came up against a stone wall?
Did he turn and walk away, defeated? Or did he adjust himself to the realities of that wall? He had talked of alternatives
to George Howard and James J. Hill. Now it was time to
face them himself: either he refused to support his striking
trackmen, in which event the American Railway Union
would dissolve into the ash-gray mist, or he changed his beliefs to fit a changing industrial world.

He found it easier to abandon his convictions than his
men. Chilled, exhausted, miserable in heart and mind, he resolved to call a strike on the Great Northern. The decision
made, he crawled in beside Theodore and was asleep at once.

When they reached the hall that evening, they found it
well filled. Theodore and Howard took seats in the last row.
Gene walked up the side aisle alone. All faces turned in his
direction; and as they turned, Gene realized how difficult his
task would be: there was no fear or hatred in this audience,
but neither was there any interest or sympathy. It was absurd
to think that the Brotherhoods would give up their contracts
and security for a handful of unskilled laborers. Some of
them knew Gene as a friend who had helped in their own
early organization; the others were simply curious as to what
he would say.

He mounted the little side stairs, passed the straight-backed
chair sitting in the emptiness, and walked out to the rim of
the slightly curved stage. A dozen of his friends applauded,
the rest sat in tepid silence. After a moment Gene took a
deep breath and began talking: he reviewed the history of the
various Brotherhoods, showing how far they had come not
only in wages but in security and status in the few years since
their inception; he described the painful and slow descending
curve of unionization from the top level of the engineer
down through what had been an irresponsible and drifting
class of trackwalkers; he proved what they already knew, that
where the Brotherhoods stood together they gained their
common ends, but when they failed each other everything
was lost. He turned their attention to James J. Hill, outlining
his vast railroad empire, giving figures on the amount of dividends that had been distributed to stockholders. He then reported Hill's categorical refusal to arbitrate.

It had been a good presentation of the facts. Nothing was
left out that was important, nothing was included that was
rhetorical or tangential. It should have convinced his listeners
that he was right. Yet his orderly array of facts had left the
men unmoved. He realized this in the very midst of a sen-

tence; he stopped short, stood gazing for a moment at the composite mass of human faces before him, then turned and walked to the lone chair. He sat down, rested his bony elbows on his bony knees and buried his long, lean face in his long, lean fingers, shutting out all sight and sound. Under his chair he could feel the trains traversing the land; clackety-clack, clackety-clack, click-clack, click-clack.

Dear God, I have failed, he told himself. There's something wrong, they don't believe me, they're not interested, their minds are one solid cold shoulder thrust upward at me. It must be my fault, it can't be theirs: I know these men too well. I know that they yield to appeals for help. There's no callousness in them. Not a man out there but has suffered hunger and unemployment. Then why aren't they listening to me? Why do they sit there, immovable, as though these trackmen are some breed of animal who don't suffer when they are hungry and cold, and have no place in the world? If only I could pray, I would pray now, for I need help. I need something that's not in my mind or my voice or my presence here tonight. I mustn't fail. If we leave the trackmen in the lurch, no group will ever go down the line for any other group; labor will be the same kind of jungle as capital, with everyone indifferent to the fate of his neighbor, and the strong devouring the weak.

He made no movement of his body, but simply lifted his face out of the cup of his hands, and opened his eyes. For the first time he heard the silence in the hall, a deeper silence than he had had while speaking. Something had gone out over that hall; where before there had been some hundreds of men, each holding fast to his separate interest, grimly determined to retain the last ounce of his advantage, hundreds of unconnected islands in a vast sea of self-protection, now they were somehow merged, the sharp outlines of the separate heads and shoulders and torsoes blurred. This was no longer a hall full of individuals. It was one man: mankind.

He rose, began speaking slowly.

". . . call them hands." He held his two hands in front of him, the fingers arched inwardly, his arms flexed. "They think it is a derogatory name, but I say it's good; for it is hands that have built this world, toil of millions of pairs of untiring hands. They are despised, these trackmen, because they have no strength, no power, just as we were despised a few years ago, because we were only hands. But now we're more than hands: we're brains and souls, we're people—and why? Because we knew that we all had to rise or fall together. We made sacrifices, we risked our jobs, our homes,

our future, with every man standing shoulder to shoulder
with his neighbor. This is the most beautiful thing in the
world, not only because of the material gains we've earned,
but because we've won something without which we are animals and our span on earth is meaningless. We fought for
brotherhood. We earned our brotherhood. This is what makes
us men. For every fellow creature we abandon, we cut away
from our own stature. If you walk out of this hall tonight,
leaving those unfortunate men and their families at the mercy
of their employers, you will be closing and freezing your
hearts against your companions who need you in their bitter
hour. If we destroy brotherhood, what have we left? The
food we put in our mouth? The clothes on our back?

"I know you men well. I've shared your food and your
bunks in the icy caboose hurtling through the night; I've
walked with you through sleet-filled yards when there was no
work and your children were hungry. Then you were humble,
you were at the mercy of powerful forces with which you
could not cope. The trackmen of the West are in that same
position tonight; their eyes are turned to you men sitting in
this hall, for to them you are all-powerful. If they could pray,
they would pray to you, pray that your hearts could be filled
with love instead of indifference, with the brotherhood that
makes us whole men."

He stopped. His eyes were blurred and he could see nothing of the faces before him.

There were several long moments of silence. No one
moved. Then a man got up in the front row. Two more at
the opposite side of the hall rose to their feet. Men rose from
all over the hall now, singly, then in groups. Soon every last
man in the hall was on his feet. They were shouting or cheering or crying, Gene could not tell which.

All men are brothers. If only they knew it.

For eighteen days the Great Northern stood still. From his
hotel room in St. Paul Gene operated an office for the American Railway Union. In his office a few blocks away Mr. Hill
tried to run his railroad. He offered inducements to the
Brotherhoods to go back to work. Promises of preferential
promotion, increased wages, a new and better contract. No
man returned to work. Mr. Hill tried to secure troops to run
his railroad, but no one would give him troops; he sought to
enforce an injunction handed down by a local judge which
declared it a criminal act for "men to combine to desist from
work." But there was no one to enforce the injunction. The
Minneapolis Chamber of Commerce, whose members were

suffering sharp losses because their merchandise was neither coming in nor going out of the Twin Cities, asked Gene to state his side of the case to a full meeting of its members. Gene did not talk brotherhood with the Chamber; he merely explained that when wages are forced below a subsistence level workingmen cannot buy sufficient to keep either their mouths or the stores open long enough to sustain either of them.

The Chamber thanked him for his courtesy, and then Charles Pillsbury, the millionaire flour miller, took a committee with him to see Mr. Hill. Late that afternoon Gene received a message asking him to come to Mr. Hill's office. Hill was alone, but the room was filled with leftover cigar smoke and the remains of unsettled arguments. The two men did not greet each other. Gene dropped into the same chair he had occupied on his first visit, and waited for Hill to speak. Hill was apparently girding his industrial loins, for it took him several moments to open the conversation.

"Mr. Debs, I have decided to grant your request for arbitration."

"Mr. Hill, you're exactly eighteen days too late for arbitration. The last time I was in here I pleaded with you to compromise this problem; if you had met us halfway, we would have met you halfway. I begged you not to force the men out on strike. You not only dared us to go out, but you spent most of the intervening time trying to divide our organization and make trouble between the American Railway Union and the Brotherhoods." He took a piece of hotel stationery out of his inside coat pocket, unfolded it, and laid it on Hill's desk. "These are the terms upon which we will go back to work."

"Less than three weeks ago you were crying for arbitration; now that I have the generosity to agree . . ."

"Mr. Hill, the men are convinced that their demands are just. If Mr. Charles Pillsbury and his committee will listen to both sides of this case, we will accept their judgment in the matter."

That evening Gene, Theodore and Howard met in Hill's office with Pillsbury and a committee of Twin Cities businessmen. Flanking Mr. Hill were a half-dozen members of his board of directors. It took seven hours for every man to speak his piece. Mr. Pillsbury then adjourned with his committee to a room down the hall. In an astonishing few moments they were back with their decision: ninety-seven and one half per cent of the workers' demands had been granted! Theodore leaned over to Gene and whispered:

"They gave Hill that lonely two and one half per cent so that he could save face."

Hill was no bitter-ender; when the room cleared, he shook hands with Gene.

"You've got a raise for everybody else on the Great Northern," he said, "where do I go to get a raise?"

"Why, you join the American Railway Union. We'll start a new order known as the Brotherhood of Railroad Presidents."

Hill laughed. "If you don't mind my asking a personal question, Mr. Debs, just how much do you make out of this victory?"

"A fortune, Mr. Hill: one hundred and fifty thousand dollars a month for the men."

Utterly depleted now that the battle was over, Gene walked down to the station and threw himself onto one of the bunks in a caboose. He could feel the wheels beneath him, but they were barely turning.

"Theo, why are we moving so slowly?"

"I'll go see."

After a moment Theodore stuck his head in from the rear platform and said, "Gene, come here."

He rose wearily, went out on the platform. Lining the tracks on either side, some in their work clothes, others in off-duty dress, stood the railroad men of Minneapolis and St. Paul: the mechanics from the roundhouse, the brakemen and conductors off the freights, the inspectors and operators, the trackmen and truckmen. Word had been sent to the engineer to pull slowly out of the yards, for the boys wanted to say good-by. They were not shouting, they were not cheering, they were not even smiling; but as the train crept slowly down the rails the men took off their hats and stood with their eyes riveted on the two men standing on the rear platform.

As the train neared the end of the yards and the end of the bareheaded workmen, Gene realized that he was crying. To Theodore he murmured, "I guess I'll never get cured of being a sentimental Frenchman."

"Don't be silly," replied Theodore. "You got the same cinders in your eyes that I got in mine."

It was a beautiful early May morning when they pulled into Terre Haute. The station and the street beyond were packed with people. Someone caught sight of him and yelled, "There's Gene Debs!" A shout went up. Several firemen

grasped Gene and Theodore and led them to the front of the
station, where they had a band and carriage all decked out in
colorful streamers. A banner along the side said: WELCOME
HOME GENE DEBS. In his confusion Gene thought, Somebody
forgot to provide the horse.

The band took its position in front of the wagon. A hundred eager hands grabbed the brothers. "Up you get, Gene
and Theo," someone cried; "we're carrying you home in
state."

Gene laughed. "I'm not dead yet, boys. I don't need a carriage. Come on, Theo, let's help pull this wagon."

There was a cheer, the band struck up and the little parade
moved through the streets of Terre Haute. When they reached
his house, Gene mounted the front steps to the porch, thanked
his friends for their kindness and grasped the knob of his
front door. It was locked. He took out his key and turned it,
but the door was bolted from within. He pounded on the
wood frame with his fist, calling out:

"Kate, Kate, it's Eugene. Come down and open the door."

Several minutes passed. He heard no sound from within
the house. He walked around to the back, unlocked the
kitchen door and went quickly through the lower floor. He
found Kate upstairs, in their bedroom, sitting before her
dressing table with her head buried on her arm.

"Kate, what's wrong, what's happened?"

Her eyes were terror-stricken.

"Eugene, that mob! I heard them coming down Eighth
Street. I thought they were coming after you."

He was flabbergasted, then burst into laughter.

"Kate, for heaven's sake, that was my reception committee.
They met me at the station with a band."

"Eugene, there's been so much talk against you in the papers. You would have been better off if you'd lost that strike.
I thought they hated you before, but when James J. Hill
conceded defeat! Oh, Eugene, if you could know the names
they've been calling you."

He sat on her dressing chair, then held out his arms to her,
pressed her to him to dissipate her terror.

"Didn't you hear the band music? Why didn't you come
out on the porch? Of course I have enemies, but I also have
friends."

She held her trembling frame tightly against him.

He talked to her quietly, patiently, showing her that there
had been no violence and no hurt feeling; that the outburst
she had read in the Chicago newspaper was not from responsible sources but from the hysterics.

"We came out on top, Kate. We got practically everything we asked for. There was no trouble, we've just been victorious."

She jumped up, began pacing the room agitatedly.

"You think you've been victorious; but sooner or later they will be the ones who come out on top, for they have the money and the power. And when they're on top, Eugene, they'll crush you, just as though you were . . . a . . . an empty grocery box lying in the way of a giant locomotive. Just you wait, Eugene, and you'll see that I'm right."

He did not have long to wait.

— 14 —

He was resting in his upstairs workroom, glancing over the evening papers, when he heard voices and what he thought was an altercation at the front door. He ran down the winding steps, but from the middle step he saw Kate on her way back to the kitchen.

"Kate, didn't I hear voices? Who was here?"

She flung over her shoulder, "Oh, just some strange men, wanting to disturb you. I told them you were asleep."

He went quickly to the front door and across the porch to the sidewalk. Three men were walking dejectedly up Eighth Street. He called out, "Hello there! Why are you rushing off mad?"

When the men turned around he saw that they were three union officials from the Pullman shops. They came back to him.

"Your wife told us you were asleep. She said you couldn't be disturbed."

He shook hands with each of the men, clapped them on the back and took them into his library. "I was just resting. Mrs. Debs thinks I'm a fragile creature. She treats me like an only child."

The men laughed. Kate appeared in the room saying, "Gene, you know you complained of a headache this morning. You shouldn't be working. But since you insist, surely you'll get this meeting over as quickly as possible?"

Her manner was curt, with so little regard for the men present that he considered it the better part of wisdom not to introduce them. He said, "Just give us one hour, Kate dear."

She left the room without signifying whether this compromise pleased or displeased her; when he heard her go upstairs he closed the door of the library, opened the windows wide, for it was a warm spring evening, and said:

"Now, boys, what's on your mind?"

There was plenty on their mind. Work at the Pullman shops had become scarce and George Pullman had taken a repair contract at such a low figure that it would mean a loss to the company of fifty thousand dollars. Despite the fact that the Pullman Company had made a net profit of five and one half million dollars the year before, and six and one half million dollars the year before that, George Pullman was determined that every penny of the fifty-thousand-dollar operating loss must be absorbed by his employees. He had reduced wages to the point where his workers' weekly income exactly matched their rent for the company houses.

The three men stopped talking as simultaneously as they had begun. While they waited tensely, Gene asked himself how it could be possible that so magnificently courageous and resourceful an industrialist as George Pullman could resort to the inhuman device known in the company coal towns as "mining the miners instead of the coal." George Pullman was one of the mechanical geniuses of his age; why then, he asked himself, wasn't this genius extended to the human beings who worked for him, as well as to the sleeping cars that worked for him?

When Pullman had been only twenty, working in his brother's cabinetmaking shop in upstate New York, he had taken his first overnight ride in a sleeping car. He was given a wooden bunk at one side of a converted coach, where he stretched out fully dressed on a rough mattress and covered himself with his overcoat. From this one trip he saw the need for a comfortable sleeping car on wheels.

He persuaded the Chicago and Alton Railroad to let him experiment on two of their old coaches. He hinged the backs of seats so they could be folded down to make a bed, hung the upper berths on pulleys so they could be closed during the daytime and would hold the bedding. The cars were upholstered in plush and lighted by oil lamps, with a washroom at each end.

Young George Pullman knew that remodeling old coaches was a makeshift, that he would have to build his sleeping cars from the tracks up. He spent four years drawing blueprints for the first complete Pullman car. The astounding part of this new car was not only its beauty and mechanical ingenuity, but the fact that Pullman had built his car too high to pass under existing bridges and too wide to be used at station platforms. Pullman, in his strength and daring, had said, "This is what a sleeping car must have; the entire railroad system of America will be changed to fit its needs."

"The men want to go out on strike, Gene," concluded the

most forceful of the three visitors. "We want the American Railway Union to refuse to haul Pullman cars."

"Now, boys, wait just a moment. None of these Pullman workers is a railway man. What you're talking about is a sympathy strike. It's never been done in this country."

"No, and neither has there ever been an industrial union. But that didn't stop you from forming the American Railway Union!"

"We have one hundred and forty thousand members throughout the country, Ed," Gene replied, "but one hundred thousand of them have never paid a penny of dues. We don't know how strong their allegiance is to us. We have got to get some kind of gauge on their loyalty before we attempt anything as difficult as a nationwide sympathy strike."

Ed's face turned a dull red. "In other words, Gene, before you can help us you want ideal conditions! When does labor ever get ideal conditions? We have to strike when we have to strike! You should have learned that up in St. Paul."

"Sit down, Ed, and stop talking at me. We're going to give you all the help we can, but first I want your word that you'll go back to Chicago and do your utmost to arbitrate your differences."

The second of the two men rose and spoke quietly.

"We'll try anything, but in return we've got a request to make of you: come up to Chicago and go through the town of Pullman with us."

Ten days later he arrived at the American Railway Union headquarters in Chicago. He had sent word for the three Pullman delegates to meet him at the office.

Ed greeted him with a growl. "Mr. Pullman told us there is nothing to arbitrate, that he could not restore our wage scales because he had taken contracts for new work at a loss."

"Ed told Mr. Pullman that if he wouldn't restore wages, he could reduce the rents on our houses. Mr. Pullman replied that it was impossible to reduce rents, for the capital invested in these houses had to have its just return. The next day the three of us were laid off."

The third member, the quiet one, said, "We fulfilled our promise to you, Gene, now you've got to come out to the town of Pullman with us."

Riding south on the train, Ed handed Gene a pamphlet called *The Story of Pullman*. "Here, read this page, Gene." He read:

"Imagine a perfectly equipped town of twelve thousand inhabitants, built out from one central thought to a beautiful and harmonious whole, where all that is ugly and discordant and demoralizing is eliminated and all that inspires to self-respect, to thrift and to cleanliness of person and of thought is generously provided."

The four men left the train, and in a few moments arrived at the village that George Pullman had created from five hundred acres of unused prairie land. The main street had bright red flower beds in the center and houses of red brick with trim lawns in front. But when the men left the center square and walked one short block, they came into another world. The unpainted wooden houses were of the cheapest construction, the rooms inside were small and dark and airless, each house was provided with one faucet, in the basement.

"We can't get a job in the Pullman shops, Gene, until we rent one of these houses. If any repairs are needed before we move in, the Pullman Company advances the money and we pay it out of our wages."

Gene felt himself getting sick at his stomach. Ed and Charlie each took him by an arm and walked him to the back part of town. Here he found lawnless tenements with four and five families crowded into each railroad flat, all the families using one toilet. Behind the tenements were slums, wooden shanties that had cost only one hundred dollars to erect, occupied by marginal families who had eight dollars a month taken out of their wages, a return to the Pullman Company of almost 100 per cent on its investment. The residents were constantly spied upon, living under a reign of terror, afraid to trust their neighbors or friends.

Riding the train back to Chicago, Gene suffered a wave of revulsion against man's inhumanity to man. Ed had informed him that a meeting of the Pullman workers was scheduled for that night and that the workers would surely go out on strike. Bitterly as he hated strikes, Gene had learned that there were depths of hunger and degradation beneath which human beings could not be submerged. His mind went back to the enigmatic case of George Pullman, owner of a fifty-million-dollar corporation, and earner of several million dollars every year for his own purse and pocket. He thought, What a pity that there is no relation between the power of the brain to create and the ability of the spirit to love! Men who care enough about machines to invent new ones are not able to care enough about humanity to be concerned over its welfare. Men who care a great deal about the fate of humanity are not able to understand machines well enough to invent new ones.

If the world were full of sentimental godunks like me, he thought, there would be no property, but neither would there be progress. People would still be living in caves and using stone axes. If the world were full of mechanical geniuses like Pullman and Hill, there would be fantastic progress, with no people to use it because they all would have been mangled in a machine, run over by a railroad, or suffocated in a bank vault.

He stood on the stubby platform of Uhlich Hall facing four hundred American Railway Union delegates from the Midwest locals who had climbed aboard the cabs and cabooses and come into Chicago. The Pullman strike was now several weeks old, the town of Pullman as quiet as death itself. Funds for the strikers were coming in not only from such sympathetic unions as the typographers, painters and carpenters, but from the people of small towns, police and fire departments, singing societies, circus entertainers, ticket brokers, department stores, and Republican Clubs. If the American Railway Union was going to strike in sympathy with the Pullman workers, this was the hour to do so; but Gene did not want to strike. It was one thing to call his men out in the clean-cut issue of the workers of the Great Northern against James J. Hill's slash in wages. But if the American Railway Union refused to haul Pullmans they would close down the railroads of the nation, tackle the General Managers' Association and its interlocking billions of wealth. The American Railway Union was a lusty infant, but one which could grow to magnificent manhood only if nurtured carefully.

All this he told the delegates, who listened to him respectfully, some agreeing, some disagreeing, some thinking with their logic and some with their emotions. The Pullman strikers had asked permission for the Rev. William H. Carwardine, who had been a pastor in Pullman for many years, to address the convention. Gene introduced him to the delegates. The Rev. Mr. Carwardine was bald on top of his head but the rest of his face was framed in luxuriant and square whiskers, the sideburns coming down bushily to meet the ends of his mustache. The plight of the Pullman workers had aroused him, and he was speaking with a tongue and a temper he had never before known.

"No man craves Mr. Pullman's position before the American people today. The very qualities that made him successful in life have, untempered with nobler elements, placed him in his present predicament before the American public. Determination and resolution have turned into arrogance and obstinacy. My sympathies have gone out to the striking employees. Never did men have a cause more just, never did a corporation with equal pretenses grind men more unmercifully. He who denies the right of the clergy to discuss these matters of great public concern has either been brought up under a government totally foreign to the free atmosphere of American institutions, or else he has failed utterly to comprehend the spirit of the age in which he lives."

Gene was relieved to see that, magnificent as had been the Rev. Mr. Carwardine's philippic against injustice, he had failed to rouse the delegates to a point of white heat. Then he saw a movement toward the back of the hall and a number of men came down the aisle with a young woman in their midst. One of them called out:

"This here is Jennie Curtiss. She's worked in the Pullman sewing rooms for five years. We ask that she be heard."

"Any man or woman who wishes to address this convention will be heard."

He went to the little side steps, descended several of them, held out a hand to the young woman and helped her up to the platform.

Jennie Curtiss went to the edge of the platform near the stairs and stood staring out at the delegates. She was slight, black-haired, black-eyed, with pale skin and almost bloodless lips.

"My name's Jennie Curtiss. My father worked in the Pullman shops for ten years. The company charged us so much rent and repairs that when he died, after he was sick three months, we owed the Pullman Company sixty dollars. I worked in the repair shop sewing room five years. The company told me I have to pay my father's back rent. I been getting nine, sometimes ten dollars, for two weeks' work. But they wouldn't let me keep my wages. After I paid all I owed for my board, the company took the rest against the rent. I been paying for months and months and still I owe them fifteen dollars. When I go to the company bank to get my pay check, and there ain't enough left over to take something against the rent, the clerks insult me and call me dirty names."

Jennie Curtiss had been speaking in an emotionless voice that pierced the quiet of the room. No one moved. Gene knew that this was the critical moment, that anything could happen if Jennie remained on the platform. If he shut her off now he could control the convention. She had told her story, there could be nothing wrong with his stepping forward, thanking her, helping her down the stairs. Yet he could not get off his chair, for Jennie Curtiss was still standing there, her

toes turned in toward each other, swaying slightly at the
knees, her shoulders hunched from years over a sewing machine, her fingers clenched and held hard up against her
belly: for Jennie Curtiss had one thing more to say . . . and
Eugene Debs was not the man to stop her.

"We workers out at Pullman are on strike, on a strike for
our lives. We ask you to help us. Not with your money, and
not with your sympathy, but with the risk of your jobs. We
ask you to come out with us, because none of us is fightin'
just for ourselves. We're fighting for freedom for workingmen
all over the country. We ask you to stand by us and come out
with us. Will you come?"

Men began climbing to their feet all over the hall. Some
introduced motions, others resolutions, but most of them just
cried out, "We won't haul Pullmans. We've got to stand by
the Pullman workers."

Gene's eyes swept over the faces below him; there was not
a man in that convention hall but was determined to go out.
He had no way to stop them; their constitution gave them the
right to declare a strike. He knew what a desperate struggle
would ensue, what forces would be unleashed against them.
He was their leader, he had given birth to this organization,
built it to its present strength; yet if the delegates wanted to
go out on a strike he must lead them, for what good is a
leader if he will not implement the wishes of his people? He
had preached brotherhood, and they had been converted all
too well. There was no way to turn brotherhood on or off as
if it were water in a spigot.

— 15 —

Any fear he might have had concerning the allegiance
of the ranks was dispelled almost too fast: the Great Northern men, grateful for their recent victory over James J.
Hill, abandoned their Pullmans at the first water tank. Gene
had to send out a series of telegrams to get them back on
their trains, to deliver the hapless passengers to their destina-
tions.

By the third day forty thousand members of the American
Railway Union were refusing to handle Pullman cars. All
lines operating west of Chicago were at a standstill. By the
end of a week some one hundred twenty-five thousand men
were out. Telegrams, letters, money, promises of assistance in
the fight over George Pullman came in from the thousands of
local unions all over America. The Chicago Labor Council,
with a larger membership than the American Railway Union,
offered to participate in a general strike. Samuel Gompers

rode in from New York to give Debs a sizable check. He and Theodore worked twenty hours a day in the office, keeping in touch with all major stations along the twenty lines that had been closed down. As in the Great Northern strike, the men went home and stayed home.

"If we can keep this up," said Gene, "we're going to win this strike."

Theodore had always been less emotional and more skeptical than Gene.

"I don't want to worry you," he said, "but have you had time to look at the newspapers today?"

He spread out sample front pages of the main Illinois papers, as well as those from Pennsylvania and New York. The headlines screamed:

NATION PARALYZED BY DEBS STRIKE

"These stories are too similar to have been made up by the local city editors. The General Managers' Association is sending handouts to the papers, portraying you to the country as a desperate revolutionist who is using this strike to seize control of the country. Governor Altgeld is getting hundreds of telegrams demanding that he send out the state militia to take over."

"Take over what?" replied Gene. "The state militia can only be sent at the request of local sheriffs and mayors when there are riot conditions they can't control. Have you forgotten, Theo, my boy, we're peaceable! We're not even blowing our nose in public for fear somebody will become alarmed at the noise."

Gene was right, but not quite right enough. The General Managers' Association went over the governor's head. Their representative in President Cleveland's Cabinet was a lawyer by the name of Olney, who had spent many years as counsel for the Erie Railway, and gone straight from the railway offices into the Cabinet. Attorney General Olney waited until the newspaper attack on Debs had been solidly built, then took the papers in to President Cleveland to prove that Chicago was in a state of insurrection, that life and property were in grave danger, and that if he did not send in federal troops immediately, blood would flow down Michigan Boulevard.

President Cleveland was the first Democrat elected since the Civil War; he was friendly to labor, he did not want to believe these reports. He told the attorney general that his fellow Democrat, Governor Altgeld, had sufficient state militia to keep the situation in control. Olney accused Governor Altgeld of being an anarchist, for had he not pardoned the remaining three men convicted of the Haymarket Riot?

The next morning Gene was wakened by the tramp of heavy boots outside his hotel window on Jackson Street. Theodore murmured sleepily from the other half of the big bed, "They're getting started awful early for their Fourth of July celebration."

Gene pushed aside the curtain and studied the soldiers for some time. He turned slowly back to his brother.

"Theo, those are federal troops!"

Attorney General Olney arrived in Chicago and appointed Edwin Walker, a lawyer for the General Managers' Association, as special assistant attorney general in Chicago, with full federal powers to act. Edwin Walker acted swiftly: he appealed to two federal judges, William A. Woods and Peter S. Grosscup, to issue him an injunction which would forbid Gene and his brother officers of the American Railway Union from "interfering with, obstructing, or stopping any of the business of the twenty railroads now under strike conditions." Judges Woods and Grosscup issued the injunction. Gene and his fellow officers were subject to arrest.

He was surprised to have Clarence Darrow drop into a chair at the American Railway Union headquarters: for the past two years Darrow had been working as legal counsel for the Chicago and Northwestern Railroad.

"I was in Springfield last night," said Darrow, "and bring you a message from Governor Altgeld. The governor said, 'By remaining peaceful, by merely refusing to move trains carrying Pullmans, the strikes are on their way to victory; their demands are just, and the public is with them. The only thing that can defeat the strike now is violence.' "

Gene nodded his head in vigorous agreement.

"I'm in telegraphic touch with every junction on the lines. I've ordered the men to stay home, to stay sober, and to keep their hands off railroad property. But, Clarence, they're swearing in thousands of federal deputies, giving them guns. Who are these men? Are they responsible citizens?"

Darrow drawled, "Let's go find out for ourselves."

They took a streetcar into South Chicago, alighting at the point where the Illinois Central and the Rock Island paralleled each other. The outside line of both sets of tracks was guarded almost solidly by armed men. Gene and Darrow walked along the tracks, passing out cigarettes, striking up conversations. After two hours they returned to the streetcar and rode back to the hotel. They were both depressed.

"You wanted to know who has been sworn in as deputy marshals," commented Darrow; "rich men aren't going to risk getting hurt; professional men have too much work piled up; men with jobs can't give them up, and unemployed workers aren't going to carry guns against strikers. Who's left? You saw for yourself: the dregs of the Chicago tenderloin: gangsters, hoodlums, petty criminals, sharpers, loafers, alcoholics. Those armed men have nothing to lose: they would burn and destroy a city for the sheer pleasure and the pillage involved."

"What superb irony!" cried Gene. "These irresponsible ones are now officers of the United States Government; they're going to defend society against workers in revolt."

"You've got to find a way to keep your men from clashing with those deputies."

Gene thanked Darrow for his assistance, excused himself and went into the office of the American Railway Union. At least fifty railroaders were crowded into the little room.

"Drop whatever you're doing, men, and get out to the yards. Tell your boys to go home and stay home. Tell them not to tangle with the railroad deputies; tell them to keep their hands off railroad property. Come along, I'm going out there too."

Once again he rode the streetcar south. When he reached the stockyards he found his men standing in the yards glowering: for on the cowcatcher of an engine were half a dozen United States soldiers with their guns outstretched, and up in the cab were more soldiers at the throttle and the boilers. Along the track beside the engine walked solidly flanked troops, bayonets fixed.

For Gene, this was the worst blow of the contest: his workmen could fight the organization of railroads on an even basis, but how could they fight the Managers' Association and federal government combined? He was seized with such a passionate anger that he began trembling all over. One of the officials who had been in the office with him only an hour before came running up to him.

"What do you say now, Gene? Do we run home and hide under our beds? Or do we prevent these troops from breaking our strike?"

This was the moment of decision. The happenings of the past twenty hours had invalidated almost twenty years of his thinking and working for the peaceable solution. This world was not a vacuum, there were no ideal situations, and other things never remained equal. Everything that he and the rail-roaders had worked and suffered and sacrificed to achieve for two long decades was in process of being obliterated. Must he step down from his command, retire to the closed and airless room of theorizing?

He looked at the men about him. They knew him almost as well as he knew himself. They felt the conflict tearing at his innards; they knew how much he would have to repudi-ate. He searched their faces one by one. A voice inside him spoke, a voice compounded of Colonel Robert G. Ingersoll and Susan B. Anthony; of Wendell Phillips and Major O. J. Smith, of all the thinking and all the manhood of the fighters he had known.

"Federal troops must not move their trains. Spike the switches, but be careful not to harm railroad property."

Word went swiftly through the railroaders. They thronged onto the tracks, leaving him alone on a slight rise. The troops were able to move the cattle train only one block, then sev-eral hours passed while they repaired the switch. Once again the train began to crawl down the yard; this time there was no convenient switch to be spiked. Gene watched his men ov-erturn freight cars in the path of the oncoming train. His heart sank, for he knew this was the beginning of a new and uncontrollable phase of the conflict. His men had deliberately disobeyed his orders. Or had they? He had told them that the car must not move; when an officer gives the command to fire, can he repudiate his men because someone has been hit?

A riot call was sent out. Swarms of deputies and soldiers moved onto the tracks, righting the freight cars, pushing them ahead of the cattle train. For many hours the contest continued. By nightfall the troops had been able to move the train exactly six blocks. The railroaders were jubilant; the overturned freight cars had not been injured, yet they had stopped the strikebreakers. But Gene lay awake all night toss-ing on his bed, talking fitfully to Theodore.

"The men think we've won, but this was only the first skir-mish. The Managers' Association is going to bring a Pullman train into Chicago over the Rock Island in the morning; that will be harder to stop. Oh, we'll stop it all right, but what methods will we have to use?"

At dawn he and Theodore and some twenty of the union officers caught the first streetcar out to Fifty-first Street. A through Pullman train from the West was creeping down the track, its cowcatcher, cab and every platform bristling with federal troops and Gatling guns. The strikers and an enormous crowd of their families and sympathizers poured over the tracks like floodwaters over a valley road. The train stopped. An officer in the cab bellowed:

"Fix bayonets! Charge!"

The human floodwater evaporated from the tracks; the soldiers climbed back onto the train accompanied by jeers and curses and stones. The train began to move again, slowly. The strikers ran ahead to Fortieth Street and overturned freight cars in its path.

Gene stood in the hot July sun, moving along slowly with the Pullman, which managed to cover thirty blocks by the end of the day. This was a sharp defeat for the General Managers' Association. Gene told his men they had victory in their hands: if no trains could be moved, George Pullman would sooner or later be forced to arbitrate.

His optimism was short-lived: that night the railroad yards burst into flame, and with it the strike.

Freight cars were burned, roundhouses went up in smoke. Governor Altgeld sent in state militia, which took up their position between the strikers and the deputies. The crowds grew larger, milling about, calling names. Fist fights began. Excitement mounted. At three-thirty in the afternoon the mob broke loose. They charged into the militiamen who were trying to push them out of the yards. The militiamen fired. Three men fell dead. The railroad deputies broke loose with their pistols and clubs.

Watching all this, heartbroken, unable to control it, Gene realized that violence is not a form but a fluid content: it will pour into any available receptacle. And he also learned what he had known as a younger man: that you cannot deviate the slightest fraction from non-violence and still remain in peace.

He picked up a bleeding child and carried her to the nearby stockyard hospital. The dead were brought in and laid on the floor beside him. He knelt down, took the burlap covering off their faces. The first was apparently a stockyard worker; the second was a railroad man, though one he did not know; the third was Pete Hararchy, a fireman on the Rock Island, an old friend and union member.

With tears in his eyes, he asked himself, Did I kill them? I started out as a man of peace. What a long road it has been . . . to violence and death!

— 16 —

He was resting in his room at the Leland Hotel when there was a knock on the door. He opened it.

"Is this Mr. Debs?"

Gene bowed his assent. The man continued:

"I am Marshal Arnold of Judge Grosscup's court. I have a warrant for your arrest. You must come with me immediately."

Theodore came in through the hall. They gazed at each other. Theodore took Gene's coat off the back of a chair and held it out for his brother. As they walked out of the hotel room two deputy marshals fell in behind them. There were two more armed deputies posted at the elevator. In a few moments they were in the Federal Building. Similar little parades kept entering the courtroom, with the American Railway Union officers surrounded by knots of deputies: George Howard's enraged face was as black as his beard; Keliher looked serene; Rogers was excited by the drama in which he was participating. Martin Elliott was cursing in his copper-mine patois, much to the amusement of his fellow Montanan, laughter-loving Jim Hogan. William Burns and Roy Goodwin were silent and serious. Gene was talking quietly to his associates when he saw Captain Stewart, a post office inspector, enter the room with a big bundle of books and papers. Gene looked at them with only half an eye as they passed, but even so they seemed familiar. A few moments later Lou Benedict ran into the courtroom, his collar and tie awry. He made straight for Gene.

"Mr. Debs, Mr. Debs, they've raided our offices and taken our records! Our bankbooks and money and files. Mr. Debs, they even grabbed up your unopened mail!"

Gene had been calm up to this moment, now he went white with anger. Marshal Arnold came to his side.

"Mr. Debs, the judge says I'll have to lock you up."

He was locked in cell 31, on the first tier. The floor was cold, of dirt-streaked cement. There was a short, splintered wooden bench on one side and an iron frame cot fastened to the wall on the other. Over everything was the stale and humid odor of refuse that had not been washed out; of food that had not been removed; of unwashed bodies inside thick airless walls; the stagnant air of men incarcerated, men momentarily dead. The only sounds were the heavy boots of the guards and the occasional horse cry or raucous laughter from one of the tiers above. A gaslight hissed at the intersection of the tier blocks, but it shed no light in his cell. Under him he felt the fast movement of a freight hurtling through the night.

He had been locked up too late to receive any supper; for this lack of interruption he was grateful. He sat on the hard bench with his face in his hands. He thought, Poor Kate, now all of her nightmares will come true. She will reproach herself for her failure to convert me, to make me desist from what she called my headstrong folly, my useless sacrifice. How can I explain to her that all this is a necessary and unavoidable part of the struggle? That my imprisonment and everything that may flow from it is part of the job, just as it is sometimes the part of a soldier's job to be captured by the enemy. What can I do to soften the blow for her, keep her from suffering a thousandfold for whatever may happen to me?

Idly he reached into his back pocket and took out his penknife, began slapping it roughly from one hand to the other, enjoying the physical pain and the comforting touch of an old friend. The knife slipped out of his hand and fell to the cement floor, the bone handle on one side smashed. He made no effort to retrieve the pieces, but sat numb with misery, thinking:

Everything has gone to smash, my knife, my organization, my beliefs.

Something whisked past him on the hard bench. His flesh crawled. Then he heard the almost noiseless scraping of claws on the cement.

At that moment he heard voices and heavy footsteps coming down the iron corridor. The guard and a visitor pulled up in front of his cell. The guard unlocked the door, the visitor entered and the door was clanged shut behind him.

"It's me, Gene, Clarence Darrow. I just got word of your arrest."

The two men shook hands in the darkness, barely able to see each other's face. The guard stood twirling his big key and gazing into the cell.

"How did you get in, Clarence? They told me no visitors were allowed after dark."

Darrow chuckled. "They think I am still the attorney for the Chicago and Northwestern Railway."

"They think . . . but aren't you?"

"Not since five o'clock this afternoon, I'm not. I told our president that when the United States Government and the General Managers' Association conspire to enjoin workers from striking, that's too much of a conspiracy for my weak stomach. I said, 'I'm giving up my job here, Mr. Hughitt, to defend Eugene Debs and the American Railway Union.'"

Gene's sadness was gone, replaced by an exaltation.

"What did the president answer?"

"He said, 'They haven't a chance, Clarence; this injunction is a Gatling gun on paper. Why give up a good position for a hopeless cause? Don Quixote only tilted at windmills; you're going to run into a high-powered locomotive under full steam.' "

The guard shoved his squarish, bony face against the bars and muttered, "You gotta talk plain English in there, Mr. Darrow, or I can't lecha stay."

Gene and Clarence smiled at each other in the darkness. At that instant Gene felt the rush across his legs once more. Darrow took out a block of matches from his coat pocket. He split off half a dozen and made a light. Two black sewer rats as large as cats were surprised in their antics under the iron cot and fled through the bars between the jailer's legs.

"We're very considerate in Cook County," drawled Darrow. "We don't let you get lonely in our jails."

The guard, who had a dim feeling that his institution was being insulted, said with a leering half-smile, "We'll take care of you the same way we did them anarchists. This is the same cell block where I guarded Parsons, Spies, Fischer and Engel. We hanged them for what they done."

Feeling slightly sick at his stomach, Gene asked Darrow, "Is it true, are these the same cells the Haymarket anarchists were in?"

"These, or the next ones."

"You're no better than them," cried the guard. "If you can make a rebellion, we can hang you too!"

"Rebellion?" Gene turned to Darrow inquiringly.

"He's seen the evening paper, Gene. The newsboys are crying, 'READ ALL ABOUT THE DEBS REBELLION.'" There was a harsh note to Darrow's voice when he spoke again. "You're in rebellion against the existing form of government, and are out to burn civilization to the ground."

"I broke into railroading as a fireman. I'm used to handling the stormy end of a scoop."

"But what you don't know," said Darrow, "is that a schoolteacher in New York City had her class debate this morning on 'Why Eugene Debs is the most dangerous man in America.'"

"Just think of it," murmured Gene, aghast. "Poisoning the minds of little children."

"We don't use poison in Cook County," said the guard; "we use the end of a rope, like on them Haymarket murderers."

The needling began to get under Gene's skin.

"Why the devil does he keep comparing me to the Haymarket anarchists? I never killed anybody."

"Neither did they."

Something inside Gene crashed. He remembered his father at the time of the Haymarket explosion saying, "They didn't do it, Gene. They had no reason." To Darrow he whispered, "But they had a public trial."

"So will you have."

"The jury convicted them, the judge was convinced of their guilt."

"So will yours be."

There was a long moment of stunned silence for Gene, then he murmured, "Clarence, is it true? Were they innocent?"

"To this very day no one knows who threw that bomb. There was not the slightest shred of evidence connecting any one of the anarchists with it. Every supposition of logic and reason tells us that they could not have been connected with it, for they had nothing to gain: they were conducting a peaceable meeting; the mayor of Chicago stayed through half of it and then left, telling his police captain that everything was peaceable. The anarchists were tried for conspiring to throw the bomb; actually the state never named anyone as the thrower of the bomb. Believe me, Gene, the only guilty men in that courtroom were the men doing the convicting."

The guard inserted his iron key into the door. "Your time is up; come on, Mr. Darrow."

The two men rose from the hard bench. Gene put his arm around Darrow's shoulder to comfort him.

"I feel much better since you've come. Now I know that I deserve to be in this cell."

"Deserve?"

"Because I believed those anarchists were guilty. I never gave them the benefit of doubt, I never examined the evidence. I entered into the mass hysteria you're talking about, Clarence; I wrote flaming articles against them in the *Locomotive Firemen's Magazine*. I should have known better, because my father told me they were innocent, and my father should have known, for he was an anarchist. But I became part of the mob. I helped kill those men."

Darrow left. Gene sat quietly on the hard bench, leaning the back of his head against the cold cement wall. From out the small cell window he saw a reddish glow: freight cars were burning in their yards, railroad property was going up in flames. Locked in his dark cell, the sewer rats scurrying past his feet, he felt the world and his heart on fire too.

— 17 —

The strike was quickly broken. The railroad lines began moving their trains. Within a few days service was back to normal. With the strikers black-listed, the American Railway Union discredited and declared illegal, its funds and papers seized, the General Managers' Association decided that it would be safe for the federal court to allow the imprisoned men out on bail. They so informed Attorney General Olney, who notified his representative, Edwin Walker, who passed on the instruction to Judge Grosscup. Gene and his fellow officers were released on ten thousand dollars bail each.

Gene went home to Terre Haute: to sit with Theodore amidst the ashes of their organization, while Clarence Darrow prepared the legal case in Chicago; to tell Daniel how terribly, bitterly wrong he had been about the anarchists who had been hanged; to assure Daisy that no jury would ever send him to prison.

Once again he found his own difficulties paralleled by the Rev. Mr. Hanford's. The All Faith Church had occupied the former vegetable store for a number of years now, but the Rev. Peter Hanford had been indiscreet; he had preached a fiery sermon praising Eugene V. Debs and the American Railway Union, and had then secured publication of his sermon in the *Gazette*. One noon the preacher reached the All Faith Church to find his desk, box of Bibles, and oddly assorted string of benches out on the sidewalk. Gene asked his Terre Haute local if their meeting room could become the All Faith Church on Sundays: and so the All Faith Church and the Terre Haute Local of the Brotherhood of Locomotive Firemen merged.

At home no mention of the strike or the impending trial was ever made. Kate went stolidly about her household tasks, and in the evening when they sat together in the library they talked of other things. He was proud of the way she was bearing up under the strain.

At last the day came for his return to Chicago to stand before the bar of justice. When his bag was packed he went into his wife's room to see if she were ready. He found her standing in the middle of the floor, gazing downward at nothing. He saw no suitcase, nor had any wearing apparel been removed from her bureau.

"Kate, you must hurry. We'll miss our train."

Without raising her head or looking at him, she said:

"I'm not going."

"You're not going? But the trial may take weeks, even months. Don't you want to be with me?"

She looked up swiftly.

"I just can't make myself go."

Gently he whispered, "You don't have to, Kate. I thought you would want to be by my side."

"I couldn't stand the torture. Every time they accused you of something new, it would be like sticking a knife into me."

"Then put on your heavy suit of armor."

"Armor? What are you talking about? This is no time to make jokes."

"Don't you remember, Kate, what we used to say when we were children? 'Sticks and stones will break my bones'? There's no reason for you to be hurt by their charges or their name calling."

"My dear, when they accuse you of those horrible things before the whole world, who will there be to believe you? That's what hurts me so dreadfully, Eugene, the things their name calling will convict you of in the eyes of all the good people, and the right people."

She suffers so terribly, he thought. He took her in his arms, ran his fingers tenderly over her cheek.

"Kate, come with me to Chicago. You will see that we are not alone, that we are not defenseless. It isn't I who will be convicted in that courtroom, but George Pullman and the General Managers' Association."

She pulled away from him, shaking her head in despair.

"How can you be so childish as to think you can convict the greatest men in the country?"

"Kate, we have only fifteen minutes to train time. Let me help you pack your bag."

"No, Eugene. It's in your best interests if I stay home. Oh, don't you see? I've always been against your work, and this dreadful tragedy proves I was right. Haven't I predicted this would happen? If I sat in that courtroom, where the judge and the jurors and newspapermen could see my face, they'd know how I felt, Eugene. . . ."

"You mean they'd know you were against your own husband?"

Impetuously she threw her arms around his neck.

"Oh no, Eugene. I am for you. I have always been for you. That's why I've tried so hard to get you to go into a respectable business, into a safe and secure position where no one could ever harm you."

"No one is going to harm me, Kate."

She held her cheek against his, and he could feel the wet, salty tears against the corner of his mouth.

"Darling, they're going to convict you. Everybody knows that. They're going to send you to prison. And that will kill you. It will kill your spirit. Oh, Eugene, I've pleaded with you, I've offered you opportunities . . ."

Sternly he said, "I've done nothing wrong. I've broken no laws, and you can only send a man to prison in this country when he breaks laws. But even supposing the worst happens, suppose I am convicted, I shall be a political prisoner, Kate, not a criminal prisoner. If we are to be happy together for the rest of our lives, you must come to understand this difference."

She broke away and stared at him with wide-eyed terror.

"I knew it! You've realized all along they would send you to jail. You've tried to hide it from me. But now you gave it away." She dropped onto a chair. "Oh, Eugene, how could you have done this to us? You had so much promise. Your future looked so brilliant, and how do you end up? Hated and reviled by the whole country, convicted of starting a bloody revolution, sent to prison for your crimes, crimes you never intended, I know that, but crimes that had to come when you insisted on taking your own headstrong course, fighting the government and the powerful men of the country."

There had been a light but insistent knocking on the front door. Georgie and Aggie stood there owl-eyed.

"Mr. Debs, we've brought our penny banks for you. I have eleven dollars and Aggie here has three."

"We want you to give them the money, Mr. Debs," chirped Aggie, "so they won't make you go to jail."

Gene felt hot tears behind his eyelids. He crouched down, one coin-juggling container in each hand, and hugged the children.

"Thank you, Aggie and Georgie. When I come back from Chicago, I'll bring you the most beautiful toys ever seen in Terre Haute."

He returned to the bedroom to find that Kate had not moved. Her face was pale. She took a few steps toward him, then stopped, began to speak in an almost inaudible whisper.

"If you go to prison, I will go to prison too. This house will be my prison. I will lock the windows, lower the blinds, bolt the doors. I will eat only the severest food, just enough to keep me alive. I will see no one, I will talk to no one. I will allow myself no moment of pleasure or happiness. I will never set foot out of this house until the day you return. So you see, Eugene, you will not be alone; I will be with you; I will be with you in spirit every moment of the night and day; I'll be in prison with you, suffering just as you suffer."

He wanted to answer, Kate, all this is useless. I have no intention of suffering. Only men who have done wrong suffer. But he could not say this to his wife, for she would not understand, and it would not lessen her anguish. Her burden would be a hundredfold greater than his, for he would be sustained by the belief that what he had done had to be done; she could have no such solace, for she had known all along that he was wrong and that his conduct would bring them to grief.

His heart ached for her. He wished that there were some comforting thought, some word of wisdom he could give as a parting gift.

"I am sorry to leave you all alone, Kate. If we had had children . . ."

Her eyes flamed; she cried out, "I'm glad we have no children! I hope we never have children! Then I won't have to fear for them, fear that every moment of their lives other children on the street will taunt them."

"Taunt them with what, Kate?"

"That their father is a . . . a . . ."

She could not finish the sentence. Stricken, Gene finished it for her, ". . . a jailbird?"

She did not answer, but he saw her nod to herself.

"Kate, you mustn't say things like that, you mustn't even think them. We're going to have children, lots of children. You know I'm not superstitious, but those words, they might put a curse . . . Kate, we don't want a childless home, an empty house."

He heard the long low whistle of the train coming across the prairie. He went out the front door without looking back.

BOOK FOUR

WALLS AND BARS

THE SNOW WAS BEING DRIVEN BY A HARD WIND WHEN GENE and Clarence Darrow entered the courthouse. They took off their heavy overcoats, still white and wet, and started down the center aisle, focus for every pair of eyes on the jammed rows of benches. A railing in front of the judge's dais enclosed the jury box and broad mahogany tables for the prosecution and defense. The press table directly across the enclosure from the jury box was occupied by some thirty newsmen, including representatives of the British and European newspapers. Gene murmured:

"This is going to be the greatest opportunity labor has had to educate the American people."

"Haven't taught school since I was a youngster," said Darrow, his big shoulders hunched over. "Had a great time then, boarded around with the parents of my pupils; they fed me pie three times a day."

"Nobody's going to feed you pie for defending me."

"Couldn't eat it if they did: spoiled my digestive system lawyering for the railroads."

Gene walked over to the front row of spectators to kiss Daisy and Daniel, who had come up to Chicago the evening before, Theodore remaining behind in Terre Haute to take care of the grocery store. Then he pushed open the little railing gate and joined his brother officials at the defense table.

He was about to seat himself when his glance encountered the battery for the prosecution. His heart pounded: for leaning over the portfolios, handsomely garbed in a gray suit, stood Ned Harkness, his full black hair combed back to fit the fine contour of his head, his face freshly shaved and powdered, looking more handsome and successful than Gene had remembered him from their meetings in Terre Haute.

Harkness looked up from the sheaf of papers on his table, saw Gene, straightened to his full height, the documents pushed aside. Silent thoughts ran between them; their eyes held. Then the contact was broken. Gene sank weakly into his chair: for into the front row behind the prosecution table slipped Paul Weston, Mrs. Weston and Gloria. She sat between her parents, her hands buried in her lap beneath her mink cape, her face partially concealed by the brim of her fur hat.

She's more beautiful than ever, Gene thought. And so cosmopolitan. Only her eyes were unfamiliar; they were grave, not unhappy, perhaps, but brooding. His own eyes became glazed; his insides felt hurt and hollow.

Judge Grosscup entered from his chambers. The clerk cried, "Everybody rise!" but Gene could not get off his chair.

Why has she come? To see me accused, humiliated? To prove to herself that she was right in marrying Ned Harkness? It's seventeen years since she said she loved me; has time changed her so much, have wealth and social position so captured her that she believes me a miscreant, and takes her place behind the prosecution?

Or was she only demonstrating her loyalty to her husband? For he knew that if Gloria had been his wife she would have been sitting in the front row behind the defense table.

Judge Grosscup said, "If both sides are ready, we will proceed."

Darrow, who had been sitting slumped forward in his chair, rose quickly.

"Your Honor, the defense protests against the presence of one of the prosecution's attorneys."

To Gene's lips flashed the words, Oh, Clarence, don't do that, Gloria will think . . . He tugged at Darrow's coattail.

"I have no objections to Mr. Harkness."

Darrow had not heard his client, nor would he have paid any attention to him if he had.

"Mr. Harkness at this very moment is legal counsel for the Chicago, Milwaukee and St. Paul Railroad. When a railroad counselor becomes at the same time prosecutor for the federal government, then the railroads and the federal government become one and the same agency."

Gene watched Gloria's face while Darrow made his

charge, saw her lean forward intently, her face strained, her hands clasped tight in her lap.

"The Court sees no reason why Mr. Harkness should not assist in the trial. The government may open its case."

He watched her settle back on the bench, her face pale. Then he forced himself to study the selection of a jury, the eight farmers, the dealer in agricultural implements, the real estate agent, the insurance broker and the decorating contractor who had it in their power to convict him of "criminal conspiracy to obstruct the mails" and to send him and his friends to Atlanta penitentiary for as long as ten years.

—2—

At the end of the day the defendants were taken by deputy marshals to the jail. He found himself placed in a large cell with five other men, all accused of crimes but not yet tried. The three-bunk tier on either side so crowded the cell that half the men stretched out on their beds in order for the other half to sit around a table on the cement floor.

He quickly became acquainted with his cellmates. There was a winsome little pickpocket called Harry the Dip, a Negro by the name of Bass Huggard, accused of cheating his landlord out of two months' rent, a big square-jawed, flaxen-haired Norwegian arrested in a barroom brawl, an Italian accused of stealing sacks of cement from a warehouse, an old man, toothless, with white hair falling over his ears, picked up as a beggar.

At five o'clock armed guards came through the corridors to unlock the heavy doors, and the men were marched into the mess hall for supper. Here he had a chance to ask Keliher and Rogers how they were faring. He could not touch any of what the prisoners called slumgullion: boiled hogback with a few slivers of meat hanging to the bones.

After supper they were returned to their cells. He heard familiar footsteps ringing down the cement passage. While the guard stood rattling his keys, a voice cried out:

"Who's in this cell, a burglar or a poet?"

A laugh sprang to his lips as he replied, "A burglar."

"Good, then I must be the poet!"

The guard opened the door and James Whitcomb Riley entered the cell. He almost wrung Gene's hand off.

"I always figured some of my verses would land me in jail. But what is a big business executive like you doing in the clink? Have you absconded with the company's funds? Have you been cheating the public with short weights and measures? You should have been a versifier like me: then you could have been a guest at the White House, and had high society fawn over you!"

Gene examined his old friend: when last he had seen Jimmy Riley he had been an impecunious hall-bedroom lodger, eating when the opportunity presented itself, writing stanzas on such scraps of paper as might be available. Now he saw that Riley wore a good broadcloth suit with a gold watch chain strung across his vest.

"By all that's wonderful and miraculous," he exclaimed, "whatever happened to you? Did you marry the boss's daughter?"

"Even better!" replied Riley. "You know Bill Nye, the humorist? He was invited to perform before New York's famous authors at the National Arts Club. Took me along with him and introduced me as his encore. I gave them *Frost Is on the Punkin.* They ate it up, made me give six encores. Mrs. Grover Cleveland asked me if I wouldn't come to the White House and give my poems for the president."

"Well, what do you know!" murmured Gene.

"Remember how you had me to Terre Haute three times, and hardly took in enough to pay for my railroad ticket? Now I go to the theaters and find them hanging from the rafters by their tails."

"Well, what do you know!"

"So what do you care if the court fines you ten thousand dollars, Gene? I'll come get you out of hock."

"Time's up, Mr. Riley," said the guard.

Riley pulled on an expensive pair of kidskin gloves. "Here's a copy of the *Times;* you'll find something on page three that might interest you."

Gene opened the *Times.* In the center of page three was a poem called *Terry Hut.*

> *And there's Gene Debs—a man 'at stands*
> *And jest holds out in his two hands*
> *As warm a heart as ever beat*
> *Betwixt here and the Jedgement Seat!*

The guards turned out the lights, plunging the prison into inky blackness. Gene stretched out on his bunk. He was warmed by Riley's visit, miserable over Gloria's appearance at the trial, curious as to the sympathies of the jury after hearing Darrow's aside, "We are supposed to find twelve of your peers from among this group, but federal jury panels never include an employee!" Self-reproaches flooded his mind as he went back over the steps that had led him to this impasse. He should never have permitted the American Railway Union to go out; he had allowed his sentimentality to betray him. If a railway manager needed to be hard as rock, then a union manager needed to be hard as granite. He should have fought the convention, used all manner of strategems in turning down the Pullman workers: then his own organization would not have been destroyed.

His cellmates stirred restlessly, some asleep, some awake. During the daylight hours they could present a hard façade to the world, but now he heard them murmuring and groaning, all pretenses down, frightened children in the dark. From the adjoining wing came the soft weeping of the women prisoners, locked away from their families and their love, helpless ones imprisoned in steel and concrete for who knew what transgressions of the flesh or the purse? His own confused thoughts vanished, and in their place came heartbreak for imprisoned mankind, struggling upward through the darkness and the centuries, suffering untold torture at the hands of their fellow men: mendicants, like the white-haired old man in the bunk opposite, plodding their weary way up the road that leads from birth to death.

For six straight days he and his companions sat at the table directly below the witness stand, across which paraded newspaper reporters, railroad superintendents, police, businessmen, stockyard executives, nearby residents. Ned Harkness adroitly extracted from them the story of the strike, the stoppage of train service, the attempts to bring in cars over the Rock Island and the Illinois Central, the overturning of freights, the spiking of switches, the resistance of the strikers to federal troops, the ultimate clash, the burning of railroad property.

Halfway through the recital Gene leaned over Darrow and asked, "Why are they going to such elaborate pains to establish what we do not contest?"

"That's their only case, Gene. They must prove that you conspired to obstruct the public highways."

"But we offered to run the mail through on special trains."

Darrow looked up sharply at the jury.

"I'm on your side; the ones you have to convince are those twelve jurymen."

As though from an inner need for collaboration, he turned his head the full half circle to where Gloria was sitting. She was bending a little forward, tautly, listening to her husband's every sharp sentence. How strange, he thought, for himself and Gloria to be sitting in the same room these several days and never once to have spoken, to have let their eyes meet in the avowal of friendship.

The nights would have been long had he not been allowed one visitor each day after court closed. Daisy and Daniel left this visiting hour free for his friends. Susan B. Anthony came one evening, her hair white at seventy-five, but her eyes as spirited and determined as the day he had protected her from the rowdies at Terre Haute. Samuel Gompers arrived to explain that the American Federation of Labor had had to repudiate Gene's industrial union in order not to hurt their growing membership. Terence Powderly came back to the cell block to remind him of his prediction in Scranton that trade-unionism was little more than a soporific. Robert Ingersoll entered the cell with a fatherly smile on his face, twitting Gene for having supported the reactionary Democratic party, advising him to embrace the truly liberal Republican party. Major O. J. Smith visited several times, once with galleys on a laudatory story about the American Railway Union, a second time with a signed check made out to Gene, the amount left blank.

When he awoke on Sunday morning he felt that the prison was smothered under a brooding sense of loneliness and dejection. Week-days were workdays, men handled themselves in the cold, rat-ridden prison as professionally as they could; but Sunday was family day. No one smoked or talked or told stories; the men lay dispiritedly on their bunks with their eyes closed, trying to shut out the immediate world of cement. He missed Kate terribly; missed the crisp white apron over her go-to-meeting dress, missed her glow of satisfaction at the beautifully shining silver on the Sunday dinner table, the warmth of his own study, and the convenience of Kate's marble bath.

His depression grew acute as the dinner hour approached, the moment when Daisy and Daniel gathered their clan about the dining table: Theodore with his Gertrude, Mary and her three children, Jenny and Louise each with her child, Daniel presiding happily and proudly at the head of the table; Daniel, whose beard had grown white, who followed his son's expression and the testimony with intense interest. Gene had forced himself to go to the prisoners' mess for some watery mush and black coffee that morning, but he knew that he would not leave his cell for dinner, even though Harry the Dip had told him, with the first spark of life among the prisoners, that they had roast pork for Sunday dinner.

A few moments before the guards came to lock-step them

to dinner, a voice called from down the corridor. Gene sprang to the bars.

"Theo!" he exclaimed. "I'm so happy to see you, that homely old phiz of yours looks absolutely beautiful."

Theodore was carrying an enormous wicker basket. While the guard unlocked the cell door, he replied, "I've always been beautiful, Gene; the only reason you haven't thought so is that I look too much like you."

The brothers embraced. Their happiness was a vast hole cut in the wall, a summer sun pouring down its light and warmth to dissipate the heartbreak of the cell.

"Boys, I want you all to meet my brother," Gene exclaimed radiantly. "Theo, this imp is called Harry the Dip; hold onto your hat while you shake hands with him. This Paul Bunyan out of the north woods is Sven Christofesen. This is my friend Bass Huggard, and I'll bet you that it's his landlord should be in this cell instead of him."

Theodore shook hands with each of the men. Then he put the wicker basket on the wooden table, unstrapped it, began taking out delicious-smelling foods.

"Since Daisy only got back to Terre Haute last night, Gertrude knew she wouldn't have time to prepare anything for you. Look, Gene, a roast turkey with walnut dressing, a ham baked with sliced oranges, and three pies, apple, mince and pumpkin."

Gene watched Theodore lay out the feast; his cellmates stood by, their eyes enormous.

"Fall to, everyone!" he cried.

—3—

Theodore came again at eight the next morning with a new shirt, collar and tie, saying, "As long as you are going to be the prima donna of the day, you might as well get all spruced up," then wrapped his brother in a blanket while he took his gray tweed suit to a tailor to be freshly pressed and his shoes to be shined.

The Sunday newspapers had announced that Eugene V. Debs would go on the stand early Monday morning. When Gene entered the courtroom through the rear door he saw Theodore and Louise in the front seats; and when he saw Gloria in the row opposite he realized how passionately he had been hoping she would be there to hear his side of the story. Even as he walked to his seat at the defense table he sensed that this group of spectators had a different feel from those of the week before: they seemed more sympathetically disposed. He mentioned this to Darrow, who scanned the audience, smiled and nodded several times before turning back to his client.

"You have attracted a distinguished audience, Gene; there are several professors out there from the University of Chicago, surrounded by their students, and at least half a dozen members of the Sunset Club. They'll provide good background for the story you're going to tell."

Gene was sworn in, then went to the witness box and stood in front of it for a moment, gazing out at the courtroom: tall, lean, angular, fair of complexion, his wide mouth raised slightly to one side, his eyes more gray than blue. A murmur went quickly over the spectators as he stood there, but Judge Grosscup banged his gavel, the courtroom quieted, and Gene sat down in the same box where fifty witnesses had sat in the prosecution's effort to portray him as a conspirator against the public peace.

Darrow began very quietly, leading Gene into the story of his life: that he had gone to work scraping paint off railroad cars at fourteen; that after a year of this work he had become a locomotive fireman, sharing the hard, dangerous life of the men who went down the rails for their living. Gene told of the depression year of 1873, when he had gone on to St. Louis to look for work, joined the thousands of unemployed who walked the streets cold and hungry, begging food for their children. He told of spending years as a clerk in Hulman's grocery store while in his mind he searched for his niche in life, for a job which would have meaning and purpose over and above the earning of necessities. To the jammed and hushed courtroom he explained how his imagination had been captured by the men who ran the trains; how he had suffered for them because they were being brutalized by a seventy-hour week, drinking themselves into insensibility for momentary escape, pushed about by a force they could neither understand nor control; maimed, crippled, killed on their job, often for no failure of their own, and then disinherited as no longer useful to their lines. He told of how Joshua Leach had come to Terre Haute to organize a local of the new Brotherhood of Locomotive Firemen, how the opportunity to work with the railroaders he loved, and the chance to help their poverty-ridden families, had brought him the joyful knowledge that here at last was a chance to serve.

Ned Harkness was on his feet constantly, protesting, "Your Honor, this material is irrelevant!"

But Darrow worked his way forward from Gene's first meeting with the firemen in the hall in Terre Haute, through the obstacles placed in their way by management, the indolence and ignorance of the railroaders themselves. He told how he had entered the labor movement for the simple purpose of providing benevolent insurance; of how he had progressed from this to the basic trade-union objectives of shorter working hours, higher wages, safer working conditions. Leaning forward eagerly in the chair, his rich warm voice sounding a clackety-clack, clackety-clack, click-clack, click-clack over the years, he addressed now the jury, now the judge, now the newspapermen at the press table, now the throng of spectators, now Louise and Theodore, who had their long, lean Debs faces turned up to him.

But mostly he was speaking to Gloria. Never by the slightest expression did he show that he knew she was there. She gazed at him intently, absorbing every word, revealing no emotion. In his heart he knew he was trying to justify himself to the love of his youth, and to that youth itself, wanting desperately for her not to condemn him, think him a misguided fool who had squandered his years and his patrimony, bringing little but trouble and confusion in his wake. He must convince her in order to convince himself, he must prove that what had been done could not have been left undone.

Ever since his arrest he had been portrayed in the big city newspapers as a dangerous and destructive character. Now for the first time as his own story poured forth, as his devotion became manifest to all people who ate their bread with the sweat still caked on their faces, millions of strangers came to know him as a man, as a cause, as a passion, as a voice crying in the wilderness, crying out for them, wherever they might be, in whatever dark or distant arena, in whatever plight or pain.

His repatriation was fleeting: Ned Harkness had a sharp legal mind and a driving will behind it. At last the two men faced each other; the silence in the crowded courtroom was tactile.

"Mr. Debs, you call yourself a railroader, do you not?"

"I work with railroad men."

"How long is it since you have done any actual labor?"

"Since your bosses put me in jail, Mr. Harkness."

"I am talking about the labor you do with your hands and your arms and your muscles, Mr. Debs. Actually it is twenty-two years since you turned in a full day of hard work, is it not?"

Gene suppressed a smile as he recalled Engles's similar accusation that he did his laboring safely behind a desk.

"It is that long since I shoveled coal into a boiler," he replied.

"And in the interim, Mr. Debs, you have been the manager of labor organizations, have you not?"

"I have been the secretary of several unions."

"Were you paid well for your efforts, Mr. Debs?"

"Yes."

"How much money were you earning at the time you declared your nationwide strike?"

"Three thousand dollars a year."

"I heard you tell the gentlemen of the jury that you started the American Railway Union at a wage of seventy-five dollars a month. That's a phenomenal rise in salary in one short year, is it not?"

"It is a good raise."

"Mr. Debs, who raised your wages from seventy-five a month to three thousand a year?"

"The officers of my union."

"You made no effort to refuse this enormous raise?"

"No."

"The various unions you have worked for, Mr. Debs, they give you an expense account, do they not?"

"I have had an expense account."

"Did anyone actually keep books on your expenditures?"

"None that I know of."

"Then you could have spent as many thousands of dollars on yourself, your traveling and your pleasures as you saw fit?"

"I never thought about it that way, Mr. Harkness."

"How much money was there in your treasury at the time you began your strike?"

"About forty thousand dollars."

"Who had control over this money?"

"The defendants you see at that table down there, Mr. Harkness."

"And also the defendant at whom I am gazing in the witness box, is that not so?"

"Yes."

"How much of that forty thousand dollars were you planning to spend on a higher salary for yourself and your expense account?"

"As much as I thought necessary to continue building our organization."

"In other words, Mr. Debs, there is very little control exerted over you, is that not so?"

"The General Managers' Association makes up for that, Mr. Harkness."

There was a quick laugh from the spectators. Ned Harkness did not like the sound of it, and turned to glare. Gloria sat with her head down, her face concealed.

"But actually, Mr. Debs, what is the essential difference between you and your distorted conception of a manager? You run your organization with autocratic methods; you spend as much of its money as you wish, without accounting for it; you raise your salary whenever it pleases you and to whatever extent you think safe at the moment."

Darrow was on his feet, exclaiming, "Your Honor, counsel is not cross-examining the defendant, he is making speeches to this court, and libelous speeches, in my opinion."

"Counsel will confine himself to cross-examination."

"Your Honor, every word I have elicited from the defendant is directly relative and material, for it is my thesis that this man sitting in the witness box is no leader of labor, but a vulture preying off them; a man who has not soiled his hands for twenty-two years, but like every demagogue has used labor's varying fortunes to cry havoc and fatten his own purse."

Ned Harkness leaned over the prosecution table, opening a sealed envelope. "Your Honor, I ask permission to offer this photograph in evidence. Mr. Debs, do you recognize this photograph?"

Gene saw it was a picture of his home in Terre Haute, standing in all its serene Queen Anne dignity, and looking very lovely.

"It is a picture of my home in Terre Haute."

"You built this home for yourself, Mr. Debs?"

"Yes."

"And you paid cash for it?"

"I did."

"And it has been completed for many years, has it not, Mr. Debs?"

"Mrs. Debs and I have lived in it for five years."

"Your Honor, I ask that this exhibit be passed among the jurymen."

Judge Grosscup nodded approval. The clerk handed the picture to the foreman, who looked at it quickly and passed it down the front row of the jury box. The spectators craned in the hopeless effort to see the picture; but they had no trouble in seeing that the jurymen were impressed by the Debs home.

"Mr. Debs, how much did it cost you to build that house?"

"I don't know."

"You don't know, Mr. Debs? Then who does?"

"My wife. I turn all my earnings over to her and she built the house."

"Did Mrs. Debs have a private source of income at the time this house was built?"

"My wife invested my earnings."

"Invested? In what, Mr. Debs?"

"Stocks and bonds, I suppose."

"Ah, I see. From your meager earnings as an employee of the Locomotive Firemen, your wife was able to build up an estate of first-rate stocks and bonds. What is the extent of your holdings today?"

"I don't know."

"You don't know?"

"Mrs. Debs handles all the business affairs of our family."

"I am glad you put it that way, Mr. Debs. For I want to make it doubly clear to this jury that you are a businessman, not a worker; that your stock in trade is the employees of the railroad; that you keep them at work or send them out on strikes as it suits the purpose of your business interests and your profits."

Once again Darrow was on his feet, but Gene waved him down.

"That is correct, Mr. Harkness, I am a businessman; the purpose of my business is to protect the employees of the railroads, to secure them a just and adequate wage, to build for them the security which every workingman and working-woman deserves as the price of his labor."

Harkness turned to Darrow, saying sardonically, "Perhaps counsel for the defense would be so kind as to tell his client to come down off his soapbox and back into the federal court, where he is under indictment."

"My father made a living off of soapboxes in his grocery store for thirty years," interpolated Gene. "I have nothing against them."

Harkness left the defense table, walked between Gene and the jury box, took up a position alongside Gene, facing the courtroom.

"Mr. Debs, isn't it true that a strike is war, and that your primary purpose is to so intimidate the opposition over the potential loss of its equipment that they will surrender?"

"We simply refuse to work when conditions become intolerable."

"In this strike you were the leading general of your forces, Mr. Debs?"

"If the farfetched figure of speech pleases you, Mr. Harkness."

"It doesn't please me. It revolts me, revolts me to the very core of my nature, just as it revolts every right-thinking and right-minded American citizen. For it is now perfectly obvious, Mr. Debs, what you are after. You have built a union of one hundred forty thousand members, you have forty thousand dollars in your treasury, a three-thousand-dollar wage, and God alone knows how many more thousands for your private expenses. How many railroad employees did you hope to unionize?"

"The entire million men and women employed in every phase of railroading."

"And when you have your million members, how much money will you have in your treasury? A quarter million dollars? A half million?"

"Perhaps."

"And how much salary would you be taking for yourself, Mr. Debs? Twenty thousand dollars a year? Thirty? Forty thousand?"

This time Judge Grosscup sustained Darrow's objection to Harkness's harangue as being incompetent. Harkness drew himself to his full height, then turned to the jury box and smiled.

"The prosecution has no further questions to ask of Mr. Debs, for we are confident that we have portrayed him in his full light, a freebooter who has lived off the backs of labor for some twenty-two years, and has grown too big for his own bailiwick; who was waging a class war against American industry for the sole purpose of seizing control over the railroad empire and using it for his own selfish ends and personal advantage."

In the excitement-charged silence of the courtroom, Gloria Harkness suddenly rose and walked down the center aisle as quickly as she could. Gene bolted upright in the witness box; he watched Gloria's back until she had disappeared through the far door.

— 4 —

Clarence Darrow had subpoenaed George Pullman to the witness stand the following morning. Gene hardly slept that night, tossing and turning on his hard bunk with the anticipation of hearing Mr. Pullman explain the twenty-six million dollars of undistributed profits which lay in the company's treasury, and the three-million-dollar cash dividend which was distributed to the stockholders at the exact moment when the workers' wages were cut to match the sum owed by them for rent of company houses. Gene believed that the most important fact of the trial, and the one he most wanted to see spread across the front pages of the land, was that a mere hundred thousand dollars taken off the dividend and left in workingmen's wages would have avoided the starvation, desperation and industrial warfare. Just how would George Pullman justify his conduct before a civilized world?

He could have saved himself the sleeplessness: when Judge Grosscup convened court in the morning, with hundreds of spectators jammed into the side aisles and the press table occupied by some of America's best-known writers, George Pullman was eminently conspicuous by his absence. Deputy Marshal Jones, who had tried to serve the subpoena, testified that Mr. Pullman had fled from his office just as he had entered.

Gene thought it advantageous for the American public to have an opportunity to watch George Pullman flee from a subpoena.

"Send a marshal to cover his home as well as his office," he suggested to Darrow, "you'll have him in here tomorrow morning."

Gene had underestimated his adversary: the following morning Mr. Pullman's lawyer, Robert Todd Lincoln, announced to the court that his client had left on his private train for the East the night before.

"I insist that Mr. Lincoln tell this court," stormed Darrow, "whether his client did not know that there was a subpoena out for him?"

"Yes, Mr. Pullman heard about it, but he thought that a subpoena had no effect until it was served, and so he went ahead with his plans to vacation."

The son of Abraham Lincoln helping to keep the white workers of America in slavery! thought Gene.

Darrow declared belligerently, "Your Honor, I ask that George Pullman be arrested for contempt of court, exactly as my client was! We hereby serve notice that we will subpoena every last member of the General Managers' Association to testify on this stand everything they know about their own sharp practices in conspiracy!"

The next morning, just as Gene was being brought in through the rear door of the court by the deputy marshal, George Pullman entered through the front door with Robert Todd Lincoln on his left, a second attorney on his right. The three men made their way to Judge Grosscup's room. Fifteen minutes later Mr. Pullman emerged from chambers, smiled to the courtroom and walked out. Judge Grosscup took his place upon the bench, declaring that Mr. Pullman had explained his absence satisfactorily and would not be required to testify at the trial.

Before Gene or Darrow could recover from their astonishment, Edwin Walker arose and announced that due to the illness of juror John Coe the prosecution asked that the case be adjourned and put on the calendar for retrial at a future date.

"Your Honor, I demand that court be recessed for a few days," said Darrow, "until John Coe can recover his health."

"I am afraid that would do no good," replied Judge Grosscup. "Prosecution has brought me a doctor's affidavit that Mr. Coe will be ill in bed for at least a month."

"Then the defense asks Your Honor to conclude this case with eleven jurors; we cannot be more than a couple of days away from completion."

Ned Harkness sprang to his feet.

"The prosecution cannot accept any such illegal proposal."

"Then I move that the defendants be discharged!"

"That will have to be denied," answered Judge Grosscup. "It is not agreeable to the government, and it is not practicable. I will set this trial for the first Monday in May." He rose, turned to the jury, and said, "Gentlemen, thank you for your close attention to this case. You are now dismissed."

Pandemonium broke loose as Judge Grosscup made his way quickly to his chambers. Gene went to Daisy and Daniel, who had come to Chicago to be by their son's side when the verdict was announced. When he turned back to the defense table to clasp hands with his comrades, he saw the jurors streaming out of their box. Before he knew what was happening, they had surrounded him with broad smiles on their faces, were shaking his hand, clapping him on the back. Everyone began speaking at once.

"You're not guilty of anything we could see. Too bad we didn't get Pullman up on the stand. You're all right, Mr. Debs. Nothing that Harkness lawyer could say would make us think different."

The foreman, who had waited for a moment of silence, spoke up. "Mr. Debs, when we were sworn in, several of us felt that five years in Atlanta penitentiary for you would have been about the right punishment. After listening to your story on that stand, every last one of us felt differently about you and your work. We would have acquitted you like a shot."

Clarence Darrow insisted upon taking the Debs family to a victory luncheon at the Bismarck Hotel. Everyone was jubilant. Darrow told them, "The prosecution is licked! They'll never haul us into court again: George Pullman and the General Managers' Association took too bad a mauling."

It was the first enjoyable meal Gene had had since the Sunday Theodore had arrived with Gertrude's basket. But he did not have an opportunity to finish his coffee: from the street outside they heard the cries of the newsboys, faint at first, then growing louder and clearer as they approached the hotel.

"EXTRY! EXTRY! Eugene Debs gets six months! Sentenced by Judge Woods for contempt of court! Read all about it, American Railway Officers go to prison!"

He turned white, then a bilious shade of green. At length he was able to whisper:

"Judge Woods? But how did he get jurisdiction: Judge Grosscup set our new jury trial for the first Monday in May. Clarence, can they turn around now and deny us a jury trial?"

The lawyer was even more stricken than his client. Judge Woods had co-signed the injunction which ordered Gene to put an end to the strike. If Judge Grosscup now saw fit to withdraw from the more serious case of conspiracy and hand jurisdiction over to Judge Woods on the lesser charge of contempt . . . Who was to stop Judge Woods from handing down a bench order, sending the seven men to jail for refusal to obey his injunction?

"You mean, can they do it legally? That all depends on whether you think the law was written for the protection of property or for the protection of people. The General Managers' Association was determined to send you to prison for conspiracy, and now they have conspired to get you there."

Daisy reached under the table for his hand and squeezed it. Daniel's eyes, fogged over with tears, found his son's and smiled reassuringly. Gene thought, Daisy and Daniel, they'll survive it. But poor Kate, what has she to sustain her? She knew all along I would go to jail. She understands her own people better than I do. How will she take the blow, all alone, with nothing to solace her?

— 5 —

He had twenty-four hours in which to surrender to Marshal Arnold for the trip to Woodstock. He and Theodore were discussing the plans to move the American Railway Union's headquarters to Terre Haute when the office door was thrown open and Ray Eppinghauser burst in. He was the fireman to whom Gene had given his new winter overcoat that freezing night in the Terre Haute yards. Ray had moved to Chicago a number of years before, married and taken over his father-in-law's prosperous coalyard.

"What you need, Gene," declared Ray, "is a drink, a good stiff drink."

Gene considered the idea soberly for a moment.

"You're right!" he replied with his eyes snapping. "When a man's been double-crossed by his own government . . ."

"Let's go down to Harvey's; we can get a booth and drink like gentlemen."

Harvey's was still quiet at this early hour, the waiters' aprons white and crisp, the snowy linen on the front tables gleaming as the three men walked to a secluded section at the rear. Eppinghauser exchanged greetings with the waiter, an older man with swooping handlebar mustaches.

"Oscar, these men are my friends. I want you to break out the best bourbon in the safe."

"Yes, Mr. Eppinghauser, and shall we make all three of them doubles, as usual?"

Oscar returned in a few moments with three tall glasses, clinking icily, the pure amber fluid just an inch from the top rim. The bourbon tasted acrid against Gene's palate, for he was not accustomed to anything so strong: he drank beer with the boys at their various meeting places, and very occasionally a single scotch and water, half of which he would leave in his glass. He took a long draught of the bourbon; it didn't taste quite so unpleasant the second time. But his stomach seemed to have changed places with his mouth. Then his gorge slowly settled back down into the cavity in his chest, and as it got lower and lower, finally reaching its rightful place, a great sigh escaped him and he felt as though someone had snapped the taut cable which ran straight through his body, holding his feet and head rigidly on either end. He took another long swallow of the bourbon.

"Say, this is good stuff. The trouble with me is, I don't drink enough."

He threw his head back and emptied the remainder of the long drink.

"Take it easy, boy," said Theodore, "that's more liquor than you've had in the last year."

Gene heard only part of Theodore's remark.

It's funny, he thought, all your life they tell you you've got blood running faster'n hell up and down your veins, and the only time you ever believe it is when you cut yourself. But I can believe it now: I can feel that old blood tearing through me a mile a minute.

"I wish I could have felt this way in court, today, boys: I would have told 'em all what I thought of 'em." He turned to his brother, who was watching him with a tiny, indulgent smile. "Theo, you know what's the matter with the courts?"

"Yes," replied Theodore, "the judges."

Gene heard himself laugh an unnaturally loud laugh.

"What I'm talking about, in court you've got to watch your manners. A man like Harkness with greenbacks sticking out of his ears and calling you every vile name in the dictionary, can you tell him that he's contemptible? Oh dear no, you have to think of court etiquette. When Harkness calls you an extortionist, battening off helpless workers, all you can do is say 'Yes, sir' and 'No, sir'! Ah, Oscar, it's good to see you again. The trouble with me is, I'm too sober. Fill up my glass, double."

"I should have smuggled in a bottle of bourbon to your cell," said Ray, "then maybe you wouldn't have been so polite."

Gene raised his glass, closed his eyes, and swallowed half the liquid. He could no longer feel blood in his veins, now it was like ants, millions of little ants racing up and down on the outside of his arteries. He turned to Theodore.

"I propose a toast to King Pullman, monarch of that beautiful kingdom where all that is ugly and discordant is eliminated."

"You drink to him," said Theodore. "One of us is going to have to stay sober."

Oscar picked up the empty glasses. "Wouldn't you like to order now, Mr. Eppinghauser?"

"What do you want to eat, Gene?"

"Another bourbon."

"Oscar, bring Mr. Debs another bourbon, then bring us your special green cucumber salad, and thick steaks with french-fried onions."

Oscar brought the green cucumber salad with razor-thin slices of pumpernickel. But now the maggots had ceased to crawl up and down on the outside of Gene's veins, and his body had gone numb. Ideas raced brilliantly through his mind. Theodore fed him buttered slices of pumpernickel, while he devoured the cucumbers. Suddenly he leaned across the table to Ray.

"You think the American Railway Union is gone, don't you? You think it's dead and buried under Emperor Pullman's monument? That's what everybody thinks today, but they're wrong, do you hear me? The American Railway Union is alive, yes, and it's going to stay alive, it's going to grow stronger every day. In a month we'll have a quarter of a million members, in three months a half a million, by the time I get out of jail we'll have a million loyal members, every last person who works on the railroads."

"Here's your steak, Mr. Debs," said Oscar.

Gene tried to cut the meat, but the relation of the knife and the fork to the food on the plate was vague.

"Let me cut it for you," said Theodore.

Gene bolted the steak, the onions and several of the hard-shelled rolls. Oscar arrived with two more double bourbons. Gene took a liberal gulp.

"Easy, son, easy," cautioned Theodore. "I'll admit you're entitled to a good drunk . . ."

"You're right! I got a drunk coming. I'm sick of the whole mess. I'm tired of all this sentimental nonsense called service and usefulness and brotherhood. I say to hell with it all! You hear me, Theo, I'm satiated." He ran his right index finger in a sweeping gesture across the middle of his mouth. "Fed up, to the teeth."

"Right you are, Gene," agreed Ray. "You just become a grafting millionaire like that Harkness called you."

Gene's thoughts did a back flip. "And what's more," he exclaimed, "we're not going to stop when we have a million members in the American Railway Union: we're going out to organize every other great industry in America: steelworkers, miners, lumberjacks. You didn't know I had a great dream in the back of my head, did you, Ray? Well, I have, and it's even got a name. Society of Industrial Unions: twenty million workers and their families! It won't take us long, a few years at the most, and every man and woman who works for a living in America will be a member of one big union."

"My friend, you're drunk," announced Ray.

It was nine o'clock when they left Harvey's to go to Ray's house. Gene no sooner hit the fresh air than he felt as though someone had dropped his stomach down his gullet at the end of a string, and at any moment would pull it up. Theodore helped him into the hansom.

The three men were admitted to the brownstone house by Ray's wife, who took a quick look at her husband, murmured something about ". . . the town again," and then disappeared. Ray went to a cabinet, opened a new bottle of bourbon and announced, "Now we can get down to some serious drinking."

"Take it away," groaned Gene.

"The head of twenty million workers in the Society of Industrial Unions unable to handle his liquor! How do you expect to hold together a vast industrial union if you can't even hold four bourbons?"

Gene clutched the tall glass, swallowed. Mrs. Eppinghauser

called in, "I fixed the bed in the spare bedroom, Ray, in case your friends can't get home under their own traction."

Ray sprang up. "My beautiful, wonderful Hannah: even when I am drunk she is indulgent. May you and yours prosper unto the seventh generation."

Mrs. Eppinghauser laughed. "If you don't stop spending our hard-earned money on hard liquor, we won't even prosper unto the second generation."

With tears in his eyes, Gene said, "How wonderful to have a good wife! I have a good wife, too, haven't I, Theo? But she has a bad husband, a jailbird. Poor Kate, all she wanted was to be respectable, and to keep in the right element. And what do I do to her? I break her heart, I ruin her social position, I use up all her savings. What does she get out of it? A prison sentence! Yes, Theo, Kate is going to prison, too . . . and what has she done to deserve it? Nothing but make me a good home and be a faithful wife."

He took several long gulps from his glass, then found himself in a rage.

"You know why Harkness did it, don't you? You think it was only to make himself look good to his bosses? Sure, he had to stage that attack so that they would raise his salary, but that wasn't what he was thinking about, he was just trying to make me look bad to his wife, that's all."

"Easy, Gene," cautioned Theodore.

". . . trying to prove to her that she made no mistake in marrying him. That it's all right to leech off big corporations, because everybody is leeching off everybody else. If I am living in a mansion I built off the backs of labor, that makes him look like a man instead of a lackey."

"You surely are drunk," announced Ray. "Here, let me fill your glass, it'll sober you."

Gene turned to Theodore, his face pale, his eyes big and hurt. "And she believed him, Theo. She didn't miss a word, an accusation. She never took her eyes off him for an instant, you saw that, didn't you, Theo?"

Suddenly he knew that he must have fresh air or he would suffocate. He went out into the back yard, then decided that he had to write to Kate, took out his pocket knife to sharpen a pencil, and promptly dropped them both into the fishpond. He murmured:

"Sleep now . . . sure wake me . . . four o'clock . . . train leaving for Woodstock at five."

"We'll just put Gene to bed," said Theodore. "I have to catch a train back to Terre Haute."

"Don't worry about a thing," said Ray. "I'll have him up by four."

Gene woke several times. When he tried to lift his head the pillow started going around as though it were on a circular motor. Ill and nauseous, he managed to get back to sleep. When at last he awakened, and was able to reach for his watch, he saw that it was seven o'clock; a quick look out the window told him that it was seven o'clock in the evening.

"I've missed the train," he groaned. "I gave Marshal Arnold my word I'd be back by four."

His eyes ached, his head throbbed, and his insides felt as though they were on fire, yet he managed to stumble into his clothes. Ray was seated at the table with his family, calmly eating dinner.

"Ray, for heaven's sake. You know I promised to be back by four!"

"You were so sound asleep, Gene, and I thought you needed the rest."

Gene collapsed onto a dining-room chair. "I have never felt so wretched."

"Get a good night's sleep for yourself, you'll be a new man in the morning."

Gene stumbled back to the bedroom, took off his clothes. All through the interminable hours of the night he tossed and rolled, sick to his stomach and sick to his head. The only comfort he could find was that Kate was not there to see him.

Ray came in at seven in the morning.

"Why, Gene, you still look under the weather. Whatever happened to you, laddie boy?"

"It must have been those green cucumbers I had at Harveys. I never could eat cucumbers."

Ray shoved the morning paper under Gene's nose.

"The whole town's looking for you, including the sheriff's posse. We'd better get downtown before they smoke us out."

Shortly after eleven the two men rode up to the fifth floor of the Monadnock Building. Marshal Arnold's anteroom was crowded with newspapermen. Gene's entrance raised a hullabaloo and a barrage of questions.

"Where you been, Mr. Debs? Is that a mint you're chewing?"

"I've been sick, boys," said Gene lightly. "Friend Eppinghauser here took me to Harvey's where I had a green cucumber salad."

Marshal Arnold appeared in the doorway. "Will you two gentlemen kindly come into my office?"

Arnold closed the door behind him; he was white with anger.

"Mr. Debs, you have broken your promise and your word of honor. I came to respect you during the trial, and now you have forfeited that respect."

Gene blanched. The marshal was right. Stumblingly Ray explained about the cucumber salad and Gene's illness.

"Then why didn't you send a message that Mr. Debs was sick?"

Flabbergasted, Ray replied: "I am sorry. I didn't think it made any difference . . . whether Mr. Debs went to Woodstock yesterday or today."

In a towering rage, Marshal Arnold shouted, "Doesn't make any difference!"

Weak and sickish, Gene began to tremble. Deputy Logan came into the room. He was to take Gene to Woodstock; they had become friendly during the weeks of the trial.

"Marshal Arnold, Mr. Debs does look pretty bad. I know you don't want to send a sick man up to Woodstock. Sheriff Eckert might refuse to accept him. Why not let me set up a cot in the jury room? I'm sure that if Mr. Debs could have a few hours' sleep . . ."

Gene flashed him a look of gratitude. There was a pause, then Marshal Arnold said, "Well, all right, but be sure to lock the door on him."

It was cool and quiet in the jury room. Gene slept until three o'clock. He awakened feeling considerably better. In a few moments Logan looked in, then took him down to the dispatch cell to wait until train time.

He did not hear her enter, did not even know she was there until she sat beside him on the bench and turned her eyes full on his. In maturing she had fulfilled all the promise of the young girl: her eyes were deep, safe harbors for anyone's pain; her cheeks had slimmed, her bosom deepened, yet even after having borne two children, her figure was as slender and graceful as the seventeen-year-old who had leaned up high, very high, to get her hands locked about his neck while he held her supple body against him and kissed the sweet loving lips. All so many, many years ago.

"Gloria," he whispered.

It was obvious that she did not know exactly why she had come, but had followed an impulse. They would have only five minutes together, five minutes out of a lifetime, and yet the seconds were ticking away while they sat in silence, knowing how surely and wondrously they had once been in love.

When she did speak, it was not about the memory pressing hard against their hearts: the day in the storeroom office behind the grocery when she had tried to say good-by, to give him fair warning that she was about to marry Ned Harkness. She talked about the friendly little practice her father had built up in Chicago, of his nostalgia for Terre Haute and the gay house on Tenth Street. Then, abruptly, her voice changed.

"Gene, you didn't mind my being in the courtroom?"

"No, Gloria. I was glad to see you sitting loyally behind your husband, even if it had to be against me."

Her voice was like Daisy's: soft, kind.

"No, I . . . I found out . . . you were alone, that your wife stayed in Terre Haute. Oh, Gene, I heard them planning what they would do to you . . . right in my own home, the railroad presidents and their lawyers! I had to let you know that you weren't alone, that someone was by your side . . . every moment in the court."

He held her hand in his.

"I sensed it then, Gloria, but now I know. Each day I brought the image of your face back with me into the rathole of a cell. You turned it into a cool green bank of the Wabash."

She sprang up with the quick, lithe movement he remembered. There was a radiance in her eyes.

"Some part of me will always love you, Gene, no matter how many years pass or what happens to us. There's nothing disloyal about it."

They were silent, each wondering how it was that human lives got so terribly, so meaninglessly scrambled. The guard knocked on the bars with his key.

"I'm sorry, Mrs. Harkness, but I can only give you another minute."

She stood facing him.

"Gene, I think you were right and they were wrong. They're fighting for dollars, you're fighting for human life. They are the ones who are in prison, Gene, the prison of their own insatiable greed. I've watched them, I know. The country thinks you lost and they won, but someday they'll find the decision has been reversed. Oh, Gene, there's no prison in the world that can have bars for you."

Then it was time to go, time to be parted again. For one

blinding flash her lips were on his, her fingers locked tight behind his neck, and he held her to him, closely.

Then she was gone.

He looked up. The bars had vanished.

— 6 —

He was sitting by the window, Logan at his side and Cur-
ran opposite, when the train's fireman and engineer in their
striped overalls and peaked caps came marching down from
the head of the train. The engineer was Benny Balken, a former member of the Terre Haute Local; the fireman, Ed Ainsworth, had been a Great Northern switchman during the contest with James Hill.

"Hello, Benny and Ed. Nice to see you again," said Gene.

Benny growled. "Is this here the train that's taking you up
to Woodstock?"

"The very same, Benny."

"Then they're going to have to get themselves another engineer."

"Yeah, and a fireman too. It ain't never gonna be said that
Ed Ainsworth fired the engine that took Gene Debs to jail."

"It's all right, boys. It has to be this way."

"Not with us it ain't all right, Gene. Let them use a horse
and buggy."

Already conscience-stricken at the trouble he had caused,
Gene persuaded the deputies to walk him up to the engine.
The four men climbed the steel rungs into the cab, Gene took
off his coat, collar and tie, and rolled up his sleeves.

The train moved out at its scheduled time, with Gene handling the stormy end of a scoop. The shovel felt wonderful in
his hands, and so did the heat of the boiler as he gradually
worked the pressure up to 140. Soon his arms grew tired and
his back began to ache, then blisters puffed up on his palms.
At the end of a half hour he was in misery: Ned Harkness
had been right in saying that he had grown soft. Yet he
would not put down the shovel. This ordeal would be his ret-
ribution; he would sweat out the last of the alcohol. When
he stepped down from the cab at the Woodstock station, exhausted, his face caked with sweat and coal dust, and every
muscle aching, he felt whole and clean again.

Woodstock was a quiet village set in the midst of prosperous farmlands. They crossed the smooth green slopes of a
park bordered by elm and maple trees. Some of the townspeople recognized him from the pictures in the newspapers,
others knew by the appearance of the two deputies that this
was the last of the American Railway Union prisoners. He

felt their undisguised hostility: why did they have to have
federal prisoners foisted upon them?

When they had crossed the public square with its bandstand and iron fountain, they came to the red brick jail.
Sheriff Eckert, a brown-haired, brown-eyed man, was waiting,
an unlighted cigar between his teeth. Deputy Logan handed
over a batch of papers, saying, "Sheriff Eckert, this is Mr.
Eugene V. Debs. If you will sign this delivery paper, I will
leave him in your care."

Sheriff Eckert scrawled his name at the bottom of the re-
ceipt, then turned to Gene. He was courteous but cool.

"We play no favorites in this jail, Mr. Debs; neither do we
discriminate against any of the prisoners. The rules are well
established. We will expect you to abide by them."

"You will have no difficulty with me, Sheriff," replied
Gene with a slow smile.

He turned to Deputy Logan and thanked him for his kind-
nesses. The sheriff unlocked a heavy iron door. Gene entered
the prison quarters, which occupied the rear half of the jail
building. There were twelve cells lining the wall which
backed onto the sheriff's living quarters in the front half of
the building. In front of the cages was a thirty-foot corridor,
with a hanging kerosene lamp, and barred windows overlooking a quiet street; the bars across the windows were not unlike those across the front bedroom window of the house in
which he had been born.

His seven colleagues set up a terrific din.

"Why, Gene, what do you mean by keeping the federal
government waiting? Were those cucumbers aged in the
wood? Why didn't you invite us on that party, President
Debs?"

His pale face flushed with embarrassment as he walked
down the row of cells, shaking hands with each of his associates.

"Don't squeeze the paw too hard, boys, I earned passage
from Chicago shoveling coal."

Sheriff Eckert remained standing at the head of the cell
block. Gene continued down the line, introducing himself to
the four county prisoners occupying the remainder of the
cells.

Then he was locked into his cell. It was clean and without
malodor. By dint of spacing themselves systematically along
the side bars, his comrades could see Gene and he could
watch their faces as they exchanged the news of the past few
hours.

At ten o'clock Sheriff Eckert returned to extinguish the

hanging lamp; the rules forbade conversation after the light was out. Gene bade his fellows a quiet good night, got out of his street clothes, pulled down the narrow iron cot from the wall, covered himself with the rough-textured institutional blanket, and lay staring up at the ceiling. His comrades had been given three-month sentences, but this cell was to be his home for the next half year.

Sometime during the night it began to rain. At six in the morning when the sheriff opened the connecting steel door and banged on it to awaken the prisoners, the water was streaming in torrents against the corridor windows.

"Breakfast is at seven. The prisoners must clean themselves and their cells before food is brought in."

"Is there hot water available?" asked Gene.

"No, Mr. Debs, you will be obliged to wash and shave in cold water."

"I wasn't thinking of the shaving, Sheriff Eckert; if we had hot water and brushes, we could scrub the floors."

Eckert stared at Gene over a cocked shoulder, then replied, "Any two of you can come down into the basement and light a fire in the stove. Knock on this door when you are ready."

Elliott and Hogan insisted that only Montanans knew how to stoke a potbellied stove. They returned with two washtubs full of hot water, heavy brushes lying on the bottom. Each man took his turn scrubbing the cement floor, then Gene washed down the iron bars of his cell while the others laughed at him for being a spinster.

It was part of Mrs. Eckert's duties to cook for the prisoners; the breakfast was stone-cold by the time the sheriff got through his several round trips from the family kitchen to the end of the long cell block.

"I don't see why we have to eat off our knees on these bunks," growled George Howard from a middle cell. "Can't they just as well let us eat at that wooden table out in the corridor?"

Gene replied quickly, "I don't think we want to begin by asking favors, George; if those are the prison rules . . ."

Lou Rogers, in the cell next to Gene, whispered through the bars, "I don't know what's gotten into George; he has complained at everything in the jail, but I think his real grievance is against us."

Gene raised his eyebrows. Rogers answered, "Far as I can gather, he thinks we behaved stupidly and ruined ourselves for no gain whatsoever."

"George has been angry for a long time," said Gene, "but I thought it was at the authorities."

The rain-swept days that followed kept the cell block cold and damp. The central lamp did not shed enough light for good reading, and the inclement weather deprived the men of the exercise period in the yard. Gene had difficulty adjusting himself to life within a six-by-eight-foot world. He had brought along a number of books, but found himself unable to concentrate. He caught cold, his ear began to run, and the nerves of his eyes seemed to twist themselves into a cable in the center of his forehead. The dark brooding hours of the day merged into the dark pain-fraught hours of the night. The only activity he could force was the writing of a daily note to his wife in which he fabricated pleasant stories about his well-being. Through his mind pulsed her omnipresent stricture: "Eugene, be careful, be careful what you say; Eugene, be careful, be careful what you say."

Perhaps Kate had been right?

At the end of the first week his worst fears were being realized: they were disorganizedly urging the time to pass, sinking into long, meaningless reveries, more tinged with regret for the past than hope or plans for the future. Months spent in this kind of animosity, and they would come out confused and rudderless. They must get hold of themselves and organize their stay. But when? How?

Sheriff Eckert was a fair-minded man. He explained:

"Mr. Debs, we've had dozens of requests for interviews, people have been here from the newspapers and magazines. I hope you understand there's nothing personal in my not letting them in? It's just that the county rules prohibit visitors before two weeks." The sheriff champed the cigar across his mouth and back, then continued, "The whole country's watching this jail, Mr. Debs; if I should be too lenient . . ."

"I agree with your procedure, Sheriff," replied Gene. "I would do exactly the same in your place."

In his loneliness he reached into his back pocket for his penknife to sharpen a pencil, then realized that he had not seen it since he had come to Woodstock. Through his mind flashed an image of himself by the fishpond in the back yard of Ray's house in Chicago. He wrote to Eppinghauser, asking him to retrieve the knife and mail it to Woodstock.

— 7 —

The rain eventually lashed itself out. Two of the local prisoners completed their sentences, the third was released on parole. George Howard, after an acrimonious quarrel over reli-

gion with Hogan, requested his transfer to the county jail at
Joliet, walking out on his comrades with the flat announcement that he was through with the labor movement forever.
And on the morning of the seventeenth day the sun came
out, warm and gloriously bright, filling the jail with light and
hope.

At six o'clock, when Sheriff Eckert entered the cell block,
he said, "Mr. Debs, I cannot treat you and your friends as
though you were thieves."

"You haven't done so, Sheriff."

"No, but I've been severe with you. I see that you are a
fine lot of men, in jail for doing your job for your union." He
took a batch of keys out of his back pocket. "From now on
there's no need for you to be locked in your cells. Just follow
the rules: up at six, the cells cleaned by seven, lights out at
ten. I know I can rely on you not to do anything to get me in
trouble."

"We'll live up to your confidence, Sheriff."

"And from now on, you can take your meals in our dining
room. The food will be better, and it'll be less work for Mrs.
Eckert."

After breakfast the men took a brisk walk in the high
walled yard behind the jail, arm in arm, glad to be alive
again.

"Every time the sun comes out," said Gene, "a new world
is born. Maybe it wasn't our fault, maybe the rain and the
darkness caused it, but we have wasted seventeen precious
days of our stay. I haven't been to school since I was fourteen; Keliher and Hogan never did get past the second grade.
This may be the last opportunity in our lives to take a university course; we won't be able to say we graduated from Harvard or Yale, but we can always brag about our degree from
the Woodstock jail, providing we use our time wisely."

"What do you plan, Gene?" asked Martin Elliott.

"I propose a rigid routine of study and discussion. I propose that we bring the *Railway Times* back to life. I propose
that we write letters to our friends outside and ask them to
send us every book they can find that has to do with American history and social conditions. Lou, you were a schoolteacher out in Iowa before you became a brakeman on the
Quincy; if it is satisfactory with the rest of the boys, I name
you professor and ask you to take charge of the study
course."

"I accept the nomination."

"Martin Elliott, you've had experience running hotels, I

suggest you become the inspector in charge of rules and quarters."

"Leave that to me, Gene." Elliott grinned. "If every man isn't up after I yell 'Six o'clock' he's subject to a fine of ten cents."

"Jim Hogan, you were in the army, I suggest you become the colonel in charge of morning and afternoon exercise periods."

Hogan grinned his pleasure.

"I will wield the birch rod during the debates. Lou, can you name a subject for tonight?"

"I can always name a subject: *Resolved, That the State Has a Stronger Claim on the Child Than the Parents.* I will take the affirmative. Keliher, how about you taking the negative?"

"I'm the best negative argufier ever turned out by the state of Montana," replied Keliher.

"Suppose we appoint Bill Burns general secretary to take care of the correspondence. Roy Goodwin is the right man to be treasurer in charge of fines and assessments."

The plan had a galvanizing effect; by the time they sat down to their one o'clock dinner William Burns had changed the name of Woodstock jail to Liberty jail, Gene had been elected president of what Roy Goodwin called their co-operative colony. Sylvester Keliher, who had been a carpenter, had secured some old wood from the sheriff and built bookcases on either side of the windows in the corridor to house the volumes that comprised their library: the poetry of Poe, Shelley and Burns, the novels of Victor Hugo and Nathaniel Hawthorne, and such social studies as *Criminology* by John P. Altgeld, *Christ Came to Chicago* by William T. Stead, Henry George's *Social Problems,* Laurence Gronlund's *An Essay in Ethics,* Carlyle's *French Revolution.*

The rules were tacked onto the wall above the bookcase, with a ten-cent fine charged against anyone speaking during the study period, a costly stipulation for Gene, who could not help exclaiming aloud every time he ran across something interesting in a book.

After the years of emotional turmoil it was not easy for the men to get down to disciplined study. For Gene Debs it was even more difficult; he was no longer content merely to look for information: what he wanted now was wisdom, a faith arising out of that wisdom which would enable him to reconstruct his life. Up to this point his thinking had been not only piecemeal but vulnerable: no matter how deep-

grained his conviction, something always had happened to
knock it into invalidation. He did not consider himself vacil-
lating or weak, one who could be swept away by every new
opinion let loose in the world; nevertheless, he had been
obliged either to relinquish or to revise nearly every one of
his working beliefs. What he wanted now was a fluid social
philosophy within which he could think and work, modify
and challenge, in much the same fashion that any good arti-
san plied his craft within the framework of its technique.

Having reached mid-passage sore and disabused, what was
left for him to believe in? Money? Religion? He recalled yesterday's interview with the excitable Nellie Bly of the New
York *World,* who had gained fame by circling the globe in
eighty days. In her long string of questions, peripatetic
Miss Bly had asked, "But have you no ambition to get rich?"
and he had replied, "Money getting is a disease, as much as
paresis, and as much to be pitied."

"But you must have some ambition in life, Mr. Debs?"

"If I had my choice of the gifts that come to men, Miss
Bly, I would ask for the power to move people."

"You mean as an orator?"

"Yes, but as an orator with a vision by means of which
men could achieve brotherhood."

Nellie Bly had drawn a bead. "Now we're getting somewhere, Mr. Debs. Exactly what is this vision? Surely it can't
be religious? I've heard you called an infidel."

Gene had smiled gently. "There are few epithets I haven't
been called. I am not an unbeliever; I simply don't subscribe
to any creed. I wouldn't, if I could, disturb the religion of
any human creature. But as for another world, I haven't time
to think about it. I'm too intensely interested in this one."

Ah yes, he thought as he lay with his feet dangling several
inches off the end of the iron cot, it is very simple. All I need
is a faith. But what kind of faith?

His hunger was sharp and clear, and there was plenty of
solid substance in the hundreds of books that kept pouring in
from their friends. Yet all that he could find were negative
answers: the United States Constitution had not been written
to give all men political freedom and equality, but only those
who possessed property; the precious ballot, which was to
create a great and free culture, was even today, after the heroic efforts of Susan B. Anthony and her comrades, denied to
the feminine half of the American population. The Supreme
Court, which had been evolved as a check on the power of
the Executive, from the very moment of its inception under
the hand of John Marshall had set itself up as the champion

of property over person. What was the philosophy that would resolve these ironies and bring actual freedom to a people who had achieved its external forms?

He found a detachment about being in prison which enabled him to think more sharply than he ever had on the outside; being in prison was like being on a high mountain peak: the exclusion of the little sounds and the little sights, the little anguishes and the little accomplishments lent one a penetrating objectivity. It was as though he had retired from the world and, wanting nothing further from it, was able to look at its civilization with the point of view of an anchorite scholar. There was one universality he could not escape: for the eight thousand years of recorded history mankind had been kept enchained by a ruling caste and a ruling dogma. Was it religion that had been in power? Then the peoples of the world were told that any attempt to challenge the Church constituted blasphemy and would result in their eternal damnation. Was it monarchy in power? Then the weapon held at the people's head was the divine right of kings, the military defense of the Fatherland. Was it property in power? Then once again there was a superstructure so elaborate, and by now so legalistic, that the ignorant masses had been led to believe they would perish without the sustenance provided by capital and private enterprise. The external formulas had changed; what had remained constant were the poverty and the helplessness of the people.

His testing hour was the quiet and blackness of the cell block after his comrades had gone to sleep, when he sorted out his impressions of the day, clarifying, reorienting, sometimes rejecting everything he had thought during the fourteen hours of study.

Ray Eppinghauser had written to say that he had recovered the penknife from the fishpond, but the hinges had become so rusted that the hardware man said they would have to be replaced. Wouldn't Gene rather spend the money for a new knife? Gene wrote back that the knife was precious to him because he had bought it on his way to his first union meeting with Joshua Leach, and to please have new hinges put in no matter what they cost.

When the knife finally reached him in Woodstock it was like the past come back. As he turned it over in his hands and opened the blades to inspect the new parts he realized that very little of the original knife was left: the big blade he had snapped trying to open the window of the meeting hall in Terre Haute after vandals had wrecked the room; one of the bone handles he had smashed on the floor of the cell in the

Chicago jail on the night he watched the railroad yards go up
in flames; the little blade which he used to sharpen his pencils
now resembled a scimitar more closely than a straight-edged
blade. In another year or two he would have to replace that
small blade, and the other bone handle that was growing so
brittle. Then it would be a completely new knife, and it
would bear no relationship to the knife he bought the night
Joshua Leach asked him to the meeting.

How like my own life that is, he mused. I started out as
the organizer of a benevolent, self-help society; soon I had to
throw away that blade and replace it with trade-unionism;
trade-unionism rusted in the waters of changing times and
had to be replaced by new hinges called industrial unionism.
But industrial unionism was like the bone handle on my
knife; I dropped it on the dirty cement floor of the Chicago
jail and it smashed to a thousand pieces.

For that matter, what is there left of the original Eugene
V. Debs? I married to have children and a warm, open house
for my friends, but I am childless, in a cold house, its front
door locked against new people and new ideas. I start out to
resist not evil, and now I am in jail on charges of having used
force and violence against the federal government. A few
more changes and every part of the original Gene Debs will
have been replaced; I will think I am still the same man; I
will go about telling people that my name is Eugene V. Debs,
son of Daisy and Daniel Debs of Terre Haute, but it will be
a lie; I will be a different man, and there will be nothing left
of that young fellow I remember who worked so surely and
believed so surely and had such considerable faith.

The half hour after dinner and supper, while the men were
still around the sheriff's table, was spent in making puns and
laughter, with shop talk prohibited; as the warm spring days
came on they played rough-and-tumble football on the back-
yard lawn. The spirit of comradery and devotion was high;
each man's problem became every man's problem; they
helped each other through whatever dark hour or despondent
mood may have seized them, when the brain and flesh ached
with loneliness for a wife, for a child, for freedom.

— 8 —

They were gathered about the two study tables on Saturday
afternoon when the cell door opened, and Sheriff Eckert
showed in Daisy, Daniel and Theodore. Daisy evidently had
not believed Gene when he wrote that Mrs. Eckert was feed-
ing him well, for she began to unload a basket filled with the
rarest delicacies from Daniel's store. If they had any consciousness of visiting their son in jail they gave no intimation

of it. Daisy was a gracious hostess, urging the men to eat and drink, and Gene laughingly teased, "Daisy, this is just like one of your Sunday afternoon coffee parties at home."

Later, when the other men went out for their exercise and left the Debs family alone, Gene asked for news from Terre Haute. Daniel told him of the death of the Rev. Peter Hanford, and of the fine funeral the firemen's local had given him. Remembering Clarissa from the last time he had seen her, swaying down Main Street in her high heels and tight-fitting red dress, he asked if she were all right. Theodore told him that Clarissa was going steady with the son of a wealthy Terre Haute family, and was expecting to marry him soon.

"Gene, we're worried about Kate," said Daisy. "Could she be away somewhere, visiting relatives? Have you heard from her?"

"No, but I write every day, and I'm sure she stays home to get my letters."

Daniel leaned across the table to his son.

"The house looks deserted, boy, the blinds are down, no one goes in or out, not even her sisters. We're afraid she might become ill; she could die in there and no one would know."

"Have you knocked on the door," demanded Gene, "sent messages?"

"I go there nearly every day, Gene," interrupted Theodore. "I draw blue circles around the interesting stories about you in the papers, and underline the favorable comments. I leave them by her front door, but no one ever takes them in."

Gene knew that to the casual observer Kate's conduct would seem strange, yet to him it was a portrait of her devotion. She could not agree with his ideas, she could not work by his side, but that did not make her the less willing to share the rigors of his fate. Aloud he said:

"You mustn't worry about Kate. She is all right. This is her way of sharing my punishment, of going to jail along with me. I think it proves how deeply she loves me."

The family did not reply, but by turning his face slowly from Daisy to Daniel to Theodore he could read their thoughts as clearly as though little Lou Benedict were typewriting them on a sheet of paper. Their loyalty to him embraced his wife. They said nothing further.

Reporters from the country's leading publications came to interview Gene and his brother officials. The prisoners put on neither show nor front for their visitors: they were welcomed into the afternoon workshop, handed a scissors and paste pot to help put together the clip page of the *Railway Times*. Day

after day reports went out over the press wires that these
were not bloody-eyed, long-bearded revolutionists, but serious
and honest men, working at their studies from eight in the
morning until ten at night, receiving thousands of letters of
allegiance not only from America but from Europe as well.
Gene took a merciless ribbing from the boys when a clipping
came from the St. Louis *Dispatch* in which the reporter observed that the moment Debs started talking the room fairly
crackled with electricity. When the lights were extinguished
at ten o'clock, Elliott or Hogan would call:

"Gene, would you start talking and light up this dungeon
with your electricity?"

Word came back to the people of Woodstock that, instead
of being humiliated and disgraced by the presence of these
national enemies, their town had been obliquely honored. On
a Saturday afternoon, when Gene and his colleagues were led
out of the prison yard and permitted to walk past the adjoining homes and the Baptist church, the townspeople smiled in
friendly fashion.

At last three months were up, and it was time for the other
men to leave the jail. The hot sun pried open their eyelids
before six that morning; they shaved carefully and put on the
clean, starched shirts and collars they had been saving against
this day of release. At the breakfast table they all agreed that
they were determined to remain in the labor movement. Gene
joshed the men and himself on their foibles during their stay,
but their laughter could not conceal their sadness at leaving
him alone. He shook hands with them one by one, and sped
them into the sun of freedom.

He heard the whistle of the train coming into Woodstock,
then heard it again going south to Chicago. Suddenly he felt
lonely. He sat down at the table Sylvester Keliher had built
for him, and he could hear Keliher's voice booming out in its
strong miner's jargon. He could look across the second of the
two tables and see Lou Rogers making up the pages of the
Railway Times. He could see William Burns facing the long
corridor at night, opposing all co-operative ideas on the
grounds that they were Utopian and took no account of
human nature. He could hear redheaded Martin Elliott mur-
dering the English language, but giving them all a penetrating
insight into the thinking processes of the uneducated laborer.
He could hear tall, loose-boned James Hogan satirizing the
weaknesses of their arguments with hilarious broadsides.

These were good men; if for nothing else he would consider the prison stay worth while for their comradeship. The

time spent in debate and discussion had been profitable, but he understood that for him the hour of decision had struck. Time moved too swiftly for one to search long amidst the debris of broken plans and broken faith; one learned from experience, one salvaged what one could, but there was no way to go back. The road lay ahead.

He sat down at the table with its pile of labor and metropolitan newspapers, began writing an article for the *Railway Times*. His loneliness slipped away as he became immersed in the task. He did not hear Sheriff Eckert enter.

"Mr. Debs, I'm getting two new prisoners in tomorrow. I don't think they'll be here long, but I'm afraid . . ."

Thinking that the sheriff felt obliged to rescind his privileges, Gene replied, "I'll clean off this desk right away, Sheriff; perhaps it wouldn't be against the regulations if I could take a little writing bench into my cell?"

"I have a better idea than that; I wrote to Chicago for permission. Follow me."

Sheriff Eckert led him down into the basement of the jail, then along an underground corridor which led to the courthouse. Gene saw a tier of abandoned cells crammed with broken furniture. By now they had reached the farthest corner of the courthouse. The sheriff opened a door, admitting them to a small, low-ceilinged room, its walls covered with a bright paper, its floor several feet below the level of the ground outside. As Gene looked through the barless windows, across the park, he could see groups of sunburnt farmers standing before the stores. In the room was a table, several chairs and a rocker with a broken spring.

"The Chicago court also said you could have your young typewriter man come in and work during the day, but he must bring his own machine. You could use this as an office; I wish I could let you sleep here on the couch, but I can't, I'll still have to put you in your cell at ten o'clock."

Gene didn't even hear the last sentence, he was so pleased with the new office.

"I deeply appreciate your kindness, Sheriff; I'll move my papers down here, and then I'll disturb no one."

Little Lou Benedict arrived two days later with his typewriter in a box, and several thousand letters that had piled up in the Chicago office. Many of these were protestations of loyalty, but others were specific demands for information and leadership. What was Gene planning to do about this travesty of justice? Would he come to Seattle or Galveston or Atlanta or Pittsburgh or Albany and set up a new union? Would he travel to Omaha or Los Angeles or Boise or Buffalo and give a lecture, tell the story of what happened to him and what he planned to do about it? Would he write a series of articles for this paper or that magazine; would he go out lecturing for the Redpath Lecture Bureau in Chicago if he were guaranteed a three-month tour? Gene tried to answer them all, dictating in the morning, writing longhand in the afternoon.

He was leaning back in his rocker answering the morning mail when he heard strangely familiar footsteps echoing through the basement corridor. He continued dictating without looking up. In the very middle of formulating a sentence he dropped his papers and strode to the door. There stood Kate, dressed in a traveling suit, twisting her purse in her hands. Before he could cry out her name she was in his arms, and neither of them could speak. He had closed his mind so hard against thinking about her, since he could not see her for another three months, that the unexpectedness of her visit broke something resolute within him.

Lou Benedict discreetly disappeared. Gene led Kate to the rocker, then sat on a corner of the chair facing her and holding her hand between his.

"Kate, you don't know how much this means to me, your coming to Woodstock. I know how difficult it must have been for you."

Kate took his face between her hands.

"When I learned that they had left you all alone, oh, darling, it was horrible, thinking of you abandoned here! With no one to talk to, no other face to see . . . in solitary confinement . . . I just couldn't let you suffer that way, Eugene."

"Kate dear, you're so pale and thin."

"I kept my promise to you; the first time I set foot out of the house was to come here. I saw no one, no one." Her expression veered for an instant, but it was away from her own thoughts rather than Gene's eyes. ". . . except Danny. He was with me . . . for a few days. You knew that I would keep my promise, didn't you, Eugene? You knew that I wouldn't let you suffer here while I was comfortable at home? I had only one meal a day, and ate just as little as I could to keep going."

He kissed her, filled with emotions of sadness and joy.

"Yes, my dear, I knew that you would keep those promises, for you are ever faithful. But, Kate, look at me! I have had an hour of sunshine and exercise every day, I have eaten well, better than I ever did while traveling for the Brotherhood. The only part of me they locked up was my battered carcass; my mind has been free to roam the world. I have had quiet and peace, an opportunity to study and think."

Sternly Kate replied, "Then it was right that I should have suffered doubly, Eugene, for someone had to be punished!" Her tone became gentle once again. "I have a room at the little hotel across the park. I shall stay until we can go home together."

Gene was aware of how much this move had cost his wife: once she came to Woodstock she acknowledged to the world that she approved of her husband and the things he did. This was bitter medicine to Kate Metzel Debs; shedding her pride and her convictions in public had required courage and inner fortitude.

— 9 —

In the late afternoons Kate would sit with him for a while in his basement office; usually she waited until the last of his visitors had left. Sometimes when a caller stayed late, she did not come in at all, such as the time Gene entertained Keir Hardie, the British labor leader, who argued that unionism was but a way station on the road to freedom, a freedom which he thought was obtainable for humanity only under socialism.

One day there was a knock on the office door. A man's voice asked, "Is Mr. Debs at home?"

Debs's eyes twinkled as he replied, "I imagine he is!"

Victor Berger was carrying a brief case under his arm as tenderly as though it were the family Bible; actually, with his brown hair brushed back pompadour style, his narrow, steel-rimmed spectacles, his high choke collar and the formal black bow tie, he looked for all the world like a Lutheran clergyman out to win a convert. Gene welcomed the younger man with considerable warmth, for he knew that the former German teacher was one of the most articulate battlers for reform in the country. Having reached America at the age of eighteen, Berger had not been able to divest himself of what he called his Milwaukee accent, but he had such a gift for lucid and colorful phrasing that one soon became oblivious to the heavy gutturals.

"Well, Gene," boomed Berger, "I hope you are now convinced that trade-unionism by itself will get you nowhere."

"It got me in jail." Gene smiled.

Berger was too passionately in earnest to pause for laughter.

"Without a political class movement, Gene, the trade-union struggle is hopeless. You remember how Ferdinand Lassalle described the unions: 'A soporific reconciling the workingman to his fate.'" He jumped up, loosened the straps of his bulging brown leather portfolio, laid a number of newspapers before Gene's eyes. "Here, read these telegraphic reports: they tell of demonstrations of starving workingmen in London and Birmingham."

"I've read those reports, Victor. Keir Hardie brought them to me."

"So? Good! Then perhaps you have come to the same conclusions: that the economic movement alone is insufficient to improve the conditions of the working class."

"Sitting here in jail, I would be the last one to be able to disprove that."

Berger began circling the worktable.

"Gene, let me be honest with you, I am in Woodstock to convert you to socialism."

"That does not come altogether as a surprise, Victor."

"But what does come as a surprise, Gene, is that you are still walking about with blinkers over your eyes. Trade-unionism and socialism are two arms of the identical movement. Each arm has its work to do."

Gene rose, stood at the small ground-floor window and gazed at the busy stores across the square.

"The fact that this is valid in Europe means less than nothing here in America," he said without turning about. "Whenever our trade unions worked with the radicals they used us for their own political purposes. They smashed our unions whenever their policy decided it would be strategic to do so. I think the Populists have the right idea: a people's party, electing its own congressmen to put through favorable legislation, and oversee the people's proper representation in the federal courts."

Berger hauled a straight-backed chair across the floor, then sat leaning against its back, his arms clenched over the wooden top.

"Listen to me, Gene, that's like cutting off a dog's tail a piece at a time so as to spare him the pain of losing his whole tail at one clip. The world has moved slowly from dynastic slavery up through feudalism and serfdom and into capitalism. Capitalism has served a valuable purpose: it has developed the land, built the great machinery of production. But by its own processes it has outworn itself, Gene, by overthrowing its basic premise of competition in favor of vast interlocking trusts. The industrialists and bankers have created a commonwealth for their own profit! There is but one deliverance of the rule of the people by capitalism, and that is the rule of capitalism by the people. If we are to remain a politi-

cally free people, we must take possession of the country's resources, its production machinery."

Gene turned sharply and faced Berger, looking through the
narrow steel-rimmed glasses into the younger man's deep
brown eyes.

"I believe in non-violence, and if I ever started working for
your socialism . . ."

Berger stared fixedly at Gene.

"My dear friend, we know that you can kill tyrants and
scare individuals with dynamite and bullets, but you cannot
develop a system that way. We know that an overthrow
achieved by force and violence breeds dictators, and that dictators promote subjugation, never liberty. As long as we are
in the minority, we have no right to enforce our opinions
upon an unwilling majority. But we want to convert that majority."

Gene sat down and began sharpening lead pencils with the
small blade of his knife.

"Victor, what are the owners of our industries going to say
to all this? Surely you don't think the Goulds and the Armours, the Morgans, the Hills and Pullmans are going to let
you expropriate their holdings?"

Berger dove into his portfolio. "Frederick Engels wrote
only last year: 'We do not consider the indemnity of the pro-
prietors as an impossibility.' Even Karl Kautsky, the most
radical theorist of the socialists, says: 'There are a number of
reasons which indicate that a proletarian regime will seek the
road of compensation and payment of the capitalists and
landowners.' "

Whimsically Gene replied, "That settles half the problem.
You socialists will not try to take their property at the point of
a gun. But suppose they don't want to be bought out, what
then? Do you force them to sell? You know as well as I what
will result: bloodshed and destruction."

"Not if we have educated the majority of the people!"

"No, Victor. We have got to build our own political party
and work inside the framework of the existing system. When
the unions have become so strong that no federal court can
destroy them . . ."

Berger rose, put his arm about Gene's shoulder for a moment, then murmured, "Ah, Gene, I thought you were ready!
I thought you had learned your lesson. But I am a patient
man. I will come back."

Berger kept his word: he came back, not in the flesh, but
in the argument, in the dark quiet hours of the night when

the lint sifted away from the discussion and the woven fabric remained.

Berger had left behind him a representative library of socialist pamphleteers, Ferdinand Lassalle, Karl Marx, Karl Kautsky, Frederick Engels, Emile Vandervelde, Wilhelm Liebknecht. In his trade-union practices Gene had always resisted the idea that the European pattern could be used as a model for thinking in America. After going through the story of European socialism he came back eagerly to the domestic scene, reading with high excitement Edward Bellamy's *Looking Backward,* Henry Demarest Lloyd's newly published *Wealth against Commonwealth,* Maybell's *Civilization Civilized, The Human Drift* by Gillette and *Better Days* by Fitch. Looking at America through this tele-microscope, he evolved a picture of contemporary society as a pyramid, the tens of millions of have-nothings forming the base, the priests of high finance the apex. It seemed senseless that in the year 1895 eighty per cent of society should be composed of underprivileged humans, living in a state of ignorance and anxiety and semistarvation. It did not even add up to good economics. If the industrialists could make millions out of a civilization which deprived the majority of its people of the products their labor created, then why would there not be billions for the owners if every American were able to purchase the goods produced? And if he, head of the largest single union in America, could be dumped unceremoniously into jail, how defenseless was the individual American with no organization behind him?

Slowly, carefully, he came to the conclusion that the world based upon man's enslavement of man had to be reconstructed if the festering fear at the center of men's souls was to be eliminated. For it was fear which had created the rapacious man, gobbling up all he could against tomorrow's drought; fear, which had created the cruel man, destroying others so there would be more of the world's goods left for himself; fear, which had created the craven man, who dared not think or act lest he offend the established morality; fear, which had created the bitter man, hating God, nature, humanity; fear, which had created the confused man, sensing that there is light and warmth but ever stumbling over man-made obstacles; fear, which had created the blind man, living out his days in the darkness of prejudice, intolerance, ignorance.

It was not necessary for man to believe that his breadbasket would always be full, only that in lean times all men would fare alike. The issue was joined, plain for everyone to see: either men protected each other, or they destroyed each other on the sword of fear.

All men were brothers. Would they ever know it?

— 10 —

The last half of his term passed quickly. After breakfast he took a brisk walk, saying good morning to the early Woodstock risers, receiving greetings in return. A week before his release Kate announced her plans.

"Eugene, if you won't be too lonesome these last days I think I ought to prepare the house for your return. I left it in . . . well, you would be ashamed of me, Eugene. I just threw some things into my valise and came to you. I wouldn't want you to find the house in that condition; I'd like to make everything beautiful and comfortable."

Gene said that her plan was a wise one. Mrs. Eckert walked her to the station.

The night before his release he was sitting at the table in the corridor reading Eli's *Political Economy* under the central lamp, when Sheriff Eckert came in.

"Mr. Debs, you have a visitor, a Mrs. Harkness. I told her I didn't know . . ."

Gloria in Woodstock! Why had she come?

"Mrs. Harkness is a childhood friend, from Terre Haute."

He stood with his eyes fastened on the iron door through which she must come. She was dressed in black, with a heavy black veil before her face. Sheriff Eckert closed the door behind him. They took a few steps toward each other, then stood in silence. He saw nothing of her face through the veil, only the glow of her eyes.

"What a poor host I am, Gloria; every time you come visiting, I receive you in jail."

He went to her side, took her by the arm and led her to the wooden table. He drew up a chair opposite and sat gazing at her intently. He knew there was something wrong, and that it was connected with her black dress and black coat, her black hat and veil. When he spoke again it was in the hope that he might make them both more comfortable.

"You are a good prophet, Gloria; there have been no bars. For the first time I have achieved real freedom. We are behind the bars in front of our minds, Gloria, and as we grow older they become more numerous, harder to see through. But now they have been dissolved, and I can see for miles and for years ahead of me."

Gloria did not reply directly, but said in a soft voice:

"I think I came in the hope of hearing you say something

like this, Gene; in the hope that there would be no rancor in
your heart against . . . against those who . . ."

A perception began to grow at the back of his mind.

"I couldn't bear to think that you held your imprisonment
against him. He meant you no harm, Gene. There was nothing personal in his case against you."

"Gloria, has something happened to your husband?"

She lowered her head so that he could see only the top of
her black hat. Her voice was so low that he could hardly be
certain he heard her aright.

"Ned is dead, Gene. The funeral was this morning."

For a moment he could not think, let alone answer. Finally
he managed to ask stumblingly, "But how? He was so strong,
so well . . ."

"A hunting accident. The first vacation he had taken in
years. One of his friends . . . He was killed instantly."

He wanted to take her in his arms and comfort her, but he
could not rise from his chair. Neither could he utter any of
the formalities of condolence that came halfway to his lips.
Gloria lifted her veil, placing it back on her hat. Her eyes
were more beautiful than he had ever known them.

"Ned was a good man, Gene, always kind and gentle with
me and the two girls. He hurt no one, he had no enemies. I
couldn't think of him lying in his grave with someone . . .
hating his memory."

"Oh no, Gloria," he protested, disturbed that she should
believe him guilty of rancor; "no, I don't hate him. Not an
hour, not a moment has passed since that trial that I haven't
vowed to fight the General Managers' Association, and its
corrupt hold over the courts, but your husband was just
doing his job."

"Then you forgive him, Gene?"

"There is nothing to forgive. Ned Harkness derived no personal gratification from my troubles."

The tears came into her eyes as she murmured:

"Oh, you must believe that! His daughters loved him,
Gene; I loved him; his friends were fond of him. If you can
think of him with kindness, then he has harmed no one; he
will rest more quietly that way, and so will I."

She gave him a grateful smile, then slipped her hand into
his.

"It would be only human for you to be bitter, Gene. You
were innocent, and you should have been vindicated in that
court."

He got up, walked to the window to hide the grimace of
pain that swept his features as he recalled his wife's avowal:

"Then it was right that I should have suffered doubly, for someone had to be punished." He heard Gloria saying:

"It was strange for me to watch that trial, Gene. You were facing years in a federal penitentiary, yet there was no fear in you. But my husband was frightened."

Astonished, he could only cry out, "Frightened? But of what?"

With pity in her voice, she answered:

"Ned came of a poor family. The ugly kind of poverty, Gene; he was raised in one of those miserable hovels that border the iron foundries. He grew up ragged, starved. His father was a laborer, working an eighty-hour week at the furnaces. Ned's name wasn't even Harkness; his father was a Czech: Jan Plavachek."

"Then all the more reason for him to have been on our side! We were only trying to help people like his father, and himself, when he was hungry and ragged."

"He knew that, Gene. But if you could have felt his fear that someday he might be forced back into that wretchedness . . ."

Ah yes, thought Gene, our friend fear: born in our blood, carried in our bone.

"It wasn't only the physical deprivation that frightened him, it was the humiliation of poverty. That's why he was dissatisfied with twenty thousand a year the moment he had it, and yearned for thirty thousand, and then when he had thirty thousand, relentlessly pursued forty thousand. He needed to reassure himself constantly."

"And you, Gloria?"

"Gene, I never wanted money or an elaborate home. All I ever wanted was love, and laughter, and children."

He sat with his head down, the years and memories flooding upon him. Kate would have been happy with Ned Harkness. While he . . .

He looked up. Gloria had gone.

Theodore arrived the following morning with a new black suit, and a trunk in which to ship the six months' accumulation of papers, books and correspondence. Gene heard Sheriff Eckert's footsteps in the corridor; then the door opened.

"Mr. Debs," said the sheriff, "you are now a free man."

At luncheon Gene presented the sheriff and his wife with the gifts which Theodore had brought from Chicago. At one o'clock he and Theodore went back into the jail corridor to finish packing the books and papers. Around midafternoon Gene remarked:

"Better keep your eyes on your watch, Theo. We don't want to miss that five o'clock train."

Theodore smiled.

"I don't think we'll miss it."

The trip to Chicago was exciting; it was good to feel wheels over rails again. The train pulled into the Wells Street station. A hard rain was falling. As the train stopped a cry went up. The platform was a mass of cheering, waving people, and beyond them the stairs leading down to the station were jammed solidly with more pushing, jostling, shouting, grinning friends. Outside in the rain-swept streets, standing in mud and puddles of water, was the most enormous throng he had ever seen. There was a lump in his throat, and he could not speak. He was hoisted to the shoulders of strapping workmen, who tried to make their way down the platform.

"Move down the stairs! We want to come out!"

But the people below on the street and in the station wanted to come in, to see Gene, to touch him, to speak to him. All movement was impossible. Finally the police pushed their way through the throng and cleared a small path.

Feeling the hot, sentimental tears which always pushed hard behind his eyelids at such moments, he persuaded his friends to set him on his feet. Hundreds of hands rose up to shake his, thousands of voices cried out their greetings.

After some twenty minutes he was at the entrance of the station, where six white horses were hitched up to a carriage, bedecked with banners and placards. The horses were wet and bedraggled, but not so the spirit of the crowd, which cried out for him to get up on the seat of the carriage so that everyone could see him.

"If the rest walk, I walk," he called.

The Chicago police had denied the unions a permit to parade, but there was nothing illegal in going to the station to welcome home a friend. The enormous crowd now marched down to the armory of Battery D. The armory held only five thousand people; the remainder milled about in the streets. Gene found Victor Berger on the platform to welcome him, and a woman delegate from the Shoe Operatives' Protective Union who presented him with a bouquet of chrysanthemums.

He stepped to the front of the platform, the chrysanthemums in his arms. The audience became quiet.

He gazed into the faces below him, excited, happy at the reception. And there came to him the realization that this demonstration was not a personal triumph, but an indication of mankind's will to freedom; their salute to brotherhood. In some remote corner of his spirit he prayed:

May I never fail them, or myself!

— 11 —

From the moment he swung up the steps and saw that the usually locked front door was wide open, he knew that something important was happening. It was not merely that the many windows were also open, letting in the cool fragrant air. It was even something more than the fresh flowers filling every vase in the living room. As he walked into the dining room and saw that the big table had been pulled out, the four auxiliary leaves inserted, and places set for some twenty guests, he knew that, for the first time since he and Kate had walked up those stone steps some six years before, the Debses were holding open house.

He pushed the swinging door into the kitchen and stood gazing at his wife, who was triumphantly taking a turkey out of the big oven, her dress covered with a spotless long-sleeved apron. Her eyes were full of the happiness of the moment; she was talking in German to a young immigrant girl. Suddenly she sensed his presence. She turned her head, burst into a radiant smile, put her arms around his neck, and kissed him warmly on the mouth. When at last they could speak, he said:

"I see you have killed the fatted calf."

"I wanted you to have a welcome-home party, Eugene. I invited your whole family and mine. There will be about twenty-six to dinner, and I must have sent out at least a hundred invitations for people to come in for dessert."

Her eyes were clear and strong. How far she had come since the day he left for the trial! Then she had considered that he was going to his disgrace and doom, and now she was backing him with her loyalty and love.

Kate opened the oven again, took out the casseroles of sweet potatoes, set them on doilies covering her silver platters. He wanted to call out, Oh no, Kate, not so soon; they will get cold. Instead he murmured, "Kate, can you keep a secret? I mean, from the newspaper reporters?"

"I'll try, Eugene."

"I love you very much, Mrs. Debs."

The dinner party was a wonderful success. Mary's husband, Ernst, who had grown consistently colder to Gene the deeper he got into unionism, and who had remained silent throughout the trial and imprisonment, was overheard telling two of Kate's rich half brothers that after all every man makes mistakes, and Gene had undoubtedly learned his lesson. Kate had generously seated Daisy and Daniel on either side of their son; it was the first time they had been invited for dinner in several years. They were so choked up by Gene's homecoming, and this incredible hospitality, that they could hardly touch their food. Under the brilliant glare of the dining-room candelabra, Gene saw how white-haired and thin they had grown, and he understood that there were no troubles of the children which did not inflict grievous wounds on the parents; that Kate was not the only one who had paid a price for being related to him. Theodore found it difficult to take his eyes off his brother; he had missed him sorely the past six months. Gertrude was too shy, after having been precluded from this house for three years, to do anything more than make a pretense of eating.

He slept late the next morning; when he went down to the kitchen he found that Kate had prepared his favorite breakfast: hot cakes and sausages and biscuits. She also announced self-consciously that Theodore would be along in a few minutes to take their walk through the woods.

The trees were on fire with deep autumnal colorings. Gene plucked brittle leaves from the plants and bushes, exclaiming over the purple and burnt-orange colorings.

"Theo, these trails are in bad shape. I see you haven't been using them."

"Not since you went away, Gene; walking is not fun alone."

They came to a clearing brilliantly lighted and warmed by the overhead sun. The two men dropped down into the grass, their long bodies stretched out, Gene lying on his back with his hands under his head, gazing up at the cloud-tufted sky, Theodore leaning on one elbow.

Gene's thoughts went to his immediate problem.

"What condition are the books in, pard?"

"Bad, my boy. We're twelve thousand dollars in debt."

"Twelve thousand, eh? That's the same amount the Brotherhood of Locomotive Firemen owed when we took over."

"But there is one unfortunate difference, Gene: you were determined to put the Locomotive Firemen back on their feet."

"And you think I consider the American Railway Union dead?"

Theodore remained silent.

"How long has it been since you took any salary?"

"About four months."

"What have you been living on, ozone?"

"Gertrude is economical."

Gene sat up and pulled his knees sharply under his chin.

"You know, Theo, I've never in my life spoken for money. But I've got to pay back that twelve thousand dollars. Fred Pelham, manager of the Redpath Lecture Bureau, said he can book me every night for a number of months. Susan B. Anthony told me years ago that she went lecturing to earn back the ten thousand dollars her newspaper had gone in debt."

"A man has to earn a living as best he can, Gene. So far you have only talked to unions; maybe it would be a good thing to get out and meet the general public, find out what they are thinking."

"My dear old pard," murmured Gene with a smile. "One sentence from you and I am convinced."

Theodore grunted, rolled over and leaned forward.

"And would you mind giving an extra lecture or two with me as the beneficiary? Gertrude says I'm going to be a family man, come spring, and any niece or nephew of yours is sure to have a large and expensive appetite."

"Why, Theo, you old devil. You beat me to it, and I had all these years' head start." He jumped up. "Come on, let's go to your house, I want to kiss Gertrude."

When he arrived home he again found the door wide open, the house thronged with his old friends, mostly the railroaders with whom he had grown up and worked these past twenty years. Kate and her flaxen-haired German girl were bringing in trays of hot coffee and *Käsekuchen*. She moved serenely through the rooms, offering hospitality, food and drink. When she passed him in the library without noticing he was there, he put his arms about her from behind and kissed her low on her neck.

"Kate," he whispered, "it's like being on a honeymoon."

She seemed both doubtful and pleased about his plan for a lecture tour. The doubt emerged first.

"Gene, who will come to listen to you?"

"Well, I don't know, people."

"But what have you to tell them that they'll want to hear?"

"The story of everything that happened to me."

"But, darling, they know what happened to you."

Indulgently he replied, "Americans are funny: they'll go to listen to any man whose name and face have been in the newspapers."

"You mean, famous people?"

"Yes." He smiled. "Or infamous people."

"Eugene, I'm afraid you'll go from one town to another, wear yourself out traveling, and then there won't be enough money to pay your expenses."

He thought, She knows that she wouldn't go to hear such a person as myself, so why should anyone else? Aloud he said, "But I'm not taking any risk, Kate. The Redpath Bureau is guaranteeing me seventy-five dollars to a hundred and a quarter for each performance, depending on how far I have to travel."

She gazed at him with sheer incredulity, unable to decide whether he was telling an untruth or someone was trying to cheat him. He went to his desk, took out the contract with the Redpath Bureau, and showed her the sum of money involved.

"This is a legal contract, Kate; the Bureau has bonded itself to pay me for so many appearances."

The sight of the contract brought Kate back to solid ground. She did not know how it had happened, she was convinced that somebody was going to lose a lot of money, but evidently it was not going to be her husband.

"That's just fine, Eugene. I haven't wanted to worry you about money. I've been very good about it, haven't I?"

"Yes, Kate, you've been wonderful."

"But this past year has been very hard on me; I've had to eat into capital. Your lecture money will pay that back and put us several thousand dollars ahead."

Sadly he said, "Kate, this money is not for us."

"Not for us? But you signed the contract, Eugene."

"I'll get the money all right, but you see, the American Railway Union is twelve thousand dollars in debt. The only reason I'm going out to lecture is to pay back that debt."

Kate digested this intelligence carefully.

"What you mean, Eugene, is that the American Railway Union is bankrupt?"

"I suppose you could call it that."

"Then you don't have to pay the debts, Eugene! The law says that when a business goes bankrupt it's no longer responsible for what it owes."

"But we borrowed this money from people who trusted us, Kate, old friends like Major Smith."

Excitedly she said, "You have no legal obligations whatever!"

He tackled her resistance tangentially.

"Kate Metzel, I am surprised! You come from a wonderful business family, and yet you don't realize that a man must not destroy his credit. I have many years ahead of me, and no one knows how many new ventures I might want to start. If I have once gone bankrupt . . ."

"Nonsense, Eugene, some of the most successful men of America have founded their fortunes on a bankruptcy."

"I'm not trying to found a fortune, Kate. I can't have people saying that the first industrial union in America not only failed, but went to the wall owing its friends a considerable sum of money."

Kate ventured a tiny smile.

"Since you are so anxious to protect your credit, don't you think you ought to protect mine too? My funds are getting pretty low. You wouldn't want Kate Metzel to go bankrupt and embarrass the entire Metzel family?"

Grateful for the humorous approach, he exclaimed, "Kate, you're right! I'll use two thirds of the contract to pay off the American Railway Union debt, and the other third goes to you."

"Half would be fairer," she said, "but under the circumstances I'll settle for a third."

— 12 —

Once again he was riding the rails; once again the rhythmic movement was pulsing through his long lean body: clackety-clack, clackety-clack, click-clack, click-clack: Milwaukee, Grand Rapids, Detroit, Buffalo, Toledo, Cleveland; clackety-clack, clackety-clack, click-clack, click-clack: Lima, Evansville, Washington, East St. Louis, Marion, Atlanta, Macon, Athens, Augusta, Charleston, Savannah, Birmingham. Now there was money coming in from the lectures, money to be spent for comfortable Pullman berths so he could sleep between towns, but he would not patronize George Pullman, and so he sat up all night in coaches, his elbow on the window sill, chin and cheek grasped in his long, bony fingers, his overcoat collar turned up against the cold, his hat pulled down over his eyes to shut out the light.

Everywhere he went the pattern was the same: throngs of people filled the halls, consumed avidly his stories of the strike, the violence, the imprisonment, applauded heartily when he demanded that the Constitution be recast so as to admit the initiative and referendum, when he maintained that laboring people had to become politically powerful if they were to make any advances and if the federal government were to be rescued from the corporations. They applauded when he stated Susan B. Anthony's case for women's suffrage, even applauded when he stood with one leg over the footlight trough, leaning forward from the waist with his great arm and long finger extended, telling them that the trade union could go only so far, that America could never achieve its great potential for civilization until the profit system was modified.

Financially he was doing well; he had been able to send several thousand dollars to Theodore, and each week he enclosed a large money order with his letter to Kate. But when he went into the railroad yards, trying to locate the members of the American Railway Union, he learned that they had been fired and black-listed, hounded out of the railroad centers and the railroad industry. Some of the more skilled members had been kept on by individual managers; these he brought together in small union meetings, urging them to remain faithful to the American Railway Union, to rebuild their ranks. But within a matter of weeks even these skeletal meetings had to be abandoned. The union meetings were being attended by private detectives hired from the Pinkerton Agency, and every last man, no matter how valuable, was fired the next day, barred throughout the railroad empire.

He returned home in the spring, physically exhausted and so tired mentally that he could not speak without stuttering. His next tour was not scheduled until the fall. Kate was determined that he should rest and relax during the coming months.

By the beginning of summer he was well again. He resumed his early morning walks with Theodore in the woods. He did miss one night's sleep, when Gertrude's baby was born. He and Theodore had several drinks just before dawn to toast the beautiful little Marguerite.

He and Kate were happy together. She pampered him until the flesh was back on his shoulders and chest, between his bony ribs and hollowed-out cheeks. The hours they enjoyed most were the quiet ones in the library after dinner, when they were alone together and all the world was locked out. He sat smoking his pipe, reading *Huckleberry Finn* and laughing aloud at the boisterous humor. Kate sat in her favorite chair, her endlessly busy fingers working on a new piece of petit point for one of the parlor chairs.

Then it came time to tell his wife that he now believed in the philosophy of socialism.

With the exception of the small group of Germans who had formed the Socialist Labor party in New York City, and centered their activities around a German-language newspaper, there was as yet in America no socialist party, no movement, no organization, no cause. There were just a few scattered men and women, unconnected except by their common interest, who believed that the utilization of the vast American wealth for communal consumption rather than individual profit could produce a saner, more just and more durable culture.

He marshaled quiet arguments which he hoped would reassure her, if not by their content, then at least by their manner, that his new work would cause no change in their way of life; that he would not bring socialism or socialists into her home, any more than he had unionism or unionists; that through his lectures and writings on the subject he would soon be earning a good living for them. She would have no cause to worry about the reverberations of his change in faith: socialism was merely an educative movement, a humanistic philosophy, a faith in mankind's potential for freedom, a highly spiritual economic religion. He would assure her that socialists were revolutionaries only in the historical sense.

He looked up from the book he was reading.

"Kate, there is something I want to tell you."

He spoke in his quietest and most intimate tone, reviewed for her the background of his work with the labor unions, showing her how he had been brought to a dead end. He characterized the plight of the mass of American workers who were buffeted by every economic storm. Slowly he argued his way into socialism, which to him meant the public ownership of the land, of the minerals and oil which lay below the surface of the earth and the forests which stretched above it; of the factories, machinery and scientific skill for the production of goods, and the replacement of production for profit by production for mankind's well-being, with every producer: farmer, mechanic, clerk, doctor, paid according to the value of his contribution, but no man left unemployed, unwanted, unclothed, unfed. He stressed that his philosophy was American in character and method, that it set out to achieve its ends by full legal means, that he was not asking for equal distribution of wealth, but for the right of every man to work and to share in the full benefits of that work. He said he was a socialist because it promoted an opportunity for better living and greater liberty for all mankind.

She offered no objections; she did not break in, argue, contradict, ridicule or deny the truth of anything he said. The only effect upon her that he could notice was that her lids were stretching higher and higher over her eyes. When finally he reached the point where he had to make it clear that he was determined to devote the rest of his life to the cause, Kate's teeth began to chatter, she shook as though in a seizure, her eyes rolled upward to the far corners of their sockets.

Then she fell onto the floor in a dead faint.

BOOK FIVE

NO PEACE IN PARADISE

KATE LAY UNCONSCIOUS FOR THIRTY-SIX HOURS, HER HALF
sisters keeping vigil by her bedside, Daisy and Daniel remaining downstairs with Gene. Gene could hold nothing on his
stomach, not even Daisy's black coffee. He had been prepared to face any possible resistance on Kate's part: tears, accusations, arguments, but how could he justify prostrating his
wife? She had been so kind to him these past months, sacrificed her convictions to be at his side in jail, thrown open his
home to his associates. Fate was cruel to Katherine Metzel:
no matter how far she came, or at what personal cost, it was
never far enough: during the months of her struggle to reach
her husband's side, he had been undergoing his own struggle
and had reached some new and hostile horizon.

Dr. Reinche, the Metzel family physician, summoned Gene
to Kate's bedroom, where the two men sat on either side of
the bed. Dr. August Reinche was known among his patients
as a squarehead, an impolite but accurate description. He had
thick stubby fingers and was without small talk, yet he won
respect by his insistence upon bludgeoning people back to
health.

The doctor said, "You say that your wife was in *goot*
health *aber* that she suddenly fall on the floor while you talk.
Tell to me all what to Kate happened."

Hating himself for his cowardice in not having revealed
the truth at once, Gene murmured, his eyes small and red,
"I'm the one who made my wife ill. I told her that I had be-

come a socialist; that I was going to spend the rest of my life working for the cause."

"*Dummkopf!*" exploded Dr. Reinche. "You tell a Metzel that you go for socialism in America, *aber* when she falls into faint, you do not understand! People only part of the time get sick from hemorrhages or germs. More times sickness comes from ideas we can't see under a microscope. Kate is not sick in the body *aber* here up in the head." Dr. Reinche excitedly struck his head with a hard glancing blow of his palm. "Look at your wife, Mr. Debs. When she wakes she must face the fact she is married to a socialist. That is worse for Kate Metzel than a scabrous second-story man to find in her bed."

Gene sat with his head in his hands, wretched. Try as he might he could think of nothing to think.

"As long as socialism in this house is, your wife will be ill. Stand over her and shout, 'I have not meant it! I am not socialist!' And well will she be again."

"She hated unions almost as badly when we were first married. . . ."

The doctor took off his gold-rimmed spectacles and waved them across Gene's face.

"To a Metzel, labor unions are bad, they interfere with *goot* business, *aber* they don't challenge the right of business to live. To a Metzel socialism to unionism is like consumption to a head cold."

Brusquely he picked up his bag and left the room, his heavy steps pounding down the stairway, then down the silent street.

All night Gene sat by his wife, his bony elbows on his bony knees, watching her pale, lifeless face as it lay on the pillow. Was he going to become another of those misguided wretches who set out to reform the world, leaving behind him cruelty and chaos in his own family? Certainly his first obligation was not to abstract causes, but to the one person for whom he had taken responsibility, whom he had promised to love, cherish and protect?

But what would he do and where would he go if he abandoned socialism? What was left of his own life? He did not want to limp through the rest of his days, sick in spirit and dead in heart because he had found a road to freedom, and had then failed to follow it.

Shortly after dawn Kate opened her eyes. He brushed her hair back from her brow, spoke quiet words of comfort, went down into the kitchen to make her a cup of tea. She accepted the tea, wordlessly.

He continued to sleep in the adjoining back bedroom

where he could hear her during the night if she wanted anything. The room was drab and cold, for it faced the freezing winds whirling down from the north. Kate had never furnished it; the narrow cot reminded him all too vividly of Woodstock.

By the end of the week she seemed back to normal, and undertook her household duties.

Then a blinding snowstorm struck Terre Haute. Cold seeped through the window cracks of the rear bedroom. Gene asked Kate if it was all right for him to move back into their bedroom. She did not reply. When he returned from his office late that evening he found that she had moved the last of his belongings out of her bedroom.

He stood in the cold, cheerless rear room, gazing at his nightgown, robe and slippers on the cot. Kate was not putting him out or repudiating him as a person: it was his beliefs with which she could have no intercourse.

He closed his eyes, swaying slightly to the movement of the train beneath him: clackety-clack, clackety-clack, click-clack, click-clack. From now on this cubicle would be his confine of the house; the rest would be Kate's.

Cold, heartsick, forlorn, he threw himself down on the narrow cot, his face in the pillow.

— 2 —

Theodore sat in a tiny room downtown trying to run the *Railway Times,* struggling to keep it alive for some two thousand die-hard survivors of the union. Gene asked himself, How the devil has he managed to get the paper out? And what has he been living on? There can't be enough money coming into that office to feed a family of birds.

He climbed into his heavy overcoat, pulled his hat down over his ears and walked through the heavy snow toward Theodore's office. During all these years they had been as close in understanding as any two humans could be; he had always known that no matter how greatly he erred Theodore would stand by him. Now suspended between two points in time, with the American Railway Union dead but not yet interred, and socialism conceived but not yet born, he had to admit to himself that his work and his years added up to little but failure.

The *Railway Times* headquarters was a third-floor cubbyhole, its only attractive feature the four dollars a month rent. In it there was space for Theodore, his desk and the file. When Gene pushed open the door it hit the desk, and he had to edge sideways to close the door behind him. Theodore was correcting galleys.

"Theo, can I have a word with you?"

Without looking up, Theodore replied, "I have no time for social dallying right now, son, the printer's waiting for this copy."

"Then let him wait, this is important."

Theodore tossed his pencil onto the desk and looked up, unspeaking.

"I have been letting you run this without any help from me," said Gene. "I haven't even had the decency to ask whether or not you are taking in enough money to eat."

"I haven't asked that question myself," replied Theodore quietly. "Gertrude is the only one who knows."

A tiny smile came to Gene's lips.

"Frankly I wasn't worried about your breadbasket; I know its elasticity. But I am concerned about your future, Theo. Things have happened to me, some of them pretty drastic; the sum total of what I have lived through has converted me to socialism. But you have always been more practical than I, Theo; I don't recall your saying anything against socialism, nor do I remember your making a declaration in its favor. In short . . ."

". . . you are giving me a chance to declare myself."

"That's right."

"You walked all the way down here in the snow just to tell me that if I don't approve of socialism I don't have to throw in with you?" Theodore pulled his long, lean frame up out of the rickety swivel chair, pushed a mess of exchange newspapers aside, then perched on the edge of the desk and gazed into his brother's grayblue eyes. His voice was low and ruminative. "It is true I didn't spend weeks in the Chicago jail, nor was I locked up in Woodstock for six months. Neither have the newspapers called me incendiary or an evil creature plotting the downfall of my own country. Nevertheless I came out of your experiences a socialist. Does that mean I am abjectly following or echoing you?"

His insides warming slowly, Gene could only murmur, "It would be the first time."

"I didn't make any great speeches about how I suffered when you were in jail; but I lived through that strike too, I watched the federal troops and the General Managers' Association's hired thugs break up the union. I knew why Victor Berger visited you, so I read the same books you were reading . . ."

"And if you disagreed with me, you would take to the tall and uncut?"

"Of course I would, Gene. Do you think I'm a hopeless idiot?"

"Yes, and in addition, the worst liar in Terre Haute."

Theodore swung in his swivel chair so that his eyes no longer met Gene's.

"Anyway, it is an abstract question. As it happens, I agree with you. So there is no problem."

"My dear old pard," Gene murmured, "you are just a no-good sentimental Frenchman and no one will ever beat any sense into your head."

"Suppose you go waste somebody else's time," replied Theodore, "and give me a chance to send this paper to bed."

Gene paid no attention to him.

"Do you remember that day, Theo, when you helped me clean out the storage room behind the grocery, and white-wash the union meeting hall? We weren't respectable, we weren't wanted, but with the passage of time we built a union and became so prosperous that we occupied the entire floor above Riley McKeen's bank."

"That practically made us bankers, too."

"It took us twenty years to end up, not only in jail, which is bad enough, but in debt, which is worse. Now we have to begin all over again: penniless, ignored, feared . . ."

There was a heavy knock on the door, which was pushed open and hit Gene in the back. Ed Boyce, president of the Western Federation of Miners, stuck his head in and murmured with an apologetic grin, "Did I smack somebody?"

"Oh no," replied Gene, "you just buried your pick in me, that's all. Come in, Ed."

Boyce squeezed his way in past the door and the room became crowded with the three men; Boyce was tall, though spare, a fighting Irishman dressed in respectable broadcloth.

"How is the strike going, Ed?" asked Theodore.

"There hasn't been a man jack go down into those mines for six months. But the managers have a union of their own, and they've got a million dollars left for every one we started with." His black eyes were smoldering. "Gene, you've got to come out and help us, the men are beginning to weaken."

Gene took a deep breath before answering.

"Ed, the day the strike is over, I will be on hand with my prayer book and sermon. But if I went out there and talked now, they would label your strike socialism, and that would hurt you."

Boyce pushed away this argument with a rough sweep of his hand.

"Gene, you got a family doctor?"

"Sure, Dr. Reinche."

"Would he refuse to come see you when you were sick?"

"No."

"Then you got no right to refuse us; our members are sick over the strike, and our union may die."

Gene slipped past the opposite edge of the desk and went to the window, staring out at the brown snow slush in the gutters, remembering his own death struggle with the Railroad Managers' Association.

"The interesting thing about our family doctor, Ed, is that he is never satisfied with a cure; he keeps pursuing the cause of the illness even if he doesn't catch up with it for years. I'll go out to Colorado with you, Ed, but winning that strike isn't going to do the boys any permanent good. Samuel Gompers says there is no basic disturbance in the body politic, that the patient is completely well and normal and that all he needs is sufficient food and drink to keep up his strength. But I say there is a disease eating at our vitals. I know its manifestations: fear, insecurity; I know its contagion centers: trusts, managers' associations."

The Rio Grande Depot in Leadville and the streets beyond were filled with some three thousand miners, railroaders and members of the Leadville trades assembly. The townspeople and the merchants, who were paralyzed by the strike, were already seated in the Western Opera House. On the stage Gene was silhouetted against a solid mass of eager faces; there was no room for him to move up and down while he spoke.

The applause that had greeted his entrance was sharp and short. Within a matter of seconds he had plunged into his analysis of the seven-month-old conflict; deplored the need for strikes, but declared that when it became a choice between a strike and degradation, then he was in favor of a strike because there was a condition more to be feared than being out of employment, and that was when the workers submitted to being stripped of their manhood and independence.

He told of the vast army of three million men in America who were tramps, tramps because they could find no employment at home and had gone on the road to seek a few dollars for their families; mendicants created by a machine system which steadily threw men out of work through no fault of their own. He quoted Christ, who had said, "The foxes have holes, and the birds of the air have nests, but the Son of Man hath not where to lay his head."

"This is because we have deified the dollar in this country," cried Gene. "We call it the Almighty Dollar as though it were a synonym for Almighty God; the standard by which we measure man's success or failure is the dollar. I believe that American manhood and womanhood are of infinitely more importance. A few people in this country have vastly too much and the masses of the people are being subjected to impoverishment; I believe there is something radically wrong with a system under which these injustices are possible. The time is not far distant when this system will be abolished. Workingmen are beginning to think; they will soon begin to act."

At the end of two hours he was exhausted, but the audience had no intention of letting him go. The crowd was eager for knowledge, and people began clambering to their feet to ask questions:

"Is it possible that the mines can ever be owned by the miners? Does the government seize them, or do we buy them? If we buy them, where in tarnation do we get the money? Who gets the best jobs after everybody is an owner? Who decides how long we work, for how much?"

The townspeople also threw steel-barbed inquiries.

"I own a grocery store: what happens to me under socialism?" "I'm a barber: who tells me what chins I've got to scrape?" "I am a schoolteacher: who tells me what I have to teach?" "I run a real estate office: does socialism plan to own all the land, and if so, where do I go to make a living?" "I'm a Western Union operator: will socialism force me to stick to my job for the rest of my life?"

It was seven o'clock before he got back to his hotel. He threw himself across the bed. Early the next morning Ed Boyce burst in with a triumphant expression on his face.

"Gene, you old turkey gobbler, Governor Adams wants you to come to a conference at the Hotel Vendome. The mine managers are there: they've agreed to arbitrate at last!"

Traveling back to Terre Haute in the coach, Gene had an opportunity to review the tumultuous happenings in Leadville. He was happy to have helped secure a compromise settlement of the strike, yet he knew that he had failed abjectly when the people had asked him specific questions about socialism. He had been able to offer only generalizations and theories; these hard-bitten people with the lines of hunger etched deep in their faces had known you could not operate a single mine, let alone all of society, on theory. In order to create the new society for which he was pleading, they would have to have an architectural plan and an engineer's working drawings. He had felt like a child caught fabricating a fantastic story before a group of adults, and he vowed that his next task would be to draw up a blueprint for socialist America. He was glad that he had complete time and freedom ahead, months in which he could sit at his desk, ask himself questions, unrelentingly pursue the answers.

— 3 —

For years Gene had passed the old Weston house on his way to see Daisy and Daniel, noting that the people who had bought it were letting it run down. But this Sunday something unusual was happening: from a full block down the street he could see that carpenters and painters had been at work; on the side of each set of windows were new shutters, painted a fireman's red. When he reached the front door he found it standing wide open. The wall between the living-room windows had been torn out and plate glass put in its place.

Then he heard a woman's voice. He walked slowly up the front steps and went a little way into the hall. From the kitchen he heard voices coming closer. The woman stopped short. They stood gazing at each other, the mass of broken plaster and sawed-off planks across the twisting paths of their lives.

"Welcome, Gene."

They came the few intermediary steps to each other, then gripped each other's hands hard.

"Gloria, this is a surprise!"

Happy laughter tinkled through the open spaces of the hallway.

"Why should you be surprised to see me in Terre Haute? I never liked Chicago. I bought back our old home, Gene, just as I always planned I would."

He let go of one hand.

"But why are you tearing the place down? There won't be anything left."

"Oh yes, there will: I am simply taking out walls and throwing all the little rooms into big rooms. Then I'm putting in more windows for sun and light. Everything will be gay and cheerful. You remember how Mother used to have chintz when everyone else was hanging velours draperies? And how she covered the muddy brown plush chairs with flowered prints?"

"Of course I remember, Gloria. It was the happiest house I have ever been in."

She flashed him a grateful smile.

"That's what it's going to be all over again, Gene. We are putting in an enormous fireplace; anybody can walk right into the kitchen and help himself to anything from the icebox. Will you come visit us, Gene?"

"Who is 'us,' Gloria?"

"Well . . . not Mother. She passed away a few months ago. Father is with me; I'm buying him a new smoking jacket, just like the one he always wore. And of course my two beautiful daughters. I'm an inveterate matchmaker; I kept hoping you would have sons."

A voice said softly behind him, "Hello, Gene," and he turned to find Paul Weston gazing up at him. Into Gene's mind flashed the picture of his meeting with Gloria's father, practically on this very torn-up spot, when Paul had offered to train him for the law and take him in as a partner. Except for the wrinkles which began at his nostrils, circled the mouth and then disappeared into the chin, Paul Weston seemed little older.

"It's good to see you here again, Gene," Weston was saying; "makes our return to Terre Haute seem kind of official."

Two months later he received a rough water-color impression of the Weston abode, inviting him to a Saturday night housewarming. He took the invitation to Kate, hoping that she would accept. Kate's sense of the proprieties was offended by the informality of the announcement.

"No, thank you, Eugene, I wouldn't be in my element."

"But there will be lots of people, Kate, and I'm sure everyone will be able to find his own . . . element."

"These people," said Kate sternly, running a finger over the painted invitation, "they will all be shouting from soapboxes before the evening is over."

Gene took a light supper and walked over to Gloria's house as dusk was falling. While mounting the steps he saw that a wooden plaque had been attached to the door. Standing with his hand on the knob, he read half aloud,

> *Whoe'er thou art that entereth here*
> *Forget the struggling world*
> *And every trembling fear.*

> *Here all are kin of God above*
> *Thou too, dear heart; and here*
> *The rule of life is love.*

He entered the front door and found himself in one of the largest rooms he had ever seen. He had arrived early, and had the place to himself. The walls were covered in knotty pine, lined with bookshelves on which stood hundreds of volumes. Facing south was an enormous window which would admit every last vestige of sun from dawn to dark, while in the back there was a fieldstone fireplace in which a man could stand upright. There were long, low divans and a dozen tables holding magazines and the latest publications.

Gene walked about, touching the comfortable chairs and the tables, the gay hangings, the books and magazines, the open boxes of candy, the bowls of fruit and cookies. He walked to the fire and stood gazing down at the crackling logs. Wherever there was an available space of wall there were sun-drenched landscapes, the like of which he had never seen, but which made him feel warm and excited inside.

This was what he had dreamed of; this was the kind of home for which he had married; nothing so big nor half so beautiful, but an atmosphere that was warm and hospitable, a home which welcomed every man and every philosophy, the adventuresome, the stirring, the changing, the growing: filled with life and laughter and companionship.

Paul Weston was the first to come into the room and greet him. His white shirt was open at the throat, exactly as Gene had remembered him, and he was wearing the new blue velvet smoking jacket Gloria had bought for the occasion. With him was a broad-shouldered, stumpy man whom Paul introduced as Richard Hurtz, professor of mechanical engineering at Rose Polytechnic. The three men sat on a divan facing the fire, while Professor Hurtz exclaimed.

"I hear you've become a socialist, Mr. Debs!"

Gloria came in from the kitchen with Professor Hurtz's wife, and Gene gasped audibly when he saw that both women were wearing some kind of modern contraption with a divided skirt, very handsome, he thought, and very daring. Gloria exclaimed:

"Gene Debs, take that shocked expression off your face; no man who is trying to change the structure of our political economy has a right to complain about a change in women's clothing. This is the Jeness Miller style of dress; no more of those horrible bustles and corsets. Besides, they are a great social asset: Mrs. Hurtz and I were the first to wear them here in Terre Haute, and that is how we met."

Guests began coming in. First to arrive was Max Ehrmann, who had written the poem inscribed on the front door. Gene remembered him as the young Harvard student who

had dragged half a dozen of his unwilling classmates to hear
him lecture at the Prospect Union in Cambridge. Then came
four young musicians who were trying to get concert engagements as a string quartet. Next came a group whom Gene
recognized as the founders of a Sunday painting group
known as the Salmagundis; then there was another ambitious
group who called themselves the Terre Haute Thespians, and
put on plays for their own entertainment. Some of the people
Gene had grown up with, others were newcomers to Terre
Haute or people with whom he had just a nodding acquain-
tance. Separate discussions were raging in every corner of the
room and around each separate coffee table, for in the few
months of her return to Terre Haute, Gloria had either met
or sought out every last one of the town's writers, artists, musicians, intellectuals, social renegades.

Gene met Gloria's daughters. Imogene, the older, was a
slender redheaded girl with her mother's oval face, delicate
ankles and flashing green eyes; the younger daughter, Nedina,
had dark brown eyes and shiny black hair. The string quartet
began playing Debussy's *Premier Quatuor*. After several encores an argument broke out about music versus cacophony.
Soon the Thespians took over, playing the first act of Brieux's
Three Daughters of M. Dupont. Some of the guests had recently been to New York and told of plays being done on
Broadway. Gloria called on Max Ehrmann to read some of
his new poems.

Gene was astonished to find that it was midnight. He
thought he should be going home. At that moment Gloria
and Mrs. Hurtz put a white apron over his suit and a white
cap on his head and declared him to be the official chef of
the steak sandwiches. Everyone sat around eating steaks and
drinking beer or wine. Then the men lit their pipes and the
group remained about the fire with the lights turned off,
while they discussed the new book by Dr. Buck, called
Cosmic Consciousness.

Gene sat to one side of the fire watching Gloria, thinking
how beautiful she was with the flames dancing in her eyes.
Nothing in this room or in Gloria's life could ever be hack-
neyed, cold and formal. Gloria's mind and Gloria's heart
could go anywhere because she was utterly without fear.

He slipped out the front door without telling anyone he
was leaving. In the east, dawn was seeping a light gray awakening into the purple sky. It had been one of the happiest
nights of his life. Everyone had been so completely alive and
enthralled; no, wait, Nedina had not been happy. He had
seen her come and go several times; while she was in the

room her expression had been dark, almost thwarted, as though she could not understand these strange goings on and hated these people who were confusing her. She resembled someone he knew. He stopped in the gray darkness of Eighth Street. Ned Harkness. She had Ned's big brown eyes, the sleek black hair and high cheekbones. But why should she be unhappy? This was her home, these were her mother's friends. All of that nice music and poetry should have been exciting to her young mind; and there had been several attractive young men present.

As he reached the steps of his own house the answer came to him: Ned Harkness would have hated these people, hated their bohemian dress, their arty talk, their dissonant music, their radical ideas. This was Ned Harkness's daughter, a stranger in her mother's house, fighting her father's fight.

He inserted the key in the lock, then stood with his head down, thinking. There was no such thing as the present, there was only a given moment in flight, the sum total of the accumulated and irretrievable past.

By the time the churches had let out at noon, all of Terre Haute had heard of Gloria's housewarming, and most of Terre Haute was aghast. Because of the red window shutters and red door, the residence had already been named the Red House, with overtones which implied that it was both a center of radicalism and also had something to do with the red-light district. When Gene came downstairs for his combined breakfast and lunch, Kate did not return his greeting but asked instead:

"Aren't you ashamed of yourself?"

Gene did not know about the Sunday morning church gossip.

"Ashamed of what, Kate?"

"That immoral party!"

"Immoral! Why, Kate, that was one of the nicest . . ."

"And I suppose you are going to deny that you were out all night?"

"As a matter of fact I did get home at dawn," he laughed, "but I was the first one to leave. That party may be going on yet, for all I know."

"You mean with everyone lying around on the floor, drunk?"

"Oh no, Kate," he protested. "We had wine with our steaks at midnight, but nobody got drunk."

"There's no use your standing up for them, Gene. I know that those fast and loose women wore men's trousers."

"Not really trousers, Kate, they are just a new style, kind

of a divided skirt. But it's conduct that counts, and all of the women behaved as decorously as you would at a party."

"Have you ever seen me sit on a floor?"

"No."

"Have you ever seen me act out a love scene from a play?"

"No."

"It's that Gloria Harkness . . ."

He broke in before she could finish her sentence.

"Mrs. Harkness lives with her father and two grown daughters . . ."

"I know her kind, Eugene. Her only thought is to have men about her, making love to her. But she will never get away with it in Terre Haute."

She turned back to the stove, broke some eggs into a pan.

Dear God, prayed Gene, don't let Kate know that Gloria and I were once sweethearts.

— 4 —

Ernst Zobel said jeeringly at a businessmen's luncheon that if Mr. Debs thought socialism was the pot of gold at the end of the rainbow he would very soon learn that it was all pot and no gold. A New York newspaper accused him of being the kind of idealist who wanted to run upstairs twenty-five steps at a time. Now he was anxious to crawl up the steep steps of socialism on his hands and knees, carefully building each step above him with his hammer and nails before he attempted to set foot on it. He knew that Kate had assembled the house of her life over a long period of years, cutting out hundreds of drawings and photographs from magazines, copying descriptions from fashion books, future-shopping in the stores so that she would know precisely the fabric for her draperies, or covering for her floors.

For some twenty-two years he had spent his days and nights in every kind of structure that society had erected; he had shopped in railroad yards, coal mines, foundries, factories, slums and hospitals for fabrics with which to cover the bare boards of his furnishings so that mankind could be warm and comfortable. Now it was time to decide the size and flow of the rooms, chart the fireplaces and the plumbing, put together society's house of tomorrow, working so carefully and scientifically that the foundations would never crumble, the doors warp, the pipes stop up, the fireplaces smoke, the stairs sag. And yet it was less possible to be rigid in building a new state than in building a house, lest the structure itself become more important than the occupants.

Above all, the new society must become a home, not a
prison.

But when he sat at his desk trying to think his way through
the social maze, he always ended by feeling trapped and im-
potent. His eyes burned and his head burned and his insides
burned. The best brains of men from every nation, from
every race and religion and epoch in time, had fumbled and
fought, fashioned and experimented, succeeded a little and
failed a great deal over the eight thousand years of history.
Did man have to stumble through still another eight thousand, another eighty thousand, victimized, hungry, cold, beset
on all sides by uncertainty and fear? He felt himself lacking
in scientific training for the task, and yet the fact that he
must seek the whole solution while knowing that during his
lifetime he could find only a few fragments must not deter
him.

Having preached against the evils of money for so long, he
now began to know the boundaries of a moneyless world: he
had returned from Colorado without a dollar to his name. He
couldn't bring himself to ask Theodore for any of the few
greenbacks that came into the office of the *Railway Times*
and he and Kate were on too formal terms to discuss money.
She fed him and kept the house warm and took care of the
laundry; she was far too conscientious a housewife ever to
neglect what she conceived to be her husband's basic needs.
Sometimes he shivered for fear she would find out that he
hadn't a cent, for he knew that she would say:

"A man without a penny in his pocket is going to tell us
how to make a better world!"

He had on hand an adequate supply of paper, pencils, pen
and ink: he walked to and from Theodore's office, and when
there were letters to be mailed, Theodore sent them out with
stamps of the *Railway Times*. It was a rarefied feeling to
exist with no money whatever, and after a few days he began
to feel like a disembodied spirit wandering loose and unob-
served in a materialistic world. The only external evidence
that he was penniless was that his hair began to grow long on
his neck.

While trying to answer the hundreds of questions fired at
him in Leadville he had used quotations from Gordon's *Hard
Times, Cause and Cure,* Watkins's *Evolution of Industry,*
Rogers's *Six Centuries of Work and Wages.* Trade-union publications in the West had reported his speech. Letters began
reaching him enclosing coins for copies of the booklets to
which he had referred. When the requests were for Bellamy,
Lloyd or Gronlund, he turned the money over to the local

bookstore, but most of the pamphlets were unobtainable. Deciding that he would have to make them available, he went to see old man Langen, who was now deep in his seventies and wore a skullcap to keep his bald head warm. A considerable portion of the money the American Railway Union owed to Moore and Langen had been paid during Gene's lecture tour, but he still owed them something over a thousand dollars. He explained to Mr. Langen that he wanted some books and pamphlets printed but that as usual he was broke, had no immediate source of income, didn't even have an organization to stand responsible for his losses. He showed the printer copies of the pamphlets he wanted to put out.

"I'd like to sell them for five and ten cents."

"It will cost you that much to print them, Mr. Debs; there will be no margin left for profit."

"I know, Mr. Langen, but I am not doing this for profit; I want to get these books out to the people at the lowest possible cost. They are all just working folk, and anything over ten cents involves hardship and deprivation."

Old man Langen shook his head despairingly.

"You are a bad businessman, Mr. Debs: you don't even have enough sense to take advantage of the bankruptcy law when you fail, and thus save yourself paying your back debts."

Gene flashed him a quick grin.

"That's not bad business, Mr. Langen, that's good business: it makes you willing to print my little books even though I don't have a bean in the world."

Mr. Langen shook his head in agreement.

"I guess we are both too old to change our character, Mr. Debs. You didn't have any money when I printed those Ingersoll posters for you more than twenty years ago, and you were thousands of dollars in debt when I bought the new presses for your *Locomotive Firemen's Magazine*. But somehow you always pay off! What name do you want me to put down for your publishing house?"

"Publishing house?" asked Gene, crinkling his eyes behind his spectacles. "Maybe I am going into the publishing business, at that. A chap by the name of Hill offered me a good proposition a while back publishing a series of lessons on the rudiments of firing, combustion and engine problems. As long as we are going into business together, I might just as well undertake that project too. The profits we allow ourselves on Hill's course will cover our expenses for printing the socialist literature."

He was working in his upstairs study when he caught the sound of an altercation at the front door. Phrases drifted up to him:

". . . his brother Theodore said he was here . . . we came a hundred miles out of our way . . ."

He ran quickly down the stairs, crying out in cheerful tones, "It's all right, Kate. I came in the back way just a few moments ago."

He had never seen the two men before, but he remembered their names: they had started an organization known as the Brotherhood of the Co-operative Commonwealth. Myron Reed was a tall, middle-aged man with a full gray beard and a gentle expression, who had been fired out of his church for preaching the socialism of Bellamy's *Looking Backward*. Lermond was an economics professor dressed in a shiny blue serge suit, pudgy in form, full of a bouncing vitality. Gene took the men to his upstairs study, passed his bowl of tobacco.

"Gentlemen, what brings you to my neck of the woods?"

Lermond jumped up. "We have been scouting around in Arkansas and Tennessee to find a spot for our co-operative colony."

Gene could only exclaim in astonishment, "A place for your colony! Do you actually have enough members to set up a colony?"

Myron Reed gave Lermond a gentle but benign smile.

"Actually, Mr. Debs, it is a case of which comes first, the cart or the horse. Apparently we can get no one to join the Brotherhood of Co-operative Commonwealth until we can tell them precisely where the colony is to be, and provide them with a complete physical description."

"We have taken an option on a tract in Tennessee," broke in Lermond, "but we have expended the last of our money on this trip. That's why we have come to you, Mr. Debs."

Gene threw back his head and laughed wholeheartedly. He stopped abruptly when he saw the pained expressions on the faces of his guests.

"Forgive me," he said, "I was laughing at myself, not at you. Never in all my life have I been in more straitened circumstances."

Reed replied quietly, "We are not seeking funds from you, Mr. Debs; we are here to effect a merger. You announced publicly that you have become a socialist. Why can we not put our plans and our friends together?"

Gene thought this an interesting idea, but to all his practical questions as to how they would raise their funds, provide transportation, erect their houses, insure their first year's living, neither Reed nor Lermond had any practical answers. He shook his head sadly.

"Gentlemen, when I first announced that I had become a socialist, a newspaper editor commented that socialism was not a program but a pious wish, a gaseous feeling around the heart. That is true of me, and alas, it is also true of you. But even if you were practical men of high finance, what makes you think such a colony could work when all other experimental colonies in America have failed?"

"The Mormons didn't fail out in Utah," rejoined Reed. "Nor did the Harmony Society in Pennsylvania."

"No, but they were held together by religious discipline and by religious ecstasy. Even granting that you could create a successful colony, what have you proven beyond the fact that a small group of idealists in an isolated community are able to live co-operatively? We have to prove that socialism can work among a heterogeneous mass of some sixty-five million Americans."

Reed rose, stretched a long arm across Gene's desk and said, "We socialists need friends, you know."

Gene rose, walked the two men to the front door.

"You are quite right, Mr. Reed, we need friends: we also need money, plans, programs, organization, influence, newspapers, magazines, schools, mayors, governors, senators, and everything else you can think of. In fact, gentlemen, I find socialism in America in much the same position as my own financial condition: at the bottom, with nowhere to go, except up."

— 5 —

Myron Reed had said that socialists needed friends. Gene decided that he must visit Daniel De Leon, head of a group of German-language immigrants calling themselves the Socialist Labor party, and existing for the most part in New York City. Perhaps he, De Leon and the Reed-Lermond group could unite?

With the first few dollars brought in by Hill's training course, Gene made the trip to New York. He pushed through the crowded and noisy tenement blocks of Reade Street, and then made his way up three long narrow flights of stairs to De Leon's office. Through the open door he saw a white-bearded man sitting in a three-cornered angle where the curiously shaped room came to a point. He knew that De Leon was about his own age, and yet the white beard and mustache, the deep burning seriousness of the eyes, gave the impression of a very old and at the same time an ageless man. De Leon had been born in Curaçao, a Dutch West Indies island, and had come to America at the age of twenty-two.

Before either of them spoke, Gene had another impression: dust, dust over the hundreds of tomes lining the walls, dust over the newspapers, magazines, pamphlets and manuscripts which littered the desk.

De Leon did not rise or extend his hand; there was recognition in his eyes but no friendliness. He was wearing a black silk coat, but in place of a collar there was rolled a soft and spotless handkerchief tied at the back of his neck. Short, massive, with a round chin and high, bald, powerful head, he reminded Gene for all the world of James J. Hill, the creator of the Great Northern Railroad. But where Hill had built iron rails and steel locomotives and opened dark forests to settlement, garnering millions on his powerfully ruthless plunge through virgin territory, De Leon had donned snowshoes and fought his way through the blizzard-swept wasteland of social revolution. On his voyage Daniel De Leon had picked up a few followers, a host of enemies and no money whatever. Yet Gene felt that Daniel De Leon could have become as rich and as powerful in the industrial world as had Hill, for he had won all honors at Columbia Law College, taught there with a fiery brilliance and a keen perception of the law which made the other faculty members predict that here was one of the great legal minds of the day. Then, at the age of thirty-five, De Leon had read Henry George's *Progress and Poverty;* he campaigned when George ran for mayor of New York. Later he had gone into the works of Karl Marx and Engels, joined the Socialist Labor party, and within a few years had taken over the party and its press. Fanatically honest and sincere, he despised material possessions, living with his wife and children on whatever occasional dollar came into the party till. Gene noted that he had soft white hands: the intellectual in a proletarian revolution.

"I read that you have become a socialist, Mr. Debs," began De Leon in a low, restrained voice. "Precisely what kind of socialism, may I ask?"

"I don't know yet, Mr. De Leon, I am like a man who has suddenly gotten religion but doesn't know what church to join."

He had meant it as a little joke, assuming that De Leon would smile and get them off to a pleasant start. But Daniel De Leon did not like jokes; he called American humor a nar-

cotic fed to the people by the capitalists in order to keep
them content with their lot. His eyes flashed with what Gene
decided was the most knifelike passion he had ever seen.

"Do you think that socialism is some kind of game, Mr.
Debs, that you can put sticks in a hat and then decide your
convictions on the basis of a gambler's choice?" De. Leon's
voice was picking up power and intensity with every word.
"There is only one socialism, Mr. Debs, and that is the socialism of the Marxian dialectic. Of that true socialism I am the
official interpreter and leader in America."

Still trying to establish some kind of amiable basis for their
discussion, Gene murmured, "I have read some of your pamphlets, and the brilliant articles in your paper, *The People*.
Now I am going to make a confession to you, Mr. De Leon,
but I don't want you to print it: I am not a great intellect; in
fact I am hardly an intellect at all. You were educated at the
famous University of Leyden. I had to leave grammar school
when I was fourteen. Oh, I have read lots of books and I
have written a lot of words, but frankly I have a little trouble
with what you call the dialectic. I have read some of *Das
Kapital* but I must admit I understand it only in snatches. For
you see, Mr. De Leon, I can't qualify to be a socialist of the
mind; I am a socialist of the heart."

When he finished he found himself leaning far over the
desk, his face just a couple of inches from De Leon's. He
wished his host would invite him to sit down, but there was
no other chair in the room. De Leon put his hand under his
chin and rolled his fingers inside the white neckerchief.

"You are a sentimental socialist, Mr. Debs, and that is
even worse than being a Christian socialist, for you have no
solid base; all you can do is wail against the injustices of capitalism, beg a handout for the unemployed and the under-
paid. Bah! You crybabies do the movement more harm than
good! Anybody can defeat you in an argument, any half-wit-
ted fool can make your socialism sound like a schoolgirl's
effusions. You convince no one with tears. You convince the
workers with cold logic, and the capitalists with hot lead!"

There was enough truth to De Leon's accusations to get
under Gene's skin, yet he knew he had to control himself if
anything good were to result from this meeting.

"Let me ask you, Mr. De Leon, how much success have
you had with your approach to the American workingman?"

"Success!" spat De Leon, as though an insect had flown
into his mouth. "That is the most detestable of all bourgeois
concepts. Do you think I need millions of men and millions
of dollars to bring about the revolution? When the right mo-

ment comes I will seize the government with a handful of well-trained and obedient lieutenants."

De Leon's voice was now booming to the back hall and ricocheting around the three-sided room. Gene glanced out De Leon's one window to a neighboring roof where an iron trumpeter was blowing on an iron trumpet.

"Be that as it may, Mr. De Leon, it can do you no harm to bring the American workingman to your side. I am here to suggest that we join forces: I still have several thousand friends among the railroaders."

De Leon pulled himself up quickly.

"Very well, Mr. Debs, you come here to put yourself in my hands, and to lay your followers at my feet. I am willing to take in you and your organization, but you must understand the terms and conditions."

"What we want is a merger, Mr. De Leon, one which will double our strength . . ."

De Leon bored deep into Gene's eyes.

"Try to understand me, Mr. Debs, there are no mergers: you and your people come into my organization as obedient subjects. Your main task is to understand my will and carry out my orders. There are no questionings in the Socialist Labor party, Mr. Debs, no arguments, no housewife demands. Alone I have created the form in which Marxian socialism can and must be achieved in the industrial world. We have no room in here for labor fakers like Samuel Gompers or the Eugene V. Debs of the Brotherhood of Locomotive Firemen, men who are tools in the hands of the capitalists."

While Gene stood blinking, trying to understand the convolutions of De Leon's mind, the man with the firm jaw and aggressive mouth began outlining his demands: Gene's followers would have to abandon their trade unions, and work to destroy them. They would publish no newspaper, no pamphlets or tracts except those written by De Leon himself, or edited and approved by him. All new members were to be trained in De Leon dialectics and utter no word except that which he had approved as the party line. Gene and his associates must empty their minds as completely as their bowels would be emptied by castor oil, then they would be given a new content by De Leon, one which they would never have to change, question or discard. They would all act as one, think as one, believe as one, do as one: and Daniel De Leon would be that One. In unquestioning obedience lay the future of the revolution! To their enemies they might appear as automatons, might even look foolish if required to reverse their positions in mid-air, like the humming bird. But only through this solidity of purpose and strength could they, so few in number, conquer the flaccid, directionless masses, and destroy the capitalist system.

"Are you able to accept this discipline, Mr. Debs?"

"I . . . I . . ."

"Understand me, I have no covetous bourgeois ego to placate; I do not rule and command because it gives me any pleasure; it is a burden I carry most unwillingly. I am not seeking power for its own sake, but only to achieve the dictatorship of the proletariat."

Gene said to himself, This man is more like James J. Hill than Mr. Hill himself. Aloud he asked, "Once your revolution is successful, Mr. De Leon, and we have a socialist government in America, you will relax your controls, will you not? Men will then be free to think as they wish, to express their own opinions, to start independent action if they believe . . ."

De Leon edged out of his tight corner.

"Never," he shouted, "that is when the danger is the greatest, when the capitalist thieves will be plotting behind our backs to overthrow socialism. It is doubly important then that every man, woman and child in America act as I tell them to act! These bourgeois illusions of freedom of speech, and press and assemblage, they are the most invidious snares in all capitalism, deluding the people into thinking they are free men when actually their every thought and belief is dictated and controlled from above, formulated by their slavey newspapers, their corrupt politicians and their prostitute preachers. Ah no, Mr. Debs, when I am the ruler of socialist America I will not fool our people with such cheap imitations of freedom. I will give them real freedom, freedom from poverty, from unemployment, from cold and hunger. When I am the master of America they will not need freedom, they will have it!"

Gene stood awkwardly, nervous tremors of fright running through his abdomen. Was this socialism? he asked himself. He had thought of socialism as a philosophy which preached the flowering of the human spirit. De Leon's socialism apparently meant a flowering of man's intestinal tract. He did not want to quarrel with the passionately earnest man before him, yet he could not leave without making himself clear.

"I like a comfortable bed to sleep in, Mr. De Leon, and I like a good pot roast for dinner. But there are things more important to me than a soft bed or pot roast: the right to speak my mind, to form my own opinion, to act as an independent man. If you turn man into a machine, if you paralyze his right and his ability to think for himself, to create for himself, how does he differ from the machine which he tends in the factory?"

De Leon clenched his hands until his fingers were white. His eyes dismissed Gene contemptuously. He went behind his desk, picked up his pen, dipped it in the ink, and continued work on the manuscript before him. Just as Gene reached the door and started down the long stairs, he heard De Leon's voice behind him.:

"You sentimental reformers are more dangerous to us than the Armours, the Pullmans and the Fricks. We will have to destroy you first, before we can meet our enemies with a solid phalanx and drive them into the sea."

There was a saloon on the corner. Gene went in and downed two whiskies as fast as he could drink them. After a few moments he stopped trembling. He had never been so frightened in his life. De Leon had made his dictatorship of the proletariat sound even worse than the dictatorship of the capitalists! De Leon was aiming to change the nature of mankind's chains, not to dissolve them; to substitute the dictatorship of dogma and doctrine, moral, spiritual and intellectual serfdom for the economic serfdom of the American workers. Gene felt certain that if the American worker had his choice between economic slavery and mental slavery, he would tighten his belt, straighten his shoulders and cry for all the world to hear: "I am my own man! I think as I like, believe as I please, speak as the spirit moves me!" But then De Leon had no intention of giving the American worker his choice. De Leon's political belief was a throwback to the Middle Ages, to the absolutism of the divine right of rulers; man's most valuable achievement over the centuries, his freedom to think and act upon his own motivation, this would be obliterated.

Then and there Gene Debs made a number of mighty resolves: there shall be no czar, no master, no boss, no dictator, in any movement in which I participate. Any man who swallows doctrine whole and undisputed will be invited to resign. All policy, platform, plans, action, will be democratically worked out in open discussion, then decided by majority rule. There shall be no secret meetings, no conspiracy to deceive. There shall be none of De Leon's hot lead. The philosophy of socialism is democratic; socialists, through education, through voting majorities, will achieve economic security without broken heads, bruised and battered liberties, or mechanical slave brains.

— 6 —

The laconic report of the arrest was already several days old when he came across it in the Terre Haute newspaper. Gene half ran to the police station, went straight to the desk sergeant and asked:

"What are the charges against Clarissa Hanford?"

The sergeant automatically turned the pages before him.

"Soliciting. She was warned to stay in the red-light district."

Gene felt his heart drop in his chest.

"Red-light district! But she is only a child!"

"Don't lay it at my door, mister," replied the officer. "After all, she was picked up three times for prostitution."

"What will the sentence be, Sergeant?"

"Ninety days."

Gene remembered the beautiful little Clarissa in the study of the parsonage; he remembered her as a lonely child living in the austere furnished room with her father while he carried on his mission work; he remembered her in her tight red dress and her high heels, out to enjoy the world at any cost; he remembered the soft night crying of the women prisoners in the Chicago jail.

"May I see her, Sergeant?"

"Guess so; she hasn't had any visitors since the officers brought her in three days ago."

The matron walked him down the steel corridors, then stopped. Gene saw a form huddled on a cot, as abject and lifeless as a half-empty sack of meal. But no, it was not lifeless, for Clarissa was crying, noiselessly now after three days and three nights, with a kind of fatigued twitching spasm. The matron unlocked the door, admitting Gene to the cell. He sat on the edge of the cot and put his hand on Clarrisa's shoulder.

"Clarissa," he said, "it's Eugene Debs. You remember me. I was your father's friend. I've come to help you."

Clarissa raised her head. Her face was puffy and swollen from crying. She was still wearing a gay dress with silken flounces, now crushed and soiled. She stared at Gene without recognition.

"Clarissa, I loved your father; he was one of the best men God ever put on this earth . . ."

"Don't speak of God to me!" she cried.

There was no good in talk. that was plain. Gene rose, signaled the matron to open the door.

The new police chief, Orin Flanner, was a stranger to

Gene. There were methods of securing an advantageous introduction, but time was of the essence. Gene sat restlessly in a drafty corridor for almost an hour until the official came in by way of his private entrance. Gene introduced himself and got quickly to the point.

"Chief Flanner, could you release Clarissa Hanford in my custody?"

The chief made a rolling movement of the cigar between his lips.

"Clarissa Hanford? Now which one might that be?"

"She is the Rev. Mr. Hanford's daughter. You remember him, he had that mission over behind the Union Station for years, then he held services in our union offices. The girl has been locked up for three days now."

"And what might the charges be?"

Gene's throat was dry.

"Soliciting."

The chief blew a mouthful of smoke at the ash ring of his cigar. After a moment he nodded, picked up the telephone. Clarissa was brought in.

"You understand, Mr. Debs, that you are now an emergency probation officer, and this girl is being released in your care. If she is picked up on the streets again, we'll take her right before the judge and she'll be in the county jail before you will have a chance to intercede."

Gene sent a messenger for a carriage. They had ridden only a few blocks when Clarissa lifted her head and gazed at him for the first time. She was relieved to be out of the jail, but otherwise her attitude had not changed.

"All right, you can let me out now."

"Let you out? But, Clarissa, where would you go?"

"Never mind about that," she replied, "I can take care of myself."

He took the girl's hand in his. She wrenched it away. He said quietly, "Forgive me for disagreeing, Clarissa, but I'm not sure you can take care of yourself. At least, not right now."

"So now you're going to take care of me," she sneered.

He ignored the insinuation.

"I am taking you home with me. This is what your father would have wanted me to do. You need rest and good food and friends around you. When you feel better and are ready to go to work, Mrs. Debs and I will find you a job."

Kate was sitting before her dressing table, her hair wound into a knot at the back of her head, running the comb through the bangs on either side of her forehead to fluff them. She was wearing a highnecked black dress decorated with white embroidered flower insets. Gene thought it a good omen that Kate was fluffing her bangs and wearing a fine dress: this must mean that she was in good spirits. But when he told her that Clarissa Hanford was downstairs in the library, she dropped her comb to the floor and whirled on him, her eyes blazing.

"Eugene Debs, have you gone crazy? How dare you bring a . . . a . . . into my house."

Gene recoiled.

"She's just confused and unhappy, Kate." He sat down on the bench beside his wife. "Kate, please help me to help this girl. Her father's troubles began when I asked him to introduce Robert Ingersoll at the Occidental Club lecture. And if he had not spoken out for me during the American Railway Union trial, he would never have lost that little church behind the station. Clarissa's mother died when she was a baby; she has never had any woman to help her or guide her; they lived on the very barest of necessities . . ."

Kate sprang up, walked to the door, then leaned against it.

"Are you trying to tell me you approve of what she did?"

"There is nothing in this whole sordid affair that I approve, Kate, but we must not let Clarissa be destroyed."

Kate laughed harshly.

"Destroyed! How naïve. Those harlots have the easiest time of anyone: dancing and drinking all night with no obligations or responsibilities. . . . Eugene, send her back to where she belongs, to where she will be happy."

"Please, Kate. If we don't help her she will be in prison in a matter of weeks."

He felt his wife pull up to her full, majestic height.

"Kate, if you had ever been in prison as I have; if you could know what it is like to have iron bars locked behind you, to have for your only companions the rats and vermin of the cell . . ."

Kate had not been listening. When she spoke she enunciated every syllable with terrifying precision.

"This is free love. that's what it is, and it's part of that whole intrigue you call socialism."

Gene shook his head sadly.

"Socialism has never advocated free love, you know that as well as I."

"Then it's the influence of that Harkness woman. If you hadn't fallen under her spell you would never have thought of defending this sordid creature."

Slowly, painfully, he replied, "Gloria is a fine woman. She has never done an immoral or ungenerous thing in her life."

"She'd probably be delighted to take Clarissa Hanford in, she's her own kind."

"Yes, Gloria would take Clarissa in. But she shouldn't be asked to take the responsibility for a stranger; it would only bring more malicious talk down on her head. The Rev. Mr. Hanford was my dear friend; it is my responsibility to help his daughter."

Indulgently, with an almost kind tone, Kate said, "There are charitable institutions that will take such a person."

"The only institution that will take her in is the county jail. If we could keep her with us until she finds a young man she loves, and who will marry her . . ."

Kate's face flamed crimson.

"Eugene, how despicable of you! To foist a public woman on some good and innocent young man. And as for keeping her in our house, don't you know what that will do to us in Terre Haute? It would create a scandal. We would never be able to regain our position."

Smiling wistfully, he said, "Kate, my dear, we have almost no position left. Ever since I have become a socialist, even my own brother-in-law won't let me in his house. So you see, we have nothing to lose."

A chill ran through Kate's body.

"Let's say you have nothing to lose, Eugene, for you have thrown away every opportunity, every chance to make something of yourself in this world. But I still have my place in society. If I let that girl remain here even one night, people will say bad things about my house."

Ah, thought Gene, Kate would not object to my helping the girl in any other way, it's her house I must not endanger.

"But I have no other place to take her."

"What about Theodore and Gertrude's? They always approve of any wild scheme you think up."

"But they have only the one bedroom. We have a guest room."

"This girl will be no guest of mine. If she stays in this house tonight, I shall move out of it. And may I remind you that I am the one who has been keeping up this house? I have just finished paying the taxes out of my own savings account."

She went to her closet, took out an overnight bag, began putting things into it from the bureau.

"Do you put that girl out or do you drive me from my own home?"

He could think of nothing further to say. All he could do was plead, "Please, Kate, please . . . do this for me . . . just for a few days . . . until I can find a good home for her . . . please . . ."

Kate put a kimono into her night case, snapped the lock, placed a coat over her arm and walked out of the house.

He took Clarissa up to the guest room, suggested that she rest, then went as quickly as he could to Theodore's flat.

"Eugene, you know I would do anything you ask," said Gertrude in her quiet voice, "but how can I stay in your house when Kate has invited me there only once in the years since we came to Terre Haute?"

Gene put his arms about his sister-in-law.

"Gertrude, I have never been so miserable. Please do this for me."

He could feel the revulsion that ran through her at the idea of going uninvited into Kate's house; but at last she lifted her plain, honest face and said, "All right, Gene, if it means so much to you."

They stopped downtown to buy Clarissa a suit, shoes and some night clothes. When they reached home, they found that she had locked her door.

For the next three days Gene and Gertrude tried to become friends with the girl, giving her companionship and understanding. Clarissa gave nothing in return; her expression was blank, as though all spirit had been permanently killed. They tried to find out what kind of work she might like to do if they could get her a job; they tried to learn whether she had friends in other towns where she might make a fresh start. Gertrude tried to interest her in cooking and taking care of the house, but she did not respond.

Gene had tried to keep the affair secret, but he learned that there could be no more private life for him. Reporters got wind of the story, and on the morning of the fourth day the front pages of the nation's newspapers were splashed with the tale, headlined by his own question:

"Why not war on the immoral people in high places, instead of persecuting penniless and defenseless girls?" Several of the reporters asked him if rescuing fallen women was part of the socialist platform, to which he replied that socialism aimed to help all defenseless Americans.

The formal New Year's Day announcement of his conversion to socialism had earned him not one stick of type in the city papers; through Clarissa's misfortune, great segments of the public learned that Eugene Debs was now a socialist.

Kate returned home in the company of the attorney who

advised her on her investments. No one exchanged greetings. Gertrude gratefully gathered up her things and left by the porch door. Kate was the first to speak.

"That girl is still in the house?"

Wretched, Gene replied "Yes, Gertrude has been taking care of her."

The lawyer announced, "Either the girl will be out of the house by nightfall, or you will be out."

Gene looked dazedly from the man's face to Kate's; there was nothing in their expressions to give him further illumination.

". . . or I will be out? I don't understand."

"This house is in Mrs. Debs's name," said her counselor. "She owns it. You have no legal rights here."

Kate came to Gene, put her hand on his cheek.

"That isn't what we mean, Eugene; we only mean that the girl must go. She has been here long enough."

Gene walked to a chair and sat down heavily. It was incredible that Kate could be threatening to dispossess him. If he left this house, what else did it mean? That he was also leaving Kate? Were they dispossessing him of his marriage, declaring it to be at an end? He turned his face up to his wife.

"Kate, surely you don't . . ."

Kate's lawyer took her by the arm and led her to the front door. He said over his shoulder, "We will be back at five. Either you are here alone, or you're not here at all."

He heard the front door slam. He felt deathly ill, as though he could never again raise his lids over his eyes or his body out of the chair. He swayed with the movement of the slow freight going down the line, clackety-clack, clackety-clack, click-clack, click-clack. He felt stifled inside of Kate's walls. Slowly he rose, went to the front door and out into the street. Soon he found himself in the railroad yards, walking the tracks, stumbling over the ties, bruising his feet on the hard rock of the roadbed. He did not know how far he had walked, he knew only that he must be back at the house before five, get Clarissa, find temporary refuge for them both.

He was relieved to see by the clock in the front hall that it was only a little after four. He still had time. He slid into a library chair. His feet hurt. Then he sensed that someone was in the room with him. He looked up. Clarissa stood there. She was gazing at him, her eyes no longer bitter or blank.

"I heard what they said, Mr. Debs. They're going to put you out of your house."

"It's all right, Clarissa," he murmured. "In just a few moments, as soon as I can get up, we'll collect our things and go to Theodore and Gertrude's. We'll work it out together, somehow."

"You mean you would give up your home . . . just for me . . . a stranger to you . . . ?"

"You aren't a stranger, Clarissa; the first thing I told you at the jail was that I loved your father. He was a great man. Now that he is dead I cannot do less for you than I would do for my own flesh and blood."

Clarissa dropped to her knees beside him, buried her head in his lap and wept; but these were not the same tears she had shed on her cot in the jail; these were not tears of hatred and defiance. She lifted her streaked face to him.

"You don't have to worry about me, Mr. Debs, I'm all right now. There'll be no more trouble."

He knew from the quality of her voice that this was the simple truth. He no longer had to fear for Clarissa.

"I'd like to go to a new town and make a fresh start, Mr. Debs. Do you know anywhere I could get a job?"

"Yes, Clarissa. I have a friend who runs the restaurant at the Union Depot in St. Louis. If I gave you a letter to him he would hire you as a waitress, and I'm sure his wife would board you."

Clarissa rose, straightened her dress, took a deep breath.

"When you write that note, will you tell them that my name is Clarissa Smith?"

"Of course. Bring me that writing pad and the pen from my desk. There's a train that leaves for St. Louis a little after five."

— 7 —

Lake Michigan sparkled in the clear June sunlight while the seven former officers of the American Railway Union walked arm in arm along the beach, each telling how he had occupied the months since they had campaigned for William Jennings Bryan and his progressive program. Gene took particular pleasure in the young ones: James Hogan, twenty-four, Irish, good-looking; Roy Goodwin only a year older, fair and blond; William Burns, tall, spare; Lou Rogers, the gently scholarly man; Martin Elliott with a reddish beard; Sylvester Keliher, saturnine.

That evening the seven former comrades from Woodstock jail sat around a seminar table on the stage of the otherwise empty Handel Hall, officially closed the books of the American Railway Union, and declared themselves ready to be absorbed into the new organization which they had decided to call the Social Democracy. Gene remarked:

"We must all believe in life after death: I never saw a group of men so optimistic about the future while attending their own funeral."

Victor Berger and Frederic Heath were waiting in his hotel room, having come down from Milwaukee after their day's work. They were delighted to learn that the American Railway Union was to be reborn as part of the Social Democracy, but their enthusiasm evaporated when they heard about the colonization idea. Gene told them of his plan to open a recruiting office and take in unemployed carpenters, bricklayers, plasterers, plumbers, machinists, this vanguard to be shipped to the colony immediately to build the houses and worships, school and church. He could see that Berger and Heath were only temporarily mollified.

The doors of Handel Hall were thrown open at nine the next morning. By the time Gene arrived several hundred delegates had assembled from twenty-odd organizations: the Ruskin Union, the Mutual Co-operative Union, the Humanitarian League, the Trade and Labor Alliance, and a number of unions such as the Metal Polishers and Buffers, Carpenters and Joiners. He spent two hours outlining the plan for the structure of the Social Democracy, and its specific list of demands. He put one foot at the edge of the platform railing, leaning over at the waist, his right arm extended far out with the index finger pointing heavenward.

"For immediate relief we demand reduction of the hours of labor in proportion to the progress of production; the inauguration of a system of public works and improvements for the employment of the unemployed; all useful inventions to be free to all; the establishment of postal savings banks; and the adoption of the initiative, the referendum and proportional representation. For our ultimate society we are demanding the public ownership of all industries now controlled by monopolies, trusts and combines; all means of transportation and communication, the railroads, telegraph and telephone; such public utilities as the water works, gas and electric plants, all oil and gas wells, all gold, silver, copper, lead, coal, iron and other mines."

The next days were spent in attacking or defending ideas with the delegates. On the seventh day they called in the newspapermen, gave them an outline of the Social Democracy's plan, then adjourned the convention until the same time the following year. Back at the hotel, he locked the door, threw himself onto the bed and slept the clock around.

The morning news brought a distinct shock: the papers reported no part of the Social Democracy's political platform, writing up only its colonization scheme.

The morning news brought a distinct shock: the papers reported no part of the Social Democracy's political platform, writing up only its colonization scheme.

To his brother Gene groused, "Theo, the colony is only a small part of our program. Why do the papers make it look as though we are interested in nothing else?"

The newspaper coverage brought staggering results. By the end of one week Gene's mail had reached the volume of ten thousand letters a day, almost all of them from people wanting to join, offering money, services, advice, asking how they could set up local branches of the Social Democracy. In a few weeks several thousand dollars in contributions had poured in; applications had been received for two hundred and fifty charters of the Social Democracy; enough skilled mechanics had applied for the immediate trek west to build a hundred colonies. Among the new members were fifty clergymen of all creeds, enough professors to start several universities, more than a dozen doctors, several of them women, and a sufficient number of lawyers to write a new legal code and a new constitution. Gene hired a room in the Trude Building, changed the name of the *Railway Times* to the *Social Democracy*, moved Theodore to Chicago and continued him in his job as editor. Young Lou Benedict was taken away from Sweet Orr and Company, the overall manufacturers, and put in charge of the office. A committee was selected to travel the country and select the best site.

Interviewers from all over the country shot questions at Gene:

"Won't your colony destroy the competitive principle for which Thomas Jefferson contended, reduce life to a dull plane of board, lodging and clothes?" "If you become an industrial colony, won't you have to use labor-saving machinery and thus throw your own people out of work? What will you do with the artists, poets, painters, will you feed them even though they don't produce?"

He answered all questions as fully as he could.

"Jefferson lived in different times: the invention of labor-saving machinery and the organization of trusts have filled the country with over four million idle and homeless men." "The competitive spirit in man will be used against poverty, ignorance, hatred, disease." "The choice of labor will settle itself; if a man works in the mines he will work three or four hours a day; if he prefers to be a clerk he will work six or

seven hours a day. Labor-saving machinery hurts only when
private industry fires the displaced men."

Then came an invitation from Governor J. R. Rogers of
Washington, which was published in most major newspapers:

*The Debs colony will be welcome in Washington. We have
wonderful natural resources waiting for the hand of labor:
forests of magnificent timber . . . mountains of iron and coal,
mines of precious metals, and in Puget Sound, the Pacific
Coast's great port. We do not fear the colony; we welcome
them! They will be subject to our laws, which will remain in
place until constitutionally changed. . . .*

The colony had found a harbor.

Gene thought it would be helpful to have his first meeting
in Terre Haute, and so he asked Kate for permission to use
the house.

Kate replied, "But, Eugene, I am not unemployed. I have a
job, managing this house. Besides, if I lent my house it would
seem as though I were giving sanction to this absurd colony
idea. I don't think you ought to attempt to involve me in
these fly-by-night vagaries you have grown so fond of lately."

He knew that he should not have embarrassed his wife
when of necessity she could give him but one answer. He
picked up his hat and walked to Gloria's house. She was in
the kitchen, broiling squabs, the color high in her cheeks. She
threw him a welcoming smile before examining the meat
under the gas flame.

"Why, Gene," she exclaimed, "however did you know we
were having pigeon tonight? I do declare you can smell it a
mile away."

"Now, Gloria, I didn't come for dinner," he protested,
"and you know that perfectly well."

Gloria laughed.

Over the supper table he explained his need for an organizational meeting.

"For example," he said, "we have to find out how many
acres of land must be cultivated to feed the people in our factories. We need not only schoolteachers, but teachers who
can write us new textbooks. We must somehow distinguish
between the unemployed and the unemployable. We are starting from scratch, we know nothing, and we have so much to
learn."

Two hundred men and women filled Gloria's house, seated
on folding chairs and covering every available portion of floor
space. Gene had drawn up an agenda for the evening and run

off a series of sheets containing the major problems which had been posed. Then he threw the meeting open for discussion: was Washington the best place to get the colony started? Should they move the colonizers on foot across the country in a spectacular march? Should they limit the size of the families they would accept? Should they refuse to move until they had the correct ratio of farmers to builders and factory workers?

After a time Gene began to feel a pair of eyes fastened on him, boring fiercely into the back of his head. He turned and saw that it was Nedina Harkness, standing at the edge of the crowd, one hand on the knob as though poised for flight, her whole being permeated by contempt.

"Won't you come join us, Nedina?" Gene asked. "I am sure we could use your good counsel."

A flush mounted to Nedina's high cheekbones. There was an uncomfortable silence. She turned halfway toward the door as though to flee, and then with a sudden decision faced the room, her big brown eyes blazing. For Gene it was like being thrust back several years into the courtroom at Chicago, with Ned Harkness accusingly before him.

"No," she said in a strong clear voice. "I won't have anything to do with your stupid talk. You are frauds, the lot of you, with your arty ways and your cheap bohemianism, sitting on the floor, as though that made you superior to people who sit on chairs and have good manners."

Gloria had risen quickly and was making her way to her daughter's side.

"Nedina, please, these are our guests."

"They are not my guests," denied Nedina, her eyes traveling swiftly over the assemblage. "My father would never have invited them into his house."

Gloria had reached her daughter's side. She put an arm about her and said quietly, "Nor would your father have approved of offending visitors in his house, Nedina."

Nedina turned and fled. No one could think of anything to say. The spirit of the meeting had been broken. After a few minutes of desultory discussion the people began to file out.

At last Gene and Gloria were alone. Gloria said:

"I'm worried about Nedina, poor child. She hates Terre Haute, and everyone in it. Even her cousins who invite her to society parties. And she seems to think that everybody hates her."

Gene felt wretched at having been the cause of Nedina's outburst, of bringing this unhappiness to Gloria. What right did he have intruding in her life and her home, causing conflict in her family and shattering her peace of mind, simply because his own home was unavailable to him?

— 8 —

For four months money, members and enthusiasm poured in to the Social Democracy. Little Lou Benedict had a hundred thousand applications filed in the Chicago office, and nine thousand dollars in voluntary contributions; locals of the Social Democracy were organized in every state of the union. Then suddenly the stream of enthusiasm vanished as completely as though a plumber had disconnected the main lead-in valve. Gene was met by skepticism, then doubt, and finally indifference; even among the members of the Social Democracy the sweet milk of human kindness began to curdle. Southern members refused to join the colony if Negroes were to be included; in the Midwest he ran into religious bigotry: no Catholics or Jews were to be allowed. Native-born Americans objected to taking immigrants; immigrants from northern Europe demanded that no immigrants from southern Europe be permitted. Members who lived in the big cities threatened to resign if the colony were started too far from civilization; farming groups informed him that they could not participate if the colony were to become industrialized. No two individuals wanted the colony in the same spot: Washington was too far away and too wet; Utah was too barren and too close to the Mormons; Wyoming was too high and too cold.

He was beginning to realize that socialism was no cure-all for the afflictions of human nature: men were not rendered divine by a blinding flash of conversion which melted down their prejudice, ignorance or conceit. He had assumed that only the most sensitive and self-sacrificing would be willing to participate in a co-operative colony, yet he found these good souls attempting to carry over to the new society the privileges and poisons of the old. His months of effort taught him that man could agree very easily on preserving the *status quo*, but that when it came to re-creating the world, no two individuals had the same vision.

He also became convinced that his colony was an impossibility.

Sitting in a day coach on his way to Chicago, he told himself that he had been naïve: were people to shed their outer skin, one which had grown horny and scabrous from thousands of years of exposure to the jungle of beast and man, merely because they had become excited by a new idea? Socialism was not the end of the road, it was a milestone along the way. One had to start with the heartbreaking premise that man was still a predatory animal, covered only by the thinnest gauze of culture and unselfishness; the converting of this predatory animal into a social-minded human being would be a long painful task which might show no progress whatever for centuries on end, for the human brain had to be emptied of its emotional terror; faith had to supplant fear, understanding and liking of one's fellow man had to supplant intolerance and the desire to kill.

When he reached his office he found even worse news awaiting him. The committee in charge of purchasing a site for the colony had fallen into the hands of an unscrupulous promoter who had sold them a tract of land high in the Colorado mountains, uninhabitable in winter, and too far from any metropolis to survive.

By the following morning the newspapers had the story:

UTOPIANISTS BUY GOLD BRICK!

Within a matter of hours Social Democracy had become the laughingstock of the nation. The derision being lavished upon the colonizers embraced all socialism. Too late Gene realized that he should never have let the colonization scheme grow to be so large a part of his program.

The ensuing months passed laboriously, his organization caught in the twin tornadoes of indifference from without and dissension within. The Chicago trade-unionists had been convinced by Samuel Gompers that socialism was inimical to the interests of labor; the liberal and intellectual clubs which had thrown in with Social Democracy had been persuaded by William Jennings Bryan that any socialist party would necessarily take its followers and its voters from the Democrats, who needed the radical support to defeat McKinley in 1900. Those who believed in colonization were convinced that the political aims of the group had alienated the American public. De Leon and his Socialist Labor party had been boring from within, sowing factionalism, hoping for a quarrel and explosion so that they could take over the remnants.

As the second convention drew closer Gene pleaded for tolerance and cohesion. But just the day before the meeting he discovered that the colonists had formed eleven new branches, each with the legal minimum of five members, for the purpose of outvoting those members of the organization who believed that their primary aim was socialism. That night Gene slept not at all.

The air of Uhlich Hall seemed crisscrossed by dissecting cleavages and resentments. He walked slowly down the center aisle, then up the short flight of steps, a smile frozen onto his face. He went to the front of the stage and stood gazing out at the mass of faces. Slowly the people below him eased in their seats.

". . . there are differences among you. Many will disagree with my opinions. My friends, that is not bad, that is healthy. The fact that we have divergent opinions means that we are thinking for ourselves. I don't fear the man who says, 'I don't agree with you.' But I am mortally afraid of an ignorant supporter."

He saw a few faces break into tiny smiles. Searching out the groups that he knew were for colonization above all else, he told them that he still believed in their theory, but that it was still too unplanned, too uncharted to succeed. Very well then, if their first approach was not workable, must they cry out in their anguish, "This we will have, and no other!" Why could they not go on to a broader vision of socialism, one so desperately needed for those other millions of workingmen who could not pack up and escape to a colony?

"We must make our Social Democracy broad enough to reach all America. We must merge and compromise our differences so that we can accomplish the major tasks of socialism. Go along with us, give us time to build our membership, to build our political party, to achieve the beginnings of public ownership. Within a few years we will make your colony possible in every state in the union. But if we split into a dozen fragments, if we hate each other for our differences instead of loving each other for our agreements, then none of us will accomplish any part of his dream for humanity."

He made his way to the edge of the platform, slowly went downstairs and then out the center aisle. Theodore was waiting in the rear of the hall.

"Are you all right, Gene? You started to look green up there."

"Just put me in a carriage," he replied, "they'll need you here to preserve unity. Whatever else happens, Theo, don't let them split up."

He knew that he could not make the long ride out to Theodore's flat. He gave the driver the name of the nearby Revere House, sending word inside to his brother. He paused at the desk only long enough to ask the clerk for a doctor, then went upstairs and fainted. When he awakened he found himself between the covers, an elderly man with a beard applying instruments to his chest and running his fingers over his abdomen. The bearded gentleman said, "So you are awake. I am Dr. Harrison. What have you been doing to yourself?"

With the faintest whisk of a smile Gene murmured, "My wife would say I have been trying to save the world, when I haven't enough sense to come in out of the rain."

"Well, drink this mixture. It will soothe your insides."

He drank the obnoxious mixture, closed his eyes and was asleep before the doctor had left the room. He had fantastically wild dreams in which the hundreds of people he had known since childhood played strange and incongruous roles. Finally he dreamed he was in the midst of an excited caucus being held in heaven, with his bed floating among the clouds and a half-dozen committeemen sitting around the edges with their feet dangling and arguing heatedly some point of parliamentary procedure. He opened one eye to find that although he was not in heaven, a half dozen of his friends were sitting around his bed arguing whether or not their opponents had captured the meeting by legal procedure. Gene turned his head to the window, saw that it was still black outside. His mouth and lips were parched.

"What time is it?" he murmured.

Theodore came to him, ran his fingers over Gene's forehead.

"It's three in the morning. I managed to keep them down in the foyer for an hour, but they just couldn't be held any longer."

"What happened?"

Everyone began speaking at once, with Victor Berger in the lead.

"The colonists took over. They passed a resolution against forming a political party. We did everything we could to compromise the issues, Gene, but it was no use. They were hell-bent for the colony."

Gene struggled up to his elbow and gazed from one face to the other. His expression asked the question more clearly than any words.

"We had no choice, Gene, it was a case of bolt or be frozen out. And so we bolted."

Gene fell back onto his pillow, wearily. A year's work gone for nothing, ended by a factional dispute. Everything he had done since his release from Woodstock had come to complete and ludicrous failure. Despair seized him. He said to himself, We'll never get anywhere, we'll never accomplish anything. Profit making settles all doubts and differences, keeps men together in bonds of gold. But those of us who want a better world, all we can do is quarrel over the best means to achieve it.

Aloud he asked, "How many are left?"

"Us five," replied Frederic Heath, "and about twenty more down in the lobby, waiting to find out whether we are dead or alive."

"Why don't we bring them up here?" asked Seymour Stedman. "Now that Gene is awake . . ."

"We couldn't get twenty more men in here with a shoe-horn," murmured Gene. He threw aside the covers and put his long lanky legs out of bed. "I'll dress and come down."

Theodore remained behind to help. Gene's teeth were chattering as he slipped into a shirt. Theodore had to fasten the tie.

The parlor of the Revere House had been set aside for birthdays, parties and committee meetings. There was a huge chandelier cascading from the ceiling, but only the sleeping superintendent knew how to light it. Two side gas brackets had been lit, but air had gotten into the pipes and they gave off more hiss than light. As Gene entered the room he saw the faces of some of the comrades whom he had come to love during the past year: names he felt relieved and happy to know would be in the fight. Then his heart sank when he saw that Sylvester Keliher was the only American Railway Union officer there; Hogan, Goodwin, Burns, all had gone over to the opposition. He sat numbly on the edge of a curved-back mohair sofa.

"Well, gentlemen, I understand we are now twenty-five men in search of a party."

Victor Berger rose, adjusted his glasses, hunched his coat over his shoulders, came to the middle of the room, looking for all the world like a college professor about to begin a lecture.

"Gene, we bolted the Social Democracy at midnight and it is now four in the morning. In my opinion four hours is exactly long enough for the United States to be without a socialist party."

Gene gazed at Victor Berger for a moment, remembering his first visit to the Woodstock jail. Then his eyes roamed about the room, recalling what each man here stood for and how steadfast he would be.

"If I sense the will of this group," he murmured, his voice barely audible over the hissing gas jets, "it is that we form our own party here and now."

"That's right, Gene," cried a dozen voices.

"Very well, gentlemen, you have just voted us into a new

political party. A few hours ago we all belonged to the Social Democracy. Now the Social Democracy has jumped the tracks. Therefore I think we have a right to call ourselves the Social Democratic party."

"What about the newspaper, and the office, and the money in the bank?" asked Eugene Dietzgen. "Aren't we entitled to our proportionate share?"

Gene turned to Berger.

"How about it, Victor?"

Berger shook his head a dozen times before the words came out.

"When you bolt, the majority keeps the newspapers, the furniture, the records and whatever money there is in the bank."

There was a silence while the men examined the dark brown carpet under their feet.

"It's all right, boys," Gene murmured, "we each of us came into the world naked, and we managed to survive. Back in 1880 when the Brotherhood of Locomotive Firemen asked me to take over, our total cash assets consisted of three black pennies I found in the safe of the abandoned Indianapolis office."

They went through the lobby of the hotel. The sun was just rising over Lake Michigan. Gene walked with his friends to the front door, where a young porter was washing down the sidewalks. He murmured, "It is the dawn of a new day."

Seymour Stedman said, "We ought to give three rousing cheers for the Social Democratic party."

"You would wake the neighborhood," reproved Berger sternly.

"Let the boys cheer," said Gene, "maybe it will wake the nation."

— 9 —

An old fireman friend put him to bed in the caboose and fed him from his lunch pail, but he could hold nothing on his stomach, not even the black coffee that was kept boiling on the little wood stove in a corner of the car. A Terre Haute brakeman insisted upon walking him home from the depot. His head burned, he could barely get one leg in front of the other. He did not need to tell Kate he was ill; she asked no questions and offered no sympathy, yet the formality of her manner was gone as she led him up to the guest room overlooking the street.

She put him to bed and sent a neighbor's child for Dr. Reinche. In his illness he called forth her maternal instincts.

The moment the doctor arrived she went into the kitchen to prepare the weak tea and soft-boiled eggs which, through the years, had been his best medicine. Dr. Reinche asked him no questions either, but in the midst of his examination gave him a lecture.

"You want to die, is it! You don't like life any more? Around a grave you want us all to stand and say, 'What a fine fellow was Eugene Debs; too bad he died so young.' When for the railroad you worked would you treat your train so bad? *Nein,* because the engine would have broken down and been out of work. So now out of work you are because your own engine you let break down. Broke without enough food, without sleep, without rest, without an end of worry. Tell me, Mr. Debs, why do you do it? How can you be so wise in the heart and so stupid in the head?"

Gene had to smile at this.

"Maybe you could perform a little operation, put my heart up where my brains should be?"

"*Nein,* that I cannot do, *aber* something better I can: in bed for one week will you stay, eat good food, a little at a time. Some solid flesh on these bones first, and heal your poisoned insides with nutritious food." Dr. Reinche closed his worn brown medical kit and exclaimed, "*Aber* complain I shouldn't. If people were not such *Dummkopfs,* how would I make a living?"

Gene heard the doctor talking to Kate in the lower hall. He fell into a half sleep. Kate came in with medicine, and a little later the tea and egg. Then he slept again. He awakened feeling a little better. He saw his wife look in, and in a few moments she returned with a bowl of broth and a small piece of chicken, finely shredded.

It was good to be cared for, even though Kate in her crisply starched white apron was more the nurse than the wife. As the days went by he enjoyed her rigid discipline, getting out of bed very little, sometimes sitting in an armchair by the window, an afghan tucked securely around him, his face in the sun, reading a few pages from *Slow Train Through Arkansas,* or *Connecticut Yankee in King Arthur's Court.*

She left him alone only once, toward the end of the week. When she came into his room after luncheon he saw that she had changed from her blue gingham house dress to a purple afternoon gown. At the high neckline was pinned her garnet brooch, and as she pulled on her long doeskin gloves the diamond in her solitaire sparkled.

"You will be all right for a couple of hours, won't you,

Eugene? Mayor Eberle's wife has invited me to tea. It's her biggest party of the year and I wouldn't want to miss it."

"Why, that's wonderful, Kate," Gene exclaimed with pleasure. "You go along and have a fine time for yourself. I'll be right here when you come back."

She returned about five-thirty, flushed and triumphant. To his inquiry as to how she had enjoyed the party she replied, "It was the most important social function of the year. Everybody was there. I was right in my element." She put her fingers on his forehead to see if he was warm, then continued the thoughts she had been thinking so ardently on the way home. "You could have been the mayor of Terre Haute, Eugene; you were so popular as city clerk; then we would have had a gorgeous home like Mayor Eberle, with gardens surrounding the house, and Saruk rugs."

"I wouldn't envy the mayor's wife her finery, Kate, it's likely to prove transient. Eberle has been patterning himself after Boss Tweed of New York. He has gotten away with thousands of dollars of the taxpayers' money."

"I refuse to believe you, Eugene. You are saying these things out of pique."

Gently he expostulated, "Kate dear, the mayor gets four thousand dollars a year. How do you think he built that mansion? How do you think he bought those Saruk rugs you loved so much?"

"That's not our business," snapped Kate. "I never ask a man how he makes his money, once he has it."

"But the grand jury says it's their business. They've asked for an indictment. I'm afraid he is going to end up in the Indiana penitentiary."

"Why should he be sent to the penitentiary," she cried angrily, "just because he earned himself a few dollars on the side? My brothers say that honest graft is natural in America, that's the price we can afford to pay for good government."

Gene was unable to contain himself.

"Good government! When he stole about half a million from the treasury? Mayor Eberle's a burglar . . . worse than a burglar. He not only stole our money, gave us a dangerous water system, and no lighting to protect us at night, but in addition he struck a serious blow at democratic government."

By the end of the second week he had recovered sufficiently to think of returning to Chicago. He knew that this week of convalescence would make no change in Kate's feelings, yet he could not go away without thanking her, without trying to justify himself.

"Kate, I'm sorry that I've been able to send so little money home; I had to cut off my hundred dollars a month wage when the colony began to fail. I know that those occasional ten-dollar bills don't help very much . . ."

The mention of the ten-dollar bills made Kate draw up stiffly.

"Just what are those . . . those . . . greenbacks?" she managed to get out. "Are they something to stuff into an envelope when you manage to remember you have a home to support?"

"No, they are all I have."

There were half a dozen warring emotions on Kate's face; the only one he recognized was incredulity.

"But you are out on a lecture tour, Eugene. You made a great deal of money when you were with the Redpath Bureau."

"I know, but I'm not with any bureau now, and I am not on a tour. I'm just a traveling salesman, the main difference being that I don't have any kitchen utensils or yard goods to sell. All I have is ideas."

"Which nobody wants!"

"Quite so, Kate, which nobody wants."

With a sudden warmth she slipped her arm around his shoulder and patted him reassuringly.

"Then there's no great harm done, Eugene, particularly now that we have you well and on your feet again. Every traveling salesman knows that if he can't sell one line he has to switch over to another. People just don't want your . . . your . . . socialism, Eugene. You admitted that yourself. Then why waste another moment on it? When those letters arrived with the greenbacks in them I was very angry at you, Eugene, because I thought you were taking in a lot of money and were not willing to send it home. But when you told me that that was all you actually made, my feeling of anger changed to one of . . . pity."

He flinched under her fingers. She hurriedly added:

"No, no, Eugene, it wasn't your fault. It's just that people don't want what you are offering. Very well, then, that's no problem to a man of your talents. There must be a dozen jobs where you will be wanted and your work will be welcome. You heard what Dr. Reinche said, Eugene; you'll kill yourself, and for what? To peddle European radicalism that is distasteful to good Americans? Why can't you make socialism your hobby . . . your avocation? I'll strike a bargain with you, Eugene: work at a respectable job during the day, and practice your socialism at night. I won't protest or complain. You can even bring your socialists into the house on week ends."

He hesitated before answering, for he knew that Kate was making a difficult concession.

"Kate dear, when have I ever been a part-time man?"

They had been standing at the window gazing with unseeing eyes down at the street. Kate slipped her arm around him and kissed him on the cheek.

"Stay home with me, Eugene, let us get back our marriage and our love. What are we without it, either of us? Because I do love you, Eugene, I have loved you since that first moent I saw you come into your mother's parlor. . . ."

He held her against him, her warmth entering into him. He had had no affection these many months, nor any caress, and he felt starved for the sense of human communion, of being loved, wanted. He thought how nice it would be to remain home for a few weeks or a few months, writing newspaper and magazine articles to keep the pot boiling, even turning out some educational pamphlets when Kate wasn't looking, so that he would not feel that he had deserted his comrades or his cause.

But even as he held his cheek against hers, even as he welcomed her lips and her kiss, he knew that he could not resign or go on sabbatical leave. He had influenced other men to throw in their lot with his, moved Theodore and his family to Chicago to help with the work. He ached to remain at home with Kate, to end this separation between them, to end the lonely frustrated days and the cold, sleepless nights on the road. There wasn't much to go back to, a beginning all over again, but he had made his pledge and he knew of no way to break it.

All of this he told stumblingly.

"Kate, why can't you just ignore my ideas, the way everyone else does!" He hoped that she would think this a joke. "In the past you have managed to overlook my job; you did your work and I did mine, we were happy together. Why isn't that possible now?"

She sank down into the rocker, covered her face with her hands.

"All right, then, if you love everything else in the world better than you do me . . . go back . . . let people despise you . . . make yourself ill . . ." She looked up at him, her eyes blazing with resentment. "Go to your . . . your comrades. But stop sending me those cheap little greenbacks. And stop coming back to me every time you think you are dying."

— 10 —

The brothers went shopping for the smallest secondhand desk they could find, but even so they could barely get through the doorway of Theodore's bedroom.

"This room is about the same size as our first little office behind Daniel's grocery store," commented Gene.

"Yes, but I don't think the landlord will let us tack grocery boxes on the walls."

"By the time you accumulate enough papers to file," replied Gene, "we will be able to rent an office. The first thing we have to do is get out a circular telling people what we stand for and why they ought to join us."

Theodore stole a quick look at his brother.

"Which one of us writes the circular and which one raises the money to print it?"

"That's easy," Gene replied, "I have an idea and you have a gold watch."

By the time Theodore returned from the pawnbroker with the fifty-dollar loan, Gene had most of the little pamphlet written. He stopped scrawling with the noisy pen as his brother entered the bedroom.

"Theo, listen to this, see if it sounds all right: 'The motto of the Social Democratic party is pure socialism and no compromise. The party stands for united political action and proposes to enter the national field this fall by nominating candidates for Congress in every district in which the organization has a foothold. The convention which resulted in separation has not weakened, but strengthened, the political movement. The cause of socialism cannot be sidetracked, it is a living force in human affairs and in due course of time it will abolish the slavery of capitalism.' "

"Amen," exclaimed Theodore, "may you prove to be a prophet."

That evening the executive committee assembled to edit Gene's statement, to fix the dues, twenty-five cents per quarter, and to write an urgent appeal for new branches and members. "As we are entirely without funds and require office equipment, printing supplies, we earnestly appeal to each branch and each member to send at once such an amount, however small, as can be spared to meet immediate demands."

"Speaking of immediate demands," said Gene, "since the present government can't be expected to rejoice in our plans to change its character, we are going to have to buy stamps to mail out these circulars. Brethren, shell out."

William Mailly pulled a bill out of his pocket and dropped it onto the center of the parlor floor, saying, "I'd like to add a zero to that five, but they tell me there's a law against forgery."

Jesse Cox added a two-dollar bill, while Seymour Stedman, Sylvester Keliher and George Koop added one-dollar bills. Gene went through his pockets: he had only a few coins. He tossed them among the greenbacks on the floor, then began looking again. In his upper vest pocket he found the little chamois bag in which he carried the three pennies from the safe of the Brotherhood of Locomotive Firemen. He opened the strings, took out the pennies and gazed at them affectionately.

"Boys," he said, "we built these three black pennies into one of the strongest unions in America, raised the Locomotive Firemen from starved and despised laborers into a group of respected craftsmen. I never thought the day would come when I would part with these three black pennies, but it seems to me a highly delectable piece of symbolism that they should also be used to start the socialist movement in this country."

Theodore's flat became their workshop, with the executive committee assembling every night to address the envelopes, mail out the circulars and, as Gene succinctly put it, "to find out whether we are still alive."

The volume of return mail they had anticipated never materialized; except for the active organizations sponsored by Berger and Heath in Milwaukee, and James Carey and Margaret Haile in Massachusetts, no new locals were formed anywhere. To his vast disappointment Gene found that the split in the convention was thoroughly indicative of the membership: at least half of all those who had been interested in the Social Democracy had been drawn in solely by the appeal of an experimental colony; others dropped out because of their disappointment at the factionalism. Many of Gene's old friends wrote that they were going back to trade-unionism and would participate in no more socialistic experiments. Others refused to join an organization which would split again at the next convention, perhaps into four segments this time, instead of two.

"There is no way of building an organization by sitting here in your Woodlawn flat," Gene exclaimed to Theodore. "I'm going to have to go out on the road again, exactly as I did in the early firemen days, hold open meetings, convince people that we are here to stay."

"What will you use for money?"

"Theo, that's not like you!" cried Gene angrily. "We don't dare ask ourselves that question! If we wait until we have enough money to finance socialism, it will never come. We've got to act as though we have unlimited funds . . ."

"Get off the soapbox, my dear old pard," murmured Theodore. "I am thinking of you, not socialism. You are not as young as you were in the days when you organized the union. You can't get thrown off freights into snowbanks: you can't go without nourishment and sleep for days on end."

Gene playfully punched his brother before replying, "I'm sorry I barked at you, Theo, and I don't mean to make heroic speeches; but what's the use of fooling ourselves? We have no assets except our faith and our physical strength. If we are not prodigal with them, if we don't spend ourselves recklessly, then we are through."

There was silence in the little bedroom.

"And just to add to your troubles," continued Gene, "we have to start a newspaper before I leave on my tour. Let's go call on Eugene Dietzgen. He is the only socialist I know who has any money."

They rode into town late that afternoon, gathered Keliher, Cox and Stedman and went together to Dietzgen's home. Dietzgen greeted the committee heartily, though he knew that so large a representation could be coming for only one purpose. His hospitable wife brought in decanters of wine and her husband's box of Havana cigars. Gene told Dietzgen about the failure of their new pamphlet to awaken interest or bring in funds, and of his intention to go on a swing throughout the country in an effort to organize locals and build up the membership. Dietzgen agreed that they had to have a newspaper to stay in existence. Without any further cue he asked how much money would be required.

All eyes turned to Theodore as the business manager. He said, "We can establish a small paper for three hundred dollars."

There was a ruminative pause while everyone watched Dietzgen's face. Then Gene said softly, "Could you lend us that much money?"

"I could," replied Dietzgen with a smile, "and I will."

His wife brought his checkbook, Dietzgen wrote out a check, handed it to Theodore. The committee expressed its thanks and went to the front door. Suddenly Gene had a twinge of conscience.

"I am afraid we haven't been completely honest with you," he said as he stood on the front porch. "We asked you to lend us the money, but I have a suspicion that you will never get it back."

"I'll try to be cheerful about it," replied Dietzgen.

On the way to Theodore's flat Gene said, "There is just one thing more we ought to do before I leave: set up an office downtown. You can't expect people to believe you have a world-shattering movement if you operate out of your own bedroom."

By noon the next day they had found an office in the Chicago Opera House, the darkest and dirtiest room they had ever been in. The paper was hanging off the walls in strips, the ceiling was festooned with cobwebs and flaking plaster; the room had not been occupied for several years and the dirt lay thick on the floor and window sills. Jesse Cox paid a month's rent in advance; the ten-dollar rental included heat but not janitorial service. While the rest of the executive committee worked with pails of hot water and clean rags, Theodore pulled the old sheets of paper off the walls, after which Gene applied a coat of white paint.

It was reminiscent of old times.

The beginning of his tour in Massachusetts was gratifying. Socialists James Carey and Lewis Scates, who were running for the state legislature, were popular in their districts and were backed by strong locals. For several weeks Gene spoke to large and enthusiastic crowds. He then swung over to Wisconsin where Victor Berger and Frederic Heath packed the meeting halls for him. By now Theodore was publishing the *Social Democratic Herald* and Gene was able to take hundreds of subscriptions. Before he left the friendly confines of Wisconsin, Carey and Scates were elected to the Massachusetts legislature, a fact which the nation's press found so startling that they gave the new Social Democratic party the first publicity it had achieved since its birth.

Heartened by this success, he struck out for the mining regions of Idaho and Montana. It was as though he had crossed an ocean to a distant and foreign land. His first meeting was scheduled for Boise, Idaho, a sizable railroad stop. Theodore had mapped his itinerary from Chicago, communicated with each town in advance, reserving the town hall or the local opera house, written to the newspapers. Gene knew that he had many friends in Boise, yet he sat alone in the hotel room watching the hours pass. Finally there was a timid knock on the door; Gene admitted a switchman whom he had known for years. The man got out his message in quick gulps: the railroad and mine managers had issued a warning that anyone seen at the Debs meeting would be fired; there would be a mine superintendent committee at the hall to listen very closely to what Mr. Debs had to say.

When he reached the hall he found a group of eight men standing about the potbellied stove with their hats, coats and mufflers on. Not another soul was present in the huge room. Gene went to the men at the stove, introduced himself, asked them one by one what their names might be, then launched into a history of the capitalist system. He told them that the superintendents had their men cowed, that they themselves became cowed when they came in contact with the managers, that when the managers stood before the board of directors the managers winced, which was true of the directors when they were called up by the president of the railroad.

"The lowers are always cowed by the uppers, and the system makes cowards of you all!"

He did not try to take up a collection.

At Boone the railroad threatened not to move the goods of any merchant who attended the lecture. When Gene reached the hall he found an audience of exactly two men: the editor of the local paper and a wholesale whisky dealer. He delivered his full lecture, after which the whisky dealer pressed a twenty-dollar gold piece into his hand, saying:

"The address you made tonight was worth that to me, so you needn't have any hesitancy in taking it."

"If that's the way you feel about it," replied Gene, "when I get home I'll send you twenty dollars' worth of socialist literature . . . at wholesale prices."

The days and nights that followed were even less fortunate; sometimes when he reached a town after dark the hotel clerk would inform him that although Theodore had made reservations far in advance there were no rooms left for Mr. Eugene Debs, socialist. The local newspapers, which had been sent advance notice of his arrival and meeting, thought the matter of insufficient interest to report. Half the time he could not speak because no one would rent him a hall without money in advance, money which Theodore could not send from Chicago. At other times he walked into a hall for which he had agreed to pay twenty-five dollars rent, only to find that he had a handful of people who contributed nickles and dimes when the hat was passed. By the time he paid the rent on the hall he was completely without funds for his hotel bill. Once again he had to deadhead over the rails.

At first he thought that the audiences were staying away solely because of threats, but he soon learned that the genuine cause of his failure to attract people was their indifference to what he had to say. As he faced empty hall after empty hall he remembered what Susan B. Anthony had said that night of her lecture in Terre Haute:

"It's easy to be the opposition in front of big audiences; the most difficult of all things to fight is silence and neglect."

At Helena, Montana, the meeting was such a dismal failure that he could not even collect the five dollars which he had pledged to pay for the hall. The owner informed him that he could not leave town until his bill was paid. Gene spent a sleepless night thrashing on his bed, fearful lest news of his embarrassment get into the papers. About two in the morning he heard unsteady footsteps coming down the hall; an old union printer burst into the room.

"Sshh a dirty shame nobody in thissh town comes ta hear you, Gene. Yeah, but tomorra night there's gonna be a girly-girly show, lotta bare legs kicking over their heads, every ticket in the whole place been sold out."

Gene smiled for the first time in days. The man continued:

"Can't let you go out of town like this, Gene, sshh a disgrace, gotta do something for you."

"Find me five dollars. I have to pay the owner of the hall five dollars in the morning or he won't let me leave town."

The drunk searched fumblingly in his pockets for money, turned a sad face to Gene and said soberly:

"Where am I going to find five dollars in Helena at two o'clock in the morning?"

"I don't know," replied Gene, "but if by any miracle you do locate the money, see if you can't find a bottle standing alongside of it."

Several hours passed. Gene again heard footsteps. He jumped up, flung open the door; there stood his printer friend with a five-dollar bill in one hand and a bottle of bourbon in the other.

"Hallelujah!" cried Gene. "I don't know which I am happier to see."

He doubled back into the Midwest, Omaha, Topeka and Wichita. Everywhere it was the same story: people said, "There is no such thing as socialism, there is just you standing up on a platform and talking about it."

When he reached the South he faced a new type of opposition: in each hotel lobby he found a committee of clergymen awaiting him.

"Are you an atheist, Mr. Debs? Do you intend to deny the existence of God? Is it true that you negate the Immaculate Conception?"

When he was finally able to convince the gentlemen that

he was not on an anti-religious tour, that no word against Christianity would escape his lips while he was in their town, the clergymen gave their grudging consent to his lecture. He had good audiences throughout the South, and after a while he understood why: entertainment was rare in these small towns. People would go to hear anyone for diversion, but they would ask no questions when the lecture was over, take away with them nothing of what had been said, leave behind nothing in the contribution plate.

When he could stand the bad food, the all-night freights or the dreary hotel rooms no longer, he would crawl back to the loving care of Theodore and Gertrude. Each time he returned he was more heavily in debt than when he had left. Enough subscriptions for the paper were coming in to pay the more pressing back bills, but Gertrude had to address the mailing wrappers at night in order to save a couple of dollars on each issue. Theodore pawned his gold watch so often that his wife commented:

"All you have to do is throw that watch out into the street and it will find its own way to the hock shop."

The last occasion on which the watch made its pilgrimage was on Daisy's and Daniel's fiftieth wedding anniversary. The entire family was collecting in Terre Haute, and Gene insisted that Gertrude and baby Marguerite must have new dresses, he and Theodore new shoes, shirts and ties. By the time they had acquired all this finery there was only enough money left for Gertrude's railroad ticket.

"I never thought we would have to deadhead to our parents' fiftieth anniversary," mourned Gene.

"We'll probably deadhead to our own funerals," replied Theodore grimly.

Gene left Chicago the day before the event. He had to let several trains go by until he found a friend up on the locomotive cab who would let him ride along.

— 11 —

His step quickened as he neared Daisy's and Daniel's. When he reached Debity Debs's grocery store he found the door locked and the merchandise removed from the windows. He stood gaping at the now dead store, unable to understand what had happened. He felt uneasy as he walked up the long flight of stairs, but when he reached the parlor nothing seemed to be wrong. Daniel was sitting in his poets' corner, a volume of François Villon's ballades in his hand. He was reading, his lips moving with each phrase; he had heard his son's footsteps but waited until he finished his line to look up.

"Nothing to be alarmed about, son, I have simply retired."

"Has someone left you a fortune, Daniel? Your oldest son, perhaps?" He studied his father's face, closely.

Daniel smiled. "My oldest son is an idealist; he will never leave money to anyone."

"You're an idealist too, Father, and I wouldn't be surprised if you left me a hundred dollars in your will."

A smile cleared the film from Daniel's eyes.

"Gene, I never told you why I came to America."

"You had heard it was a land of freedom . . ."

"Ah yes, but freedom for what? To cut paving blocks of gold out of the streets? No, son, it was because I wanted freedom to believe in new ideas. In Europe they wouldn't let a man believe in new ideas; they put him in jail for his thoughts. That was why I felt bad when they sent you to jail, Gene; it was like visiting the sins of the father upon the son."

Gene crouched down by his father's chair.

"Why, Daniel, now I know where I inherited my bad tendencies."

The old man threw his head back with a flash of spirit.

"I smuggled forbidden pamphlets into Alsace. Those printed pages set me on fire, Gene, and I set out to preach the new truth as I saw it."

"When somebody issued an order for your arrest?"

Daniel chuckled.

"I was too fast for them. I fled to America. . . . In you, son, my dreams come true: all of America knows you are a socialist, you write articles and pamphlets, you travel freely from city to city giving lectures, and your government does not order you arrested." He ran his hand lovingly over Gene's head. "Freedom is no illusion; it may evade you for half a lifetime or half a century, but if you stay with it always, you will end by grasping it with your two bare hands."

"I'm happy you approve my working for socialism, Father."

He sat in silence on the floor, then recalled the empty windows of the grocery store and the locked door. He looked up sharply. Daniel's eyes were wide open . . . but they were not looking at anything. Gene raised his hand, moved it slowly back and forth before his father's face. Daniel made no motion, gave no sign.

Daniel Debs was blind.

Gene wept, soundlessly. Fifty years of selling groceries, of carrying one-hundred-and-seventy-pound barrels of sugar and flour on his back over muddy sidewalks and up back stairs, always dreaming of the day when he would retire to his poets' corner. And now . . .

Daniel had picked up his book once more, was holding it in his two hands and reading aloud. Gene was bewildered, then the realization came: Daniel had not been cheated after all; he had handled each volume for fifty years until he knew these books by heart, every cadence, every rhyme, every thought. His memory would serve as his eyes and his last years would be as rich as he had ever dreamed they would be, living amidst his books and his poetry. What was it Daniel had said?

"Freedom is no illusion: it may evade you for half a lifetime or half a century, but if you stay with it always, you will end by grasping it with your two bare hands."

The next morning Gene and Theodore were in the woods by a little after five. It was an Indian summer day, the air warm with early morning sunshine, the leaves just beginning to turn. They walked for several hours along the trails they knew so well, stopping by old landmarks, exclaiming how certain trees had grown and noticing wild flowers that they had never seen before.

"You know, Theo," said Gene, "these walks are what I miss most."

"We'll be back," replied Theodore confidently, "Chicago is not our home. We belong in Terre Haute, and as soon as we get the party organized . . ."

"Oh, Theo, how in the world are we ever going to get anything organized? The first year's work went down the hopper because the colony idea failed. And what do we have at the end of this second year's work. Debts, a few sympathizers . . ."

Then he remembered Daniel and Daisy, and was ashamed. What had they had at the end of the second year of their marriage? Two children born, both of them dead. Daniel working in a pork-packing plant to accumulate the few dollars needed to open a tiny grocery store in their front parlor. After fifty years of brutal labor, with little compensation other than the love of his wife and children, Daniel could still proclaim proudly: "Freedom is no illusion!" Into his mind flashed a picture of his father bent almost double with a huge sack of potatoes or a barrel of molasses on his back, loading the springless cart for the early morning delivery.

To Theodore he exclaimed brusquely:

"Do we still get Daniel De Leon's paper at the office? I must find out when they're having their next meeting in

New York. De Leon has two thousand members, and that's a working nucleus."

The bare, cheerless Labor Lyceum on East Fourth Street was crowded when he arrived; since there was no place to sit down, he leaned unobtrusively against the rear wall, studying the group on the platform: De Leon and his two lieutenants, Vogt and Abelson. There was no general hum of conversation, no friendly exchange of greetings. De Leon rose, went to the small podium and announced:

"Delegate Abelson will call the meeting to order."

Abelson called for nominations for a permanent chairman. A man sitting immediately in front of De Leon sprang up to nominate Kuhn. At the side of the hall a man called out his nomination of someone called Buck. Abelson called for a vote of hands, but Vogt straightened up from a whispered conversation with De Leon to cry:

"Only delegates who have been members of the general committee for the past six months will be allowed to vote."

Bedlam broke loose. Delegates stood on their chairs, shaking their fists and calling names. A man with an almost imperceptible limp pushed his way up to the platform and cried in a voice that rang out above all the others:

"Let the credentials committee report; they have the right to say who can vote."

A man flanking De Leon yelled, "Hillquit, sit down!"

"I will not."

"Then I'll smash your jaw!"

He swung and caught Hillquit on the point of the chin, sending him sprawling on the floor. There was silence while everyone watched Hillquit slowly pick himself up, walk to his assailant and knock the man halfway across the platform.

Men fought in couples, in bunches. Hats were smashed, clothes torn, noses bloodied. Gene, who was watching De Leon, saw him run out the front door to safety. Vogt also tried to fight his way to the door but was trapped.

Several times the fighters took a swift look at Gene to see which side he was on, but they were baffled by his pained smile. He was saddened to find these Socialist Laborites fist-fighting to perpetuate themselves in power. He asked himself, Are they more interested in salvation for others or self-expression for themselves? What would happen if a conflict arose between their personal interest and that of the cause? Would they submerge themselves, or would they pummel and pounce until they had brought the movement and the years of work down over their heads? Apparently a man's ego was as great and constant a danger inside a humanitarian movement as were the profit pressures from without. And yet, Gene asked himself, how could a man be separated from his ego?

The fights ended; the room began to thin out. At last there was only one man left, Morris Hillquit, the leader of the opposition. He had a cut on the cheek, his shirt was badly ripped, but he was smiling.

"Who won?"

"Nobody."

"I'm Gene Debs."

"So I gathered. I'm Morris Hillquit."

"So I gathered. Why don't you join the Social Democrats? We're peaceable."

"Oh, not so terribly peaceable," rejoined Hillquit with a chuckle. "When the majority of your Social Democracy wanted to colonize, you bolted and started your own party."

"We didn't split any heads."

"You split allegiances, that's just as bad. But you're right. I'm repelled by De Leon's dictatorial manner. He has actually said to me, 'Anyone who dissents from my views is an enemy of the movement.' There is simply no place for De Leonism in America."

"Then you and your friends will join us?" asked Debs eagerly.

"I don't like to walk out empty-handed from a going concern," replied Hillquit, "just to join a movement which can't get itself started. But you will join me for coffee and cake? I think we ought to be friends."

"Good! Friends is what I need."

— 12 —

Gene and his associates had called a presidential nominating convention for Indianapolis in the spring of 1900, at which time they hoped to bring their party into actual physical existence. Gene knew the meeting would do them more harm than good if it were attended by only a dozen delegates from two or three states. He also knew that no one could build a convention by correspondence; once again he would have to ride the rails, hold meetings, form locals, set up state organizations, have delegates elected.

He left Chicago without a dollar in his pocket; this time there was no chance that Theodore could grease his itinerary with greenbacks. Like a mendicant, he would have to live on his wits. He slept with comrades whenever they had a fraction of a bed to spare; whoever had a little food shared it with him. The railroaders had not forgotten his twenty years of service; they carried him over ten thousand miles on their interlocking lines, even when the only available space was a box in front of the boilers.

In most towns he was able to get a modest meeting together, have delegates nominated for the convention. But when he returned to Chicago, forty pounds lighter in weight, his eyes buried deep in their sockets and his cheekbones standing out like central tent poles for the canvas of his skin, he had no way of knowing whether the convention hall in Indianapolis would be filled or would echo hollowly with unkept promises.

There was nothing more he could do, nothing but stew in his own juice and rehearse each meeting he had called, each pledge he had extracted. At night he paced restlessly from one room to another of Gertrude's apartment; the days he spent in Theodore's downtown office, wishing the hours away.

One noon Gertrude made the long car ride downtown to bring him a letter from Kate. He had written to her every few days, telling her where he was and how he was getting along, but no word from his wife ever reached him. This letter was such an unusual event that his fumbling fingers tore the flap halfway across the top.

DEAR EUGENE,
Could you please come home? I have something important to talk over with you.

KATE

He rode a night freight into Terre Haute. It was still dark when he dropped off in the yards and walked up to his house. Kate heard him come up the stairs and was out of bed in time to greet him at the doorway. She put her hands on his shoulders tentatively, kissing him on the cheek. He saw that she was troubled. She thanked him for coming so quickly, then went into the kitchen to light the stove.

There was a comradely air in the big warm kitchen as they had breakfast opposite each other. It was not until Kate had refilled his cup with hot coffee that she ventured to tell him what was on her mind.

"Eugene, I am afraid we are going to lose the house."

Gene put down his coffee cup so abruptly that it almost broke the saucer.

"Lose the house? But how, why?"

Kate rose, walked to the sink and stood leaning against it.

"Please believe me, Eugene, I am not criticizing you, but no matter how little I spend, the expenses continue to pile up, taxes have risen, we have had special assessments this year for gas mains and paving . . ."

"But Kate, you have money coming in from your investments."

Kate did not meet his eyes. She stood hanging her head, the first time he had ever seen his wife do this.

"I have been stupid, Eugene, and willful; against my brothers' advice I sold some of our gilt-edged bonds . . . invested the money in stocks."

She looked up, apologetically.

"There just wasn't enough coming in . . . that's why I wanted the quick and easy money." There was despair in her voice now, and she had to force the words ". . . the stocks are practically worthless. . . ."

Gene thought, Gold bricks! Sooner or later everybody buys a gold brick . . . our colonizing committee . . . even hard-headed Kate Metzel.

"I'm behind in my taxes, and I owe the last assessment." She went to her kitchen drawer, took out an official paper, laid it on the table before him. "This is a notice from the city that I am delinquent; if I can't pay the taxes, Eugene, they'll sell the house."

She buried her head on the table. Gene got up quickly, said meaningless phrases. He raised her head from the table, rested it on his shoulder.

"It's my fault, Kate dear. You were quite right when you said that it is no good for a man to try to reform the world when he can't supply the barest necessities for his own home. From now on I promise to provide enough money every year to take care of the house. Just you draw me up a list of how much you need, and I will see that you get it. How much do you owe on the taxes and assessments? I'll have that money for you by tomorrow night. You have my promise, Kate, this will never happen again; there will always be enough money to take care of you and your house."

Her eyes filled with tears.

"Thank you, Eugene, I knew you wouldn't let them take the house away from me."

Riley McKeen had retired from the bank, but he guaranteed Gene's note. When Gene handed the money to Kate, a sufficient amount to cover the back debts and assessments, she did not thank him directly, but in kind.

"You were right about Mayor Eberle, Eugene. He and his

accomplices have been sent to the Indiana penitentiary. Why, they even pocked the appropriation for the orphans' building."

Now that the taxes had been cared for, he tackled the problem of providing sufficient money to run the house. He sat down at his desk and hammered out three articles, the first about Robert G. Ingersoll, who had just died, the second about Wendell Phillips and their meeting in Terre Haute, the third about James Whitcomb Riley and his boyhood in Greenfield. Then suddenly he felt his energies collapse. He went to bed and stayed there, not because he was physically ill, but because there had come over him a devitalizing *Weltschmerz*. He had worked like a demon and what had resulted? Strife, conflict, uncertainty. Even his most loyal comrades, the former officers of the American Railway Union, had gone their own way. Letters reached him every day from Theodore, from Victor Berger, Frederic Heath, Seymour Stedman, Jesse Cox, Margaret Haile and James Carey: they were getting the new organization under way, making new plans. He was so fatigued that he could not bring himself to read their letters, let alone do any of the duties that were required of him. They had a new party, they had a new plan; but at the end of a month, or a year, or a decade, wouldn't it all come to nothing? Wouldn't they again be torn by inner dissension, make mistakes which would earn them ridicule, end in a blowup which would invalidate everything they had worked to achieve?

Almost three weeks had passed when, fingering through the morning's mail, he found a letter from a magazine editor in New York. He had succeeded in selling the articles; the checks would give Kate six months of freedom from money worries. He got out of bed, brushed his hair, slipped into his bathrobe and slippers and went downstairs to tell Kate.

She put her arms around him, joy and gratitude lighting up her face.

"You are good, Eugene, and generous."

Her soft words broke something inside him, his sense of futility and frustration. He pressed her tightly to him.

"I love you, Eugene," she said. "You know that, don't you? We will be together again, won't we?"

He thought, Our love has been so badly beaten and mauled and knocked out of shape; we have tortured each other over so many years. And yet I am all she has to love, and she is all I have to love. How we cherish what little we have, for without it, what would we be?

"Yes, Kate," he replied, "you are my wife, you will always be my wife, and I will always love you."

The house, which had stood between them all these years, had served to bring them together again.

— 13 —

Reichwein's Hall in Indianapolis was decorated with flags and banners. Most of the sixty-two delegates were young, enthusiastic and excited. Gene at forty-five was the oldest man in the hall. He followed the debates closely but took no part in them, content to go up on the platform when the going got a little rough, or to sit down next to a disgruntled delegate and smooth his feathers. Nominations opened for president and vice-president of the United States. Gene had made it abundantly clear that he could not run for office.

The Rev. Frederick O. McCartney rose, made an eloquent speech about the great future of the Social Democratic party, and then cried out:

"Eugene V. Debs is the unanimous choice of this convention for the nomination for president of the United States. He owes it to the party to bear the standards this year. The party is in a peculiar sense Eugene V. Debs's own, as it owes its existence to him."

The convention rose to its feet and cheered wildly. Gene sat stupefied. White-faced and trembling, he went onto the platform.

"It is not possible for me to accept the honor you wish to confer on me. There are conditions of health known to me only which make it necessary for me to decline."

He was immediately surrounded by a protesting throng. Job Harriman of Los Angeles implored him to accept for the sake of socialism, offering a recuperative trip to California. James Carey promised that they would give him three months of rest before involving him in the campaign. Morris Hillquit insisted that he was the only logical candidate.

Unable to resist the importuning of this group of men and women he loved best in all the world, he asked for a few hours to think it over, picked up his hat and overcoat and slipped out the back door of the hall.

There were still carriages on the streets and occasional couples on their way home from gatherings. His memory went back to the first night he had walked the streets of Indianapolis. Then too he had been troubled: the first convention he had attended had rejected him. He recalled how a man had loomed up in the darkness just as the church bells had tolled midnight, and how Jimmy Riley had said to him:

"Cities are like people; when they're asleep you can read their innermost secrets."

He had made a wide circuit of one of the residential districts, his long legs eating up the blocks. Now he returned toward the heart of town; at last he was alone, and he could face his problem. It seemed that all of his important decisions were made while walking the streets at night, alone, yet aware of the sleeping multitudes behind the front walls of brick, plaster or wood.

He had vowed that he was through with politics; he had no gift for campaigning and there was something repugnant to his nature in asking people to vote for him on the grounds that he was a superior candidate, or that he was more honest or capable than the other fellow. He found distasteful the personal slander and character assassination heaped like medieval offal from a second-story window upon any crier advocating the slightest change in the capitalist economy. Through his mind ran the wail of Horace Greeley when it had been proposed that he run for the presidency against the fabulously incompetent Ulysses S. Grant in 1872: "I am a beaten, broken-down, used-up politician and have the soreness of many defeats in my bones."

Though he was only forty-five years old, he too felt that he was old, with the wounds of too many battles to undertake this most difficult of all crusades. The cold he had contracted in Woodstock kept his left ear running most of the winter; his eyesight had been squandered on the incredibly small print of radical literature. He felt that the movement being born demanded a young man, one who had not already been to the wars; that he himself could serve best as a writer and teacher. If he let himself be drawn into the violence of the political arena it would mean more tens of thousands of miles of deadheading over the lines, for there would be no money for railroad fares, at least none that he would not prefer to put into pamphlets and educational material. It meant months of sleeping in cabooses, small-town depots, cold and dreary rooming houses. It meant more months of the sparest and meanest kind of food because he was unwilling to waste money on his stomach; months of tension, of sharp abdominal pains, retching and diarrhea, days of lying flat on his back in some distant and dirty hall bedroom.

And how would Kate react to all this? In the early days she had been brokenhearted because he had abandoned politics; now he was back in politics, but as a socialist. He had spent the last few years as a visitor in Terre Haute because of his beliefs, a stranger within his own walls. If he accepted this nomination, proclaimed to all the world that he was the leader of American socialism, and hence responsible for its deeds, would not Kate lock the door against him permanently? Might she not go to court, surrounded on all sides by her influential half brothers, and dispossess him?

He loved Kate, not as an ardent suitor, nor as an enamored husband; but as a companion, one tied into the skein of his life. He loved her, too, for everything he had somehow failed to fulfill in their love and marriage. He did not want to hurt her any more, to bring further misery into the bleakness of her house. Once she had had the house of her life she had asked only one thing more of him:

"Eugene, be careful, be careful what you say."

But he had not been careful, he had gone his headstrong way, making decisions without consulting her or taking into account what the new conflicts might do to her peace of mind. At all times Kate had been the innocent bystander, he had been the troublemaker. Now they were close again, he could see her sitting in the bay of the dining room as he swung up from the Union Depot, her hands busily working on some material in her lap but her eyes glued to the streets, watching through the days and nights for his return. From the shining example of Daisy's and Daniel's half century of life together he knew that if a man fails in his marriage he fails in his life, no matter what else he may accomplish.

The last peal of the bells was ebbing away on the sharp clear midnight air when he saw a figure coming toward him in the darkness. The man was hatless and coatless, swinging along in a jaunty stride, his shirt collar open and his hands thrust deep into sweater pockets.

Suddenly the stranger stopped and called out:

"Who is this wandering Indianapolis at midnight, burglar or poet?"

Gene's delighted laughter rang through the sleeping caverns of the streets.

"Jimmy Riley! It can't be. What happened to all your beautiful clothes?"

The men came together, threw their arms about each other for an instant of joyous embrace, and then Riley stepped back.

"The prosperous and debonair outfit is at home on a hanger marked *James Whitcomb Riley, Lecturer*. The man you see before you is the same one you met on these streets twenty-five years ago: Jimmy Riley, still writing homespun, Indiana corn fritters on scraps of discarded butcher paper. But why are you looking so sad on such a beautiful night?"

Gene linked his arm through Riley's and they swung down the street together, the tall, lean, harassed, long-striding figure alongside the short, bland, quick-stepping one.

"Alas," Gene replied, "I have been to another convention."

"No!" exclaimed Riley. "You should keep away from conventions. They don't agree with you. They upset your digestion. The first time I met you on these streets you were unhappy because the delegates had found you too young, too inexperienced. What went wrong tonight?"

"I guess I am too old, too used up."

Riley stopped short, his eyes earnestly demanding an explanation.

"The Socialist party wants me to run for the presidency," Gene said.

"Why, of course you must become president," agreed Riley. "Then you can appoint me poet laureate of America. I will come live at the White House with you. And whenever you are faced with an insoluble problem I will play my guitar for you and recite my verses."

Gene laughed, some of his anxiety spent.

"It sounds like a good idea, Jimmy; certainly your guitar and verses would be sweeter music for the American people than the voice of Mark Hanna whispering into McKinley's ear."

"Who does the Socialist party nominate for the presidency if you turn them down, Gene?"

"Well, we have a number of good men: James Carey of Massachusetts, Job Harriman of California . . ."

Riley shook his head.

"I never heard of them."

"But they are all fresher, better qualified to stage a whirlwind campaign . . ."

". . . with whom? There are millions of people in America who know you, Gene. You need that campaign, don't you, to give the party its official baptism?"

Reluctantly Gene replied, "Yes, Jimmy, we must wage a unified and vigorous campaign to consolidate the party."

"Then you have no choice, Gene, any more than you had a choice of not being locked in that jail cell where I visited you. Granted that you are not twenty, as you were when we first met; granted that you have a hundred different ailments all racing to get you in first to the undertaker's; granted that you are sick of conflict, what can you do? You're going to have to go out and do battle as though you were a starry-eyed youth."

Gene stopped, gazed at the heavens, then at the tilled fields.

"Jimmy, do you know the wonderful line from the Talmud that Robert Ingersoll used to quote? 'It is not upon thee to finish the work; neither art thou free to desist from it.'"

— 14 —

He had hoped to reach home ahead of the news, but when he entered his library he saw the local paper spread open to a two-column article underneath his picture. Kate was sitting in front of her dressing table, her hair combed back in a soft pompadour. She was wearing one of her favorite dresses: a silk with its high neck and bodice covered with lace, the long sleeves elaborate with flounces billowing from shoulder to elbow, and ending in silken bands around the forearm and wrist. For a fleeting instant he hoped that she was actually pleased to have her husband nominated for the presidency of the United States.

When they went down to the library she brought him his pipe and tobacco, then went to brew a pot of tea. He was relieved, grateful, confused. He launched into a vigorous description of the campaign, then asked:

"Kate, would you come with me? Every major city in the United States is on our itinerary; you've never been farther away than Louisville, and this would be a great opportunity to see the country. We could stop for a few days at the Grand Canyon and Yellowstone National Park. And you would attract a lot of votes for us, Kate, don't smile, you would. You would lend the socialist movement a kind of . . . solidity, respectability."

Kate slowly stirred the hot tea, shaking her head indulgently.

"Eugene, you're not really going through with this folly?"

"Why is it a folly, Kate? I think you would have all the poise and dignity required of a First Lady."

Kate's hand began to tremble so violently that she spilled the tea onto her dress.

"Oh, Eugene, why do you have to taunt me so? What's the use of trying to make these trivial activities sound as though they were real and important?"

He went to her side, sat on the edge of her chair.

"Of course it's real and important, darling. Isn't it the dream of every American boy to be nominated for the presidency?"

"Yes, as a Republican. Even as a Democrat. But where is your sense of balance, Eugene: to be nominated by a handful of radicals is equivalent to being nominated . . . by the inmates of a jail, for all the honor it attaches."

He replied gently, "Then all the more reason to stage a national campaign, Kate: we want to show the country that they should agree with us rather than despise us. Once we get our program before the voters . . ."

She looked up at him sharply.

"There can't be more than a hundred people in America who agree with your wild ideas. You'll speak to empty halls, and your campaign literature will be thrown into the gutter."

"That would be bitter medicine, Kate, but if you were along to share it with me, it would be only half as bad."

Kate sprang up, walked heavily to the window and stood staring out. When she turned about there was an expression on her face that he could never remember having seen there.

"Eugene, I want to make a bargain with you."

"Excellent. Now that I am a professional politician I am open to all kinds of horse trades."

"Eugene, please be serious." She went to him, put her arms about him. "Dr. Reinche says that a woman must never interfere in a man's world. It is wiser and healthier for her to be happy inside her home and not pass judgment on her husband's job."

"God bless Dr. Reinche."

"I am asking you to forgive me, Eugene, for having let your work come between us."

"Yes, Kate."

"Then you will agree to the bargain, Eugene? I won't oppose your work any more. I won't set up my judgments against yours. I will never discuss economics or politics again. We will just be happy here together, with me doing my job and you doing yours. Do you agree?"

Trying to think through the tangled skein of the discussion, Gene could only murmur, "Of course I agree, Kate, but where does the bargain come in?"

"You will give up the nomination."

He dropped heavily into a chair, rubbing his hands over his eyes, wearily.

"But, Kate, this nomination and the campaign are part of my job. You have just said . . ."

"I have just said that if you insist upon believing this . . . this socialism, very well, that will be your own private business. But when you embark on this ridiculous campaign, publicly announce yourself as the head of a group of wildeyed, irresponsible . . ."

"Now just a moment, Kate!" For the first time he was

angry. "None of the adjectives you are using really fit us. We are not wild-eyed, we are not irresponsible."

Kate's lids raised high over her eyes and he could see her fists clench at her side.

"Oh no, you are only revolutionists. All you want to do is to destroy private property and tear up the Constitution."

She gritted her teeth together and stuffed her handkerchief hard against her lips.

"Kate," he implored, "don't you see that you are making yourself ill by minding my political business? If I am wrong, if I am misguided, then I will simply get nowhere, the American people will turn their backs on me, no one will vote for me. I shall then go to young Hulman and ask for a job behind my old desk."

She looked up at him with her eyes hard and cold.

"Then you refuse to give up the nomination?"

"Oh, Kate, I refused it a dozen times. I don't want that nomination any more than you do. I hate politics."

She rose, clenched her left hand under her bosom.

"Eugene, you always go your selfish, headstrong way. You care nothing about me, and nothing about our marriage. And now I know why: you are an egotist! You like your picture in the newspaper, you like all this notoriety, you even like the criticism and abuse because you think it makes you an important figure. You get pleasure out of posing as a martyr. All your years of talk about injustice and the poor people and how you can't bear to see them suffer, they were just lies, lies that you used as your stock in trade to get what you wanted. You never have been hurt by your injustice to me, Eugene; you have never cared that you have made my life miserable, far more miserable than the wife of any switchman or fireman for whom you pose as a champion. Ah, if the people could only know you as I know you! You may be a hero to those half-dozen tosspots who nominated you for the presidency, but you are no hero to me. I told you once before, Eugene, that I was happy we never had children; and now I am doubly happy. You would have been no better father to them than you are husband to me. You would have sacrificed their interests at every turn to promote your own career. By now they would have been sitting in this very room begging you to think of them for a change instead of the starving masses you're forever bleating about. They say that charity begins at home, Eugene, but apparently you are not a charitable man."

She stood gazing at him for a moment, letting her words sink in, then left the room. He heard her slow, heavy footsteps drag up the stairs, heard the bedroom door close behind her and listened to the key turn in the lock.

— 15 —

Once again he found himself going to Gloria for help. She converted her home into campaign headquarters; typewriters and desks were rented, volunteers thronged the house to mail out literature, arrange meetings, rent halls. When he reproved her for not keeping a set of books, she replied:

"It's not in my nature to keep books. We simply must amass at least one hundred thousand votes."

"Why a hundred thousand?" he asked. "Is there some mystical significance to that figure?"

"Stop teasing me, Gene. Ned told me many things about the American people. If after the election you can say, 'The Socialist vote ran into six figures,' people will be so impressed that the party will become permanent."

"But once the excitement of the campaign is over, Gloria, I don't want you and your father to face each other across the breakfast table and have to say, 'We spent all our money on Gene Debs, and what are we going to do now?' "

Gloria's eyes flashed angrily.

"That thought could never come into our minds, Mr. Debs! The most important thing in our lives today is for you to make a considerable showing in every state."

Gene tucked her arm under his and held it for a moment; his mind went back to his first political campaign, when Kate Metzel had opened headquarters for him in a little vacant store on Main Street and succeeded in getting her half brothers to contribute to his campaign for the legislature. Now Kate had locked herself in her house, had discontinued the newspaper. She was pretending that there was no presidential campaign being waged and that her husband was not involved in it.

Gene groused to Theodore:

"I spent almost all of last year gallivanting around this country; I talked myself blue in the face and hoarse in the throat to empty halls. Now I am starting out on the identical tour, and I am supposed to attract thousands of wildly enthusiastic people. How? Why? What do I have this year that I didn't have last year?"

"That's easy," replied Theodore, "you have the year 1900 instead of the year 1899. You have the twentieth century instead of the nineteenth century. You have a people who are looking forward to new ideas, new plans . . ."

"Now don't go mystical on me, son. You are supposed to be the practical one in our partnership. . . ."

"All right. Last year you were a lone wolf, a perambulating eccentric; this time you are a political candidate. Your name will be on a ballot, even as the Republican candidate's and the Democratic candidate's. You are officially alive. We will pack the biggest hall in every major city in America. By the time you finish your campaign there will be Americans of all ages and classes who will know exactly what socialism stands for, because you are going to tell them."

"My dear old pard," murmured Gene, "you missed your calling. You should have been a traveling book salesman."

But hardheaded Theodore proved to be right. In conservative Boston three thousand people in three successive nights crowded into Payne Memorial Hall. In Milwaukee the Pabst Theater was full to bursting by seven o'clock. At Philadelphia, even with William Jennings Bryan speaking in a nearby hall, the Academy of Music was packed to the rafters. At Trenton, people stood in the aisles and on the stage of Association Hall. At Wheeling, the laboring men of the city so jammed the Arion Clubhouse and the streets outside that the police had to deal with the crowds; the local paper admitted the following morning that no such enthusiasm had been shown in Wheeling for either McKinley or Bryan.

As the campaign gathered momentum he drew ever bigger and bigger crowds; New York, Hartford, Rockville, Rochester, Toledo, Evansville, Linton. The Philadelphia *North American* gave Eugene V. Debs and William Jennings Bryan the identical amount of space on the front page for their pictures and speeches; the Boston *Globe* gave almost a full page to his tumultuous reception and his excoriation of capitalism; the Wheeling *Register* advised the workingmen of the town not to be deceived by the false promises of socialism, but reported that the meeting had been crowded to the doors, with Eugene Debs bringing the audience to its feet with cheers and applause at every cogent point in his presentation.

He stuck to principles and let personalities alone: thus he was able to indicate how America's wealth and power was centering in fewer and fewer hands, while the millions of American workingmen became nothing more than "hands," dispossessed of their tools and machines and employment. Everywhere he went he concluded with the ringing, hopeful challenge:

"Comrades, a vote cast for the Social Democratic party in this campaign is a landmark, aye, an emancipation mark in the onward and upward march of the working class, until they reach the highlands of that rightful freedom where a man owns himself, works for himself, and enjoys all the fruits of that liberty which knows no master."

Sometimes he made four and five speeches a day; sometimes he went for a week sitting up in coaches, still unwilling to patronize George Pullman's sleeping berths. Day after day he talked socialism to villagers who had never heard the word before. Reception committees met him at the train, hauled him from one meeting to the other; there was always laughter and excitement, food and drink, comradeship and the upward surge of a movement on the march. Where a year before people had refused to listen to him, had rejected every word he said as nonsense and hysteria, now because he represented a political party, because he was on the ballot, because his picture was in the paper alongside McKinley's and Bryan's, they came to understand that possibly, just possibly, all these strange iconoclastic things that Eugene V. Debs was saying were not the nonsensical inventions of a lonely lunatic.

He had told the convention, "I am too old, too ill, too used up to represent such a young and vital movement." Traveling, speaking and conferring sometimes twenty hours a day, he felt stronger than he had on that momentous occasion when Joshua Leach had come swaying down the center aisle of Hulman's. His bad ear bothered him not at all, his heart gave him no dizzy spells, his stomach behaved perfectly, for he was happy, exhilarated, gathering more clarity, force and penetration the deeper he plunged into the American countryside and the issues of the campaign.

He returned to Terre Haute on the day before the election to attend the monster rally that had been arranged for him at the Opera House. Walking down the outside alley to the stage door, holding Theodore by one arm and Gloria by the other, he recalled the lecturers he had himself escorted backstage for the Occidental Club. Eighty-year-old Susan B. Anthony was still carrying on her crusade: Robert G. Ingersoll, Wendell Phillips, Henry George, were all dead now, but their ideas were alive and flourishing. He had a burning faith that just as Wendell Phillips had helped free man from his racial chains, Susan B. Anthony from his sex chains, Robert G. Ingersoll from his chains of religious bigotry, so socialism was another idea which could in time release great segments of mankind from the chains of economic fear and insecurity.

He took a deep breath, smiled at his brother and Gloria, then stepped from the darkness behind the curtain into the full glare of the Opera House.

BOOK SIX

A NEW WORLD IS BORN

MANY OUTSIZED TRICKS WERE PLAYED UPON GENE DEBS AND the Social Democrats to keep them from amassing the hundred thousand votes which Gloria had set as their goal. On the eve of the election a report swept across the nation that he had withdrawn in favor of the Democratic candidate; in Terre Haute, where the Debs family, the Westons and a considerable number of friends had cast their ballots for Gene, not one Socialist vote was reported. Yet in spite of these handicaps more than ninety thousand votes were officially recorded. To those Americans who had never heard of Gene, or who had dismissed the Socialists as transients, the size of the vote came as a distinct shock.

The success of the campaign also united the dissidents within the ranks, and everyone agreed that they should now simply call themselves the Socialist party. Gene refused all offers of title, position, rank or authority. Theodore resigned as executive secretary.

"From now on we will be completely free, Theo. We'll do our work, make our living, and be accountable to no one. There's no need to rush; we won't weigh our results in terms of hours or days. Remember what I told you when we began our work for the firemen's local: we are going to throw away the clocks and the calendars, and treat time like it was a stick of Gloria's molasses taffy; the harder you pull on it the farther it stretches."

"Suits me fine," replied Theodore, pecking experimentally

at his typewriter, which he had just uncrated on its return from the Chicago office.

The two-roomed suite on the second floor of the Whitcomb Allen Building had scrubbed pine floors, a high ceiling and a ten-dollar-a-month rental. On the glass top of the door was lettered: DEBS PUBLISHING COMPANY. When the brothers stopped work for a breather they could hear the presses in the shop downstairs printing their books and pamphlets.

In the first of the rooms Gene and Theodore placed their desks side by side, with bookshelves hung on the wall above. The opposite wall was covered by an outline map of the United States. The rear room was used for wrapping and shipping their literature. Across the hall was a dentist by the name of Trinkle, while on the other side of the central staircase was a dancing school for children. In the late afternoons they could hear the piano music and the laughter of the youngsters.

"As long as we're back in Terre Haute for keeps," announced Theodore, "I think Gertrude and I will build ourselves a house. We have that piece of land out on Ohio Street, and Gertrude never did sell any of our Building and Loan bonds, no matter how bad things got."

Gene clapped his brother on the shoulder. "Oh, Theo, you have worked so hard for so little. At least you will have your own home."

"What shall we do about these account books, Gene? If we have to record every coin that comes in an envelope and enter it against a pamphlet shipped, we'll need a whole book-keeping staff."

"Let's borrow Daisy's big soup tureen and dump all the money into it. On the first of each month we'll take cash from the tureen to pay our rent and printing bill, buy our stationery and stamps. Whatever is left we will divide as wages. Only let's make sure there's no profit at the end of the year."

"Small chance," grunted Theodore, picking up a bulky package from his desk; "this fellow who wrote you from Little Rock enclosing ten cents, how much worth of literature did you send him?"

"I thought you didn't want to keep account books?" Gene grinned. "He was hungry for knowledge about socialism. That's going to be the main part of our job, Theo, reaching people with the things we've got to say." He turned and gazed over his high-backed chair. "There are about seventy-five million people living in those forty-five states, Theo, and we've got to bring socialism to every last one of them."

Theodore gazed at the white map, his silver-rimmed spectacles sliding down over the hump in his nose.

"That's quite a job," he murmured; "good thing you're planning to live as long as Methuselah."

Theodore thumbed through the accumulated stack of letters, asking Gene whether he intended to answer them all. "Some of them are trivial, and at least half want something from you."

Gene's eyes radiated gray and blue. "But not half so hard as something I want from them: to start a Socialist local in their home town, to serve as a distributing agent for our pamphlets, to help us arrange our lecture tours. Every letter we mail, Theo, must be a friend and a vote we have earned for socialism."

"Get off your soapbox, boss," replied Theodore. "I was only thinking of you: are you going to have the strength to answer thousands of letters every week?"

"My dear old pard, I never felt better or younger. I have a full half of my life to live."

"Happy to hear it," grunted Theodore; "from the way you complained about your illnesses to the nominating convention, you sounded to me like a gone duck."

They settled down to the happy routine they had established a quarter of a century before. They were up at five for their walk in the woods; snow, rain, sleet or heat, no weather stopped them; they rebroke the trails they had formed as young men, rediscovering the trees and shrubs with which they had grown up. Dr. Trinkle, riding the streetcar to his office at seven in the morning, would see them striding briskly in the middle of the tracks on their way home for breakfast: two tall, lanky, fast-walking men, their heads high.

At noon each brother again went home to his wife for dinner; each day Gene returned with a sack of apples, bananas or pears which he distributed among the printers, Dr. Trinkle, and the little Italian dancing master down the hall.

When Kate learned of the DEBS PUBLISHING COMPANY painted on the glass door in the Whitcomb Allen Building a radiant smile came over her face. At last her husband was in a respectable occupation, a businessman engaged in the normal pursuit of profit. When she went to her society teas and her friends asked, "What is Mr. Debs doing?" she replied brightly:

"Oh, didn't you know? He is now a publisher."

— 2 —

Monsieur Jean Longuet, Socialist member of the French

Chamber of Deputies, and editor of *Le Populaire,* came to Terre Haute on tour. Gene thought that Longuet's international position might give him sufficient standing in Kate's eyes to justify a reception. Kate made no comment about Monsieur Longuet's politics, but begged off on the grounds that she did not have the facilities with which to entertain.

"Why don't you take him to the Union Depot Restaurant, Eugene? Their food is tasty."

Gene arranged a party which included Gloria and her father, Theodore and Gertrude, and Max Ehrmann, a group of whose poems had appeared recently in the *Atlantic Monthly.* After dinner they returned to Gloria's house, to which she had invited some fifty of Gene's friends. Monsieur Longuet was astounded to find himself surrounded by the latest controversial books, pamphlets and magazines out of Europe; his debate with Gene on the best methods of achieving socialism lasted until two in the morning.

Since the days when Gene had sponsored Robert G. Ingersoll and Susan B. Anthony, Terre Haute had become an important lecture town. Now, as the American, British and European writers and statesmen made their swing about the country, they were invited by Gloria to stay at the Red House. Here they found themselves in as international an atmosphere as the best salons of New York or Boston; here they met Gene's socialist comrades, Morris Hillquit or Meyer London down from New York for a conference, Frederic Heath or Victor Berger returning to Milwaukee from a St. Louis convention, W. H. Ghent or Professor Herron touring the country in search of material for their articles and books.

When word came to Terre Haute that it was becoming known for the two persons it most strongly resented, Eugene Debs and Gloria Harkness, the more solid citizens cried, "Aren't there enough wonderful people in this town to talk about?"

"The trouble with Debs and the Harknesses," exclaimed Mrs. Trillenge, one of society's leaders, "is that they're a hundred years ahead of their time"; to which Gloria replied, "That's no worse than being a hundred years behind the times."

The spontaneous parties at Gloria's settled down to regular Wednesday and Saturday night buffet suppers. James Whitcomb Riley came over once a month to read his new poems and make changes with his flicking pencil. Gene liked to rehearse his news ideas before the group, throw the solid meat of his problems into the open pot of discussion and combat every kind of reaction before he began pacing the floor of his office, dictating the new article to Theodore's rapidly typing fingers.

He and Gloria were never alone, but were surrounded by the host of friends who thronged the Red House. Gene knew how quickly their relationship could be destroyed: one word of scandal, one ugly innuendo carried to Kate, and he would never again be able to set foot in this house. He had double protection against any such possibility, for Nedina constituted herself a chaperone, refusing to leave her mother's side from the moment he entered the house. Nor did Nedina make any effort to conceal her antagonism; he was never allowed to forget that Ned Harkness had feared and hated him, and that his daughter was carrying on the tradition.

He knew that in the late afternoons Gloria and Nedina went shopping, while Imogene practiced the piano. Sometimes when he was tired or low in spirits he would walk to the Red House, drop silently into a chair and watch Imogene's lovely face, so miraculously a re-creation of the young redheaded Gloria he remembered. As he sat with his chin on his chest, hearing the music dimly, he thought again how much he had wanted to have children, to watch them grow, to share in their joys and sorrows, to help them achieve maturity. Deep in the recesses of his mind he thought of Imogene as the daughter who might have been his, had his life been different.

Only once did he and Gloria have an hour alone, when he slipped in for a few moments to hear Imogene play, only to find that she had accompanied her sister to select some wool for a dress. Gloria was sitting on one of the divans under the big south window, the sun lighting up her hair to make it look coppery gold. She was wearing a flowered print robe which matched her slippers. He thought how strange it was that her voice had not aged.

"Are you happy with your new work, Gene?"

He sat in silence for a few moments, letting the sunlight warm his thoughts.

"Yes, I'm happy, and sometimes confused as to how it can best be done. Everyone expects the socialist to be an idle dreamer; they're waiting for the chance to say, 'You want to make a whole new world, but you can't even carry through the simplest business arrangements.' Every time we send out a letter or pamphlet, a colored pin goes up on the map in our office. When ten letters, pamphlets or books have been sent to one locality, we change the color of the pin. We can also show you by our pin system where every local of the Socialist party is located, and how many members it has. How's that for being scientific?"

Gloria laughed a deep-throated chuckle.

"Oh, Gene, you work so hard to prove all the things that you are not. You are a dreamer and a theorist and an idealist, and God knows how desperately we need your kind in a world full of profit worshipers. No, Gene, you are carrying on an educational campaign, and in education you expect to give out everything and get nothing back, or at least not for twenty years."

He had been studying her face while she spoke.

"Gloria, are you happy?"

"Oh yes," she replied soberly, her eyes full on his, "I have been very happy since we opened this house."

"But you are still young. There is so much love in your nature. Don't you ever plan to . . . marry again?"

Gloria looked down at her hands, clasping and unclasping them in her lap.

"I have a great deal of love: my father, my two daughters." She looked up at him, her expression serious. "And I have my love for you, Gene. That is something I never lost. I know that your . . . marriage . . . is permanent. But when I see you here, surrounded by your friends, when I hear you formulating ideas, or reading your articles and asking for criticism, then I am terribly happy, Gene. I feel that I am playing some small part in your life, perhaps giving you something that no one else has to offer."

She rose, walked to the fireplace and stood there facing him.

"You said I am still young, and I feel young, but not in the way I did when I loved you so terribly here in Terre Haute. I don't think I want to marry again, Gene; I want a good deal more for our friendship to continue. And I think you had better go now, before my young daughter gets back and finds me alone with you. Nedina would not approve of that."

Kate hated the Red House more intensely than anyone else because it took her husband away from her two evenings a week. She did not accuse him of participating in the orgies she was sure were going on there, but she was revolted at the idea of his being exposed to what she called loose women and loose ideas. He begged her to come with him so that she could see for herself that nothing more heretical was happening than that a group of people, some of them sitting on the floor, were discussing the new work of Ibsen, Zola or George Bernard Shaw. But Kate only replied:

"She won't get away with it, that Harkness woman. She'll get her comeuppance."

— 3 —

Across his desk poured countless requests to attend meetings, rump sessions, policy committees, state and national conventions.

"From the number of invitations we've had to attend Socialist luncheons and banquets this week," he commented to Theodore, "it looks as though our comrades expect to *eat in* the revolution."

There was a dispute waging over state versus national authority within the party; the battle between the radical and conservative elements had already begun. The left-wing minority, known as the Impossibilists, declared that it was impossible to accomplish socialism by gradual, legal means; that violent revolution was the inevitable end of the class struggle, and toward this end the party must declare war on religion, the small farmer, the craft union, demanding complete and unquestioning obedience from the rank and file. The Opportunists believed in the gradual and peaceful evolution of socialism, through reform and the ballot, as did the Fabian Society in England, which had been founded by H. G. Wells, George Bernard Shaw, Beatrice and Sidney Webb.

He did not want to participate in these unending arguments for he knew that every quarrel left behind a trail of ill will and hurt feelings. Someone had to remain outside the arena, be a disinterested party to whom the disputants could turn to have their ruffled feathers smoothed, their differences compromised.

He refused all invitations, stayed away from meetings.

Yet when the Impossibilists began a movement to have the socialist publications unified so that they would all be saying the same thing at the same time, Gene shed his calm and jumped into the ring with both fists flailing. Each socialist paper and magazine was separately and privately owned: Berger's *Social Democratic Herald* in Milwaukee, J. A. Wayland's *Appeal to Reason* in Girard, Kansas, Algernon Lee's *The People* and Abraham Cahan's *Jewish Daily Forward* in New York City. These owners had started their papers on shoestrings, struggled for circulation in hostile communities; they were individualists who would fight to the bitter end to preserve their freedom to speak their minds. The Impossibilits, who maintained that ideological differences created confusion among their sympathizers and gave comfort to their enemies, circulated a petition demanding that all party papers be held to a centrally enunciated party discipline.

Gene wired Victor Berger to meet him in Chicago, where they picked up Gaylord Wilshire, millionaire Los Angeles real estate owner and publisher of *The Challenge,* who was also known as the frock-coat socialist because he always gave his lectures attired in formal evening dress. In New York they were joined by Hillquit, London, Professor Herron, all of whom were resolved to smash this first effort at intellectual dictatorship. When Gene got back to Terre Haute, four days later, he was able to tell Theodore that a freedom-of-speech-and-press plank had been nailed into the constitution of the Socialist party.

"Fine," murmured Theodore, "but when did you sleep last?"

He was making no worthwhile progress with his Blueprint for an American Civilization, for at the critical moment in his thinking he, would find that he did not have sufficient technical information. He would go out to buy textbooks on money and banking and foreign exchange, try to master the subjects so that he could plan just what kind of money would be minted by the socialist government and whether workmen would be paid in coin or script; but after an hour of reading his eyes would begin to burn and his head grow heavy and he would tell himself that he was too old to become a student again.

Yet if his blueprint would not get itself charted, each new problem evolved as a study for one of the socialist papers, an article describing the difference between production goods, such as machines and factories, which would be owned co-operatively by the socialist commonwealth, and personal or consumer goods, such as houses, furniture, books, which would be owned privately by those who worked and earned the right to buy them.

Because he had remained aloof from personal conflicts, he now found himself the party's unofficial repairman. One of their state campaign managers was discovered in bed with someone else's wife; a wildcat scheme was endorsed by a socialist paper which sold its subscribers stock in an invention called the airplane. There was little he could do about these peccadilloes, but when he learned from a derisive newspaper article in Dubuque that the employees of J. A. Wayland's *Appeal to Reason* had gone out on strike because Wayland refused to recognize their union, he decided he had better make a little excurison into Kansas.

The prospect of seeing Wayland was pleasant, for he considered the publisher of the *Appeal to Reason* the most colorful of all the socialists. J. A. Wayland had been born just a few months before Gene, also in Indiana; before he was twenty he was a printer, journalist, and part owner of the small-town newspaper. In Pueblo, Colorado, he had set up the One Hoss Print Shop, bought real estate and become one of the most prosperous men in town. His conversion to socialism was an intellectual process in which he was helped by an old shoemaker who led him to the writings of William Morris and John Ruskin. He started his first socialist publication, *The Coming Nation*, in Greensburg, Indiana, and made it so successful that he was able to found the Ruskin Colony in Tennessee on its profits. When the members took to fighting among themselves, Wayland pulled out, leaving behind his valuable newspaper and the last of his resources. On August 31, 1895, he published the first issue of his new paper, the *Appeal to Reason*, in Kansas City. Costs were high and he had to suspend publication. After he had saved a few dollars, he headed west. When his train reached the small farming community of Girard, Kansas, Wayland looked out the window, decided this was approximately what he had been looking for, and got off.

Riding the train over the same line to Girard, Gene chuckled to himself as he recalled the consternation of the Girard farmers and businessmen when they learned that a socialist newspaper was about to descend upon them. They put every obstacle in Wayland's path, but Wayland was a strapping, two-fisted fighter; he survived the first years of Girard's opposition and dislike. By now the hidebound little county seat was glad to have the *Appeal to Reason* because it had brought them a first-class post office, and the growing staff of what they called the *"Squeal of Treason"* was buying in its stores and eating in its restaurants.

Gene took his satchel off the high rack and walked from the station up to the southwest corner of Courthouse Square, where the magazine had its print shop and offices. Catalpa trees were planted on each side of the street and the L-shaped frame houses, with their pointed roofs, were painted immaculate white or light green.

He passed through the downstairs press and mailing rooms and climbed the stairs to Wayland's office. Wayland was six feet three in height, with steady gray eyes, blunt, tactless, hardheaded, incorrigibly independent. He had to struggle to keep an oversentimental nature in check, and so he presented to the world a hard-crusted, insensitive exterior. His membership card in the Socialist party was the one concession he would make to national headquarters; for all the rest he was a maverick, clashing with the personnel and politics of the party, going his own sweet and idiosyncratic way.

Wayland greeted Gene with bluff cordiality, inviting him home for supper. Wayland's first wife had died; he had recently married his young secretary and bought a lovely mansion out on Summit which had been left over from a former boom. Gene wandered through the big, furniture-cluttered rooms, commenting:

"You are the only man I have ever seen that looks good in a mansion."

The first glimmer of a smile came to Wayland's face as he said, "Well, you know how it is with us socialists, we are always satisfied with the best."

"You know, One Hoss," grinned Gene, "you are the rarest thing the socialist movement has, a humorist. You can win people over, where us serious codgers can't get to first base."

Wayland stopped short in his peregrinations.

"You meant that comment for a purpose, Gene."

"Well, I am the last man to mind your business, but I think a dash of that world-famous One Hoss Wayland comedy could help this strike situation enormously."

Wayland was not displeased at being called world-famous.

"What's there to laugh about in a strike, Gene? These upstarts are threatening my control over the paper. If I give in to them, I will be working for the A. F. of L. If you can give me one good reason why I should let my typists and clerks tell me how to run my business . . ."

Gene leapt out of his chair, his hand extended, exclaiming, "Why, Mr. James J. Hill, how delightful to see you again! What are you doing all the way out here in Girard, Kansas? I haven't seen you since the Great Northern strike, back in '94."

Wayland collapsed onto a leather divan, his legs sprawled out lengthily in front of him.

"One Hoss Debs," he murmured.

"Look, J.A., you pay those girls four dollars a week. Is that enough?"

"It's not enough," replied Wayland, "but it's a dollar above the regular rate paid in town. When the Girard merchants heard I was paying four dollars they demanded I stop this socialistic nonsense and come down to the regulation rate."

"Excellent!" exclaimed Gene. "Raise the wages to ten dollars a week and they will run you out of town. That will make a martyr out of you and hasten the revolution by at least thirty minutes."

There was a loud knocking on the door. A servant came in to tell Wayland that a committee from the Girard Merchants' Association wanted to see him. Wayland snapped, "What are they coming to see me for? Not one of them has talked to me in the past three years."

He offered them neither seats nor drinks.

"Gentlemen, to what do I owe the honor of your visit?"

The shortest of the three men answered quickly, "We want you to know that the town is behind you solidly in this contest, Mr. Wayland. We are prepared to furnish people to take the place of every last striker."

"In case you need any money, Mr. Wayland," said another, "we have a fund that's available. We will do everything we can to help you keep Girard a non-union town."

A flush of anger spread over Wayland's cheeks and forehead, giving his white hair a colorful base. In his most pontifical voice he replied:

"Gentlemen, I don't need to tell you how heartening it is to learn that we businessmen of Girard are solidly united, going forward arm in arm, with one thought and one purpose."

The committee bowed itself out. Wayland went to a mahogany sideboard, took out a bottle of whisky and poured himself a water tumbler of it.

"You know, J.A.," commented Gene casually, "when you first moved the *Appeal* out here to Girard I thought you were making a mistake because you would be surrounded by hostile souls. That just shows you what a bad businessman I am. Here you have made yourself a fortune, and you have the best element in town solidly behind you."

Wayland took a deep draught of whisky, then threw himself down on the sofa.

"All right, I've been pigheaded. What do I do next?"

Gene pushed Wayland's heavy legs off the dark leather and sat beside him.

"You have come through a bad time, one of the most difficult for any man to handle: that moment at which your liberalism ran afoul of your vested interest. I know that you are willing to pay higher wages, but what you are unwilling to share is your power. Power is a headstrong drink, One Hoss, even stronger than your hundred-proof whisky. Compared to it, the accumulation of money is a third-rate pastime. It is the challenge to their power that makes the Fricks call out the Pinkertons and fire on the workers at Homestead, the Pullmans and the General Managers' Association hire armed thugs, the George Baers and other coal-mine owners hire their Coal and Iron Police."

Wayland poured another drink, then whirled on his accuser.

"Get me out of this mess!"

"There is only one way of doing it, and that is by satirizing yourself. You have made the socialists a laughingstock by fighting this first union ever formed inside the cause. Now let's see if we can earn some laughs for you and some sympathy for the movement along with it."

"Sure, but how?"

"Give your staff not only the things they have been demanding, but a dozen others in addition: a forty-seven-hour week; you'll be the first paper in America to establish it. Two weeks' vacation with pay . . ."

"And perfume in the ladies' lavatory?"

The following evening Wayland appeared before his assembled employees and townspeople. The committee from the Girard Merchants' Association was sitting in the front row. Wayland told them that he had been wrong to oppose the union, that socialism endorsed all unionism; he recited the list of concessions he was making, which included several items he had thought up for himself, such as life insurance and a pension. There were amazed gasps from the work group; the merchants' committee held a whispered conference, rose and left in protest.

Gene leaned back in his chair, chuckling.

— 4 —

Theodore was pacing the floor when Gene returned from Girard.

"Have you forgotten that we are starting on our lecture tour tomorrow morning?"

By the time they reached the Texas Panhandle the train was stifling, but they could not open the window because of the dirt and dust that poured in. At Big Springs it was a hundred and eighteen in the shade, and no shade. The chairman met them at the station, said, "One of our comrades has a hotel here, we would like you to stay with him."

The hotel turned out to be a few rooms over a storehouse. Gene said to the owner:

"It's too hot to eat anything heavy, but we would be mighty grateful for some soft-boiled eggs."

"Better not try eggs, boys," replied the man. "I cracked three dozen this morning and only found one good one."

"Then what do you suggest?" asked Theodore.

"The only thing I've got that's safe is a can of beans. Would you settle for that?"

Gene's molars locked but he replied courteously, "We would be glad to settle for it, if only we can take a bath."

"I'm sorry, comrades," said the owner, "but we don't have any bathtubs."

They had eaten a few spoonfuls of the beans when they were interrupted by the delegation arriving in front of the storehouse. The chairman entered the little restaurant and cried:

"It's time for the meeting now. We are parading out to the camp grounds."

The midsummer sun beat down fiercely. It had not rained for months and the dust was a foot thick. Gene and Theodore took their places at the head of the procession. They paraded along the lonely road for three miles to the grove where several acres of wagons were assembled. Some of the farmers had driven seventy-five miles to attend the meeting, bringing along their families and turning the junket into their annual vacation. There was only one tree for miles around, but under it a platform had mercifully been built. Several hundred men, women and children, who had made the long journey over the prairie in springless wagons, were sitting on the hard ground in front of the platform, protected from the relentless sun by parasols and straw hats.

Within a few moments the tree became useless for the purpose of shade, and Gene found himself speaking in the full heat of the Texas sun. The perspiration flew off his finger tips onto the people sitting immediately in front of the platform. Theodore was worried; the intense heat could not be good for Gene's heart. He flashed his brother a signal to stop speaking.

The real ordeal began when finally he did stop, for every man, woman and child in the audience wanted to shake his hand and hold a conversation. After three hours the skin between his fingers had worn through, and his arm was so paralyzed he could not lift it from his side. At last Theodore helped him into one of the wagons and they made their way back to the little room above the storehouse.

They drew the mosquito netting about them. Gene fell asleep. Within a few minutes he awoke to find himself nearly devoured by the mosquitoes. Crouched by the side of the bed, his face swollen by enormous bites, was Theodore, futilely trying to patch the holes in the netting. They lay in torture the rest of the night, alternately beating off the insects and rubbing their welts.

The next morning they took a train called the Orient which had no roadbed and was just laid over the prairie. The bumps threw them into the aisle. They reached Bad Well at sundown, went to the post office for their mail and asked about a restaurant.

"Only place to eat is the butcher shop down the block," replied the postmaster.

The butcher shop had one table at which a cowboy was working over a steak, the perspiration rolling off his face and onto the plate. Myriads of flies were eating off the half beef which hung on an open hook behind the counter. Theodore asked the cowboy:

"How is the steak?"

The cowboy grunted without looking up, "Best I ever eat."

"Think you would like one, Gene?"

Gene took a quick look at the butcher's bloody apron and replied:

"You know our parents raised us to be vegetarians."

"We don't have no vegetables," said the butcher, "but I can sell you some Uneeda biscuits."

"Just what we need."

They left the butcher shop, each munching a cracker, and found a general store that had some bananas for sale. This was the first solid food they had eaten in four days. Since Gene was not scheduled to speak until the next day, no one had met their train. Theodore asked a small boy if there was a hotel in town.

"We had one," replied the boy, "but it burned down."

They went back to the depot, asked the stationmaster who was to be in charge of the camp meeting the following day.

"They weren't expecting you until tomorrow," explained the man; "they've all gone out to the camp grounds to sleep overnight and visit with their friends. But I'll take you out to their house."

It was pitch-dark when the men reached the chairman's house. The stationmaster left the brothers in the bedroom, returning in a few moments with a bucket of water with a big piece of ice in it.

"I would like to fall right into the bucket," said Gene.

"Gene, you are mortally tired," said Theodore. "It's going to be too hot for both of us to sleep on that narrow bed. You have to speak tomorrow, so I will just stretch out here on the floor."

"No, Theo, I couldn't sleep, knowing you were uncomfortable."

"Then you can sleep in the bed the first half of the night, and I'll take the second shift."

"You can't fool me that way, son; it's going to take a club to wake me."

"I am your lecture manager," said Theodore, "and I give the orders around here. Get into that bed."

But when Theodore pulled back the bedspread they both let out an agonized gasp: under it was nothing but bare slats. The chairman and his wife had taken the mattress and bedclothes with them, along with every cushion in the house. The brothers gazed at each other with tears in their eyes. Gene made a wide sweeping gesture toward the bed.

"You first, my dear Alphonse."

"Oh no," replied Theodore, bowing low, "you first, my dear Gaston."

"This story is going to be very funny to tell next winter in Terre Haute."

"If we live that long."

Gene slept on the floor with his satchel as a pillow. Theodore stretched out on the cedar chest. At dawn they got up, every bone in their bodies aching. Just as they finished dressing they heard a carriage draw up. The chairman burst in, welcomed them to Texas, then picked up their bags.

"Come along with me, I'll find you a place with a comfortable bed and you will be able to sleep as long as you like."

Gene and Theodore trailed behind the chairman to a white house with a clean cool bed. They fell asleep instantly, but an hour later the children started slamming the screen door, and further sleep was impossible. The chairman broke into the room.

"Get up quickly, I found a better place for you to sleep."

Once again they dressed, trudged a few blocks and were given twin beds in a doctor's house. By now they had been without sleep for so long that they were too jumpy to close their eyes. Shortly before noon they drove out to the camp ground. It was a picturesque sight, with families grouped around hundreds of little fires, cooking their midday meal. Gene did not think he could summon sufficient energy to stumble through his speech, but when he saw his comrades surrounding the little bandstand, smiling up at him and calling friendly greetings, he forgot his troubles and cried out with an embracing voice and gesture:

"The spirit of socialism is abroad in the land, arousing the people from their slumber. What do we mean by socialism? The end of class rule, of master and slave, of ignorance and vice, of poverty and shame, of cruelty and crime. The birth of freedom, the dawn of brotherhood, the beginning of man. That is the demand. That is socialism."

By the time they got back to the doctor's house, five hours later, the parlor was crowded with the comrades, all wanting to carry on the discussion.

The next day they had to change cars four times in order to reach Denison. At one juncture Gene announced: "I am going to see the station agent and ask if he knows an easier route." When he returned a few moments later he reported, "The agent says there isn't any difference; if you take the one you will wish you took the other."

The Poages Restaurant had the longest lunch counter they had ever seen. The brothers sat down, scanned the menu and ordered chicken pie. Just at that moment Gene saw two cockroaches sticking their whiskers out of a pie on the counter. He canceled their order and bought some chewing gum to soothe their appetites. When they asked the owner about a room, he escorted them upstairs.

The room was small and blazing hot. The frying meat odors wafted up from the kitchen, turning their empty stomachs and making them nauseous. Things had been bad on former trips, but this was the worst they had ever encountered.

At the first light of dawn they heard noises in the kitchen below. Gene went downstairs, asked for a glass of milk. It was sour.

"There must be an easier way than this to make a living," he groused.

Their meeting that afternoon was held in the ball park on the outskirts of town. It was the largest meeting so far, with a band and a canopied platform. By the time Gene got through his talk he was green in the face and shivering with fever. The crowd had no intention of letting him go, thronging around so thick that Theodore could not rescue him.

At dusk the brothers were deposited at the railroad station. They had to sit up all night in order to make the following day's meeting. At noon they reached Wichita Falls, Texas. The platform was paved with asphalt; they practically left their shoes in the hot liquid at each step. On the tracks they saw jack rabbits lying about, cooked by the sun. They found a good hotel and a clean room with two beds, but when they turned on the bath the water from the Red River was the color of clay, and almost as thick.

Gene flung himself face down on the bed.

"Theo, I don't think I can finish. I think we had better take the train home."

"You're right, Gene, we just can't go on: no food, no sleep, no baths."

In the morning Theodore heard Gene stirring about. He went into the bathroom to see his brother sitting in the bathtub on top of several inches of red mud, delightedly splashing water over his chest and head. He turned when he heard Theodore.

"We can't go back, son. All these people came through this heat; they'll be terribly disappointed."

"They will be even more disappointed when they read your obituary in the *Appeal to Reason*."

"It would hurt me worse to disappoint them than this heat will. Another month or so, and we'll get used to it."

— 15 —

The colored pins on the map multiplied. Theodore was kept busy arranging tours. For some of the lectures Gene took the fee needed to keep the Terre Haute office running, but most of his talks were given under the auspices of the Socialist locals which had been unable to accumulate the funds needed to stage membership drives.

It was clackety-clack, clackety-clack, click-clack, click-clack over the rails again, while he watched the flashing panorama of America, all the way from the prosperous farm country of Iowa to the deepest, darkest slums of overcrowded cities. Whenever he was feeling discouraged or disillusioned he would make for the tenements of the East Side of New York City. Here he saw the party opening schools and holding classes for people who had no other opportunity for education; saw the party fighting for the sweatshop workers jammed into railroad flats, organizing protest meetings and waging an unceasing battle for a reduction of the twelve-hour day, the eradication of filth and disease from the factories and the raising of the piece wage so that families working in malignant holes would be able to buy enough food to keep their bodies alive.

For the chained thousands of the slums, socialism was the only brightly burning light of their existence; all the rest was darkness, brutality, exploitation, slavery. He went with them on a Sunday to their picnic in the park or woods or at the beach, saw the children romping in the sunshine, singing with fervor the new Young People's Socialist League songs: for these were the abandoned of the earth, abandoned by God and Man. Socialism alone cared for them. When Gene rose to tell them how they must work to educate themselves and free their children, so that they could go out into the world and work to free all other oppressed peoples, their faces became suffused with hope and serenity.

The word "comrade" had special meaning for Gene: any man, woman or child who came into the Socialist party was his comrade, for it involved sacrifice to become a socialist, to give up those few precious pennies each week for the sake of the cause, to risk the displeasure of the community and the anger of the employer; to work nights and Sundays carrying the planks to put together the platform for the street-corner meetings, or to wash the dishes after a supper given to raise funds for strikers. When he met a socialist in Buffalo or Spargo or Makin, when he put his long, thin arm around a new member, clutched him by the shoulder and called him comrade, he felt he had gained another much-needed brother in the long and desperate fight for freedom.

He gave Kate her expense money on the first of each month. She did not ask where the money came from; all dollars looked alike to Kate, and were equally interesting. At first he thought that it might be a hardship on her to be left alone month after month in the big house on Eighth Street, but he was reassured by the answer she gave to one of the Terre Haute elite.

"No, I don't mind Mr. Debs being away. After all, every man must take care of his business, and Mr. Debs's lecture tours earn a great deal of money."

Theodore was not always able to go on tour with him, for the work of the office was too heavy to be left behind. For months on end Gene found himself traveling the hard itinerary of train to hotel to lecture hall, to train to hotel to lecture hall. Nor was there any rest once the local comrades had let him retire, or the train had pulled out for the next station: newspaper articles had to be written for the *Social Democratic Herald* and the *Appeal to Reason*, letters had to be answered, letters reaching him in bundles at each stop, forwarded by Theodore, marked, "Need your personal attention."

Whenever possible he would return to Terre Haute, sit rocking on the wide veranda on warm nights, regaining his strength and composure, having dinner with Theodore and Gertrude in their new home. He spent many evenings with his parents, for Daisy was now confined to bed with attacks of rheumatism. She would get up for supper only if Gene were coming. These were the happiest hours in the Debs household, when they would sit companionably about the dinner table, Daisy asking if her tureen was being kept as full of coins as she had kept it full of thick soups. After supper Gene picked his mother up in his arms and carried her into the parlor, wrapping an afghan about her while he read for an hour to Daniel out of Malherbe or Alfred de Vigny. He could see Daniel's lips murmuring the lines, word for word. Daisy was listening to her son's voice too, but she was not hearing poetry, she was reliving the memories of her half century in Terre Haute.

Sometimes there were children in his house, Kate's nieces and nephews. She kept a glass jar of butterballs on the dining-room buffet; when one of the children came to visit, Kate would say:

"You may take *a* butterball from the jar."

He concealed a box of chocolates in the back of his desk in the library, and crayons and drawing paper as well, with which to tempt them further. There was one beautiful child of ten with blond pigtails whom they called the Cricket. Gene walked unexpectedly into the kitchen one day to find Kate at the center table, holding the Cricket on her lap, plying her with ice cream. When the child finished her dish and ran out the back door, Gene sat down at the kitchen table opposite his wife.

"How beautiful you are at this moment, Kate, with those high spots of color in your cheeks. If only you could have had children, how much richer life would have been for you . . . for both of us."

Kate replied slowly, "Actually, Eugene, I never wanted children."

Gene could not believe that he heard right.

"Kate, you mean that when I gave up politics . . . when you saw that I would always be in the midst of controversy . . . ?"

"No, Eugene." Her eyes were full upon his. "I made that decision when I was a young girl. I never liked the muss that children made in the house, the dirt they tracked in with them, the way they soiled the walls with their dirty fingers. I wanted most to have my house always immaculate, with a place for everything and everything in its place."

Feeling sick inside, he stumbled upstairs, sat on the edge of the bed, thinking, How little we really know other people, even when we have lived with them for twenty-five years. He would never have married Kate if he had known she didn't want children. All these years he had believed that they couldn't have them; only now did he learn . . . How completely she had made the house of her childhood come true, with nary a soul to displace a piece of furniture or leave fingerprints on a shiny surface. But the things he wanted most from marriage: children, a hospitable home, a wife who would be his partner, who would stand by his side, all these had passed him by.

He knew there would be no point in reproaching Kate, even in saying, But why didn't you tell me you never wanted children? He had married on the assumption that this was one of the primary purposes of marriage, that everybody loved youngsters and wanted them. Well, he had been naïve, he had deceived himself; surely that was no one's fault but his own?

During the months preceding the 1904 convention he took every opportunity to tell his friends that he was not a candidate for the presidency. He refused all invitations to come to Chicago, and yielded only to the plea of Professor Herron, who was chairman of the platform committee.

As their educational objective, Gene and Professor Herron defined socialism as meaning that "all those things upon which the people in common depend shall by the people in common be owned and administered; that all production shall be for the direct use of the producers." For its immediate reform program the Socialist party pledged itself to work for shortened days of labor and increases in wages; for the insurance of the workers against accident, sickness and lack of employment; for pensions for aged and exhausted workers; for the public ownership of the means of transportation, communication and exchange; for the graduated taxation of incomes, inheritances, franchises and land values; for the complete education of children and their freedom from the workshop.

His job finished, he was packing his bag when Victor Berger and Frederic Heath wandered into the room.

"Better come on over to the convention hall, Gene," said Berger.

Gene looked up sharply from his packing.

"What for?"

"The delegates have just drawn you up a new lease on the White House," replied Heath.

Gene started speaking the instant he stepped onto the stage from the wings, forestalling any applause.

". . . don't nominate me again. The American people have neither interest nor patience in a loser. The voters are entitled to a new face, a different personality, a fresh voice. I can't tell them anything new . . ."

John Spargo, editor of *The Comrade,* rose and cried to the

audience, "We want Gene Debs for president; he drew the milk of revolution from his mother's breast."

Someone in the gallery called back, "Aw heck, he was a bottle baby."

Gene laughed hard. A member of the nominating committee said:

"Before you make your decision, I think you ought to know that your running mate is going to be Ben Hanford."

Eager hands seized Hanford from the middle of the New York delegation and handed him up to the stage. Gene put his arm fondly about the shoulder of the sickly little printer who had three times run for the governorship of New York on the Socialist ticket. A slight and gentle face, with dreamy eyes, gray-and-black hair, Ben Hanford had fallen ill years before; not an instant of his life was spent free of pain, and yet he wrote, lectured and organized for socialism with untiring energy.

As Gene stood clutching Hanford's bony shoulder, he knew that he could never refuse to do any job the party asked of him. Without releasing his grip on Hanford, he said, "Comrade Chairman and comrades, I accept this nomination because of the duty it imposes. I shall be heard in the coming campaign as often and as emphatically as my ability and my strength will allow."

He spent the long summer months storing up energy for the campaign, writing during the mornings, during the still nights rocking in the coolness and quiet of his porch. His nomination, which had been ignored by the press during the Chicago convention, took on significance when the Democratic party rejected William Jennings Bryan as being too radical, and in his place nominated Judge Alton B. Parker of New York State on a conservative gold-standard platform. Elated by this development, which practically merged the Democratic and Republican parties for the purposes of the campaign, Gene issued a statement which the national press services gave important space:

"Democrats, progressives, liberals, humanitarians: you now have no place to go except the Socialist party."

The fruits of their four years' work became evident the moment Gene officially opened the campaign: the white map with which they had covered the rear wall of their office was populated with thousands of variegated pins, all of which represented interest awakened, contacts established. When he spoke in the small towns of Ohio, Michigan, Wisconsin and Minnesota, when he swung down through the Dakotas and Nebraska into Kansas, when he turned south from Wichita to speak in Joplin, Fort Smith, Memphis and Nashville, the faces of the people were no longer hostile or uncomprehending: in every audience there were friends to whom he had written letters, sent packages of literature, clasped hands on a former lecture tour.

He made a stop at Woodstock to renew his friendship with Sheriff Eckert. In a small railroad junction he met the former brakeman who had found him reading by candlelight and said, "One of us is a danged fool, and it ain't me." The grizzled seventy-year-old, who was eking out an existence as a crossing guard, whispered hoarsely:

"I was the danged fool. Just think, boy, you read some books, and now you're going to be president!"

During his visit to New York he was taken to the Aquarium, where he thrilled to the multicolored fish behind their glass walls. While going up Broadway he saw a pushcart of apples standing by the curb. He picked out three red beauties, handed one to each of his comrades. The next morning he was astonished to find their picture spread over the New York papers. A heated debate ensued as to whether his informality had won or lost support.

But no one, certainly least of all Gene, was prepared for the outcome of the election: for he and Ben Hanford accumulated almost half a million officially tabulated votes. The Democratic vote fell off so sharply that if the Socialists could continue their geometric rate of progression, quadrupling their vote at each election, they would have six and a half million votes by 1912, replacing the Democrats as the second largest party in America.

After the close of the campaign Gene received two newspaper articles from Ben Hanford with, "Gene, our efforts were not wasted" scrawled across them in blue pencil. He read the articles aloud to Theodore while they sat before their desks in the bright winter sunlight. In the first the president of the National Association of Manufacturers declared that in order to offset the heresies of socialism, there had to be reforms in the administration of corporate properties. The *Wall Street Journal* editorialized: "We must raise still higher our standard of commercial ethics, and we must insist more and more upon those fundamental principles of our country, equality before the law and obedience to the law. In no other way can the advance of socialism, either revolutionary or evolutionary, be checked."

"Just think," Theodore murmured, "the *Wall Street Journal* and the National Association of Manufacturers are growing concerned about us."

"Yes, sir." Gene grinned. "We are now being discussed by the best element."

— 6 —

He was always tired, always underfed, needing sleep and quiet, but he never stopped: there was so much work that had to be done. There was no such thing as meeting him for the first time. Were you not a part of humanity? Then he had always loved you. When he stood on a platform, doubled over at the waist like a jackknife, his enormously long arms wide outstretched to reach his entire audience as though it were one human being, to pull it up against his bosom, he glowed as radiantly as a blazing stove in winter. The lonely, the blind, the unhappy, the dispossessed thronged about to warm their fingers at his fire.

Watching his face, listening to his words, people knew that he was eaten up with the wrong and the injustice still abroad in the land. After the meeting they came forward to the platform to feel, to touch this creature who apparently cared more for them than for himself, regardless of their shortcomings or their just desserts. To man and woman alike he opened his arms, holding them for an instant in an embrace which said, All men are brothers. He never refused to see or talk to anyone, not even the fools, the time-wasters, the vengeful. Nor did he ever forget any man, woman or child that he had held in his arms, though the years passed and the number mounted into the hundreds of thousands.

If only he could cover every square foot of America, meet every last person within its borders, gaze into their faces, hear their voices, envelop them in his understanding and sympathy, he could persuade them to forget their differences of race, religion, class. The more he listened to the dialectics and intellectual arguments, the more deeply he was convinced that conversion to socialism lay through the heart and not through the mind; he could quote irrefutable facts, argue theory and logic until he was hoarse in the throat, and he would accomplish nothing, nothing until he could move the people to a deeply felt emotion. All his life he had worked for the education of the mind; now there were others better qualified than he to carry on this teaching. It was his task to work for the education of the heart.

He looked ever leaner, more fleshless; only his enormous height remained, and the deep-buried, burning eyes. New papers sprang up constantly, each local attempting to establish its own voice in print. They turned to him first for contributions. He did not care how small their distribution, he sent them his best effort. If through this publication he reached even one new mind, was that not compensation enough?

He stopped lecturing to socialists: they already agreed with him. Now he spent his time taking on new groups. The Young Men's Christian Association offered him an extensive lecture tour, and he signed the contract over Theodore's protestation that six months of lecturing night after night without rest would be too severe a strain.

"Yes, Theo, it will be a difficult grind. But it will add immeasurably to the number of outsiders who, for the first time, may look upon socialism as slightly respectable."

Within a few days he came to know the nature of his YMCA audiences, learned that he could not be dogmatic, doctrinaire, passionate or emotional. At the end of each lecture he would say with a quiet smile:

"I don't expect you to be converted to socialism just by listening to me. If you could become a socialist so easily, after one hour's talk, someone might come around next week and convert you to something else. So buy our literature and study for yourself."

He had only one nightmare: a split in the party similar to the one which wrecked it back in 1898. To this end he worked incessantly to keep factions together, to bind wounds, heal hurts, show the amiable and democratic way to compromise. He knew that the movement had attracted crackpots as well as humanitarians, egoists as well as sacrificers. He met men and women who had come in for every wrong reason: to secure themselves a husband or a platform or a clubroom; lusting for self-expression or gratification of their egos, for power; scattered souls who hoped that socialism could do for them what their doctors had failed to accomplish.

Theodore no longer dared to give him a flat sum when he left Terre Haute, for he soon stripped himself of his money. While waiting for a train in Fort Worth he encountered a group of European immigrants who had come to Galveston by boat and traveled this far before their money ran out. They were hungry and miserable at the fact that they could not reach their destination in California. He bought them tickets to Los Angeles, gave them his few remaining dollars for food on the way. When he went back to the platform to find his suitcase, he discovered that it was missing.

"They stole your suitcase, Mr. Debs, just before the train pulled out," cried the stationmaster. "It was too late for me to stop them. That's how they repaid you for your kindness. Maybe that will teach you a lesson."

"No," replied Gene wearily, "I am too old a dog to learn

new tricks. They are the ones who must learn lessons. Perhaps when they have lived in a democracy for a while, they will come to understand that you don't rob your neighbor, particularly when he has helped you."

Theodore arranged to have a registered letter with money at each town on the itinerary, and always he struggled to have this sum sufficiently large to take care of his brother at a good restaurant and a good hotel. But Gene had reduced himself to a bare minimum of creature comforts; he ate in the poorest restaurants, slept in the most humble rooming houses.

"I don't want to grow attached to good things, Theo," he explained. "I don't want my mind to dwell on comforts and luxuries. That's the way to grow soft and to begin thinking in terms of rewards and possessions. I am happy as I am, and that happiness is much more important than any luxurious hotel room or thick steak. And please don't urge me to stay with the comrades, just because you think they will take better care of me: every time I have to get up in the middle of the night and stumble through the darkness to the outhouse, I fall over the furniture and half kill myself. Here, look at these barked shins from the last place I stayed!"

Sometimes the more prosperous comrades in the big cities, knowing of his deprivations on the road, tried to give him special treats. After a lecture in New York a friend took him to Keen's Chop House. The waiter handed him an immense bill of fare, but he laid it down without looking at it, saying:

"If you please, I'll take a large order of hash."

"Wait a minute, Gene," said his friend. "This is a good place. You can get anything you want."

"Well, if it's a good place," replied Gene, "then surely they will have good hash."

He dropped off a Chicago train one January morning and walked up to his house shivering with the cold. Kate opened the door for him.

"Eugene, your lips are blue! What happened? Where did you leave that overcoat I bought you?"

"Well I . . . I really didn't leave it anywhere . . . I gave it away."

"Oh, Eugene, no! To whom?"

"Well, to an old blind man I saw shivering in the streets yesterday."

"You mean to a beggar?" Her eyes were wide with exasperation. "You are as credulous as a child."

"He would have frozen to death in that snowstorm, Kate."

"But those mendicants, they make an excellent living. I read an article in a magazine only last week . . ."

"Not this one, Kate. You see, he was a Negro, and the white people won't give anything . . ."

"You gave your brand-new overcoat to a colored man!"

Kate sank into a chair, staring up at him as though he had gone completely out of his mind. Whatever shred of excuse he might have had was dissipated by this revelation of the old man's color.

"Now I understand," she said tonelessly. "I always said you were a play actor. You are presenting yourself in the role of Jesus Christ, returned to America."

Gene was too confused by Kate's accusation to think of an answer. Did she mean that he was insincere? That he was motivated not by sympathy but by the urge to display himself in a romantic part? It was true that he had sometimes quoted Christ in his lectures.

"I don't say this critically, but I sometimes have the feeling that you never grew up. You know that I have not missed church in years. But, Eugene, when we wake up to the practical workaday world of Monday morning . . ."

Gene recalled Daniel's saying about the Terre Haute Germans. "The Bavarian bourgeoisie have little use for a Christ on weekdays."

"I am not trying to live like Christ, Kate, but if I were, what would be so wrong about that? Christ's example is the one we are supposed to aspire to."

"In our private thoughts," replied Kate, "not our public actions. Not for the sake of making people talk about us, or getting our picture in the papers. Eugene, there are times when I think you publicly exhibit your Christ conduct in order to make a place for yourself."

"You mean, I do it in order to earn votes at election time, or bring people into my lectures?"

"I mean you do things that are not natural to you, simply because you think Christ would have done them."

"Or St. Francis. Is that a bad reason for doing good things, Kate? There were times when you called me an atheist, when you said that socialism was godless and would destroy religion. How can I be an atheist and an imitator of Christ at the same time?"

"Eugene, I remember hearing someone criticize you for saying the identical things at every lecture. You defended yourself by replying, 'Did Jesus have to say something new every time he spoke?' Don't you see, you were comparing yourself to Christ."

"All I meant was that it should be sufficient just to tell the truth, particularly when so few are telling it."

Kate rose to her full and majestic height.

"Why should you be the only one out of ninety million Americans telling the truth? Why should you be the only one to whom truth has been revealed? Because you think you are God! Oh, Eugene, this is a sickness, a terrible sickness. You must give up this foolishness. You must let Dr. Reinche help you."

— 7 —

He had never refused a union's call when they were on strike, needed funds, advice or enheartening talk; yet no matter how far he traveled or how long he spent at the scene of the turmoil, the workers refused to vote for him at election time. When next they sent him a plea for help, Gene would cry to the assembled members:

"Every time you go to the polls you vote yourself fifteen per cent of the product you create, and you vote your bosses the other eighty-five per cent. You must like this state of affairs because you keep voting for it."

He found that he was spending half his time in the mining regions, particularly in Colorado, which was a captive state, its government, judges and troops owned by the mining companies. He saw Coal and Iron Police fire into groups of strikers, union leaders clubbed and thrown into the company jails, organizers forced into freights and ridden out of the state. He wrote the story of this warfare for the socialist papers, declaring that Colorado had not only seceded from the Union but from the twentieth century as well. Wherever he went he was trailed by gunmen; he never knew when the next step in the dark, the next visit to the jails or the families of the beaten men would bring a bullet in the back. If at any time he was inclined to become frightened, there was before him the shining example of a white-haired bespectacled woman of sixty years, who had lost her husband and four children in a plague of yellow fever which had swept Memphis, and who had adopted all miners' families as her children.

Mother Jones had seen the inside of many jails but the indefatigable woman continued to fight for the miners, to organize their unions, to bring them food and courage during their strikes. She went into the roughest areas of America, was manhandled by the lowest characters at large on the continent; she froze, starved, fell mortally ill with pneumonia: but she always fought her way back.

He received an emergency call from Mother Jones,

stopped off at Socialist headquarters in Chicago long enough to secure what money the party could spare, then went on to warring Trinidad, where he set up a main relief tent. Here he heaped the bags of potatoes, sugar, macaroni, coffee. As each striker presented his union card, Gene gave him an order for provisions. Feeling between the miners and the owners was running high. The strikers formed a bodyguard.

"Boys, you are making me look bad," said Gene. "Mother Jones covers twice as much ground as I do, in far more dangerous country, and no bodyguard has ever been able to keep up with her."

That night when he left the tent he saw a man trail him back to town. When he went into the restaurant for supper, the man waited outside. When he went up to his hotel room the man kept a few steps behind him, his hand in his coat pocket. Gee closed the door of his room and locked it behind him, but he could feel the presence immediately outside. He flung open the door and cried:

"Why do you follow me? Surely I have never done you any harm."

The gunman released his hold on the revolver and stood staring at Gene with his mouth open.

"Oh, Mr. Debs, I am no thug. I heard the company's private police say they were going to shoot you, so I appointed myself your bodyguard. No one is going to shoot you while I'm around."

The climax to the years of civil war came when former Governor Steunenberg of Idaho, who had been charged with anti-labor violence during his administration, was murdered by the explosion of a bomb attached to the gate of his home. The man who had set the bomb, Harry Orchard, was a lifelong criminal; he was arrested, held incommunicado in jail, and then placed in the hands of the Pinkerton Agency, which provided strikebreakers and mine police. As a result of Orchard's deal with the Pinkertons, Charles Moyer, William Haywood and George Pettibone, officers of the Western Federation of Miners, were arrested in Denver, kidnaped by the police of Idaho without extradition papers, locked in murderers' row at the state penitentiary in Boise, and charged with conspiracy to murder ex-Governor Steunenberg.

The news reached Gene while he was in his office at Terre Haute. He had long been specially attached to the Western Federation of Miners because it had bolted from the conservative American Federation of Labor and formed the first industrial union since his own American Railway Union had been destroyed. He wrote in flaming anger at the head of a sheet of paper:

AROUSE YE SLAVES!

Murder has been plotted and is about to be executed in the name and under the forms of law. Charles Moyer and William D. Haywood, of the Western Federation of Miners, are charged with the assassination of ex-Governor Frank Steunenberg, of Idaho, as a mere subterfuge to pounce upon them in secret, rush them out of the state by special train, clap them into the penitentiary, convict them upon the purchased, perjured testimony of villains, and then strangle them to death with the hangman's noose. If they attempt to murder Moyer, Haywood and their brothers, a million revolutionists will meet them with guns.

The storm that broke over his head upon publication of the article was the most severe since violence had broken out in the American Railway Union strike. President Theodore Roosevelt issued a statement in which he called Eugene Debs, Charles Moyer and William Haywood undesirable citizens. Gene had a badge made which read *I Am an Undesirable Citizen*, and stuck it in his coat lapel. The idea caught on; within a few days workingmen all over America were wearing the badges.

Every newspaper in America denounced him. The Terre Haute papers editorialized:

Eugene V. Debs is personally popular in the city of his residence, not because of the impractical character of his theories of society, but because of his purely personal qualities. We cannot but believe that Mr. Debs himself will be heartily ashamed of his show of temper when he has cooled down and read his own words in cold print.

Nine years before he had vowed that socialism was going to be a peaceful movement, an educational party working within the country's legal framework. He knew that the Socialist party would suffer greatly for his outcry, that all socialists would be condemned as firebrands, the movement denounced as illegal and un-American. The friends of socialism on university campuses would be embarrassed; clergymen who had endorsed the movement would be endangered with their congregations; any progress he might have made in persuading trade unions to enter the Socialist party would be invalidated. He knew too that Daniel would be heartbroken at his outburst, that gentle and respectable people everywhere would be repulsed by his appeal for guns and revolution. Yet even now, forewarned, he could but utter the identical cry: unless the working people of the country were aroused, Moyer, Haywood and Pettibone would be executed in the death house in Boise. With their officials murdered and their union destroyed, the miners in the West would go down into the pits again on the twelve-hour day and starvation wage. Surely a man had the right to rise in his wrath against this shattering possibility? Had not Jesus become so outraged that He overthrew the tables of the money-changers?

He started on a tour of the Northwest to raise money and pledges of support. He planned to be in Boise for the opening of the trial. But when he finished his rally at Pocatello a telegram was handed to him. It read:

> FOR THE SAKE OF MOYER, HAYWOOD AND PET-
> TIBONE PLEASE STAY AWAY FROM BOISE. I WILL
> HAVE ENOUGH TROUBLE ACQUITTING THEM OF
> MURDER WITHOUT HAVING THE ADDED BURDEN
> OF ACQUITTING THEM OF SOCIALISM.
>
> CLARENCE DARROW

Gene read the telegram three times before he finally understood that Darrow too was repudiating his AROUSE YE SLAVES! appeal as prejudicial to the welfare of his clients.

Hurt, confused, feeling suddenly tired, he boarded a train and returned home in defeat.

When he came up Eighth Street from the depot, he saw a crew of painters working on Kate's house. Kate was standing in the middle of the parlor, directing the paper hangers who had set up a scaffold. Her hair was tied in a heavy scarf, and she moved with swift steps as she directed the plumbers who were putting modern fixtures into the kitchen, the upholsterers who were re-covering the chairs.

"Kate, what are you doing to the house?" he cried.

She tucked her hand under his arm.

"It's nineteen years since we moved in here, Eugene. Could you believe so much time has passed?"

He gazed at the dozen or more workingmen.

"But how are we going to pay for all this?"

She let him upstairs to his study.

"When my steel stock split four to one last month, I sold half of it and I'm using the money to redecorate."

He knew from her voice that she was not telling the whole truth. He sank onto a sheet-covered chair, murmuring, "Kate, there is something else on your mind."

She smiled broadly.

"Something wonderful happened while you were away: that was why I sold the steel stock. The editor of *Society Bazaar* was here two weeks ago. She wants to publish an article about this house! They are sending in photographers to take pictures of every room; of course I couldn't let them photograph nineteen-year-old wallpaper and furniture coverings."

He had not seen his wife so radiant since the day she had moved into this house: for Kate, a cycle had been completed, her dearest childhood wish fulfilled. Young girls growing up in unhappy homes and restricted childhoods would burrow through the pages of *Society Bazaar* and say to themselves: That's the kind of house I mean to have when I grow up. Then I will be in my element!

There was exultation on her face as she gazed lovingly around the room.

"So you see, Eugene, you were wrong all these years in telling me that I douldn't get into the best society. I did, Eugene, and I did it on my own."

Gene closed his eyes, swaying with the movement of the train. Clackety-clack, clackety-clack, click-clack, click-clack.

— 8 —

Kate knocked on his workroom door, then opened it and entered the room waving an oblong yellow paper in her hand.

"Eugene, this comes at exactly the right moment! Now you'll feel better about my redecorating the house, because you will be able to pay for everything yourself."

He searched his wife's face for a moment, held out his hand for the telegram. It was from the manager of the Chautauqua, offering him a summer tour at two hundred dollars a lecture.

"Two hundred dollars for each lecture!" exclaimed Kate. "Let's see now, thirty lectures at two hundred dollars a lecture; why, that's six thousand dollars! Just fancy paying you such a sum for six weeks' work. I am sure there won't be more than a thousand dollars expenses; after all, you live so economically on the road. That will leave us five thousand dollars clear profit. Oh, Eugene, I will be able to put on a new roof instead of just surfacing the old one, and take out the cast-iron fixtures in the bathroom . . ."

"I'm not going to accept their offer, Kate."

She stood staring at him in complete disbelief.

"You're not going to accept? But that is absurd. You love to lecture."

"If I take that contract, the Chautauqua will charge one and two dollars admission, and it will be my friends that will come and spend their money. The Chautauqua will take as much as a thousand dollars on each lecture."

"You mean your friends won't find your lectures worth one or two dollars admission?"

"They can hear me for twenty-five cents and get a year's subscription to the *Appeal to Reason* at the same time."

She was thoughtful for a moment, then said, "You have asked me many times to go on tour with you. I would love to go this time, Eugene."

"You really are anxious for me to make that money, aren't you, Kate?"

"Of course I am: it's the first opportunity you've had in years. Every good businessman knows that you must take your profit when it is available."

"But I am not a good businessman."

"You think that is necessary because you are a socialist?"

"Yes."

"Do you consider Morris Hillquit a good socialist?"

"Excellent."

She went to her bedroom, returned with some newspaper clippings and laid them in his lap.

"Morris Hillquit is making a fortune as a corporation lawyer. He has contracts with a coal company in New Jersey. He must earn at least fifty thousand dollars a year."

"Morris does nothing in his corporation work to hurt the workingman. The money he earns from business enables him to defend unions without charge. He gives every spare hour of the night and day to socialism."

"Do you consider J. A. Wayland a good socialist?"

"One of the best."

"Everyone knows his *Appeal to Reason* has made him rich. Victor Berger also makes money from his paper. I know that you consider Jesse Cox and Seymour Stedman good socialists, yet they practice law and make all the money they can."

He rose, reached for his wife's hand.

"Kate, there must be some men in the socialist movement who revolve in a moneyless world."

"Then you are going to refuse this contract?"

"I have to, Kate. Try to understand."

Bitterly she replied, "All I understand is that other socialists are practical men. I had to get the one hopeless adolescent in the whole crowd."

When the pictures and story of Kate's house appeared in the fall, 1907, issue of *Society Bazaar* it caused a considerable stir, for it was the first time that anyone in Terre Haute had been so honored. Kate bought a diamond lavaliere and had a new gown made by Madame Gorunder of soft dark green crepe de chine, then invited Terre Haute society to high tea. She had grown broader and heavier with the passing of the years; she received her guests just inside the arch of the parlor, her head held high and her eyes gleaming.

That evening she asked her husband:

"Don't you see how increasingly ridiculous this socialism talk is in America, Eugene? Everyone is working and prosperous and happy now. You must have a hard time getting a dozen people together at your meetings."

He knew that it was futile to argue. Determined to have her see with her own eyes whether all of America wore Madame Gorunder gowns and diamond lavalieres, he extracted a promise from her to accompany him on his next trip to New York City. He showed her the sweatshop tenements, the crowding of whole families into one room, the rickety children. Then, with Morris Hillquit as their guide, they toured the night classes and meetings where the workers were being taught the American language, history, geography. Hillquit took them to a basement where a young immigrant by the name of Sol Hurok was rehearsing an amateur orchestra. He wrung Gene's hand.

"Mr. Debs," he cried, "if not for your writings, I might still have been in Russia. But when I saw that in the United States there were men who fought for the oppressed, I said to myself, That is where I must go!"

Surprised that his articles had penetrated to Russia, Gene asked, "How did it happen that you could read English?"

Hurok's eyes twinkled.

"One does not need to read English to study your works, Mr. Debs. I read you in Russian. On my way here, I met comrades who had read you in every European language."

The revelation came at a happy time for Gene; he turned to see if his wife were impressed. Her expression was politely withdrawn; he knew that she had not heard a word of the conversation: after years of practice she had perfected an automatic filtering system which closed out all conversation not conducive to her well-being.

". . . it is not enough to think of revolution only in terms of economics, Mr. Debs. We socialists must create new music and new dancing, new painting and new sculpture, and we must teach our people to understand and appreciate these things."

That night Gene took Kate to the rally in uptown Manhattan. The crowd gave them a boisterous reception, then little girls dressed in starched dresses, with blue ribbons threading the eyelets in their skirts, came down the aisles carrying chrysanthemums. Gene seated the children on the stage behind him. After he had spoken for an hour, he and Kate were taken to the East Side of New York where the *Daily Forward* had organized its own rally. Proud and happy at having his wife beside him, he gave an inspirational talk on the full and rich life which lay ahead for Americans as the socialist ideal gradually brought economic security, education, culture and justice to all peoples.

When they returned to their hotel room he asked eagerly:

"Weren't they fine meetings, Kate? Don't you see now that we really are a living and growing movement? All these years that you stayed at home, you thought we were a half-dozen crackbrains meeting over a candle in some dark cellar."

Kate turned her face away as she replied, "Oh, Eugene, how can you lend yourself to that vulgarity?"

"Vulgarity?"

"That public display of emotion. It's so ill bred, fit for the lowest demagogue. And those little girls carrying flowers; their parents ought to be arrested."

He stared at her, stunned, as she continued her slowly articulated dissection.

"I suppose you enjoy those big crowds yelling and stomping for you. I suppose it makes you feel important. The whole thing frightened me; if you had said one word they didn't like, their cheering would have turned to hissing and they would have torn you to pieces."

"Oh no, Kate."

"And that second meeting on the East Side. For shame! You started out so brilliantly, and you are ending your life by talking to a lot of worthless Jews."

He stumbled to the bed and sat down, his eyes filled with tears.

"Kate, I know many of these men and women. They are decent, warmhearted folk who want nothing more than an opportunity to educate their youngsters and find a good life in America. Don't you know what a disservice you do by this intolerance? America is made up of hundreds of races, religions, faiths; we have to live together, be good neighbors. If each of us despises our fellow Americans, Kate, how will we ever achieve peace and good will?"

It was a long moment before he realized that Kate's filtering system had automatically closed her ears at his first critical word.

— 9 —

Death had brushed his shoulder several times, once when he collapsed from sunstroke while speaking in the blazing heat of the West Virginia mining camps; once in the Alpine Tunnel of the Colorado and Southern Railway, when the train broke into three pieces and the coach in which he was riding crashed into the engine ahead. With his back severely wrenched, he had helped several women through the black and smoke-filled tunnel, stumbled over the ties, coughing and choking until he saw a ray of light around the curb. That night he spoke at the Buena Vista Opera House, covered with court plaster and bandages. His audience had wanted to know what he had thought when he was so close to death.

"Death is just another incident in life," he replied.

Daisy's death was so gradual and quiet that it appeared indeed as just another incident in life. More and more she had been confined to her bed, and here her children gathered every Sunday to sit by her side, laughing and reminiscing about the things that had happened during their lives. Daisy was deeply religious and was certain that nothing would ever separate her from those she loved. One night, when Gene and Theodore and Mary and Louise and Daniel had all kissed her good night, she would drift wordlessly into another world, where she would be reunited with the children who had gone before her. Here she would await her husband and the children who were now kissing her good night, wishing her sweet dreams and filing slowly out of the room.

Daniel's death was to follow soon after Daisy's. Gene spent a wind-swept Sunday afternoon in the poets' corner, reading *Le Médecin malgré lui* aloud.

"Gene, it was good to hear Molière again, for this is the last time you will read him to me." Daniel reached out his hand, found Gene's, clasped it tightly. "I know that much of your life has been lonely and sad, my boy. You have lived . . . without love . . . and that is the hardest burden of all. But the real romance in life is the fight for human freedom; and that, Eugene, you have had in abundance."

Daniel was right: and that abundance was at last being harvested. A quickening of interest and an upsurge of excitement about socialism were sweeping through every level of

American life. A book called *The Jungle*, by a young socialist, Upton Sinclair, which had been serialized in the *Appeal
to Reason* because no publisher would release it, caused a nationwide furor and brought about a congressional investiga-
tion of the packing houses of Chicago. From the western out-
post of the nation came a second powerful book, *The Iron
Heel*, by a young and attractive Californian, Jack London,
who had already established his fame and money-making
power in the popular magazines, and who risked the rewards
of his years of labor on the road up from poverty and ob-
scurity to write *How I became a Socialist* for *The Comrade*.

Doctors, artists, newspapermen, teachers, preachers came
into the movement. The Rand School of Social Science was
opened in New York City; university professors like young
Charles A. Beard brought with them considerable prestige
when they journeyed all the way downtown from the heights
of Columbia University to give courses on the Evolution of
the State. The Intercollegiate Socialist Society was formed by
Upton Sinclair, Jack London, William English Walling and J.
G. Phelps Stokes, a New York millionaire. Crisscrossing the
nation on college lecture tours went Gene, Sinclair, London,
Walling, Stokes, Charles Edward Russell, brilliant young
journalist, Thomas Wentworth Higginson, famous Boston au-
thor and graduate of Harvard, Charlotte Perkins Gilman, the
great-granddaughter of Lyman Beecher, Leonard D. Abbott,
Clarence Darrow.

Gene climaxed a whirlwind tour of a hundred colleges
with a two-hour talk at Harvard. Twenty years before, when
he had wanted to talk trade-unionism to the Harvard students, Max Ehrmann had been able to round up only a
half-dozen students to listen to him; now, with the socialist
movement running at flood tide, the student body poured into
the lecture hall to see what the excitement was all about.
Gene had planned to write out his speech carefully, then sub-
mit it for correction to a friend who taught at Harvard;
however, the leisure time never materialized. When he went
on the platform he prayed, Dear God, don't let me make any
silly blunders in grammar or I will get socialism laughed out
of Cambridge. For the first three sentences he was careful,
then he warmed to his subject and words poured from him
like a torrent. At the end he asked the professor:

"Did I murder the king's English?"

"Just a split infinitive or two. Nothing that will injure the
young gentlemen permanently. By the way, did you know
that college socialists are called Debsies?"

In spite of the new and famous young men joining

the movement, many of them from the highest social, financial, academic and intellectual levels of American life, Gene
still found himself responsible for the Socialist party in
America. Morris Hillquit, with his brilliant series of articles
and books on socialism, was the intellectual spearhead of the
movement; Victor Berger, with his whiplash energies, was the
organizational engineer who kept the parts related to the
whole. Gene grew increasingly less able to define his own
function, but because Hillquit and Berger had been born in
Europe, he felt that he had to maintain his position as a na-
tive American radical with roots in the valley of Indiana.

Determined that no one was ever to have the right to say
to him, "Why don't you go back where you came from?" or
"That's not American thinking, that's European!" he stead-
fastly refused to attend the meetings of the International Socialist Society in Europe. This he conceived to be his function: the American socialist, grown in the American earth,
nurtured under the American sun and rain, creating a way of
life which would be American in its character and indigenous
to the American political heritage.

A special-delivery letter arrived at the office of the Debs
Publishing Company, informing Gene that the Socialist convention meeting in Chicago in May 1908 had nominated him
to run for the presidency a third time. It also told him of the
convention's plan for a campaign train to be called the Red
Special.

"If I know the American people, Gene," said Theodore,
"the very fact that we have a campaign train will make them
believe there are three parties of equal importance in this
country. With that Red Special we could get a million votes."

Within a few weeks a fund of six thousand dollars had been
accumulated, with pledges for many more thousands pouring
in. However when Theodore went to Chicago to rent railroad
equipment, the Pullman corporation refused to give him any
car in which they could sleep on the sixty-eight-day trip. In
the fourteen years since his battle with George Pullman,
Gene had ridden tens of thousands of miles sitting up in
coaches with his bony elbow propped on a cold window sill
and his long, thin face clutched in his long, thin fingers.
Theodore located a Mr. and Mrs. Yerkes, who managed
trains for touring musicians; the Yerkes had a contract with
Pullman, and through them Theodore was able to rent an engine, coal car, baggage car, parlor car, and one regulation
Pullman.

The national executive committee asked Theodore to take

over as general manager of the train. That left no one in Terre Haute to supervise the publishing and distribution of the quantities of literature which would be called for. Gene hesitated before he turned once again to Gloria for help.

A strange situation had arisen at the Red House. Gene had tried to be friendly with Nedina, to sit beside her on the sofa and chat, but Nedina held herself rigid until he quieted, then left his side. One evening when he was returning home from the office he had stopped at Gloria's in the hope of a few moments of conversation and a glass of wine before the fire. Gloria and Imogene were out to a concert; Nedina was in the living room poring over a worn scrapbook of the 1894 trial. She had silhouetted her father's pictures with a red pencil, outlined his name and all references to him. When she felt Gene standing by her, she closed the book hurriedly and glared up at him.

"Nedina, why do you keep yourself living so completely in the past? It's good for you to love your father, and to cherish his memory, but when those memories make it impossible for you to be happy with the people around you, then they are doing you harm. Your father would be unhappy too, if he knew about this."

"I don't need you to tell me what my father would think, Mr. Debs. His thoughts and yours could never have anything in common."

"If you think I was wrong, then you must know I was sent to prison. Ned Harkness would have believed that sufficient punishment. Why do you continue to punish me fourteen years later?"

Nedina sprang up, gathering her scrap book in her arms.

"Nothing is ever over, Mr. Debs; my father would not have felt any different about you today than when he forced the truth out of you on the witness stand."

Gene winced. The dark-eyed, black-haired girl stood before him giving no inch of ground. Paul Weston came down the stairs, an open book in his hand, his eyes remonstrative.

"What are the loud voices about?" he asked. "Sounds like somebody is campaigning for office."

"Paul," Gene said, "can't you do something about Nedina? Why does she think she must be my enemy?"

"I am afraid it is jealousy," Paul replied quietly. "Nedina has learned that you and Gloria once loved each other. She also learned about Gloria's visit to your cell . . ."

"Yes," cut in Nedina, her face blazing, "and that Mother believed you were right, and Father was wrong . . ."

She burst into tears, then fled up the stairs.

Since then he had avoided the Red House except on the nights of open house. He and Gloria made no engagements to meet, nor did they seek each other out during those evenings at home. When they came together he spent no more time with her than he did with any other member of the group; they talked of their current interests or problems, never of anything personal.

His misgivings were dispelled the moment he told Gloria that Theodore was coming along with him. She seemed delighted at the opportunity of taking over the office, and promised that she would keep the presses rolling so that plenty of campaign literature reached the Red Special at every major stop.

At the end of August he and Theodore went to Chicago to move into their train. The Pullman Company had been obliged to honor their Yerkes contract, but instead of sending a modern and comfortable car, they had dug up a twenty-five-year-old Wagner car with a single small stateroom. They left the Illinois Central Station on a trial run up to Lemont Park, where there were several thousand picnicking socialists. The train was greeted with loud cheers as Gene stepped onto the back platform. He had spoken only a few minutes when a heckler shouted:

"What is the difference between you and your mortal enemies, the Democrats and the Republicans? You use their same capitalistic paraphernalia! What is happening to the revolution while you sit here at your bourgeois picnic, eating ham sandwiches? The revolution is today! Join the Socialist Labor party and follow our great leader, Daniel De Leon!"

Angry hands started to haul him down. Gene said, "Leave him be." To the throng he cried out:

"We do not consider the Republicans and the Democrats our mortal enemies, for we do not believe that we must build barricades and let Republican and Democrat blood flow in American streets. We believe that the members of these parties can be absorbed by the Socialist program. We leave to the De Leonites all wish for mass destruction; we prefer to think in terms of mass conversion."

A few hours later the Red Special headed for the Midwest and the Pacific coast. Gene seated himself at the window, gazing out at the beautiful farmlands of Illinois.

Spectators who assembled at the first stops were disappointed that the entire train was not painted red. He saw that many of his listeners had been attracted by curiosity, and so he spoke to them with humor. His concept of winning a vote was getting someone to listen, to read a pamphlet, to begin thinking about socialism. At Davenport he told his audience:

"Under the present system people are forced to develop ti-gerish instincts. You good folks don't look to me as if you want to live out your life obeying the laws of the jungle. When you help us achieve socialism there will be no more need for tigers."

His anxiety lest the Red Special be neglected by the farm cities was dispelled when Des Moines and Omaha gave them a hearty greeting at the railroad stations. There were new and frequently young faces, people who had never heard the word "socialism" until their local paper announced that the Red Special would stop in their yards. Often the assembled groups were puzzled by the strange man, enormous in height, with a swivel waist, bending so far forward to meet them that he stood doubled over at a right angle, his fingers clasping his knees.

They had been on the road for only a week when a tele-gram arrived from J. Mahlon Barnes of the national office, telling them that contributions for the Red Special had dropped off, and the Eastern half of the campaign would have to be canceled. Gene called an immediate caucus.

"We are seeing with our own eyes what the Red Special is accomplishing. How can we collect enough money on this Western trip to pay for our Eastern junket?"

In the Colorado mining towns of Leadville and Glenwood Springs he said to his audiences:

"It's up to you boys of the West to give the boys of the East a chance to see the Red Special. Give us an ocular dem-onstration of whence the Socialist program gets its campaign funds. Let's hear those silver dollars go kerplunk."

After his third appeal, which was made in Denver, the staff of the Red Special stayed up most of the night counting the twenty-one hundred dollars which had been thrown into the pie tins. The next morning Theodore staggered to the bank carrying two hundred pounds of coins, but when the bank looked at the bags and heard there were nineteen hundred unassorted coins in the collection, they refused to accept the money. It seemed quicker and simpler for Theodore to ship the bags back to Gloria in Terre Haute.

The Red Special stopped between ten and twenty times a day. The September weather was hot in Iowa, Missouri, Kan-sas, Nebraska; Gene was drenched with perspiration at the end of each talk. The moment the train pulled out, Theodore would rush him into their bedroom, strip off his wet clothes, give him an alcohol rub to cool him down, and get him dressed again in fresh linens in time to go onto the platform and address the group assembled at the next small-town depot. Often there was a meeting scheduled for the early hours before dawn. At Everett the train was several hours late, but when they pulled in at four in the morning, they found a throng singing socialist songs and waiting for their chance to cheer their candidate.

Life inside the train had to be closely integrated because of the split-second regime. The Yerkeses were experienced managers; meals were served on time. Gene went on a vegetarian diet, and his car was filled with the fruits, nuts, jars of honey which the members of the locals brought down to the train as their gesture of welcome. There were explosions of temper and quarrels among the staff as the pressure of the itinerary tightened, but the moment he heard loud voices, Gene would come out of his stateroom and say:

"Bill, how about sharing an apple with me?" or, "Comrade, could you help me get this article written for the *Appeal?*" Because of his shining face and his shining voice, the tempers would quiet, differences dissolve, peace reign.

The Red Special had its own troubles; the plumbing failed in the washroom, and the water flooded Gene's car; if it had not been for the loving care administered to the antiquated engine in every railroad yard where they stood still for five minutes, their train would have halted permanently on some siding in the middle of the Arizona desert. When they returned to Chicago, Gene learned that the campaign committee had not allowed him one day of rest, that he was scheduled to leave immediately for Indianapolis, Detroit, Trenton, Cleveland. He insisted that the train could not leave the yards until the Pullman Company had siphoned off the water in his stateroom.

By the time the Red Special reached Syracuse, the funds were again exhausted.

"The boys of the West contributed money for this Eastern tour," cried Gene. "You don't want their charity, do you?"

Now it was greenbacks instead of silver dollars that slipped noiselessly into the circulated baskets.

On Sunday afternoon and evening he spoke to three crowded audiences in Philadelphia and Camden. Although he was wet with sweat from head to foot, the committee put him into an open automobile and drove for forty minutes through the icy wind. His clothes became glued to his body, his teeth chattered in a violent chill. The next morning he was down with fever. Theodore tried to keep him in bed, but he refused to miss the final mass meeting in Brooklyn.

They returned to Terre Haute certain that the campaign

had been a success. But in a few days the bad news reached them: their total count was only twenty thousand votes over the 1904 election. Gene turned his face to the office wall, bitterly disappointed.

"Four years of hard labor, gone for nothing."

Theodore replied softly, "Don't be discouraged, boy. Most of the people you talked to were hearing about socialism for the first time. Give them four years to think about what you said."

Gene turned to his brother, reached out a thin hand. "My dear old pard."

— 10 —

He and Kate were at the dinner table when she asked suddenly:

"Eugene, why did Gloria Harkness put in those months of work in your print shop? Was she paid?"

"No one is paid for working for socialism, Kate."

"If she didn't do it for money, could she have been working for love?"

He started to reply, Yes, love for the movement, but the words stuck in his throat.

"You are not going to tell me that she does it out of love for socialism, Eugene? You two were childhood sweethearts, weren't you?"

He thought, It's come at last. Filled with dread, he answered:

"That was a long time ago, Kate."

"And you have loved her all this time, haven't you, Eugene?"

"Once you have loved a person, something of that feeling always remains."

"Then you do love her!" Kate's eyes were wide with anger. "You have been deceiving me. All through these years you have carried that love with you."

"There are many people in the world whom I love, Kate, men and women alike."

"Don't evade the issue." She rose from the table. "That's why you could be so obstinate, why you could go against my wishes. If that Gloria woman had asked you to give up your work for the unions, you would have done so; and if she had hated socialism, you never would have gone into it. Try to deny that, Eugene."

He sat numbly.

"What a fool I've been," cried Kate bitterly, "never to suspect that another woman was the cause of my trouble and unhappiness."

He got up from the table, took his wife's shoulders firmly in his two hands.

"Listen to me, Kate. Perhaps my love hasn't seemed worth much, but I have always loved you and I have always been faithful."

"And you won't go to that Red House any more?"

When he was silent, suspicion flamed in her eyes.

"Why is it so important for you to go there? You have a beautiful home of your own."

How could he tell his wife that he went to Gloria's for the things he could not find in his own home: warmth, hospitality, laughter, an eagerness for new and exciting ideas?

"Eugene, if you love me, then you will promise never to go into that house again."

He had caused his wife pain through the years because of his work, work which he had not been able to stop merely because she disapproved its nature. But this was something different, this was a matter involving pleasure and comradeship.

"Very well, Kate, if it will make you happier, I won't go there any more."

He left the house, walking with swift, jerky strides until he had cleared the town and was deep in the woods. Here he strode along familiar trails, his emotions in turmoil. How was he going to tell Gloria? What reason could he give for terminating their friendship? He could not simply stay away; yet a formal farewell would be poor compensation for her work and devotion. . . .

It was a problem he never had to resolve. Nedina locked herself in an upstairs bathroom, swallowed poison, and died before the door could be broken down.

Kate spoke for Terre Haute.

"I blame her mother for this. Nedina was too fine-grained, too sensible to tolerate vulgar bohemianism. That house drove her to suicide. I've heard how she begged her mother to let them live like respectable people. But, oh no, not Gloria Harkness. She was the patron of the arts. When foreigners went back to Europe they spoke of Mrs. Harkness' salon, but in the meanwhile her daughter was dying of humiliation under her very eyes. Gloria Harkness killed her own daughter because she was unwilling to give up her tawdry little notoriety!"

Later, he knocked on the door of the Red House. No one

answered. He opened the door and walked in. Paul Weston was slumped in a chair before a cold fireplace. Gene asked:

"How is . . . is Gloria? Do you think she would want to see me?"

Paul replied without looking up, "I think she would want to see you, Gene. She's in the side bedroom."

Gloria was lying in a side huddle in the center of the bed, her face buried in her arms. Gene sat beside her, took one of her hands in his. Gloria knew who it was. After a considerable time she lifted her head; her face was haggard, her eyes dull. She held herself against his bosom, racked by her sobbing and misery.

"Oh, Gene, I am so unhappy for the poor child. There is nothing I wouldn't have done to save her . . . if only I had known what to do. Was it my fault? When I saw that she didn't like this house, should I have given it up, moved to Chicago, done things her way?"

He brushed the hair back from her brow.

"Gloria, my dear, there are many things we would do differently if we could know in advance how they are going to come out. Something in Nedina turned her against us, made her hate our ideas, our work, our very presence here, just as my wife has always hated my ideas, my comrades, my way of life."

Gloria covered her head with her arms.

"Now that it is too late, I am going to sell the house . . . move away. Oh, Gene, what is there left for me?"

Walking the streets again, oblivious to the bitter cold, he asked himself, What is left for any of us? For Gloria, in some strange city, her heart dead in her bosom? For me, weary and used up, without children, without love? For Kate, alone in the hollow, echoing house?

When Kate opened the door for him, she found that his gaze was vaguely focused, his mouth loose and his tie untidy in his collar. At first she was unable to believe her own eyes; but she was too well trained in taking care of her brother Danny to make any mistakes.

Gene was extremely sorry to encounter Kate at this moment.

"I . . . I just had a glass . . . too many. I'll just go . . . sleep, be fine . . . morning."

One of Kate's loose-lying rugs slipped under his foot; he would have fallen had she not grasped him strongly by the arm. She was white with terror.

"How could you do this to me? I have suffered so much over Danny all these years, and now one day they'll find you lying face down in the gutter! Oh, Eugene, this is the worst blow of them all."

Her words sobered him.

"Now, Kate, no one has ever found me in a gutter or face down anywhere, except in my own bed."

J. A. Wayland had long wanted him to become part of the *Appeal to Reason*; he had offered him a year's contract at one hundred dollars a week, Gene to contribute whatever articles he might wish to the *Appeal,* and go on lecture tours for the purpose of securing new subscribers for the paper. He knew that Kate would be satisfied if he sent her fifty dollars a week; forty dollars of the balance he could send to Theodore to keep their office open, and their publishing concern distributing the little bound books by Lassalle, Ladoff, Blatchford and Heath.

He told Kate that he was going to Girard for a year to work for the *Appeal to Reason,* that he would send her half his pay check each week. Kate made no comment. He packed two large suitcases of his belongings, carried them downstairs. Kate was in the kitchen peeling potatoes for supper; he knew that she would never touch the potatoes after they were cooked, but that his wife found it salutary to go through the normal motions of the day, even when the world about her was collapsing. He could think of no words with which to say good-by, but instead put his hands on her shoulders and kissed her upon the cheek. She paused in her work for a moment, the paring knife gashed deep into a potato, holding herself rigid, that there should be no display of emotion. Not until he reached the street did he realize that for the first time in his married life he had left for a trip without his wife saying:

"Eugene, be careful, be careful what you say."

— 11 —

The *Appeal to Reason* had just completed its new two-story red brick quarters. When Gene went into Wayland's office, he commented:

"The *Appeal* is looking mighty permanent and prosperous."

"That's just the trouble," growled Wayland. "Young Fred Warren is so much better an editor than I ever was that all I have to do is write a few witty paragraphs each week. If I get just a little more bored, I will have to go out and start an opposition paper. How about staying with us, Gene? There must be half a dozen bedrooms that I have never even seen."

"Thanks, One Hoss, but you know I never like to make trouble for people. I already rented a place in that little rooming house on the square. You know what's the matter with you, J.A.? You are too intense, you don't know how to relax."

He rose every morning at six and took a long walk in the woods, or past Wayland's house to Burnett's Park, where he could watch the ducks. He had a standing invitation to breakfast every morning from members of the *Appeal* staff, but he always ate in the cheapest little restaurant he could find, the one that needed his patronage the most.

He dictated articles and correspondence to a typist all morning. At twelve o'clock Gene, Wayland, Fred Warren and George Brewer would go to Decker's Café or Osborne's Restaurant for lunch, where the talk was always about the movement: all the things they didn't like about the New York and Milwaukee locals which dominated the party; what would happen at the next convention; what they could do to fight the Exclusion Act; what should be editorialized in the next issue of the *Appeal*. When he paid his check Gene took his change in nickels; on the way back to the office he would hand one to each of the kids on the street, saying, "Now let's see who can run fastest to the ice cream parlor."

Back in the office he revised manuscripts until four in the afternoon, then wrote a daily note to Kate; now that there was distance between them, and days and weeks in which they had not seen each other, it was easier for him to assume that they had not separated. He scooped up an armful of current newspapers and magazines, went to his little room with its iron bedstead and washbasin, and read until suppertime. Immediately after supper he went back to his room and took out his three straight-stemmed pipes. While lecturing at Harvard he had come across a wonderful tobacco which Cobb, Yerkes and Bates called *Our Special Mixture*. This was an expensive blend, over a dollar a pound, but Gene kept sending for it. When people invited him to a good hotel to eat he would say, "Oh no, I don't need all that fine food." Warren and Brewer twitted him about the tobacco, saying that according to his philosophy he should smoke the worst kind available. Gene replied with a grin:

"That's carrying a joke too far."

In spite of his friends and the solidarity of the socialist group, he suffered long stretches of loneliness and homesickness. He sorely missed Theodore's companionship, but he could not have said what he was homesick for: his wife? The house on Eighth Street? There was more laughter and comradeship at the Warrens' or the Brewers' than inside Kate's domain. But sometimes he knew what it was he lacked:

roots, a sense of belonging, of being wanted, of having a wife and children to love him and for whom he was responsible. In his depressed moods he had to confess that he was not doing anything for socialism that could not be done faster and better by the young men on the *Appeal* staff.

He remembered Horace Greeley saying, "I am a beaten, broken-down, used-up politician and have the soreness of many defeats in my bones." The progress that socialism had made toward justice and human decency after twelve years of constant activity was so small that it could cause little but derisive laughter in those circles which controlled American life. He had started with such high hopes; he had believed that the American people, once they had been made to see the cruelty and chaos underlying a fragmentary wage system, would of their own free will revise their political economy so that the wealth of the nation would be owned co-operatively, its fruits enjoyed by all the American people.

His position had deteriorated to that of the wasp, the gadfly, the irritant. In earlier years Kate had been the adversary in his house, disapproving passionately of everything he said and did. There had been no need for him to wonder very long what the world or his enemies might think, for his wife had always presented their case swiftly, lethally. Now he was accused of being the adversary in the house of America, his mind set against his own people, of being prejudiced and blind, of believing anyone who would say ill of them. The United States never had to wait to find out what other nations might say about its foibles: Eugene Debs was right there at home to tell them, in clear, hard words, all the things they would rather not have heard. It was as though the people were crying out:

"Debs, for God's sake, approve of us just once, for appearances' sake!"

He was the unwelcome guest, the poor relative who always told the truth and embarrassed the family. His audience had grown tired and bored; they no longer drained him, sapped his vitality, his enthusiasm, his love; now they seemed to say:

"Go away and leave us alone; we don't care what's happening, we just want to forget it all."

The existing world looked very black to him indeed. He had lived almost fifty-five years with a hopeful nature, but the rate of progress was so minute that at this snail's pace it would take hundreds of years to achieve any major part of the humanitarian society he had envisaged. At such times, in his loneliness, in his fatigue, in his discouragement, he turned to the magic contents of the bottle. He did not know one whisky from the other: scotch, rye and bourbon, they all tasted alike to him, but once he had begun a bottle he could not stop until its amber liquid was completely gone. Somewhere in the middle he would recall his years of work among the locomotive firemen to keep them away from just such a bottle, which took their health, robbed them of their jobs and their families of the necessities of life. At this point, while his thinking was still coherent, he would recall that moment in the Woodstock jail when his cherished pocket knife had been returned by Ray Eppinghauser, and he had realized that this was not the same knife he had bought on his way to his first meeting of the firemen's local.

The knife had long since vanished; it was years since he had replaced the last scimitar blade and the last original portion of the bone handle. What survived of his own original ideas and ideals and hopes for service? What was he any longer but that sorriest of all objects, a tired liberal? But by the time the bottle stood gray and empty on his little washstand, the harsh outlines of reality had blurred, and there was amorphous hope in his mind . . . until he fell into the sleep of oblivion.

Sometimes he could not stop drinking for a whole week; his comrades did not intrude upon his private affairs, nor did they discuss the fact among themselves. They knew he was carrying some kind of burden, and in their love for him, in their pity, they did everything they could to take him into their homes, to keep him with their families and children, to keep happy and gay the Gene Debs they had known these many years.

Now that he thought back, he could remember the pain had been with him for almost a year, a dull ache which came intermittently, low in his throat, behind his Adam's apple. During the first months he assumed it was his constant lecturing at the subscription rallies that caused the growing hoarseness. But when he returned to Girard, and schedules were drawn for several Eastern trips, Gene knew that he would have to be examined. The Girard doctor said:

"You have some kind of growth in your throat, Mr. Debs."

Dully he asked, "Growth? Isn't that . . . dangerous?"

"Why don't you go to the Mayo Clinic in Rochester and have it cut out? Only a postoperative examination of the tissue can reveal its true nature."

He returned to his boardinghouse considerably shaken. There was a bottle of whisky standing on his bureau. He murmured aloud, "This is the first time I have really had something to run away from, and I haven't the slightest desire for a drink."

He did not want Kate or Theodore to worry, so he sent them no word about the operation. The Mayo brothers, Charles and Will, escorted him through their hospital laboratories, showing him the extensive scientific work that was going on. When he marveled at all they were able to do, Charles Mayo replied:

"We are trying to get at the causes of physical disease, Mr. Debs, in much the same way as you are trying to get at the causes of social disease."

When he awakened, with a pounding sore throat and sick to his stomach from the ether, he saw a figure sitting by the side of his bed. At first he imagined it was a nurse, for it was a woman; and then he thought he had not really awakened, for it was Kate sitting there, her coat thrown over the back of her chair and her hand covering his where it lay quiet on the white spread. She leaned over, smiled at him and asked:

"Well, Eugene, how do you feel?"

He was too befuddled to talk, and his throat hurt too much to try it anyway.

"How could you even think of undergoing an operation without letting me know? Haven't I always taken care of you when you were ill? Could any wife have been a better nurse?"

Gene nodded his head, tears of happiness in his eyes. He had not realized how much he wanted her there, holding his hand, speaking just these comforting words. How good Kate really was; did she not always rise to emergencies, like that time she had thought him to be alone and abandoned in the Woodstock jail? He must never let them quarrel again, he must not let anything come between them, no, not even his work; for he could see now that his wife's face was thin and lined, and that there were dark circles under her eyes.

Charles Mayo came into the room, his black stethoscope etched sharply against the crisp white coat. He was carrying a report in his hand.

"So he finally woke up, did he, Mrs. Debs? Just in time too. I have good news for him. The microscope tells us that you had a fibroma, which is a benign growth. It probably will not recur."

Gene smiled his relief, thinking, I made those resolutions because I thought I was going to die of cancer. But how much more important it is to keep them while one is alive.

"By the way, Mr. Debs, have you been having any trouble with your heart?"

Gene croaked hoarsely, "Dizzy spells, on and off."

"Well, that old pump of yours is not as strong as it might be. Like all men absorbed in their job, you have put too much strain on it. Mrs. Debs, I suggest that you keep him home as much as you can."

"I shall fill that prescription, Dr. Mayo," replied Kate with a spirited toss of her head.

— 12 —

It was good to be back in Terre Haute again. Even Kate's house seemed beautiful and precious. She kept him in her comfortable bedroom, arranged the fresh-cut flowers each day as they were brought by friends. Their quarrels and difficulties were forgotten. Theodore and Gertrude were invited to the house once a week, and Kate made it plain that Theodore was welcome to bring the correspondence from their downtown office, and to type out the weekly articles which Gene still contributed to the *Appeal to Reason*.

When Gene was well again, the brothers sold their plates and remaining stock to Kerr and Company in Chicago, a socialist publishing house which was better equipped to handle the nationwide distribution of material. Gene then undertook a new series of lecture tours for the *Appeal to Reason;* this time Theodore went along as his manager. The brothers were happy at being together, and laughed a great deal at simple things. Riding the trains, Theodore made Gene sit at the window seat of the coach so that he could limit the conversations with people pressing around. Late at night, after they had come home from a lecture and Theodore had given his brother a vigorous rubdown, he would pour them each a glass of wine which they sipped slowly while tamping down the tobacco in their pipes.

Once again it seemed to Gene that socialism was coming into a golden era. The party now published a vigorous daily newspaper, the New York *Daily Call,* which achieved a wide distribution. *Wilshire's Magazine* and the *International Socialist Review* were highly respected for their literary quality as well as the temper of their economic thinking. A delightful new humorist, Oscar Ameringer, had come forth, and Ameringer's paper, *The American Guardian,* published in Oklahoma City, was laughed over and quoted from one end of the nation to the other. Muckraking magazines such as *McClure's* and *Pearson's,* which documented long-standing socialist charges of economic and political corruption, became popular. Emil Seidel was elected Socialist mayor of Milwaukee and Victor Berger was elected to the United States Congress. All over America Socialists were knocking on the door

of the mayoralty, city assemblies, state legislatures, guberna-
torial mansions and the halls of Congress. By 1911 the rising
tide of socialism had secured a majority of the votes cast in
twenty-one local elections: Schenectady, New York; New
Castle, Pennsylvania; Berkeley, California; Butte, Montana;
Flint, Michigan. Planks which had made their first appearance in American political history in the 1900 Socialist platform were written into the 1904 Democratic platform and
the 1908 Republican platform.

There was dissension from the left wing of the party,
which claimed that socialism had become little more than a
vote catcher and a bourgeois reform movement, but the party
was exercising such wide influence on public thinking that
Gene was able to hold down internecine strife.

The volume of his mail from Europe had increased steadily over the years as his magazine articles and publications
were translated throughout the Continent. Rarely a day
passed but that two or three letters came in from France or
Germany, Hungary or Italy, Russia or the Balkans, his comrades abroad providing him with a vivid portrait of conditions in Europe as seen from the socialist point of view. It
was their opinion that tempers in the world capitals were rising, and that a war was in the making.

For the first time, in the campaign of 1912, he moved
across the country preaching internationalism, warning the
American people that a war was impending in Europe, that
the ruling classes were doing all they could to bring it on, and
that the only force that could stop it was the refusal of the
workingmen of one country to fight the workingmen of any
other country. He told his audiences that only their refusal to
fight their masters' battles would prevent the United States
from being plunged into any war which engulfed the Western
world.

This was his fourth consecutive presidential tour. He did
not have the cheering audiences of the 1904 campaign, or the
enthusiasm engendered by the Red Special; he made a quiet
swing around the country, speaking in the large cities. His
audiences were serious, thoughtful. When he described to
them the ever-growing forces of war in Europe, told of the
messages which reached him from the comrades across the
ocean, they were not skeptical or disbelieving; they did not
jeer him as an alarmist. Sometimes when he finished an impassioned appeal for the millions of workers throughout the
world to pledge themselves against war, he would face complete silence. For what was there to applaud in his graphic

portrayal of a world striding headlong toward its own suicide?

It seemed to Gene that his own party was not sufficiently aware of the dangers of war in Europe, that they were absorbed in fighting smaller regional battles: the winning of local elections in Ohio, Utah, Minnesota; the campaign to unionize the I.W.W. members in San Diego; at Lawrence, in the textile mills, defending Joseph Ettor and Arturo Giovannitti, strike leaders on trial for the death of a mill girl who had been shot; in Chicago, exposing the newspaper trust which was crushing the pressmen's union; supporting the Harriman railroad workers who had been driven below a subsistence wage. He too had worked on these cases, lectured, written articles, raised money, marched in the picket lines, provisioned soup kitchens. And yet, even if all of these battles were won, they would all too soon be lost in a world engulfed in the brutalities of legalized murder.

He returned to Terre Haute at the end of the campaign feeling that the vote would fall considerably below that of the two previous elections. This would be a serious blow to the party; in some areas its right to survive depended more upon the numerical strength of the Socialist vote than upon constitutional guarantees. Yet the grimness and sometimes silence of his audiences only evidenced how deeply his presentation of the case against war had moved them. Almost a million men went to the polls to vote for Gene Debs and the Socialist platform. The incumbent Republican president, William Howard Taft, had received a bare three and a half million.

Gene was no more astounded at the outcome of the voting than the country itself. With thousands of votes ignored by partisan election boards, and more tens of thousands cast for Woodrow Wilson only because liberals and progressives had been unwilling to throw away their vote on a Socialist, it was now manifest that the rising Socialist force was a permanently established power in the land.

Among the letters of congratulation was one from Gloria Harkness. Though he thought of her very often, he knew that his promise to Kate implied a complete ending of his relations with Gloria. Occasionally she wrote to Theodore, sending news of Paul, and of Imogene's children. Theodore left these letters on his desk until he was sure that Gene had seen them.

But nationalism was still stronger than internationalism, man's hate more prevalent than man's love, and socialism was but a feeble instrument blown to bits by the first pistol shots at Sarajevo. Within a matter of weeks after the outbreak of war in Europe, German socialists were killing French socialists. A few stalwarts continued to hold out, but Juarès, leader of the French socialists, was assassinated; others who opposed the war were beaten, imprisoned, threatened with death.

As the Germans drove through Belgium, inflicting carnage and destruction, and then began to lay waste France, Gene found himself condemning their brutal Junkerism. He was passionately convinced that this was not a quarrel between peoples, but a struggle between rulers and capitalists for a more profitable place in the international sun. When he expressed these thoughts to his wife, he saw her go white around the lips.

"You let yourself be blinded because your parents came originally from France," she cried. "You know as well as everyone else that Germany is fighting a preventive war. The other nations were trying to choke her to death by shutting off her foreign markets. Germany had to break the iron ring being forged around her by Russia, England, France and Italy. Besides, Eugene, it is Germany's manifest destiny to bring its culture to the inferior races of Europe."

He thought, For twenty-five years she rejected my ideas whole, because she did not want to believe them; she has swallowed German propaganda whole because she wants to believe it. How little the facts or the truth have to do with human belief!

Terre Haute was predominantly German in origin, and the town's sympathy for the Germans ran high. President Wilson urged all Americans to remain neutral in their thoughts, but there was no neutrality in Terre Haute. The second-generation Germans were as fanatically partisan to the Fatherland as their immigrant parents. Kate was now busy from morning until night attending meetings, raising funds, gathering medical supplies and equipment to be shipped to Germany. The house became a beehive of activity, with committees rushing in and out, Kate holding conferences behind the locked library door, letters and telegrams arriving for her, the newly installed telephone ringing incessantly. She had become a whirlwind of energy, sleeping little, up at dawn to write her letters, formulate her appeals, draw organizational charts. Since she had come to Gene in the Mayo hospital they had lived quietly and happily together, scrupulously avoiding controversial subjects, thinking first of each other's health and well-being.

But now all this was changed: Kate had come out of her inactivity with renewed vitality, as though the long period of enforced idleness had enabled her to store up energy. With little work needing to be done at home, and with her brain fired by dedication to what she told Gene was a great human cause, she became one of Terre Haute's outstanding organizers for German sympathy and support.

As Kate expanded, moving ever faster and more forcibly, with a radiant happiness he had rarely been able to bring to her, Gene shrank within himself, feeling colder and smaller. Any concepts he may have had of human progress, or brotherhood, were but fleeting shibboleths; the dark side of man's character, the primitive killer who had but recently emerged from his cave, was the one which predominated. Man could invent complicated and ingenious machines, but these machines brought the human race enslavement in peace and death in war. Everything that civilization had hacked out over the long centuries could be destroyed in a few hours of brutality.

Day by day he sank deeper into the abyss of disillusion and frustration as he read the accounts of the slaughter in Europe. He found it difficult to get out of bed in the morning; there was no reason to get up. He found it even more difficult to eat, for he could think of little reason for staying alive. Theodore canceled his speaking engagements during the fall of 1914 and the winter of 1915. He found himself unable to write, for he could think of nothing to say which would have validity in the face of the European holocaust; and deep in the back of his mind he found himself regretting that the Mayos had been such able surgeons. He knew that on the day Germany invaded Belgium his era and his times had ended; a new epoch had begun. Whatever world might emerge from this war would be unrecognizable to him.

Now it was he who did not go down to answer the doorbell when it rang, who failed to answer the hundreds of accumulated letters for the very good reason that he never opened the envelopes, who allowed the telephone to ring itself out while he lay thin and motionless on his bed. What made him even more ill was the inescapable fact that Mrs. Eugene V. Debs was using his name and influence to gain sympathy for Germany, to secure munitions and money with which to speed the Kaiser's conquest.

— 13 —

His house had become one of the most important German centers in the Midwest; a constant stream of visitors poured in through the front door to confer with Kate, men whose official residence was Washington, New York, Bremen or

Berlin. Old German settlers like Dr. Reinche had never quite lost their guttural accents, but the German language had rarely been heard on the streets of Terre Haute, or used as a common language at gatherings. Now when Gene opened the door of his bedroom he heard the sound of a dozen excited voices rising through the stair well, all of them speaking German. He understood enough of the language to know what they were saying: the French were swine, the English dogs, the Allies a weak and decadent people who would collapse within a very few weeks, and then Germany would rise to her position as the ruler of Europe, with vast outlying colonies pouring in millions of dollar's worth of raw materials, so that German industry would become the greatest in the world. *Deutschland über alles.*

He saw nothing of his wife: when she was in the house there was always a committee meeting, a group of men and women working busily over the library table. He was too tired, too sick at heart to question her, to challenge her motives, to accuse her of violating her nation's neutrality. But when Kate finally became part of a Washington lobby of German sympathizers whose purpose it was to influence the Congress, he tried to put an end to her activities. He waited until one o'clock in the morning, when the last of the conferees had shaken hands with his wife, wished her *Gute Nacht* at the door, and disappeared into the darkness. He led her out to the kitchen, then stopped short, staring at the array of dirty coffee cups, splattered saucers, plates heaped with cigar stubs and the remnants of sandwiches which spread over the table, the sink and a dozen of her best silver trays. Slowly he said:

"We have lived in this house for twenty-seven years; this is the first time you have willingly let it be used. You don't even look horrified at all this mess."

"Why should I be horrified? These people are my friends, we work together. Why should I not give them hospitality?"

"Ah, Kate, during all these years I wanted you to let my friends in the house, to let them sit around the library table, make speeches and draw up resolutions, fill the room with their cigar smoke and drink your coffee. But you would never allow it."

"Because there was never any good reason," she flared. "You never wanted the right people. All you wanted to do was to bring in those union men and those irresponsible socialists."

"Why is it better to fill the house with bloodthirsty warmongers?"

The blood flooded through Kate's cheeks.

"Are you calling me a warmonger, Eugene?"

"The president of your country has issued a decree ordering you to remain neutral. While it is true that you did not vote for Mr. Wilson, he is still your president. When you try to implicate this country on the side of Germany, you are helping to spread the war and make it more difficult for any peace to come about."

"Ah, but if I were working for the French you would approve of that. You would not lock yourself in your bedroom day after day, you would be downstairs here, helping the committee raise money and supplies, and trying to enlist the United States on your side."

"I have no side, Kate," he said gently. "I have only a burning need for peace. I feel closer to a German or a French socialist than to an American railroad manager, and I have more in common with a laborer from Milan or St. Petersburg than with a New York stockbroker. Kate, don't you realize that by helping in this war you are making yourself responsible for the deaths of innocent men and women?"

"That's the kind of sentimental nonsense that has ruined your life, Eugene. Now why don't you go upstairs to sleep, and let me clean the kitchen? I have a group coming early in the morning."

A dull anger rose within him.

"No, Kate, you have used this house as German headquarters long enough. What you do on the outside I cannot prevent, but you are not going to turn my home into a conspiratorial chamber for Prussian militarism."

Kate gave him a black look.

"This is my home. I saved the money that built it; it is in my name, I maintained it during the years you were being too idealistic to contribute to its support. Eugene, you have a perfect genius for being wrong, for wasting your efforts on lost causes. The French are *kaputt*. The best of the English army is buried at Ypres. The Russian soldiers are deserting. Soon the war will be over, then you will see what good times will prevail, with German culture and German industry bringing enlightenment to the whole world."

He turned away, defeated.

"Militarism and war have never brought culture. They bring only death and destruction. Have you forgotten what it says in the Bible? Those who live by the sword shall perish by the sword."

The jubilation of the Terre Haute German colony reached

its height when the *Lusitania* was sunk by a German submarine.

"It's the beginning of the end," cried Kate exultantly. "With our fleet of submarines we can starve out France and Britain in a matter of months."

Aghast, Gene could only reply, "But you can't exult over the deaths of a thousand people, many of them women and children. That makes you as guilty as the man who fired the torpedo."

"The *Lusitania* was carrying supplies to Britain. Any American who takes passage on those ships is asking for trouble."

Nor, by the spring of 1915, was the war in Europe the only violence abroad: the United States seemed to be at war with itself. At Ludlow, Colorado, the state militia set fire to a miners' tent colony, massacring women and children; in California the hop pickers were fired upon and imprisoned; in Paterson, New Jersey, an organizer in the silk mills was sentenced to the state penitentiary. The Standard Oil Corporation reported an increase in its net profits of forty million dollars over the preceding year, yet American workers were living at subsistence levels, in shacks and hovels, with no more food, clothing or medication than the Terre Haute firemen had received forty years before. This too, he believed, was warfare: the destruction of a country's population by privation, ill-health, ignorance.

He went on a nationwide tour for the *Rip-Saw*, a new socialist monthly. Anyone paying twenty-five cents for admission received a year's subscription to the *Rip-Saw* and a two-hour lecture from Gene on the need for an immediate negotiated peace. With every word he uttered he fought the entry of the United States into the war: America's participation would not only prolong the conflagration abroad, but intensify the industrial warfare at home. As the German submarines continued to sink American ships, as Wall Street pressure to protect its loans to the Allies was exerted in Washington, the fever of the American people for war against Germany rose day by day. Gene issued a call to American labor unions to vote a general strike if war were declared, to force President Wilson to adhere to his statement that "We are the only one of the great white nations that is free from war today and it would be a crime against civilization for us to go in."

His tour proved to be continuous warfare: halls for which he had contracted were locked against him; judges handed down swift injunctions preventing him from speaking. All pretense that the United States was at peace was dropped. It was like the American Railway Union days all over again: tempers were short, hatreds long; in an effort to stop his voice he was threatened with arrest, physical violence. Once again the clergy was preaching against him as an atheist, schoolteachers labeling him an anarchist and an enemy of society.

Samuel Gompers and a hundred other labor leaders denounced him, pledging their full support to President Wilson in the event that he declared war against Germany. This attack did not weaken Gene's resolve, but when Kate heartily approved his plea, told him with glowing eyes and flushed cheeks that he had done a great service for German culture, he slumped in his rocking chair. How could anything that the victory-crazed Germans of Terre Haute approved be at the same time right and valid for America?

When the presidential election of 1916 drew near, he had no trouble convincing the party that he should not be a candidate. His appeal for a general strike had alienated labor; in addition he found himself at odds with the Socialist platform, for it contained several clauses about preparedness and defense which would afford justification for the party to leap into war, precisely as had the European socialists.

Out of the horror and devastation of human values that emerged from shattered Europe, there at last came for him a single compensation. In March of 1917 the Czar and his court were overthrown in Russia, and a coalition government was set up in which the Mensheviki, the equivalent of his own Socialist party in the United States, assumed power. Since there was little violence, but simply banishment of the Czar and his courtiers, most of the American people rejoiced for the liberated Russian people and welcomed them into the family of democratic nations.

Four weeks later America declared war on Germany. The activities of Kate and the Terre Haute Germans came to an abrupt halt. All of Gene's hopes for a negotiated peace in Europe were ended; the war would go on now until Germany was battered into submission, if it took ten years; more thousands of young men would be killed, cities leveled, and the great lamp of learning, of wisdom, of tolerance, of freedom, of the ever-expanding and ever-warming light of brotherhood would be extinguished. The cold dark night of legalized warfare would settle suffocatingly upon the civilized world.

The American Socialist party was nineteen years old. Gene felt that the old stalwarts, Berger, Heath, Cox, Hillquit, Stedman, would not follow the marching parades down the cypress-lined avenues toward war. But what of the thousands of members who had joined the party during its recent years? Would they keep their feet on the steep, rocky path of non-violence? Had he himself not fallen off the cliff in moments of conflict and crisis?

As he had expected, the men with whom he had founded the party in 1898 held fast to pacifism, branding the declaration of war as a crime against the people of the United States. This news was comforting to him but it caused an explosion, not only in the party ranks, but in the government itself. One hundred thousand Socialists resigned, making public declarations of their allegiance to the war; a bare twenty thousand loyal ones remained. Gene wrote anti-war articles every day, but his opportunity for expression was steadily growing dimmer: in June of 1917 Congress strengthened its espionage laws. Socialist papers were either denied second-class post office privileges or forcibly suppressed. Even his beloved *Appeal to Reason* buried its name and its traditions under the *New Appeal* and went all out for the war. Any member who remained loyal to his party walked in constant terror of his job, his security, his very life. National party headquarters in Chicago was seized, its files and literature taken to Washington. Federal agents broke into the office at Indianapolis, confiscated the files and correspondence, and smashed the place into debris. A conference called at South Dakota was raided by a combination of federal agents and policemen; men and women alike were beaten, thrown into jail, held incommunicado.

Yet, as Gene knew only too well, the beasts of war were not confining themselves to socialists: the teacher across the street was fired in disgrace from the Terre Haute school system and driven from the city because her parents spoke no English; an old German had his house broken into at two o'clock one morning, and before the eyes of his wife and children was beaten and dragged off by federal agents. It took Gene months of heartbreaking effort to learn in what jail he was being held.

Then his one compensation out of Europe, the freeing of the Russian people for democracy, turned bitter on his lips. Following the November Revolution in Russia, the Bolsheviki, or the force-and-violence half of the Russian Revolution, corresponding to the De Leonites in America, seized control of the government, and blood began to flow down the streets of Russian cities like water from the horse-drawn cleaning carts.

The repercussions in America were instantaneous. Socialists were arrested en masse, crowded into filthy, vermin-ridden jails and held without the right of counsel or trial. A considerable portion of those who had remained in the party, courageously withstanding the pressures and the terror used against them, now denounced their comrades and proclaimed their allegiance to the war. On February 2, 1918, the entire national executive committee was arrested on charges of violating the Alien and Sedition laws.

The Department of Justice had stilled Gene's pen. It was possible for him to speak to meetings, though he ran the risk of blackjacks and metal handcuffs being used on the heads of his listeners. No one molested him personally, but this brought little comfort.

I am too useless to be persecuted, he thought.

— 14 —

So preoccupied had he been over the long-dreaded split in the party that he had failed to notice the transition that had taken place in his wife. The Terre Haute Germans, paralyzed with fear lest their strong pro-German stand be remembered, took to cover in the form of hysterical patriotism.

No one worked harder or more fanatically than Kate Debs. Anyone who did not devote her nights and days to wrapping bandages, knitting scarves or attending rallies, Kate denounced as a slacker. She worked so energetically that she was finally rewarded with the chairmanship of the women's division of the Liberty Bond drive. Gene now found his house used as headquarters for the raising of war funds. In her patriotism Kate did not care that her carpets were being covered with dirt and mud and worn thin, that there were cigarette burns on her piano, that some of the delegates soiled her furniture with their hands.

They awakened one morning to find painted on the sidewalk in front of the house, in red ink:

You Are Mutts!

Kate wept bitterly at this impugning of her loyalty, insisted that Gene go out at once with a pail, a mop and turpentine and erase the insult. He stood on the front porch, gazing for a long time at the epithet.

"No, I think we will just let nature erase it."

"But, Eugene, you can't do this to me!" cried Kate. "You know how hard I have been working to be named head of the next Red Cross drive."

He did not know how long he was going to be able to remain in the Terre Haute house. One evening he heard in his library the voices of the Terre Haute businessmen who had been appointed by the Department of Justice as members of the Civilian Spy Service. Their conversation concerned itself with the new Liberty Bond drive which was to open that week end. The Spy Service was threatening to put a rope around the neck of anyone who refused to buy Liberty Bonds.

Rage rose up within him. The thought that these men could be planning to hang innocent citizens, plotting their strategy right here in his house, was more than he could abide. He ran down the stairs, pulled up before the library door and ordered the men out. They filed past him with ill-concealed hatred on their faces.

A few nights later one of his comrades pounded on the front door.

"Gene, come quickly! They're threatening to lynch old Doc Reinche because he won't buy bonds. I've got my car."

Gene's heart raced so fast that he had to grip the door handle for support while the automobile sped to the copse of sycamores north of town. As he sprang out and ran toward the mob, he saw a rope dangling over a tree limb. He tried to cry out, but no sound came from his throat. He fought his way through the crowd; at the end of a long rope was the old doctor, half collapsed, his eyes bulging and his face turning purple. Gene lunged for the rope, crying in a voice he had never heard before:

"Let this poor old man alone! He has no money for bonds. He spends it all on medicines and hospital beds."

The Civilian Spy Service had had no intention of hanging Dr. Reinche; they were simply using him as an example for the rest of the slackers in Terre Haute. The doctor actually had been lowered to the ground before Gene burst through, but with his heart pounding wildly and with his eyes blinded by anger, Gene had not perceived this. He fell on his knees before Dr. Reinche, loosened the noose around his throat, winced when he saw the red rope burns, then picked him up and carried him through the now sullen and quiet crowd to the automobile.

By the time he had put Dr. Reinche to bed, bathed and bandaged his rope burns, the spring sun was over the horizon.

In the Woodstock jail he had said, "Every time the sun rises a new world is born." But it did not look like a new world to him this morning; it looked like an old and ugly world, determined to encompass its own self-destruction. He was trembling all over, and his heart was skipping inside his breast. He entered through the side door in order to avoid Kate, then fell onto the bed in the north bedroom, lying there with his eyes wide open and rigid.

He did not know how many hours had passed when he heard the sound of band music come down the street; it grew stronger and stronger, then seemed to stop in front of his house. He pulled himself up from the cot, stumbled through the upstairs hallway into the guest bedroom. Kate was standing at the window gazing down at the band, at the several companies of state militia, the flag-bearers and the long lines of marching citizens. At the head of the parade stood the governor of the state of Indiana. Governor Warren McCray looked up, saw Gene standing at the window, shook his fist and shouted:

"Traitor, traitor!"

Gene's heart pounded, became irregular. Perspiration stood out on his brow. He put his right hand up to clutch his left breast, a look of agony on his face. Then he sank to the floor.

He recovered consciousness some hours later, feeling weak and washed out. When he opened his eyes, he found Dr. Reinche sitting by his bed, a towel wrapped around his neck.

"Dr. Reinche," he murmured. "I thought you were in bed with two nurses."

"You save my life," croaked the doctor. "I save yours. Always pay my debts."

"I almost didn't wake up from that one, did I, Doctor?"

"Angina pectoris is bad medicine."

"What have I left: a day . . . a month . . . ?"

"The attack will recur, under mental or nervous stress. The next one might be fatal. If you keep yourself calm, quiet . . . don't try to rescue useless old men when they are being hung . . ."

Gene and the doctor exchanged a fleeting smile. Gene asked, "You haven't told Mrs. Debs . . . about this?"

"No."

Theodore and Gertrude came in. They leaned over and kissed him. Dr. Reinche closed his medical bag.

"As long as you are here, I will go home and be sick for a few hours."

Gertrude stood at the foot of the bed. Theodore sat beside Gene, running his fingers lovingly over his brother's face.

"Looks like I've been on my last binge, boy," said Gene.

"Now, boss, that's defeatist talk. You've got a few fights left inside that battered old carcass."

Gene lifted himself a little on his elbow.

"Gertrude, can you take Marguerite out of school for a month or so? I should like us all to go out to Estes Park in Colorado. Enos Mills has some cabins."

"For your edification, we are still running an office in the Whitcomb Allen Building," replied Theodore. "It is almost the last Socialist office left open in America. I am still answering letters from the faithful. Once we lock that door . . ."

Gene sighed. "You're right, Theo. Stay on the job."

Theodore's spectacles slid down the hump of his nose.

"In a few days, when you get your strength back, I'll put you to bed in a train going to Colorado, and I'll wire Enos Mills to pick you up at the station. You spend the summer resting on top of the Rockies; come fall, you will be your old self again. No son of Daisy and Daniel's should think of retiring from this vale of tears before he's eighty."

— 15 —

Enos Mills gave him a log cabin with a large south window, only four miles from the summit of Longs Peak. A mountain brook flowed just a few yards beyond his bedroom window; at night he went to sleep to its soft music. In the early morning, when it was too cold to go outdoors, Gene would sit in the window with a view of the mountains and bake in the sun. Mills had assembled a library of some five thousand books; each evening he brought a dozen new titles to the cabin, as well as records.

Within a week Gene was able to dress in corduroys and a warm flannel shirt and take short walks with Mills. They stopped every few feet to exclaim over some new wild flower, plant life or flight of birds. Mills, who had recently published *In Beaver World,* took Gene to visit a beaver colony at work and explained how it operated.

For almost a month Theodore managed to keep his brother's whereabouts a secret. He dropped Gene a brief note each day just to tell him that he and the office were unmolested, that Kate was well. Only an occasional newspaper was brought up to Longs Peak from Denver or Salt Lake, and these metropolitan dailies, filled with the clash of arms, had neither space nor interest for stories about the arrest of socialists.

Then news reached the comrades that Gene was staying in Estes Park. Hundreds of agonized letters arrived, telling of mob rule, peaceable meetings broken up with clubs, party headquarters smashed, more and more of his comrades being thrown into prison until now, in April of 1918, he was the last influential socialist permitted to remain at liberty. Then came letters from wives, from mothers, from children of the rank and file, men who had no name, no money, no influence, who were rotting in jails, never brought into court, held so secretly that their own anguished families did not know whether they were dead or alive. Those who were still at liberty were waging a desperate effort to raise funds for the defense of their comrades; there were literally thousands of socialists who had to be defended, and every trial required money for briefs, for lawyers, for court costs. Gene put his last greenbacks in an envelope and mailed them to the defense fund.

That night he lay awake listening to the sweet-sounding brook outside his bedroom window. He knew that above all the others he should be down in the strife-torn world below, fighting for his belief and his cause. Dr. Reinche had told him that he could engage in no more controversies and endure no more trouble, for his next attack might be his last. He was safe up here above the world, but down below his friends were fighting in the front ranks of peace, exposing themselves to censure, disgrace, violence. While he did . . . what? Sat serenely by, removed from the clash of arms. He said to himself, I am recovering my health, but for what? To sit rocking aimlessly until death is ready for me?

He knew that the sun of socialism was going out until the war's end, and for some time after. Should he not then make the welkin ring for socialism in terms so deep, so glowing that some of the light of brotherhood would linger in the venom-ridden world? To do less in this terrible hour was to die within oneself. What did it matter if what Theodore called his battered old carcass slumped to the floor somewhere and never moved again? Man did not live by bread, he lived by the word. Down below thousands of men were being armed and trained to kill to make the world safe for democracy. But if free speech was suppressed, if literature was denied access to the mails, if free assemblage was prohibited, then the war for democracy was lost even as it began.

When the sun came up over the Rockies, suffusing the air with light and warmth, Gene got out of bed, went to the window and watched the splendor of the awakening day. He murmured:

"It's still true: a new world is born every time the sun rises."

More than a thousand residents of Canton, Ohio, crowded into Nimisila Park on Sunday afternoon to hear him speak.

While a local comrade read the Declaration of Independence, members of the Canton Protective League pushed through the crowd, hauling off men as slackers. From his position on the platform, Gene saw that the meeting was riddled with federal agents. Determined that no harm must befall these people, he opened his talk quietly.

"Comrades, friends and fellow workers, I thank you all for your devotion to the cause. To speak for labor; to plead the cause of the men and women and children who toil; to serve the working class has always been to me a high privilege, a duty of love. Yet I realize that in speaking to you this afternoon, I must be exceedingly careful in what I say."

The crowd laughed. A little of the anxiety hovering over the gathering was dissipated.

He then went on to blast capitalist newspapers for their suppression of the truth, and to excoriate the federal courts.

"Why, the other day, by a vote of five to four, the Supreme Court declared the Child Labor Law unconstitutional, a law secured after twenty years of education and agitation on the part of all kinds of people. This body of corporation lawyers wiped that law from the statute books so that we may continue to grind the flesh and bones of puny little children into profits for the Junkers of Wall Street."

The police began to reach for their clubs. Gene's old friend, fear, rose up in an almost physical body to confront him. He knew he had only a few moments left to speak.

"Socialism is a growing idea, an expanding philosophy. It is spreading over the face of the earth. I have regretted a thousand times that I could do so little for the movement that has done so much for me. It has given me my ideas and ideals, my plans and convictions; it has taught me how to serve; it has enabled me to take my place side by side with you in the great struggle for the better day, to realize that, regardless of nationality, race, color or sex, every man and every woman who toils is my comrade.

"Do not worry over the charge of treason by your masters, but be concerned only about the treason that involves yourself. If our good comrades in prison are guilty of treason for opposing this war, then I am guilty too."

Several days later, when he was about to enter the Bohemian Gardens in Cleveland to address a meeting of the local socialists, he was confronted by three federal marshals.

"Mr. Eugene V. Debs?"

"Yes."

"We have a warrant for your arrest."

Gene smiled.

"All right, I will come along."

The officers helped him into a government car, which sped to the county courthouse. A few moments later the steel door of the jail clanged harshly behind him, and he found himself once again in a cell. On the rear wall was a little window, covered by close-fitting bars. He recalled as though it were only yesterday what Gloria Harkness had said in Chicago.

He was happy because he had overcome the meaninglessness of death.

He looked up. The bars were gone.

BOOK SEVEN

MOMENT IN FLIGHT

GENE STARED AT THE GRAY STONE PILE OF ATLANTA PENITEN-
tiary in which a Cleveland jury, a federal judge and the
United States Supreme Court had said he must be incarcerated for the next ten years. The Armistice had been signed
seven months before. It was the middle of June. The massive,
unshaded building sizzled in the Georgia sun.

United States Marshal C. E. Smith unlocked the leg mana-
cles.

"There is a belief here at Atlanta, Mr. Debs, that a prisoner makes face if he walks up to the prison door without
irons."

He got out of the car and walked slowly to the prison entrance, his heart skipping like a flat stone thrown over water.
Twice on the way he stopped to gaze about him: at the powder-blue sky, the hot yellow sun, the bright green grass, the
freedom of outside.

Marshal Smith and his two deputies closed ranks behind
him. They walked through the first of the many guarded en-
trances.

A receiving clerk signed the delivery papers. The marshal
shook hands with Gene and left.

"Your number while here will be 9653," said the convict
clerk. "This way, please."

They stepped into the main corridor. Through the steel
gate at the far end Gene could see human forms scurrying
back and forth.

The guard on the inside unlocked the gate. Gene passed through. A guard took him to the shower room. He undressed, laid his clothing on a bench, bathed. He put on the faded blue denim shirt and trousers lying on the opposite bench.

He was moved to the mugging gallery. A plate showing his registration number was hung around his neck. The convict photographer took two pictures, profile and full face, for the rogues' gallery.

At the hospital he filled out forms. The chaplains asked his denomination. He was locked in quarantine.

He stood at the iron door and listened to the silence of the prison, a silence punctuated by the tuberculars coughing up their lungs in the fetid air. He went back to his cot, stretched out on top of the coarse blanket. Through the hours he heard the night moans, the men crying out in their sleep:

"Mama." "Mary."

Five days succeeded five nights. He showed no contagious disease. With a dozen new arrivals he was taken to the deputy warden's office, pushed into a semicircle in front of a desk. The deputy, former head of a Georgia chain gang, barked the list of rules and punishments. Gene looked at his comrades, black and white, their eyes glazed.

A guard took him to a storeroom. He was issued two rough white sheets. He was walked along corridors and up iron stairs. Fear overlay the penitentiary like a sodden blanket.

They stopped at Cell House B, Range No. 7, Cell No. 4. A crossbar slid back. Two guards with clubs stood behind him. The door was unlocked. Gene entered. In the fourteen-by-fourteen-foot room were two tiers, each three bunks high, and at the back, a washbowl and toilet.

It was dusk. The lights had not been turned on. The faces of the five men inside the cell were sullen. The door clanged behind him. The long bar slid into place. The three guards retreated down the stone corridor.

He felt the tension ease. Someone murmured a greeting. For the first time since entering the prison he saw a smile.

A heavy-set man with blue eyes and short cropped hair moved his possessions out of a lower bunk, throwing them up to the top bed.

"You sleep here. It's easy in and out, and the straw mattress ain't yet too flat."

A redhead sprang from a middle bunk, took the sheets from Gene.

"Just watch me now. Make it this way to pass inspection."

Huddled over a box playing checkers were a dark-complexioned chap and a rawboned Southern mountaineer. The Southerner pulled a box from under a bunk, took out his soap and comb, wiped it clean on the inside with his blue bandanna.

"Use this box now for your things. I'll find me another come tomorrow."

At ten o'clock the lights went out. Gene and his five cellmates bade each other good night. The men rolled and tossed on their creaking mattresses.

Sleepless hours passed. The mountaineer rose from his bunk, went to the back of the cell. He had never seen modern plumbing until he came to the penitentiary. He stood barefooted on the two outer rims of the toilet bowl, crouched in mid-air. The cell was filled with the malodor of his droppings.

Gene thought, In all that chains him to his animal heritage, how vile is man.

Then he gazed at the sleeping men who had befriended him.

And yet how high he can soar on the wings of love.

— 2 —

In the morning he took his place in front of the cell. His number was checked by two relays of guards. He marched in double file to the mess hall, slid onto a wooden bench between his mates. Armed guards patrolled the room. There was a heavy, nauseating odor of stale food and rancid grease. Mush and coffee were slopped down before him. His throat locked. Atfer twenty minutes he was marched out of the mess hall. The guard took him to the clothing storage room. His job was to sort the socks and shirts as they came from the laundry. The big cement room was already hot and airless. His fellow inmates showed him how best to handle his job. The work was light.

At eleven-thirty he was marched to the mess hall for the main meal of the day. He received a ladle of beans, some bread and what the prisoners called "concrete balls," a compound of old beef hearts and veiny ox livers. He ate the bread.

At four o'clock, after work, he was admitted to the stockade for a half hour of fresh air. On the thirty-foot wall walked the guards with their Winchesters. There was a well-worn path around the yard. Gene circled it slowly, several times. A bugle blew. He marched into the mess hall. Bread and oleo, strong enough to walk, constituted supper. He drank a little water. He was then marched back to his cell and locked up for the next fourteen hours.

He perceived that there were two worlds in the Atlanta prison. The first was the relation of the inmates to their guards, who controlled them with their clubs and threats of punishment. This workaday prison was brutal and fear-crazed, where no man ever smiled. But once the men were locked in their cells for the night and the guards had vanished, a second world emerged.

He had come into a little democracy. The men shared their tobacco, cigarette papers, divided evenly the candy or cookies received from the outside. Each man carried his share of the conversation, then gave his attention to the others; and each contributed his gift of belief and sympathy. They had little to give each other but kindness; this they gave in abundance. Before the lights were out, Gene learned that the heavy-set man with the short cropped hair and the German accent had been sentenced for having liquor in his boardinghouse where soldiers were quartered. The redheaded Irishman had held up a small-town post office. The mountaineer had been convicted of moonshining. The dark-complexioned youth had stolen some packages from a freight car. The blond New Yorker had used the mails to defraud.

The next afternoon, as he passed the discipline barrack, he heard his name called. He turned, waved his hand. A guard rushed upon him, his club upraised: no one was allowed to give a sign of recognition to a prisoner in the punishment block. The guard took his number, told him that he would be reported to the warden.

"If I have broken a rule," replied Gene, "I am prepared to take the consequences."

Back in his cell, he found his mates worried about him: punishment for this offense was the Hole, a dark cement cell where he would have to sleep on the stone floor and live on bread and water.

Warden Fred G. Zerbst enjoyed a reputation for fair dealing with his charges. Since this was Gene's first offense, he was not put in the Hole, but instead lost his first-class privilege of writing and receiving a one-page letter each week. He could now write and receive only two letters a month. This was a hardship. Since no socialist newspapers, magazines or books were permitted in the penitentiary, he was cut off even more completely from his family, and from his comrades on the outside. The popular magazines in the library and the ex-purgated edition of the daily Atlanta newspaper did not afford him much critical comment on the unworkable peace treaties being bludgeoned together in Europe.

One day in the stockade a prisoner brushed against him, murmured his apologies and moved on; only then did he realize that a wad of tightly pressed clippings had been thrust into his hand. His unknown friend was a clerk in the front office who had rescued the clippings from the socialist newspapers mailed to Gene and thrown into the wastebasket by the guards. From these articles he learned that a willful group within the United States Senate was sabotaging the League of Nations, the one hope of the world for lasting peace.

On Sunday morning he was marched to compulsory chapel. He stood for a moment at the end of a row, behind his mates, not knowing whether there would be space left for him to sit down on that particular bench. A guard rushed at him, swinging his club.

"Sit down there!"

He then listened to a sermon on the need for the prisoners to reform and follow the teachings of Christ.

Two weeks passed. He was able to eat nothing but a little bread and water. At night he lay awake gasping for air in the stifling cell, his eyes sunk deep into his head. The skin of his face became taut. The prison was stronger than he; he had neither the will nor the desire to fight it.

One night he saw mysterious preparations going on in his cell. The dark chap spread himself across the front bars. The Irishman and the mountaineer brought forth paper and sticks from under their mattress. The blond New Yorker started a fire in the toilet bowl. The German emerged with a piece of steak. Over the flame the steak was cooked, then set out on a clean piece of paper. The fire was flushed down the drain.

Two men stood between Gene and the corridor, shielding him from view. The steak was the most delicious he had ever tasted.

Prisoners rarely gave confidences because of the scourge of the squealer, who ran to the warden's office with the slightest piece of information in the hope of gaining extra privileges. Yet Gene's companions sat on the bunks opposite telling him about the convict employees in the kitchen, who paid one hundred dollars each to the guards for their jobs, stole the best foods and resold them to the prisoners for tobacco, the legal tender within the walls. No fruits or fresh vegetables were considered necessary to the prisoners' diet, and the dairy products disappeared in the graft chain en route from the prison farm.

The guards were engaged in an omnipresent conspiracy to defraud; the few valuables Gene had brought to the penitentiary had been stolen by the guard who took his clothing. Gifts that were sent to him and to the other prisoners: fruit, candy, cookies, cigarettes, pipes, tobacco, books, toilet articles, greenbacks: little or nothing reached the prisoners.

The following noon he was summoned to the warden's office, where he found a pleasant-looking man who introduced himself as Denver S. Dickerson, superintendent of federal prisons.

"I have just completed my inspection of Atlanta, and before I left I thought I would ask you how you are faring down here."

"For myself I have no complaints, Mr. Dickerson," Gene replied. "But for my mates in here, I have. What is the sense of forcing men to go to religious services, and then have the guards stand over them with clubs? How can the teachings of Christ make their way into such a fear-laden room?"

"I hadn't thought of it that way."

"And why, in these long, hot Southern nights, must the men be locked up immediately after supper to stifle in their cells? Why couldn't they have an hour out in the yard for exercise and relaxation? That little privilege would improve the health and morale of your inmates a thousandfold."

Mr. Dickerson rose, said, "That makes sense. I will see what I can do when I get back to Washington."

Two weeks later an order came through from the Department of Justice, granting the men an extra hour in the yard after supper. Gene found himself devoured by the eyes of the prisoners as he walked around the beaten path of the stockade.

— 3 —

By the end of summer he looked like a walking cadaver. Each morning he awakened feeling a little weaker. He now had difficulty concealing from his mates the fact that he could barely keep up the pace in the marching lines. Sometimes he had to grip the edge of his workbench to keep from fainting.

He had only one desire left, and that was to see Kate, to find those few precious words which might reassure her of his devotion, and earn her forgiveness for the pain he had caused her. He knew how much he was asking of her, how difficult it would be for her to visit a federal penitentiary, yet he felt he had to see her just once more.

When he was put back on first-class privileges, he wrote urging her to make the trip just as soon as she could.

Kate's note, telling him that she would visit Atlanta on the first of the month, brought him great happiness. His comrades wanted stories about Kate, and so he told them of how she had come to Woodstock to spend the last three months of his sentence with him; of how he had awakened at the Mayo Clinic to find her sitting at his bedside; of how she made him soft-boiled eggs and tea whenever he had a stomach-ache. These were good things, good to remember and good to tell.

He counted the hours as they slowly passed. On the day before her arrival he found a shirt and pair of trousers on his bunk which had been bleached almost white, and pressed to a razor sharpness. When he awakened in the morning the Irishman was sitting on a box, rubbing black polish into his rough prison boots.

Kate's train was due into the station at nine. Gene had suggested that she come out to the prison at noon. After his morning's work he secured special permission to take a shower. Following the noon meal he returned to his cell for the regular lockup, shaved carefully and donned the starched uniform. A messenger summoned him.

"You are wanted in the warden's office."

He walked downstairs, his heart beating wildly. Warden Zerbst handed him a telegram.

TERRIBLY SORRY STOP MOMENTARILY ILL STOP MUST POSTPONE TRIP STOP LOVE

                                        KATE

He had no memory of leaving the warden's office, trudging down the long corridor or up the steel stairs to his cell block. His mates did not have to be told what had happened. They saw him sway, his face green, his eyes closed. They caught him before he fell, took off his almost-white coat and trousers, the polished boots, and put him in his bunk. Then they sat owl-eyed on the edge of their bunks watching his body quiver. No one spoke. No one summoned the doctor.

When the bell rang for them to go back to work they told the guard that he was ill and had best be left alone.

How cruelly he had deceived himself, imagining that Kate would come, that her visit would prove to themselves and the world that they were together at the end, not separated by a thousand miles of earth or a thousand fathoms of beliefs. He felt that on his own strength and of his own will power he could never get out of the bunk again.

The bolt in his cell was shot back. Someone stood over him.

"You are wanted. You got a visitor."

Kate had come after all! He did not know from what hidden resource the strength appeared. In a few moments he was dressed again, had made his way past the cell blocks, down the steel stairs and through the administration corridor. He stepped into the reception room. The guard rose from the head of the table, motioned him to a seat. Gene walked around the table and slid into the chair. But this was not his wife sitting across from him.

"Gloria," he murmured.

The guard mumbled in a monotone, "Keep your hands in view. Speak in a clear voice so that all conversations can be heard. Nothing must be passed between the visitor and the prisoner."

Gene did not hear the sounds washing against his ear. He saw that Gloria's golden hair had turned white, that her eyes were dark, saddened.

She smiled. The darkness and defeat disappeared from her eyes. They were young and green again.

"Theodore wired me Kate couldn't come. He was afraid that you might take the disappointment too hard. Oh, Gene, it's wonderful to see you."

"Theo shouldn't have done that . . . but, Gloria, you can't know how wonderful it is to see you again."

Gloria leaned across the table, extending her hands. The guard lay his club between them. She clenched her fists against her bosom, pushing hard against the table.

"Where are you living now?" he asked.

"In New York."

"That's a long ride from Atlanta."

"Gene, there's been a report that you are dying."

"As Mark Twain said, the report is exaggerated."

She studied his shrunken face, the veins standing out like cords in his neck, his fleshless hands.

"Oh, Gene, there's hardly enough of you left to make a successful denial! What have they been doing to you?"

He was silent for a moment, then asked, "How are Paul and Imogene?"

"Imogene is fine. She has three children now. And Paul had an eighty-second birthday last month. I bought him a new blue velvet smoking jacket."

They gazed at each other, their thoughts traveling back over the years.

"You are letting them kill you," she said in a low, intense

tone. "Gene, you mustn't let brute force conquer you. No matter how many years it takes, you have got to walk out that door with your head high and a smile on your face."

Her words came now in a passionate torrent.

"I know how sick you are, and how disgusted with this hate-torn world. But if you die in prison, your jailers will know they can destroy anyone who opposes them. It is too late for you to give up. So many of your comrades are in prisons all over the country; you mustn't fail them. They say, 'If sixty-five-year-old Gene Debs can take it, so can we.'"

"But it's not a matter of choice, Gloria. As long as my heart continues to beat I will stay alive . . ."

"No, no, Gene, you are the master. If you say you are going to remain alive, you will. If you are happy because the day you walk out of this prison alive you defeat the warmongers, the secret police, the violence, yes, and the prisons with their walls and bars, then your heart will be well, you will put flesh back on your bones. No matter how many years they keep you in here, they will never be able to kill you."

The guard rose, nodded toward the door.

"Time's up, lady."

They stood opposite each other, their eyes holding fast.

"I've got a job in one of the bookstores. As soon as I can save enough money, I will be down again."

She went to the door, then turned for one last look.

"Wait for me, Gene. I'll be back just as soon as I possibly can."

That evening the mountaineer fell ill. When the trusty came on his nightly round with the pail of epsom salts, the sick man took a strong dose. During the night his appendix burst. He died the next morning.

Again Gene was summoned to the warden's office. Standing with Warden Zerbst were several newspapermen from Atlanta. In a corner was Dr. John C. Weaver, the prison physician. Warden Zerbst seemed upset.

"You are causing us a good deal of trouble, Debs."

"I'm sorry. What have I done now?"

"You've died. We buried you in the prison cemetery beyond the stockade. The Department of Justice has been on the telephone from Washington all morning, and these newspapermen refuse to leave until I prove that you are alive."

"Gentlemen, I did not die; that was another man in my cell. Tell your readers that I have rarely been more alive than I am at this moment."

The newspaper reporters asked a few questions, then departed. The Department of Justice had ordered that Gene's heart be examined. Dr. Weaver unbuttoned Gene's shirt, took out his stethoscope. He turned to Warden Zerbst.

"His heart is in bad shape. We had better put him in the hospital."

"There is nothing wrong with my heart that hasn't been wrong with it for the past fifteen years," said Gene. "As long as I am in this prison I want to remain in my cell with the other men."

"This is a penitentiary," flared Dr. Weaver. "When the warden orders you into the hospital, you go."

The doctor stormed out. Warden Zerbst sighed.

"Why couldn't they have sent you to Leavenworth? Why did I have to get you?"

He went to the chair behind his desk.

"Debs, I want you to think over this matter of moving permanently into the hospital. Some of those men are suffering pretty badly. Here's a pass to the medical building."

Gene went through the stockade to the hospital, then walked slowly through the wards. There was an aged prisoner with one arm amputated, the other paralyzed. Next to him was a prisoner suffering from locomotor ataxia. A third had gone blind. There were men recovering from major operations, with half their insides removed; there were men with broken skulls and broken legs and broken hearts; there were consumption wards, venereal-disease wards, insane wards, dope-addict wards. And there were the "kick-off" rooms, with men in their last agonized hours. These were the hopeless ones; they would die here without a relative or friend by their side, be buried in a rough pine coffin in the neglected burial ground behind the stockade.

It was lockup time when he left the hospital and trudged across the yard, his heart sick with pain. Gloria was right, but she had posed only half the problem. How much work there was to be done here, among his new comrades. Was not the world a vast prison, edged with barbed wire and high stone walls and mounted guards with guns? Mankind had always been a prisoner of the society he had created for himself, walled in by hatred, dissension, bitterness, avarice. Yet if brotherhood could penetrate to these trapped men, forced to live like beasts; if brotherhood could batter down the walls of brutality and greed, then perhaps there was still some hope for mankind on the outside.

He would live. He would serve. And in the end he would walk out the front gate of the prison, his head high.

All men are brothers. If only they knew it.

— 4 —

The kick-off room had an iron bed, a small wooden table and chair. The walls and floor were of gray cement, but there was a window overlooking the yard. His food was cooked on the range rather than steam-boiled, and everyone in the hospital was allowed a daily quota of eggs, milk, fruit and vegetables. The pain around his heart gradually lessened; in its place came a sense of buoyancy.

On his first night in the hospital he learned the meaning of "cold turkey." A young drug addict had been put in a room across the hall, his supply of the cocaine cut off abruptly. Gene was awakened by the most gruesome shrieks. He slipped into his trousers and shoes, found the young chap raving like a madman, his eyes rolling in their sockets, begging to be saved one moment and pleading for death the next. He was up until dawn trying to ease the man's suffering. During the nights that followed, twenty new drug addicts were brought to the hospital. Since they had no physical disease, no broken bones, the doctors and convict nurses ignored them, yet they seemed as genuinely ill as anyone else in the hospital.

By the end of the first week he had ample reason to wish he was back in his own cell block: the incessant spying on sick men, the sadism of the guards, all this turned the hospital into a prison within a prison. One afternoon, as he sat reading at his table, he heard the thud of a club on a human head. He rushed into the corridor to find a prisoner messenger on the floor, blood streaming from his head.

Gene pulled the man to his feet, helped him down to Dr. Weaver to have his head sewed up, then sent a messenger for Warden Zerbst. The warden looked at the injured man, interrogated the guard, discharged him on the spot. Gene poured forth the grievances and the agonies of the men in the hospital. He drew from the warden an admission that these sick men had no way of escape, nor any way of helping other prisoners to escape. Why then could not the more gentle of the guards be assigned to the hospital, all clubs and terrorism banished, so that men who were sick in body could at least have their hearts and heads working for their recovery? He urged that Jimmie Higgins, the only guard in Atlanta who refused to carry a club, be brought over to replace the discharged guard; pleaded for permission for the sick to write as many letters as they were able, and to receive all mail which might reach the penitentiary.

"Your hospital has all the latest equipment and modern

ous. Slowly Gene raised his arm, rested his finger tips on the other man's shoulder. Sam's flesh quivered. For an instant Gene thought he was going to spring. Then, with a deep moan, Sam's body relaxed. Gene allowed his hand to rest more firmly on the man's shoulder.

No word was spoken. They did not even look at each other. They sat together in the quiet darkness.

The guard opened the door.

"Time's up."

Only then did Sam and Gene look at each other.

"I thought you might be lonesome in here, Sam. That's why I asked the warden to let me come for this little visit. I'll ask him again tomorrow."

The following afternoon, when the heavy door was pushed inward, and Gene slipped through the crack, he found Sam Moore standing up, waiting for him. Gene put out his hand, Sam pressed it in his own.

"I didn't think you come. Why you come?"

"I wanted to be with you, Sam."

"Why? Everyone hates me. Every time I do something, they try to kill me."

"I don't hate you, Sam. We are all brothers in misfortune here."

"You call me your brother? A black man? A murderer?"

"There is as much good in you, Sam, as there is in me. You've just never had a chance to show it."

Sam let out a violent string of foul curses which included the courts, the judges, the white race, prison officials, everyone whom Sam conceived to be his enemy.

"Too late now to see what's good in Sam Moore."

"It's never too late until we're dead, Sam. I just hate to think of you using that fine body of yours as a sewer from which to emit such filthy words."

Sam stood clenching and unclenching his fists.

"You don't like for me to swear?"

"No, Sam, because I think it hurts you. Just as your quarreling and your violence hurts you."

Sam turned away, went to the back wall, stood staring at it wide-eyed, breathing stertorously. After a time he turned, walked to the steel door, began pounding on it.

The guard opened the door.

Sam said, "I want to see the warden."

"Quiet down," said the guard, raising his club.

Gene stepped between Sam and the guard.

"Please ask Warden Zerbst to come here."

The warden arrived, followed by two deputies. Gene and Sam had remained locked in the cell. They had not spoken.

"What was it you wanted, Sam?" asked the warden.

"There ain't no more filthy language coming out'n me, Mr. Warden, nor no more fighting nor trouble, neither."

"What's causing the change?" asked the warden.

"Mr. Debs jest asked me to," replied Sam simply. "There's as much difference between him and other people as between mud and ice cream."

On the way back to the administration offices Warden Zerbst commented, "We have less sullenness and insubordination in this prison since you came here, Debs. I even believe that Sam Moore will improve."

"Warden, I have seen mild-tempered and gentle men made vicious by harshness. I have also seen the toughest specimens of what you call 'bad men' softened and made gentle by a kind word, by the touch of a friendly hand. Take the clubs away from your guards, Warden Zerbst, and train them to treat the prisoners as human beings. Within a week you will find the morale of the whole prison changed."

He was now given a pass which admitted him to all parts of the penitentiary. His hours were mortgaged far in advance, particularly for Saturdays and Sundays when the prisoners had the freedom of the yards, could sit next to him in the stands, watching the ball game, or tell him of how they had been framed, or unjustly handled, secure his advice on how best to appeal to the Department of Justice.

There were almost three thousand men in Atlanta. He tried to know every last one of them, to call them by their first names, to have a smile and a kind word when they passed. When they broke the rules and lost their privileges, they came to him to intercede. He pleaded for them with the "fixer," the deputy wardens, Warden Zerbst. When rain swept the prison yard and they were confined to their damp, cold cells, when oppression and defeatism ran through them like dysentery and they shouted at each other. "You're just a God-damned convict with a number on the tail of your shirt," he organized entertainments to help them take their minds off themselves. When men grew desperate because they had lost their privileges and could not receive mail from wives or children, he passed the word to the grapevine so that 'etters were smuggled in.

When Superintendent Dickerson came again, he told him whe   e badly prepared, tasteless food did to the physical   ntal health of the prison. When his letters from Theodore told him of packages that had been sent to him, but which he had never received: cake, candy, fruit, tobacco, cash, he organized an espionage ring among the trusties and caught the guards selling the prisoners' gifts. The culprits were discharged; after that, the inmates received their boxes. The amount of cash that a prisoner could have credited to his account each month was rigidly limited so that no "plut" could buy his way through the penitentiary, but the men who had neither family nor friends on the outside had no way of getting a dollar bill with which to buy tobacco. Gene's comrades from all over the world sent him money, thinking it might ease his lot. This money he divided among the accounts of those prisoners whose destitution was a burden.

He found himself on the end of a continuous smuggling line. He would return to his room from an errand to discover shirts from which the prison blue had been bleached out, a chicken leg wrapped in a napkin, a box of candy, a bottle of malted milk, a bag of pipe tobacco. He knew that it was a sacrifice for the men to give away their few luxuries, yet he also sensed how much enduring satisfaction they received from the giving. He indulged himself with the tobacco; the other gifts he passed on to the patients in the hospital. There was one gift that came from the outside which brought him unending gratification: a large framed photograph sent by Clarissa Hanford, showing her with her husband and two grown, handsome sons.

Theodore came down for Christmas. The brothers had a joyful reunion, feasting their eyes on each other after the long separation. Then Theodore told him about Gertrude and Marguerite, and the home on Ohio Street. Gertrude had sent him a box of cookies. Their sisters were well; a nephew had married. They had sent him an enormous coffeecake made from Daisy's favorite recipe.

Kate too seemed to be bearing up all right; she had sent him a new meerschaum pipe; and even her half brothers were behaving generously. They had signed the petition for his release, and when they had learned that Theodore was coming to see him, they had loaded him with packages of candy and tobacco.

"Well, what do you know!" exclaimed Gene.

Only the news about the comrades was disheartening: Victor Berger, who was appealing his twenty-year sentence for his anti-war stand, had been denied the seat in Congress to which his constituents had elected him. Five prominent Socialists who had been elected to the New York state legislature were ejected from the Capitol. Kate Richards O'Hare, an editor of the *Rip-Saw,* and mother of four young children, was serving in the Missouri state penitentiary. The Allies had won the war, but President Wilson could not forgive the Socialists who had opposed him.

Gene asked how things were going in the office, whether enough money was coming in for Theodore to pay the bills and keep up his home. Theodore replied that Socialist headquarters in New York and Chicago were sending him a good-sized check each month.

"My dear old pard," murmured Gene, "every time you tell a lie, your few remaining hairs stand on end. How much have you gone in debt so far?"

"About a thousand dollars. But I'm not worried: I have several good offers to take you on a lecture tour when you get out of this pen. The Bell Syndicate wants a series of articles on your life in prison. All you have to do is promise not to insert any political propaganda. They will sign the contract the day you are released."

"I've got some of those articles written, but I tell you, boy, they're not going to like them."

"We're getting the amnesty move under way," continued Theodore. "A good many of the Socialist locals are coming back into existence. Now that the war is over, some of the trade unions you helped organize are beginning to think maybe you don't belong in a federal penitentiary, after all. The public is also beginning to feel that nobody gained much from the war . . . except the munitions makers. We're circulating hundreds of petitions throughout the country for you . . ."

"Now look here, Theo," interrupted Gene, his eyes flashing, "I don't want anyone working for amnesty for me unless the petitions include every last socialist still in jail.

"Get off your soapbox, boss. If enough pressure is put on President Wilson and he has to release you, he will never be able to keep the other comrades in jail. We are using you as a spearhead."

By the time he had been in prison for a year the volume of his mail had risen to a hundred letters a week. The warden permitted him to read them and jot a line on the margin before forwarding them to Theodore for answering. Comrades from every state in the union made the long journey to Atlanta to see him.

had never told Kate of his disappointment over her
to visit him. He put all hope of such a meeting out of
l, never mentioning it in his letters to her. All this

made his astonishment the more acute when she informed him
was coming to Atlanta to be with him on the first anniversary
of his imprisonment. He thanked her for her offer, but told
her that Atlanta was stifling in June, that he was well and
happy and did not wish to subject her to the ordeal. Kate replied calmly that she was not afraid of the heat, that she was
terribly distressed at having failed him the first time, that
Gene could expect to see her on June fourteenth.

In the following weeks her letters told of all the friends
who had brought gifts to her to take down to Atlanta, the
name of the train she was traveling on, even the number of
her compartment. Where before his happiness at his wife's
coming had been couched in terms of his own illness and
need, this time it was a matter of joy in her strength and determination, her will to surmount her fear of entering a federal prison. He was glad now that she had not come the first
time, when she would have seen him hopeless, ill, when all
they could have said to each other was a tearful good-by.

The blow fell on the evening before her expected arrival,
in the form of a special-delivery letter: rambling, incoherent,
ink-splotched where tears had fallen, with every reason given
except the real one; that at the last moment she simply could
not face it, could not walk into a penitentiary, see her husband in
a felon's garb.

He lay awake all night, watching the flashlights of the pa-
trolling guards on the walls. Kate wasn't coming now; Kate
would never come, not even if he served out the full ten years
of his sentence . . . not even if they were never to see each
other again. It was well that Kate's house was solid, that she
was happy within the walls she had built for herself. His
work, his life, what was left of it, could no longer hurt her
and when he passed on she would close her consciousness to
it, even as she closed her ears to the things she did not want to
hear. She would remember only the tall thirty-year-old who
had walked her home over the darkened railroad tracks, while
her thoughts sang, I am Kate Metzel and you are Eugene V.
Debs. I am an attractive young woman, and you are an attractive young man. We both live in Terre Haute. I am a superior
creature and you are a superior creature . . .

His unionism . . . his socialism. For Kate Debs it would be
as though they had never existed.

— 6 —

One of the early socialists, Joe Coldwell, arrived in Atlanta. Like Gene, he had been convicted of opposing the war.
He brought confidential news from the outside world, and

much of it Gene found disastrous: the depleted Socialist party had once again split. The left-wingers, the men who believed in force and violence, had formed the American Communist party and aligned themselves with the Bolshevik Third International.

The split was such a severe blow that Gene sent word to the remaining socialists urging them to make common cause with the communists. However, it did not take him long to learn that cooperation with communists was an impossibility. The very first purpose of the local communists was to destroy the socialist movement in America because it offered a similar goal, but offered it in terms of gradual evolution, of freedom of the individual to think and act as he pleased, and to develop a design for an American future which would emerge indigenously from American character.

Gene saw that the nature of American radicalism in the United States would now undergo a change. The socialists had insisted upon working inside the framework of the legal system and the Constitution. They had tolerated no thought or program which advocated violence, illegality, sabotage or destruction of human rights. The people might claim they were misguided; but not once in the twenty-four years of their existence could anyone show them attempting to by-pass orderly procedure or disrupt the democratic processes.

But these communists, they were something new in the life of a country which had been founded and sustained for almost the single purpose of freedom of thought and action. This new radical looked not to his own mind or his own judgment, nor to a majority vote of the American people for his course. Blindly, obediently, he took his shifting orders from the Third International in Moscow, whose purpose, openly published, was to conquer the world for Russian communism. The local communists despised the entire ethic of the Western world, declaring it to a vast fraud perpetuated by capitalists to keep themselves in power. Then they themselves could lie, defraud, deceive, even murder on the grounds that the end justified the means. They worked underground, their organization and activities secret. It was impossible to get them to reveal their membership, the source of their income or the scope of their activities. Their motto was "Ruin, and then rule!" This was De Leonism all over again: the arbitrary dictatorship of a tyrant who ruled, allegedly, for the well-being of his subjects.

Gene knew that from this day forward the socialist would be the conservative element in American radicalism.

Sam Moore kept his promise. Gene taught the illiterate man how to read and write, and Sam painstakingly passed on his hard-won knowledge to the other Negroes in the prison. Encouraged by his progress with Sam, Gene began to organize classes for the evening period. New and humanitarian chaplains were assigned to Atlanta; they were successful in bringing to the penitentiary interesting lecturers whose tours brought them to that city, and such fine singers as Geraldine Farrar. When Samuel Gompers arrived in Atlanta for an A.F. of L. convention, he was invited to come out and speak to the prisoners.

Gene joined the thousand men who crowded into the dining hall to listen to the talk. As he sat on the hard bench he recalled his first visit with Samuel Gompers in New York, just before the Haymarket Riots of 1886, when Gompers was formulating his plans for an American Federation of Labor. Some thirty-five years had passed since then, and as Gene looked up at short, squat Gompers with his well-cut clothes and his air of self-confidence, he thought of what a power Sam had become in the world. Despised and feared in 1886 as a radical leader of unionism, he had now become respectable and sought after, a frequenter of the White House. While he himself had become a frequenter of prisons.

It all seemed rather strange.

— 7 —

As spring came on, and with it the season of political conventions, a strong movement swept through the socialist ranks to nominate him again for the presidency. At first he resisted the idea, saying:

"Why nominate a man who can't campaign?"

Always he received the same answer.

"You can bring old members back into the fold and unite the factions within the party."

One day in May the notification committee applied for permission to visit Gene in a body. Gene stood at the end of the waiting room. Warden Zerbst entered with Seymour Stedman, candidate for vice-president, who would have to stage the nationwide campaign; Otto Branstetter, national secretary of the Socialist party; James Oneal, William Feigenbaum, Joseph Rhoden, Madge Patton Stephens, Samuel M. Castleton, Julius Gerber and David Karsner, reporter of the New York *Daily Call*. Gene motioned for them all to sit down at the long table.

James Oneal rose, spread some papers out before him and began to speak:

"Comrade Debs, we have made this journey formally to notify you of your nomination for the presidency by the Socialist party. In the struggle of humanity for liberation, its advance couriers have often spoken from a felon's cell. You defended the human mind unchained, and the right of ungagged expression of opinion. You incarnated the best ideals and traditions of American history, and the hopes of humanity. In the name of the Socialist party of the United States, and many thousands of liberty-loving men and women, we tender this nomination to you."

"Comrade Oneal, and Comrades," replied Gene, "you will understand that in my situation I am unable, because of prison rules, to issue any formal acceptance of this nomination. Our purpose should be to state the principles of the party clearly to the people. We are in politics not to get votes but to develop power to emancipate the working class. Yet I am opposed to dictatorship in every form. We are for freedom and equal rights. The communists denounce me as a traitor. That doesn't matter. I shall not denounce them.

"It was in the socialist movement that I found myself. It gave me my ideals and my inspiration. Rest assured my spirit breathes through the bars. Your devotion has sustained me in every hour of trial and darkness. Until my last breath I shall remember you with gratitude and love."

It was time for the group to leave. They went out the front steps of the penitentiary where newsreel men, cameramen and reporters were waiting. Gene saw almost a hundred of his comrades thronged solidly on the sidewalk. He stood on top of the steps. A group of children came up to him, carrying flowers. It was the first time he had seen a child in a year.

The newsreel men ground their cameras. Then Warden Zerbst pushed the steel door open. Gene gave one hearty wave to his friends. The gate closed behind him.

It was afternoon lockup time when he walked back through the cell blocks. Hands were extended to him from between cell bars, from all directions. When he got out to the stockade he was surrounded by a group which made stumbling little speeches of congratulations. He was assured that he would sweep every precinct in the penitentiary. That afternoon, to his astonishment, Gene saw that a great many of the prisoners had campaign buttons stuck into their shirts: Otto Branstetter had filled Joe Coldwell's pocket with them before he left.

The crowding, the deteriorated food, the dampness and cold had made the men dispirited and quarrelsome. Now that they had a presidential candidate in their midst, the prisoners walked with a lighter step and a sparkle in their eyes: their status and dignity had been raised.

Letters came to Gene from every part of the country assuring him that President Wilson would release him from prison for the number of months necessary to stage his nationwide campaign, but Gene knew Mr. Wilson too well to expect any such treatment. He wrote to newspaper friends that being in prison saved him many embarrassments, such as being obliged to promise a post office to each of the candidates of rival factions. When he read that James M. Cox was going to make his speeches from the tail end of a train, and Eugene V. Debs from his cell, he sent off a note to the newspapers saying that at least the voters would know where he stood.

Having been permitted to release an opening campaign statement, he criticized the administration for its failure to settle the labor problems at home and the peace problems abroad. President Wilson ordered Gene's statements cut to five hundred words a week, none of which could deal with controversial subjects. He wrote the articles in his hospital room with pen and ink and mailed them to Theodore in Terre Haute, who typed them and sent them to party headquarters in Chicago.

Within a few days his fellow prisoners had clipped from hometown papers the statements and picture taken of him in front of the spiked bars of the gate, in his torn and badly fitting prison garb. The prominence given to his picture and weekly statements gradually led them to believe that he had a chance of being elected. They whipped each other into a conviction that Eugene V. Debs would be inaugurated as president of the United States on the following March, rejoicing among themselves over the sweeping reforms that he would make in the prisons once he had entered the White House. Prisoners came up to him and asked, seriously:

"Mr. Debs, if you are elected will you pardon me?"

"Indeed I will," Gene replied with equal seriousness, "if I am elected."

The sad moments of the campaign were when abusive letters arrived: for the hysteria and violence engendered by the war and Attorney General Palmer's raids had not yet run their course. One correspondent said that he ought to be shot; a second wrote that Atlanta was where he belonged, and should be kept there the rest of his life; a third expressed the hope that the warden would have his naked back lashed every day until it bled.

After his four o'clock supper on Election Day, he was invited to the warden's office to listen to the returns. Here he found newspaper friends and telegraphic equipment connecting them with all parts of America. One of the newspapermen said with a broad grin:

"What will be your first official act if you are elected president?"

"He will pardon himself, of course!" exclaimed David Karsner.

Warden Zerbst asked with a strange smile, "I hope you have been happy in our little institution, Mr. Debs?"

"Rest assured, Warden Zerbst," replied Gene in the same mock tones, "the very moment I have pardoned myself, I shall reappoint you warden."

By eight o'clock it was clear that Warren G. Harding and the Republican party had won the election by a landslide. Gene conceded defeat, shook hands all around, thanked Warden Zerbst for his kindness, and started back for the hospital.

Then it was he saw that his fellow prisoners, locked away from the world, concentrating on their own overwhelming wish for freedom, had actually believed he would be elected, that within a matter of days or weeks they would be out of this penitentiary. There were no bright smiles or hands pushed through the bars to clasp his; instead he saw tears coursing down the cheeks of the disappointed men, saw their faces ravaged by chagrin.

He smiled wistfully: he had become inured to these defeats.

— 8 —

The discredited Socialist party amassed a million votes. From every corner of the nation there arose the cry that a man who could receive a million votes from his compatriots should not be kept a political prisoner.

The Socialist campaign machine swung into action to secure amnesty for all imprisoned socialists. Petitions were circulated everywhere, from the largest cities to the smallest farming communities. Pressure was brought on President Wilson from churches, universities, lawyers, writers, doctors, scientists, engineers. Nearly every day Gene received a note from Theodore, telling of new progress and new hopes that all political prisoners would be freed as President Wilson's gesture on Christmas for "peace on earth, good will toward men."

During the early days of December the movement gathered so much momentum, and was backed by so many liberal newspapers, that Gene allowed himself to be persuaded that he would be home in Terre Haute for Christmas dinner. Franz von Rintelen, a German agent convicted of placing fire bombs on American ships, had just been pardoned by President Wilson. If the German political prisoners were being released, then perhaps the American political prisoners could expect their freedom?

His fellow prisoners concentrated their hopes on Gene: once he was released, he would fight their battle in the outside world, bring to the attention of the nation the conditions existing inside the stone walls, secure them quick and equitable reviews of their cases.

Christmas Day was looked forward to all year by the prisoners, and Christmas dinner of pork, mashed potatoes and apple pie was eaten in imagination three hundred times instead of the beans and concrete balls of the daily fare. The dining room would be decorated with colored streamers and even the cells would be made festive. There was singing in the chapel by choirs from the city churches, a motion picture was shown, the prisoners were allowed freedom to move about and show their gifts to their mates.

Early Christmas morning Warden Zerbst brought Gene an Atlanta newspaper. In the center of the front page, stamped across Gene's picture in his prison garb, was:

DEBS DENIED

The news swept through the prison like a prairie fire, burning out the joy of the day, leaving the men's faces charred with disappointment. Only then did Gene realize that it had been as childlike for him to think that Woodrow Wilson would pardon him as it had been for his fellow prisoners to imagine that he would be elected president.

He could not have the prisoners losing their one great day of pleasure. He went from cell block to cell block, putting an arm about the shoulder of his comrades.

"We'll have another year together. Why should that make you unhappy, if it doesn't make me unhappy?"

When he reached his original cell block, and was sharing a box of candy received by one of his mates, he saw a convict who had been in Atlanta for the last fourteen years on a murder conviction walking up and down the stone corridor in an ill-fitting civilian suit. No one knew his name, but since he was the only full-blooded Indian in Atlanta, everyone called him "Indian." The commutation of Indian's sentence had been President Wilson's Christmas gift to Atlanta penitentiary.

There was dead silence as Indian walked uncertainly up and down the cell block, his high white starched collar seeming to choke his face to an even deeper brick-red color. He stopped in front of the open cell door where Gene was sitting on a bunk with his friends, then spoke in a tone loud enough for all the penitentiary to hear:

"Not my fault, Mr. Debs. Didn't ask to be free in your place. More important you go. You have work, friends outside. I have nothing. My own people not want me back. Why they make me free, keep you here?"

"We are happy to have you free, Indian. You mustn't think that you took my place. No one is going to free me. I will stay here with the rest of the men until I complete my sentence."

He put out his hand. Indian took it eagerly.

"Good luck to you, Indian. Go on your way now, and find happiness."

That evening while he was sitting at the table in his little room two prisoners entered, his redheaded Irish friend from Cell No. 4, and a Chinese. In solemn tones the Irishman informed Gene he was wanted immediately in the basement. Each took him by an arm, escorted him down the stairs and into the illuminated recreation room. He gazed with unbelief at the table, spread with fancy doilies which had been made out of the holly-stamped papers in which gifts had been wrapped, the myraid of colored ribbons strung from the light fixtures, and the vases of flowers in the center of the table.

Some thirty or forty men who worked in the hospital and the prison kitchen rose and stood facing him, their faces bright with happiness. They had pooled their gifts for this party. He gazed about the table, smiling at each of the men in turn.

"Comrades, you have transformed this drab penitentiary basement into a sunlit cathedral."

As a result of the Debs Denied story, Gloria came to Atlanta to spend New Year's Day with him. He could not hide the flush of pride that went through him when she told him how much better he was looking.

"I couldn't get back sooner, Gene. Paul is failing: I must be with him constantly. I've been able to work only part time in the bookstore."

"Don't apologize, Gloria. Your first visit was worth a hundred. You not only saved my life, but you helped me to become useful again."

She sat pensive, her eyes shining.

"That's what you told me when we were youngsters: that what you wanted most was to be useful."

"It cost me your love, Gloria."

"No, Gene, not my love. You've always had that. Just . . . proximity."

And because she liked to end a serious moment on a note of pleasantry, she said, looking about her at the drabness to the room:

"If you aren't granted amnesty soon, I shall have to come down here and put up some curtains. Red-and-white checked gingham would look well, don't you think?"

Forty-five years dissolved as though they had never been lived, and he was back in the little storeroom behind Debity Debs's grocery.

"They were lovely curtains, Gloria." He was looking at her eyes now, seeing and feeling everything she meant to him. "The most beautiful in all the world."

— 9 —

A very few days after President Harding's inauguration in March of 1921, Gene was summoned to the warden's office. Zerbst quickly closed the door to his private office. His voice was excited.

"I just had a telephone call from Attorney General Harry Daugherty. He told me to put you on the train and send you up to see him. He said, 'Don't send a guard with him. Let him put on a suit of citizen's clothes and come alone.'"

Gene was dumfounded.

"There is a suit of clothes over on the bench that will fit you, also a shirt, collar, tie and shoes. I've ordered a black hat, and here is a black bag for your toilet articles, and money for your food and transportation. I have your reservation on the eleven-forty train for Washington. Please remember that the attorney general requests you tell no one of this trip."

Gene went back to his room, gathered up his toilet articles, concealed them under a batch of papers, returned to the warden's office and quickly donned the lightweight brown suit, black shoes. The guards and prison clerks saw him leave. They stared, but uttered no word.

The warden drove him to the station. Gene bought several magazines that had been unavailable in prison. He found his space on the train and sat by the window gazing at the landscape: wives coming out of houses with shopping baskets as the train moved through small towns; farmers engaged in their spring sowing. He had not realized how beautiful were these simple sights: a field in furrow, a brightly painted house, a group of women before a market. It was also good to feel beneath him once again the movement of wheels over rails: clackety-clack, clackety-clack, click-clack, click-clack.

He was too emotionally wrought up to think of eating lunch, but he went into the diner early that evening and sat at a table with his back to the rest of the passengers. He ordered fresh vegetable soup and roast chicken, the first chicken he had tasted since he had left Kate's house.

He arrived in Washington early the next morning, had breakfast on a stool in the depot station with the brim of his hat down over his eyes. He then took a taxi up to the Department of Justice where he was seated in the small reception room between the attorney general's office and that of his secretary.

Harry Daugherty opened the door of his office, smiled at Gene, extending his hand. Gene pressed it warmly. Daugherty closed the door behind him. He had a broad, genial face, rather good-looking, thought Gene, and a thatch of silver-gray hair.

"You were a prisoner of the United States when you stepped across the threshold, Mr. Debs. Now and until you leave you are as free a man as I am."

"Thank you, Mr. Attorney General."

"I want you to remember that anything you say to me, and you can say anything you please, will not be held against you. If you do not wish to answer any questions I ask, your refusal will not be held against you either."

"You are kind."

"President Harding, prior to his inauguration, told me that he was interested in you and wanted to know all about your case. You were given a fair trial, were you not, and a fair review by the Supreme Court?"

"Yes, everyone was fair."

"Sit down here by the side of my desk. I want to ask you some questions. Does socialism advocate the overthrow of our American form of government by force and violence?"

"On the contrary, Mr. Attorney General," replied Gene with a little smile, "I am opposed to force and violence. I have been in the penitentiary for the past two years because I believed in the commandment, Thou shalt not kill. In the twenty-four years the Socialist party has been in existence in the United States, we have committed no illegal acts. Our meetings have been open for everyone to attend, and our newspapers and magazines have always been available to anyone interested."

"But your literature is shot through with such terms as 'revolution.'"

"True, but the word 'revolution' has only sometimes been identified with uprisings, bloodshed and the destruction of the legal processes. There is another kind of revolution which goes on about us peacefully every day of our lives: revolution in the arts, in the sciences, in people's concept of what makes a good and just life. The processes by which the socialists have worked can be more properly called 'evolution': gradual education, the eradication of existing evils in industry and the courts, bringing up of a new generation which will go to the polls and vote itself a socialist society."

Daugherty rose, offered Gene a cigar.

"What of the charge that socialism preaches godlessness and would destroy all religion?"

"Mr. Attorney General, the very first platform of the Social Democracy back in 1897 advocated complete freedom of religious worship. So has every platform in the years that followed. The socialist believes passionately in the Bill of Rights, which guarantees the right of free speech, press, assemblage and religion. Under socialism there would be more churches, rather than fewer, because in a society where ignorance and poverty were banished, where every human being enjoyed the basic rights of education and sustenance and a dignified place within his community, the entire nation would have more to thank God for."

"Mr. Debs, to my mind you are absolutely wrong in your ideas about government and society, but I believe you are sincere."

"Thank you, Mr. Attorney General."

There was silence in the big room while Daugherty gazed out the window and thought over what Gene had told him. In the corner a tall clock struck noon. Daugherty turned to Gene.

"I want you to know that I think you broke the law and have been rightly punished. However, I also believe that any sentence should take into consideration a man's age. I believe that you have been punished sufficiently and I shall recommend to President Harding that he commute your sentence as a gracious act of mercy."

Gene felt a speech forming itself in his mind on the subject of his punishment and any gracious act of mercy. Before he could speak, Daugherty pressed a buzzer. A stranger came into the room. Daugherty introduced him as Jesse Smith, a friend of the president.

"Your train leaves for Atlanta at three-thirty. Mr. Smith will drive you down. I believe Warden Zerbst gave you enough money for dinner on the train. If you prefer a lunch prepared, I will send it to you."

"Thank you, but I would like a warm dinner. And thank you from the bottom of my heart for your generous treatment."

Jesse Smith drove Gene down to the station. On the way he said, "Is there anything I can do for you?"

"Thank you, no."

"But I want to do something for you."

"All right, stop at a drugstore and get me a package of goosequill toothpicks. I am all out at the prison, and I don't like to put those wooden things in my teeth."

— 10 —

His trip to Washington led him to believe that he would be free within a matter of weeks. He wrote encouraging letters to Theodore telling him he would soon be home in Terre Haute.

The American Legion condemned the Attorney General for letting Gene come to Washington. The New York *World* criticized Daugherty for staging what they called a grandstand play.

At the end of a month there was still no word of his release. Since in his mind he was already free and had left the prison, he had spent fewer hours in the hospital wards and the prison cell blocks. Now he felt that he had abandoned his comrades while still within the walls. He put all idea of amnesty out of his mind and went back to his normal life within the prison.

The heat of summer came on. The prison was stifling. Each day there were new faces, distorted with grief and unhappiness, new friends to be made, men who could be helped over the misery of their first hours in the penitentiary. Neither the days nor the nights were long enough for all the work he wanted to accomplish. What was it he had said to Theodore? "We must treat time as though it were a stick of Gloria's molasses taffy; the harder you pull on it the farther it will stretch." Very well then, if he had more years to spend within these walls, then here he was useful, valuable. He had geared himself to live as long as the prison walls would hold him, to walk out the front gate with his head high and his eyes shining. But after that, what was left for him? How

many days of health and life, after his will to survive had
been severed by victory over the forces of violence?

During the ensuing months the rumors flew by the thousand. Every day saw another story published that he had
been pardoned, returned to Terre Haute. Theodore had been
disappointed so often, made so many trips to Atlanta to be
with his brother upon his release, that he was worn down to
sheer grit and gristle.

At last the barrage of rumors crystallized in the form of
front-page articles that President Warren G. Harding had
signed Eugene V. Debs's release, that he had said publicly
that he wanted Debs to have Christmas dinner at home with
his wife. Reporters thronged to Atlanta to cover the story.
Once again Theodore took the night train, arriving three days
before Christmas.

The hours passed. They began to lose hope. Theodore was
inconsolable. Gene could only sit beside him on the rough
bench outside the warden's office, telling him not to be a sentimental Frenchman.

On his third Christmas Eve in prison, while he was helping
some friends to decorate their cell with the ribbons off the
gift packages, the warden summoned him.

"Your papers have just reached me. I am ordered to release you the first thing tomorrow morning. The other socialists have been granted amnesty too."

"Thank you, Warden. That is good news."

"President Harding has asked that you stop at the White
House before returning to Terre Haute."

He rose at dawn on Christmas, packed his few possessions,
then went through the hospital, shaking hands, saying good-
by to the sick and bedridden. When he went out into the
stockade hundreds of the prisoners crowded about him, wishing him good luck. As he said his farewells he remembered
how in a thousand ways each had made his life more bear-
able within these walls. He could not help but feel that he was
deserting these men, that he should not take his liberty until
every last one of them walked out the front gate and into a
sunshine of freedom.

He came down the long corridors. The warden gave the
guard a signal. The steel door was opened. He walked down
the steps. Standing in front of a car at the curb was Theodore. He rushed forward to embrace his brother.

They were shaken by something that sounded like a violent
explosion, a rumbling of the very earth under their feet. A
roar of voices came forth from the gray stone pile of the pen-

itentiary. The whole body of prisoners had rushed through the cell blocks to the front windows and were thundering out their farewells.

"Debs! Debs! Debs!"

Gene, Theodore, the warden stood rooted speechless. Pressed against the barred windows were hundreds of faces, faces of his friends, faces of men whom he loved and who loved him, men who had rushed past their guards, broken all the forbidding prison rules, forced their way upward and to the light for one last salute of farewell.

He felt himself overwhelmed with sadness and pain for these caged men.

Theodore took him by one arm, the warden by the other. They half helped, half pushed him into the back seat of the car. There was another and still another shout until the car had gone far up the road and the prison was blotted out.

— 11 —

The Christmas morning newspapers told of his release and of the train on which he was leaving Atlanta for Washington, D.C.

His comrades from the city of Atlanta were at the station to bid him farewell. Yet no one cheered, no one cried out. The trainmen knew he was on board; they came back to his car to give him the railroaders' salute. The families of the trainmen knew too, the wives and children who gathered along the tracks, flowers in their arms.

In the outlying residential districts, in the stations of the small towns, the people were packed so tight that the train had to move slowly.

The station in Washington was jammed with restless, milling thousands, a confused crowd, strangers all, to each other and on earth. They had come in the hope of catching a glimpse of Gene.

He came into the station. There was no way for him to move. He stood there motionless, gazing at the throng.

The people saw him. The movement stopped; they fell quiet. They looked up. There he stood, his suffering carved into his face by a steel knife with a granite handle.

And they knew they were not alone. Here was one man who understood what they endured, who carried them in his suffering heart, where they were all wanted, and all equal. Emaciated, hollow-eyed, more dead than alive but, in his near death, indestructible, he reminded them that there was a philosophy of compassion.

Utterly still, they stood gazing up at him. Utterly still, he looked down at them, not at a thousand different faces, some old, ugly, distorted, rejected; but at one creature: Man. His pent-up love poured forth to them, so radiant that they were bathed in it as in some healing fluid which drove out of their hearts despair and loneliness, and assured them of their place in the universe.

Slowly the crowd began to break, to move soundlessly away.

President Harding had left a message that he would like to see Mr. Debs at three o'clock.

Theodore asked Gene what he would like to do in the hours before he was due at the White House. It was a sparkling clear winter day, the sun bright. Even the air seemed to Gene to be light and fragrant.

"I think I'd like to take a tour of Washington."

He sat with Theodore in the back seat of a comrade's car, marveling at the beautiful city that man had built.

The Washington Monument he saw as the pure white shaft of freedom, extending endlessly into the sky. Then the car reached the Lincoln Memorial, which was just being completed. He opened the door and slowly got out. Above him sat a giant figure in marble. Gene thought. This can be no stone, no statue; this is a man, this is living flesh above us. Those eyes that have seen so much misery and death, those are living eyes.

Slowly he climbed the great stairs. His friends remained behind, even Theodore.

He went alone into the presence of Abraham Lincoln, looked up into Lincoln's face and eyes. He knew that Lincoln had understood the terrible implication of man's enslavement of man.

He gazed out over the vista of Washington and the nation beyond it. In his mind he saw what Abraham Lincoln had seen as he gazed over the land: slavery, the eternal suffering of mankind caught up in its own brutality, its own ignorance, its own fear.

It was more than half a century since Lincoln's death, yet Gene had seen as much suffering and slavery as Lincoln had. The Negroes had been freed, or so the law said, but man had not freed them. The whites had been born free, or so the law said, but man kept them enslaved. Slavery, in its glistening new machine form, was on the march, increasing with each fruitful discovery, each resourceful device.

Had Lincoln worked in vain? He did not know. But Abraham Lincoln would not have foregone the struggle. The torch of liberty must somehow, in the darkness and the hurricane, be kept alive.

"It is not upon thee to finish the work; neither art thou free to desist from it."

Smiling at Theodore, he offered up to God the only prayer he knew:

"While there is a lower class I am in it. While there is a working class I am of it. While there's a soul in prison I am not free."

Slowly, he walked down the marble stairs.